# LORE & LUST
## THE VANISHING

Queer Vampire Romance Series Book Two

**KARLA NIKOLE PUBLISHING**

# LORE & LUST
## THE VANISHING

KARLA.NIKOLE

**KARLA NIKOLE PUBLISHING**

First Karla Nikole Publishing Edition, April 2021

ISBN: 978-1-7355898-5-5 (paperback)

ISBN: 978-1-7355898-3-1 (ebook)

Library of Congress Control Number: 2021902846

Cover illustration by Thander Lin

Contact@LoreAndLust.com

www.LoreAndLust.com

Printed in the United States of America

10 9 8 7 6 5 4 3 2 1

*For my parents, who always support me in whatever new and random adventure I decide to take.*

# EARLY APRIL

# ONE

Midnight. Haruka watches in awe as Nino steps out of the master bathroom. His honeyed skin radiates the luscious scent of cinnamon and mahogany. The light casts an angelic glow on his sculpted, naked shoulders.

"Grazie per avere aspettato, tesoro." Nino grins, climbing onto the bed. He folds his legs in his soft sweatpants.

*Thank you for waiting, darling,* Haruka translates as he drags himself upright from lying on his side, adjusting to mirror his mate in front of him. Nino bites his lip. Haruka raises an eyebrow. "What?"

Reaching up, Nino moves his hands behind Haruka's head and toward the large bun at the nape of his neck. He releases the tie, pulling it forward and allowing the heavy mass of Haruka's hair to unfurl and rest against his shoulders. Nino combs through the length of it with his fingers. "It's so damn long, Haru—and thick. Jesus... it's amazing. When will your barber cut it to donate it?"

"Perhaps in another month?" Haruka guesses. This is a benevolent "punishment" for being lazy about getting his haircut. When he waits too long, his barber insists that he grow it out to have it donated to human children who are unwell. Strangely, there is a large, diverse market for purebred vampire hair. "Are you ready?" Haruka asks. "You wanted to show me something?"

"Yes," says Nino. "Watch this." His palm flat, he brings one hand up between them. Nino's eyes shift from their natural, radiant amber to glow in vivid cranberry-orange. The color reminds Haruka of a fiery sunset. It is the color of their love: their unique bond and shared vampiric essence.

With his palm still open, Nino flexes his fingers. Haruka gasps when the tips glow in bright red-orange light. Nino looks up at him, smiling. "See? I can isolate my energy a little. You're always fussing that I don't take our meditations seriously, but I'm getting better."

"I do not fuss." Haruka lifts his chin. "I encourage you... passionately."

Nino laughs. "Right." He traces his fingertips along Haruka's jawline. Nino's touch is warm and fizzy, reflective of his inherent nature. He moves Haruka's hair aside, caressing up and down the back of his neck, across the delicate grooves of his upper spine. The sensation is calming, making Haruka's eyelids heavy.

"I still can't press it outward to manipulate anything yet," Nino says, quiet and soothing. "I feel a little like E.T., but it's better than nothing."

Haruka's eyes open in a blank stare. Nino pouts. *"Haruka—"*

"E.T. is..." He glances sideways, hurriedly scanning the crammed files of his mind. "An animal—no. An... alien? From a children's television show. Movie. I understand the reference. I do."

Nino lifts and leans forward to place a quick kiss upside

Haruka's nose. "I have such a good mate that listens to me when I talk about trivial things. How did I get so lucky?"

"This isolation of your aura is wonderful progress. Pressing it outward with the same level of manipulation will be our next objective. Even if in a simple way, my hope is for you to have defensive capabilities."

"I don't know if my aura is made that way, Haru."

"My essence within you unquestionably allows for the capability. It is only a matter of intent and focus, then manifesting the power according to your unique abilities. Shall we meditate to practice now?"

Nino scrunches his nose, reaching up to scratch the back of his coppery-brown head. He wears it tapered on the sides, but wavy and longer in the top. Modern, clean and easy. "We can try?"

Seizing the hair tie from Nino's hands, Haruka refastens his dark tresses into a low bun. Once secured, he flips his palms flat between them, elbows resting on his thighs, back straight. Nino takes a deep breath before grasping his hands.

Haruka relaxes, closing his eyes and opening his mind to Nino. The objective is simple—calibrate their shared energy to practice manipulating it together. Haruka is exceptional in controlling his aura, capable of wielding it in a number of specific ways. By focusing and linking their minds, he can guide Nino in doing the same.

They have tried practicing multiple times, but their experiments are always cut short... somehow.

He breathes deep, emptying his mind of all thoughts, focusing on the frenetic energy of his vampiric essence deep within. The warmth of it swells and pulses outside Haruka's body, making his eyes burn bright behind closed lids.

Shifting his attention to the strength of Nino's hands gripping his own, Haruka mentally reaches out to him as his other half—as a fundamental but autonomous part of him.

*He looks sexy in this robe... Is it new? Why does he always smell so damn good—*

"Nino."

"Sorry."

Inhaling, exhaling, Haruka presses his aura out further. Nino's essence swirls warm and vibrant into the proliferation of Haruka's cool energy. He manipulates his essence around them so that it forms a large sphere, allowing Nino's aura to pour in and fill the shape—ideally mimicking it. Nino's thoughts echo like a whisper in Haruka's mind.

*It's a sphere... Make a sphere...*

Haruka opens his burning eyes. Nino's are still closed, his brow furrowed in stern concentration.

*And he's naked—Stop. Sphere, Nino... God, he smells incredible—Shit. Sphere.*

Like a balloon popping, Haruka releases his innate hold on their combined energy. The bright red-orange light of it glimmers and fades. Nino opens his amber eyes, apology set in his expression.

Before he can speak the words, Haruka closes the distance and kisses him. He slides his hand against Nino's scalp, fingers threading and tangling into his thick hair. Haruka tilts his head, opening wider to coax Nino into letting him inside—to feel and taste him completely.

Kissing Nino is all-consuming, the force of it like being swept up into an effervescent, fiery tornado. When Nino's mouth is on his, it's as if Haruka becomes airborne, soaring across a red sky of heat and passion and losing his breath. Losing sense of himself and his rational mind.

He leans back, hands still laced in Nino's hair as he drags him down toward the bed. He needs to feel the weight and heaviness of his body. Haruka unfolds his legs and gaps his thighs so Nino can rest in between. The moment Nino settles, their mouths connect in another burst of passion: tongues twisting and sliding, hungry and exploring. He kisses Haruka, ravenous, as if his sanity is at stake. As if the taste and feel of his mouth is Nino's only solace in the face of total madness.

After pulling the belt of Haruka's robe loose, Nino lifts, then moves his hand between their bodies to open and push the material aside. He reaches down, lightly caressing his fingertips along the center of Haruka's belly. He grazes his navel and Haruka sighs, writhing from the prospect of Nino's hand moving lower.

Nino raises his head from the kiss, his voice low. "I couldn't concentrate... again."

"I heard," Haruka breathes.

"Maybe..." Nino dips to sprinkle kisses along Haruka's jawline. "I can have tonight off? Because today is special."

Haruka slides his hands up Nino's firm back, caressing the smooth contours of elegant definition and muscle. "Is it?" he asks.

"I know we usually focus on centennial milestones in our culture, but... today is our one-year anniversary, tesoro."

Tracing his fingertips along the shallow concave of Nino's spine, Haruka grins. "Has it already been a year?"

"Mmhm. Asao kept your calendar clear for later tonight, right?"

"I believe so."

"I'm making dinner for you," Nino whispers, leaning down to rub their noses together. "The menu is a surprise—and I found the Merlot we had the night we first met. Remember? You walked into my bar and I forgot how to breathe when I saw you."

The butterflies in Haruka's stomach float and dance as he

raises his chin to connect with Nino's full lips. He kisses him twice before resting back down against the bed. "I do. I love it when you cook for me."

"Look forward to it." Nino beams, lifting on all fours. He looks at the nightstand just beside the bed. "Did you put the new bottle in my drawer or yours?"

"Yours."

Nino leans past his head and Haruka admires the distinct lines of his torso, watching them move and stretch as he reaches to open the drawer. Nino's body is exquisite, like a marble sculpture of a young Greek god but drenched in golden honey.

Nino stops, frozen. "You—There's... a ring box in here."

"Perhaps you should open it?"

For a moment, Nino remains still, his eyes shifting between Haruka's face and the open drawer. He leans forward again to grab the small black box, then crawls backward, resting against his shins. Haruka sits upright to face him.

Nino focuses on the suede box, his shoulders rising and falling as he breathes. He's trying to stay calm, but Haruka can feel the subdued joy radiating from within him. Nino flips the box open. The two handsome and polished bands that Haruka has chosen glisten in the dim light.

"Do you like them?" Haruka asks.

"I..." Nino takes a deep breath, running his fingers into the top of his hair. "I *love* them. Haru, I—When I mentioned this to you, you didn't seem interested."

"I am interested in anything that pleases you," Haruka says, taking the box from Nino's hands. Wearing and exchanging rings this way is a human practice, something rarely done among bonded couples. Everything between vampires is organic—the biological pull and connection dominant over anything else, with no need for material frills or symbolism.

But if this is what makes his mate happy, then so be it.

He takes Nino's band from its small holding space in the box. The black, shiny metal is cool to the touch and the intricate amber inlay mirrors his husband's eyes. He grasps Nino's left hand. "I realize that when we bonded a year ago, it was unexpected... My behavior at that time left much to be desired."

Carefully, he guides the ring onto Nino's finger. A perfect fit. "I... I do not express these sentimentalities well. But please know that you revived me—from a place of bitterness and loneliness. You have always been pure in your kindness toward me. And I... Perhaps I can never express how grateful I am to you. How much I love you."

Haruka takes a deep breath, his heart in his throat. Speaking this way—candid and emotional—is difficult. He is unaccustomed to it, but wants to try being more open and straightforward like his mate. "Thank you for choosing me. For loving me," he says, watching Nino and waiting.

Swooning, Nino's eyes shut as he falls against the mattress —dead weight. He rolls onto his back and presses his ringed palm to his face. Haruka leans over him. "Nino, why?"

Pulling Nino's wrist, Haruka drags his hand from his hairline. Nino's wavy hair is a mess and his honeyed skin flush. Tears are silently gathered and running from the corners of his almond-shaped eyes.

Haruka bends down, using his fingertips to wipe and dab the tears. "My love, why are you upset?"

Nino's chest rises and falls in a gasp. "I'm just... a little overwhelmed."

He nods, understanding. "This is my transgression. If I expressed these things to you more often, your reaction would not be so extreme."

"Haru, I—I love you more than I can even say. You always

encourage me to be confident and you're so patient. Thank you for trusting me with your heart... for giving yourself to me."

Haruka leans down, soft in kissing Nino's lips as he holds his tear-stained face. "Will you put my ring on?" he asks. Nino nods against the mattress. Haruka grabs the box, opens it and gives the band to his mate. While Nino lies there, he holds Haruka's palm above his face, then slides the ring onto the appropriate finger of his left hand.

He reaches up and grips Haruka's collar, pulling him into his body. He removes the tie from Haruka's bun once more and the weight of his hair falls forward like a black wave. Nino runs his fingers into it, sweeping it away from Haruka's face while bringing him down to meet his parted lips.

Kissing Nino. His mate's movement is so slow and intentional that Haruka's chest tightens. When they break the kiss, their irises are alighted as they stare at each other in the warm darkness. Nino's sunset gaze is soft but unwavering. "Will you please stretch me and come inside me?"

Haruka bites his lip. He isn't sure if he'll ever be *this* straightforward, but if this is what will make his mate happy, then so be it.

# TWO

Morning. Nino enters the kitchen and Haruka is already there, sitting at the table with Junichi. The doors to the courtyard are propped open, allowing the cool, sweet air and sunlight of spring to saturate the space.

Moving toward the counter, Nino's objective is clear. Coffee pot. He smiles in their direction. "Hey, Jun."

Tall and handsome with warm, almond butter–brown skin, the first-generation vampire lifts his marble-black irises, grinning. As Okayama's local tailor and clothing designer, Junichi Takayama is suave. In Nino's mind, he's like a male peacock, except his feathers are all black. When the light hits him, the darkness of his plumage flashes like liquid iridescence.

"Good morning, Nino." Junichi nods, his English smooth and unimpeded by his native tongue, like Haruka's. "Your husband and I are at an impasse. Maybe you can help us?"

"What's going on?" Nino pours his coffee. He once told Junichi that he can speak Japanese when visiting their home (not needing to adhere to their household habit of speaking in

English), but the male had coolly refused, claiming it's "more fun" this way.

"This is for the Hamamoto-Iseki wedding in six months," Junichi explains "We're having difficulty deciding whether Haruka should wear a suit or traditional attire. Do you have a preference in his clothing?"

Junichi raises his eyebrow, waiting while Haruka sits with his arms folded at the head of the table, his gaze focused on a letter in front of him.

Nino leans against the counter with his elbows, cradling the warm coffee cup in his palms. "Well, he looks regal in a kimono... but modern and sexy in a suit. I like both. Maybe I prefer the kimono? Oh—you know what's even better? A yukata. He's always naked under those things. Just *one* layer."

Junichi laughs. Haruka shakes his head. Nino grins as he brings his coffee cup to his lips. Whenever Haruka wears traditional robes, Nino feels as if he's bonded with one of those elegant lounging figures in an ukiyo-e wood-block painting—especially with his hair so long and dramatic like this.

"That was a lot of information." Junichi smirks. "A yukata is too casual for a wedding, but your preference is noted. Maybe I'll make a couple new robes for him this month before I fly to Europe?"

Feeling accomplished, Nino beams. "You'll be traveling for three months, right?"

"Yes sir. My clients abroad demand personalized deliveries."

"You're amazing, Jun. Everything you make for Haruka always suits him perfectly. My favorite was that kimono you designed for his welcome celebration last year... Maybe I should try wearing one to the wedding?"

"You could do that." Junichi blinks, considering. "I'll have to think about a design that complements you."

"Haru has so many, should I just try one of his?"

"Absolutely not. You two are the same height but your shoulders are broader and rounder. Your physique is more defined from your exercise routine. There's no way I'd let you walk around in a tight, ill-fitting kimono."

Haruka laughs. The deep, throaty sound of it surprises both Junichi and Nino as they shift their attention toward him. "My apologies." He smiles. "The mental image of that scenario caught me off guard."

"Welcome to the conversation, tesoro." Nino stands straight and walks to the end of the counter. He leans there with his hip. "What are you reading?"

"A formal visitation request." Haruka's dark brows are drawn together as he takes a deep breath, his previous mirth evaporated.

"From someone you dislike?" Junichi asks.

"From someone I do not know and have never heard of." Haruka lifts his bright burgundy gaze toward Nino. "May I please have a cup?"

Nino nods and turns toward the cabinet to grab a mug. "What's the request for?"

"Introductions." Haruka folds his arms. "The vampire is Lajos Almeida, which is undeniably synonymous with Ladislao Almeida of Rio de Janeiro. But I have never heard of this particular vampire within the clan's family lineage."

Tense, Nino walks around the counter with his mate's coffee. In light of both Gael and Ladislao disappearing last year, having anyone associated with the Almeida Clan so close to their home feels like a bad omen.

"Why would someone from the Almeida Clan want to meet you?" Junichi asks. "I hate to say this, but things calmed down in Brazil after Ladislao vanished. It's obvious that he was the root of the problem. Crazy male..."

"You've met him?" Nino asks.

"Yeah. Only once, but he leaves an impression."

"We have a connection," Haruka says, accepting Nino's offering. "We crossed paths with one of the Almeida Clan's associates last year. There was an altercation regarding my family's research, but then he escaped and I have not seen or heard anything since."

In a fog, Nino sits down at the table beside Haruka. The associate is Gael Silva, a large, domineering first-generation vampire they met in England more than a year ago. He'd attacked Haruka after learning about the *Lore and Lust* manuscript—an impressive compilation of accounts on forming vampiric bonds. The research is invaluable, giving shape to a topic shrouded in much mystery.

Gael's brutal response had convinced both Nino and Haruka that they should avoid revealing the manuscript's existence. At least among strangers.

With his fingertips, Nino slides the request within his line of sight, then reads the details. The appeal is for one month from now—the exact minimum amount of time considered proper when making formal requests of purebreds. Nino pushes the letter away so that it sits in the middle of the table, unsettled by the sense of foreboding emanating from it.

Junichi picks up the paper to read it, his black irises scanning. He pulls the letter to his nose and inhales. "Smells strong —like sage. This Lajos is probably purebred?"

Haruka blows out a breath. Concern is etched in his forehead. "So it would seem."

"I don't like this." Nino shakes his head. "How did he even find us? When we legally registered our bond, I made sure that all of our records were kept private. Nothing comes up if you search us online."

"Oh, the two of you registered your bond with the human

government?" Junichi asks. "Most bonded couples don't bother with that step."

Haruka brings his coffee cup to his lips. "My mate is of a meticulous nature—much more so than myself."

"It... just makes sense?" Nino grins, embarrassed. The decision is unconventional. But in Nino's mind, if anything serious ever happened, it would be better for them to have legal responsibility for each other. No questions asked.

He looks down at his left hand against the table and flexes his fingers. Another unconventional desire. He sighs, his heart light from the beautiful ring wrapped around his finger. It's black zirconium, but the inlay is textured with amber stone. It's perfect and looks like something found and cultivated from a dense rainforest... maybe from behind a waterfall.

Remembering Haruka's words and seductive actions last night gives Nino a rush of warm goosebumps. When Haruka lets loose, he reminds Nino of a panther—dark, seductive and devoted in his every movement. He'd given Nino what he'd asked for and much more.

"When I met you at the welcome celebration last year, it was obvious that you were a vampire with a plan." Junichi raises his eyebrow at Nino, teasing.

Nino shakes his head. "No, I—I didn't... not exactly—"

"The way Haruka took your hand without question and let you sweep him off into the woods spoke volumes."

"We did not go into the woods." Haruka frowns.

"Everyone went wild," Junichi says. "Like, 'Who is this stunning amber vampire that just walked in and stole our realm leader away?'"

"They bonded on the *first* try—"

"*Asao.*"

Haruka's manservant walks into the room—salt-and-pepper and broad-shouldered with his head high. Despite Haruka's furrowed brow, the older vampire grins as he takes hold of the coffee pot. "Jun, did he ever tell you he freaked out afterward? Tore up the house?"

"Asao, none of that information is necessary right now," Haruka admonishes.

"It's your anniversary." Asao shrugs, unbothered. "It's good to reflect. You've come a long way, hasn't he, Nino?"

Nino scratches the back of his head. "Please... don't include me in this conversation." Haruka and Asao have a unique relationship. Asao is much older and third-generation, his purebred vampire origins twice removed. When Haruka was twelve, his parents died and Asao was named his guardian.

The two vampires feel more like goading father and mortified son than manservant and master. In joining their household, Nino has learned to keep his mouth shut during their disagreements.

"Happy anniversary." Junichi smiles. "Wow. Bonded on the first try? That *never* happens. You two were meant to be. Like fate."

"I think so..." Nino shifts his eyes, meeting Haruka's vintage wine–colored gaze. "But I'm always told that I'm a 'romantic.'"

Haruka reaches over and grasps Nino's hand, bringing it up toward his mouth. "I am grateful that the stunning and romantic amber vampire is always so patient with his pragmatic mate." He locks eyes with Nino as he presses his lips to his fingers. Nino's stomach flips.

"We need to leave in the next five minutes to get to the Fujihara Clan's estate on time," Asao says, just before taking a long sip of his coffee. Haruka does the same, then stands from the table.

Nino looks up at him. "I'll be back home around seven to start dinner."

Nodding, Haruka pushes the chair in and meets Nino at his side. He bends down and places two swift kisses on his mouth. "Good luck in Osaka today."

"Thank you." Nino grins. "Good luck with the translation."

Haruka stands and lifts his chin toward Junichi. "Kimemashita. Suitsu ja nakute, kimono wo kimasu. Jaa, mata atode."

Junichi offers a firm nod, then winks at Nino. "Yappari kimono desu yo ne. Dewa boku ga tsukurasete itadakimasu. Are we still on for lunch this Saturday?"

"We are," Haruka confirms. He walks toward the door and Nino turns to watch him, long and elegant in his dark slacks. He wears a crisp, subtly patterned white shirt layered underneath a handsome gray sweater. The heavy weight of his lustrous hair is pulled back, neat and tidy. The quintessential Historian off to do research.

"Have you met the Fujiharas?" Junichi asks when they're alone in the kitchen. "They're the family with twins."

"Yeah..." Nino says. He knows who they are because they'd unknowingly shown him something important. Something he's been privately grappling with since the day he first met them and witnessed the way in which his mate interacted with their twins. Nino is still taken aback with how calm and doting Haruka had been. He knows his mate to be affectionate. But seeing him with children exposed Nino to a new, hidden layer of Haruka's character.

"I met them a couple months ago," Nino says, keeping his revelation about his mate to himself. "They seem nice. They're both first-gen, right?"

"Yes, they're great—and the kids are obsessed with Haruka. Such an interesting family. Sora's purebred father was a victim of the Great Vanishing. She said he was pushing her on a swing at the park one afternoon and then poof, she looked back and he was gone. Maybe she was five at the time? She walked home alone, and when she got there, her mom was doubled over in pain from the sudden separation of her mate. She ended up dying about a week later."

Nino shudders at the mere mention of the Great Vanishing: the unexplained cultural event that happened nearly two centuries ago. Several purebreds across multiple communities and continents had slowly disappeared—like mist into thin air. No explanation. Not even now, so many years later. The entire purebred vampire population declined as a result.

"I didn't know about Sora's parents. That sounds horrible." Nino sighs.

"Right?" Junichi agrees. "So Kosuke, Sora's husband, can't withstand direct sunlight very well. His first-gen father used to casually feed from humans in his youth—like for fun? Fucking nuts. His mother is purebred, but she wasn't vanished. They're living in Shimane, I think?"

"Haru told me feeding from humans too much will destroy a vampire's bloodline for a whole generation—maybe even longer. My family's bloodline wasn't clean until the mid-1800s. But I think Haru's has been clean since... something crazy like 200 CE."

"Ancient blood." Junichi shakes his head, the phrase weighted as it hangs between them. "Yayoi, Queen Himiko blood... I bet his ancestors were terrifying. They probably sucked other vampires dry when they fed. Anyway, Kosuke himself has never fed from humans, so the twins are fine. Sora works full-time as a nurse at my mother's hospital in Himeji, since she can day walk. Kosuke stays home to take care of the kids. They might be better off finding a nocturnal society, but they're pretty loyal to Haruka as a realm leader—and now you too, of course."

"We have a lot of interesting families in our realm," Nino

says thoughtfully. "Some are humble and normal. Others are ridiculous. Have you met that new clan that just moved here from Tokyo?"

Junichi's face falls flat. "Yeah."

"We went to their house to welcome them and it was crazy —marble statues, huge paintings and a dramatic staircase. It was like something out of a cheesy drama. The son is some kind of underground rock star?"

"He's a little *shit*," Junichi says with a sneer. "He comes by my shop at least once a week to pester me—making me order Versace and Gucci, Dolce & Gabbana, then asking me to custom fit everything for him before he picks it up. Was I that arrogant and frivolous when I was his age? I couldn't have been that bad..."

Nino leans on the table with his elbows, smiling. "You know, Jun, you can swear like this and be yourself in front of Haru. I know he's old blood and a little pretentious, but you don't need to put on airs for him. He thinks of you as his friend."

Junichi raises his eyebrow in a smirk. "Me? Swear and gossip in front of my gracious, poised and diplomatic purebred realm leader? My father would turn over in his grave and climb out just to smack me."

Nino understands. He's purebred himself, but he'd felt the same way when he was first getting to know Haruka. Over time though, his stoic façade cracked, revealing someone compassionate and patient.

"You should give him a chance—he'll surprise you." Realizing something, Nino narrows his eyes. "Why do you swear and gossip in front of me?"

"Because you swear and gossip in front of *me*. You broke the seal, my young friend."

"That's fair."

"I know Haruka is a good male," Junichi says. "He's easy to work with and not as pompous as he could be, considering his ancient bloodline. Not a nightmare like my selfish, dramatic shrew of a source. Plus, Haruka is bonded with you. Even if I knew nothing else about him, that would give me all the validation I needed."

# THREE

The morning weather is warm and clear, the air fresh with the scent of damp earth and new life. Haruka looks up, examining the puffy white clouds drifting overhead as he waits on the front porch. When the door swings open, he diverts his attention forward and smiles.

"Good morning, your grace," Sora says, returning Haruka's grin as she pulls the door open wider. She bows at her waist, making the giant, messy bun on top of her head shift forward. When she's upright, she adjusts her red-framed glasses. "Thank you so much for coming."

"Please, just Haruka is fine, and it is my pleasure. My apologies for the delay. The past few weeks have been exceptionally busy." Haruka steps into the cool foyer. The house smells of bitter green tea, clean tatami and something sweet.

"I can imagine," Sora says. "Since you've come back, everyone's been so excited and we all need something from you. Not to mention the social events and—"

The sound of small, eager feet racing toward them grows louder, making both Sora and Haruka turn their attention toward the long hallway. Haruka takes a step back to plant his feet, bracing himself for the impact of tiny vampires.

"Shion, Amon, *stop*—"

Haruka opens his arms just in time as the small girl pulls ahead of her brother, jumping at full speed into his embrace. He sweeps her up, while the boy crashes into his long legs, arms wrapped around Haruka's knees.

"You *cheated*, Shion." The boy looks up from Haruka's knees, a stern crease set in his adorable brow. "It's not fair!"

"Good morning, Haru-sama." Shion smiles, ignoring her brother and settling herself in Haruka's arms. "Me and Dad pressed mochi for you. We have tea, too. Will you have some?"

"I helped too," her twin brother asserts, indignant.

Shion glances down at him in a pointed moment of silence, then focuses her rich brown gaze back on Haruka. Her face is indifferent. "Amon helped too."

"I'm so sorry about my wild kids," Sora says, bending down to peel Amon's determined six-year-old frame from Haruka's legs.

"There is no need to apologize. I would love to have mochi and tea. Thank you for the wonderful treat." Indulgence. While Haruka doesn't need to consume table food as a pure-bred, he enjoys it nonetheless. As a family of first-generation vampires, the human blood entwined within the Fujihara Clan's lineage requires it. They need both food and blood to thrive as creatures born of vampiric biology.

Shion squeaks and wraps her small arms tight around Haruka's neck. He steps out of his shoes and onto the hardwood floor to follow Sora down the hallway. She drags her son by the hand as they walk toward the kitchen. The scene reminds Haruka of an owner pulling its obstinate, untrained puppy.

"They've been going berserk for the past month over your

visiting us." Sora's smile is strained as she wrestles with her little boy. "It's all they talk about—they've been driving Kosuke and me *crazy*. 'When's Haru-sama coming? Is it today? Is it today? Why isn't it today?' Oh my God—we'll never tell them anything in advance again. Everything's a surprise from now on."

Haruka laughs as they turn the corner into the kitchen. The bright sunlight spills in through the open windows and the musky scent of green tea is strong. Kosuke, Sora's mate, smiles in greeting from the counter, an apron wrapped around his narrow waist.

"Good morning, your grace. Thank you so much for helping us with this project."

"Please, just Haruka. It's my pleasure. I apologize for the delay in getting started."

"Don't worry about it. We know how busy you've been..." Kosuke frowns at his daughter. "Shion, seriously?" He holds his palms flat, urging her to transfer into his arms, but she turns away. A distinct "No thank you." Her shiny black ponytail bounces as she snakes her arms tighter around Haruka's neck.

"It's okay," Haruka says quietly. "I don't mind."

Kosuke shakes his head in exasperation as he turns back toward the counter. Haruka watches him for a moment, considering. "Kosuke, does the bright light in here not bother you?"

"Oh no, I'm okay as long as I don't go outside or sit in direct sunlight. Thankfully my sensitivity isn't as bad as some other vampires with my similar genetic background—not enough to make our household nocturnal. It's too hard in this day and age, living that kind of lifestyle."

"Agreed, it would be difficult to maintain such an outdated existence." Haruka moves to sit at the small kitchen table with Shion in his lap, taking the seat washed in direct sunlight. Sora joins him, still pulling an excitable Amon at her side.

"Haru-sama?" Shion whispers, lifting her face and blinking brown eyes. "You smell *really* nice—"

"Shion, good grief." Sora frowns behind her trendy glasses. "Like, who's raising this child? Someone call her parents—"

"I think so too!" Amon chirps from across the table. "He smells good 'cause he's a purebred."

"Can I sit with you while you read today?" Shion asks, batting her eyes. Amon bounces up in his mother's lap.

"I wanna read Latino too!" he says.

"It's *Latin*," Sora says, rolling her eyes. "Haruka needs to concentrate. You two can't be fighting and climbing all over him while he's working."

Shion directs her attention to her brother. "We won't, will we, Amon?"

"We won't—we promise."

"Depending on the complexity of the will and trust, it might be nice to have company at least some of the time?" Haruka strokes his chin, playful. "Certainly for the occasional tea break?"

"Mom—he said sometimes!" Shion pleads, her bouncy ponytail slapping Haruka in the chin as she whips her head around.

"For breaks, Mom!" Amon adds.

Sora gives Haruka a hesitant look, but he nods to reassure her. "Alright…" Sora sighs. "But you have to behave and listen to Haruka when you're in the study with him."

A chorus of small voices rings out in celebration. Kosuke carries a large tray of tea and pressed sticky rice to the table. The oval-shaped sweets are powdery pink and wrapped in green leaves—cherry blossom mochi to celebrate the spring.

"Haru-sama, what's your favorite color?" Shion asks.

"Hm… I like amber."

"Me too," Shion says.

"Me too!" Amon echoes.

Sora snorts. "Shion, you like green—"

"Nuh-uh, I changed." Shion raises her chin. "I like amber now."

"What is amber?" Amon asks, puzzled. He bulldozes on. "Haru-sama, do you like to read manga?"

"I've never read any," Haruka says. "Perhaps I should? Which one do you like?"

"*What?*" Amon bounces in Sora's lap, his eyes wide. "You've never read manga? *No way.* Dad loves manga. When Mom is at the hospital, *all he does* is read manga—"

"Alright, that's enough," Kosuke interjects, reaching down to snatch Amon up from his mate's lap. "You see what we deal with every day? Small creatures that never, ever, ever stop talking."

Haruka breathes a laugh as Shion leans forward in his lap, stretching and reaching for the mochi. He understands Sora and Kosuke's exasperation. It is natural.

For Haruka though, this environment is special. Whenever he visits the Fujihara family, his heart warms. But the edges are painted with a gentle melancholy. When he was still very young and on the cusp of forming his first bond, he had imagined his life to be something like this. At least he'd hoped.

After a while, it became clear that he should give up. So he did. He buried the quiet desire deep down, never giving it another thought.

Things haven't turned out the way he'd imagined, but he is infinitely grateful. He has Nino. A second bond. A serendipitous meeting and miraculous circumstance that he never anticipated. He couldn't ask for anything more. He wouldn't.

BY THE TIME Haruka returns home, it is night. The house is silent. He walks into the kitchen and the white moonlight spills in from the glass courtyard doors and onto the sturdy oak table.

As Haruka moves forward, he's amazed at the decadent sight before him. Thick black candles occupy the center of the table, flickering and burning softly. Beside them, a tall glass vase filled with long-stemmed red roses in full bloom. The atmosphere glows with dark elegance and romance.

Suddenly, Nino is behind him, snaking his arms around Haruka's waist to embrace him and pull him into his chest. He plants a firm kiss just underneath Haruka's ear. "Tesoro, bentornato a casa."

*Darling, welcome home.* Grinning, Haruka leans into the hug. "Grazie, amore mio. This looks exquisite."

"It reminds me of you." Nino reaches up to pull his collar away from his neck. He lowers his head, placing a soft kiss at the top of Haruka's spine. "Your aura and eyes haven't glowed in that brilliant rose-red color since we bonded. I miss it."

Haruka turns in his grasp, embracing Nino's shoulders. "I don't," he says. "I much prefer my nature entwined with yours." He leans in to kiss Nino, indulging in the rich, cinnamon-infused taste of him.

When Haruka bonded with Yuna the first time, his inherent nature hadn't changed so drastically. In this new bond with Nino, *everything* is different: their open communication and overall dynamic. The passion and love he feels is more consuming—almost feral. Submitting to the allure of it... Haruka still hesitates, but he's growing accustomed to it.

Nino lifts his head, amber eyes shining. "Have a seat and I'll pour you a glass." Obedient, Haruka moves toward the table as Nino speaks from behind the counter. "I have another surprise for you, but it's not quite ready yet. I need more time."

"When can I anticipate this surprise?"

"Mm... maybe next month?" Nino chuckles. "I bit off a little more than I can chew. How's the translation project so far?"

"Challenging. Excellent." He makes himself comfortable at the table and glances out the window. The cherry blossom trees in the courtyard flutter in shadowy pink hues, swaying against the nighttime breeze. "I read many things in Latin for pleasure, but my comprehension of legal terminology is rusty. I will need my lexicon and dictionary next time I visit."

"How are the Fujiharas?" Nino asks, setting a generous glass of Merlot before him.

"Wonderful." Haruka picks up his glass and takes a sip before continuing. "Their nest is always warm and welcoming."

"I think... we have that too," Nino says from the counter, arranging the plates.

"Of course we do." Haruka watches him, confused. "It was not a point of comparison."

Nino walks around the counter, two dinner plates in his hands. "You really like the twins, right? What are their names?"

"Shion is the girl and Amon is the boy. Yes, they are delightful. What do we have?" He looks down at the artfully plated food. It smells of fresh herbs—warm, buttery and rich.

"First course is pan-seared scallops with salsa verde. We'll have three courses altogether."

Haruka's mouth is already watering as he picks up his fork. "Il secondo?"

"Second course is breaded filetti di cernia with sesame seeds and roasted vegetables. We have a little molten chocolate chili cake for dessert."

*God help me.* How did he end up with this creature? This handsome, wholesome vampire that nourishes him and indulges him. That loves him and helps him. Haruka has faced much hardship and tragedy—the loss of his parents as a child, an unprecedented broken bond. With the appearance of Nino, it feels as if life has offered sincere recompense in one incredible, sweeping gesture.

"You have outdone yourself," Haruka says. "This is divine. When you give consulting advice to your clients in Kansai, do you also suggest recipes?"

"Sometimes, but... I try not to stick my nose into their menu too much, especially if it's food I'm not familiar with. If I see a need because it's impacting their financials, I do give some general advice."

"Such as?" Haruka asks, taking another bite of seared and buttery scallop. It flakes and practically melts in his mouth.

"I tell them to keep their menu small. Large menus with too much variety can be a business killer. For one, it's expensive to keep so many ingredients in stock. Two, it impacts quality."

Haruka nods. "They freeze things to extend the shelf life."

"Exactly, and I don't like that," says Nino. "My philosophy is, make your food fresh and make it well. A smaller menu will help set them up for success. Most family-owned restaurants in Japan are good about that. I haven't run into anything too crazy, which is why I avoid taking on major chains as clients."

"Yes, with a larger business, I imagine it would be strenuous to make changes across various locations. Frozen foods are also inevitable for distribution." Haruka takes his final bite of scallop, excited for the next course. He looks over at Nino, and his mate is staring into a half-eaten plate.

"My love, why are you not eating?" Haruka asks.

Something is distracting him. Unless they're both receptive to it, they cannot explicitly read each other's minds. As a general rule, they have decided it is better to give each other privacy.

Nino takes a deep breath before flickering his radiant eyes up at him. "I... I've had something on my mind the past few weeks. It feels like a topic we should have talked about by now, but I just never really..."

"Nino, what is it?" Haruka asks, his chest tight from the sudden shift in the atmosphere.

"You... and Yuna. You were bonded with her for ten years, right?"

"Yes," says Haruka, his voice patient but his body tense. The last thing he ever wants to discuss is his previous mate. Especially on the night of their very young anniversary.

Nino rakes his hand through his hair, a clear indicator of his stress. "Why—why didn't the two of you have children? Being together so long, it seems like you would have."

Sighing, Haruka sits back against the chair, his appetite ruined.

# FOUR

*My timing is shit.* Nino's heart is racing. He's been wondering about this for months, the topic nagging and clinging to the edges of his consciousness. He's always stifled the urge, knowing how much Haruka dislikes talking about his first mate.

Yet here it is. Awkward and spilling out over their anniversary dinner.

"Yuna did not want children," Haruka says, his eyes unblinking. Nothing more.

"So... that's it?" Nino asks. "End of story? The two of you never tried..."

Haruka takes a visible breath, his gaze shifting toward the patio doors of the courtyard. "We did. She became pregnant once, but eventually lost the child. We did not try again."

*Dammit.* Nino feels like he's been punched in the chest. His throat is tight. "I—I'm so sorry..."

Haruka nods. "It is not something I like to think about."

In Nino's mind, the next natural question is whether or not Haruka still wants children. Does he want a big family? Should they seek assistance to try to have kids themselves someday?

But Nino can't answer these questions himself. He doesn't know what he wants, only having recently contemplated the topic.

He still feels like an adolescent in some ways. He can't imagine being responsible for the lives of young vampires—teaching and guiding them between their ancient culture and the complexities of modern society. He's still figuring it out for himself.

Picking up his wine glass, Haruka brings it to his lips, then tilts his head back to drain its contents. When he's finished, he pushes up from the table. Panicked, Nino stands, blocking his path.

Haruka frowns. "What are you doing?"

"What are *you* doing?"

"I am getting more wine."

They're frozen in silence. Just as Haruka moves around him, Nino acts on impulse. He steps into him and crouches down. In a swift motion, he chops his arm at the back of Haruka's knees, making them buckle so that he can sweep him up and cradle the bulk of him against his body.

Haruka's eyes widen from the surprise attack. He squirms. "N—Nino, put me *down*."

"I shall carry his grace to the counter—"

"*Stop*."

Laughing, Nino places his flustered mate back on his feet. "His lordship doth protest—it amazes me that we're the same height but you're not heavy to me at all."

"*Please* do not do that."

"Why?" Nino frowns. "You let me pick you up when we're having sex?"

"That—that is different."

"How so?"

"There is context," Haruka says, avoiding Nino's gaze as he

tries to move past him. Nino steps into him again, scrunching his nose.

"So I can only pick you up if I'm sliding my cock—"

Gasping with wide burgundy eyes, Haruka reaches up and pinches Nino's mouth shut with his fingers. Nino breathes a muffled laugh. Haruka laughs as well, bringing his free hand up to cover his flushed face.

Nino grabs his wrist, pulling Haruka's fingers away. "Seriously, Haru? Nobody else is here but us—even Asao and his supersonic hearing are gone for the night. Why do you get embarrassed like this whenever I try to talk about our sex life? We talk about everything else."

"Because discussing it is redundant." Haruka breathes out, running his palm over the top of his smooth black head. "I am there. I know what we do."

Stepping even closer into him, Nino squares his hips and presses Haruka's backside into the table. He rests his hands against Haruka's waist, then leans in and kisses the sexy little mole just off the center of his nose. "The lord of the manor just isn't accustomed to someone talking dirty to him. It could be fun... You can tell me what you like?"

Haruka shakes his head, grinning. "You know what I like based on my reaction... and I do not know those words in English."

"Lies. You can say them in Japanese?"

He pauses, his eyes shifting to the side. "Those words don't exist in Japanese."

They both laugh. "Stubborn," Nino chides. "Alright, I give up for now. I'll ignore the fact that you know about fifteen other languages, and that those words definitely exist in Japanese."

Haruka leans into his mouth and Nino drops his jaw, letting their tongues touch and slide, tasting each other like two lovers reacquainting themselves. Haruka's mouth is always a few degrees cooler than his own and with a hint of fresh roses. The sensation reminds Nino of spring—a rainy day when the air is crisp and sweet. How can a kiss create such vivid imagery in his mind? The feeling like being swathed in a dreamlike haze —an entirely new setting where he's sheltered and deeply loved. He's never experienced anything like this until Haruka.

The kiss is fierce. When Nino tilts his head, Haruka pushes back, meeting his intensity. Just before breaking the affection, Haruka grips Nino's hair in a fist and pulls his head to the side. He leans down, lips brushing along the concave of his neck. Nino tightens his arms around his waist and Haruka bites down into the left side of his neck and pulls.

Nino groans, exhaling from the familiar heat rushing down his belly and settling in his groin. Haruka never feeds from the opposite side, careful to avoid the permanent scars at the curve of Nino's shoulder. The wounds are old but forever tender from abuse Nino experienced as a child.

Haruka sucks hard at Nino's flesh, his sharp fangs sinking further into his neck. Nino closes his eyes from the sheer euphoria of the intimacy. Haruka always pours the most elegant thoughts into him whenever he feeds. It feels like poetry: love and passion flowing in profound verse and expression.

He sucks harder and Nino's eyes flash open. Burning. His nature deep at the base of his core shifts, wanting to release. To submit to Haruka's will. Nino closes his eyes and exhales a breath, allowing Haruka to take it from him.

The heated rush of Nino's aura releasing is like an effervescent wind racing and swirling up his spine, then wildly dispersing from every pore of his body. It radiates in a blazing glow of deep orange light. The sensation is incredible, as if Nino's insides are being set free and entrusted to his mate. Sometimes, Nino physically orgasms when Haruka does this, depending on where he feeds. Now, Nino keeps his body in control, his mind recalibrating from the pleasure and focusing.

The moment Haruka pulls up from feeding, Nino bends to wrap his hands behind his mate's thighs. He lifts and urges him to sit against the table, their dinner dishes clattering and shifting aside.

His burning gaze is focused while he unfastens Haruka's pants, but then Nino flickers his eyes up. "This context is appropriate for me to pick you up, yes?"

Haruka laughs in his deep, throaty way. When his pants are undone, he lifts himself. Nino makes quick work of guiding everything around the curve of his firm ass, then down the length of his long legs. He tosses Haruka's clothing to the floor.

Sitting half naked in the moonlight and framed by flickering black candles, Haruka looks like something out of Nino's wildest dreams. Maybe Nino isn't even creative enough to dream of someone so seductive and otherworldly. He's always thought of his mate as beautiful. Sophisticated. But with this long and heavy hair, he isn't even like a vampire. He seems like something from a different species altogether.

Nino grabs the hem of Haruka's sweater and guides it up his body. His mate is obedient in lifting his arms, allowing him to remove it. He unbuttons Haruka's dress shirt, selfish in wanting to see all of him before indulging in his body.

Haruka's deep voice cuts through the silence. "Have I become il secondo?"

They both laugh as Nino finishes his task and separates the material of Haruka's shirt. He smiles. "Cheesy." Reaching up behind Haruka's head, he dismantles the tie holding his heavy bun. He drags it forward, letting his hair unfurl thick and wavy like liquid onyx against his creamy almond skin.

"My love, do you prefer my hair this way?" Haruka asks quietly. "If... you like this, I will not cut it."

Nino pulls a chair up from behind, situating himself in front of Haruka's gaped thighs. He wraps his fingers around the backs of his knees, urging him forward as he meets Haruka's gaze. "Tesoro, I don't care what your hair looks like. *You* are what I prefer. I just want you to be free."

Haruka's irises morph, gradually shimmering in vivid sunset orange. The heady scent of his rosy aura radiates from his lean body. He's opening himself. Letting his true nature breathe and expand. He's not as restrained as he used to be (the way he was in the very early days of their relationship), but it still takes a minute for Haruka to relax. They're getting there.

Smiling, Nino bends down, softly kissing the tops of his creamy thighs. Haruka squirms as he moves higher, but Nino shifts his head up and leans forward, playful in kissing and licking his tight belly.

Nino grasps the back of his knees again, and Haruka inhales when Nino pulls him even closer, resting one of his bent legs on top of Nino's shoulder. He kisses and nips the inside of Haruka's thigh, feeling his mate's body shiver with need. Nino glances up at him, and Haruka's glowing eyes are desperate, his exposed chest heaving as he laces his fingers into Nino's hair. He isn't always capable of breaking through Haruka's composed façade, but in these moments when he's successful, it gives Nino a sublime high and confidence like he's never known.

He takes Haruka's hard shaft in his fingertips, then dips to lap his tongue against the tip. Haruka sucks in a shaky breath, eyes clenched shut.

"You taste so good, Haru..." Nino shifts, gripping his mate's hardness with one hand, then using the other to slip deeper between his legs. He teases and strokes the softness of Haruka's opening with his fingertips.

Haruka tenses, arching his neck. The wild length of his hair falls back behind his shoulders. *"God help me—"*

"Tell me what you want, tesoro," Nino says. He flicks his tongue against the wetness of him again to taste. Incredible. "Should I put your cock in my mouth?"

He looks up at Haruka, waiting as he continues caressing and playing, enticing him with his fingers. Haruka finally looks down, his Adam's apple bouncing in his throat from swallowing. He takes a visible breath. *"Please."*

Nino smiles, then bends and takes the length of him into his mouth, slow and smooth. Haruka groans in a throaty sound as Nino works, running his tongue along his ridges—greedy in consuming him. Within minutes, his mate cries out and shivers in ecstasy, deliciously spilling over from Nino's seductive actions.

Haruka's body is trembling when Nino finally lifts his head —dragging his tongue and licking, making sure nothing is wasted. He stands up from the chair, but Haruka surprises him when he grips Nino's pants at his waist. His long fingers are aggressive, unbuckling and unfastening with urgency. Nino smirks, leaning forward to press their foreheads together. "Was there something else I could help you with?"

"Take off your pants," Haruka whispers, his breathing ragged.

Compliant, Nino does as requested. Before he can shift his pants and underwear past his knees, Haruka clutches his shirt and tugs Nino back down to sit in the chair. His mate looks wild as he stands from the table, then steps forward and straddles his thighs. As soon as he rests his weight against Nino's lap, Haruka takes his mouth. The passion behind the kiss makes Nino's heart beat like a drum in his chest.

When Nino pulls away, it's like coming up for air after

being swept deep into the undercurrents of the ocean. He swallows, unable to catch his breath. "There's olive oil behind you."

Haruka looks back, then leans and grabs the deep green bottle from the table before opening it. Once his fingers are slick, he reaches down and wraps them around Nino's stiff length in between them. Nino sighs, the warmth of climax already pulsing within him from Haruka's weight and touch.

"What do you want me to do to you?" Nino smiles, lazy. Haruka's fingers are marvelous as they stroke and move— talented, as if he's playing an instrument. His scent is making Nino's head fuzzy, like he's had one too many drinks.

With his dark eyebrow lifted, he takes Nino's hand and guides it behind his back and toward his naked ass. "You *know* what I want."

Using the slick residue from Haruka's hand, Nino slowly presses his finger inside him. Haruka shifts in pleasure and Nino can feel the tight, warm canal of his mate's body flexing and yielding to him. Nino bites his lip, breathless. "It would be nice if you told me... openly."

He drags his finger out, careful as he switches and presses two fingers inside, making Haruka arch and groan as he pulses them deeper. When Haruka brings his head down, his irises are bright sunset. He takes hold of Nino's chin so that their eyes meet. "Enough talking." He places a quick peck on his lips before shifting up and away from his fingers. Gripping Nino's shaft, Haruka guides himself down to meet and gradually take in his length.

When they're connected, there is no more talking. Or thinking. There's just the two of them and their innate need to be entwined. For their natures and bodies to exist as one. Haruka rolls and rocks his hips while Nino grips him, his fingers digging into his flesh. Within moments, they have both ascended to something that feels like paradise.

MAY

# FIVE

For three days straight, the rain has swept through western Japan. The sky weeps, relentless and gray, stripping the cherry blossom trees clean of their delicate flowers.

6:50 p.m. Haruka sits in the front tearoom of the estate, arms folded while his knee bounces from stress. Lightning flashes against the window, shifting his attention there. The maple tree outside the glass bends and sways in hypnotic rhythm and a rumble of thunder echoes in warning. The weather is *not* helping his unease about this meeting.

The front door to the estate opens, then shuts in a bang. After some loud shuffling, Nino appears in the doorway, his jacket and hair damp with rainwater. Asao passes behind him, likely headed to the kitchen to prepare tea for their impending guest.

"The train delays today are awful." Nino shrugs out of his jacket and disappears for a moment to hang it in the closet beside the tearoom. He calls out, "At least I made it before seven?"

A moment later, he steps down into the room, running his

fingers into the top of his wet, coppery hair to brush it back. Despite being flustered and rain-soaked, he looks handsome in a patterned dress shirt and dark khaki pants. Haruka lifts his chin when he's standing over him. Nino places two neat kisses on his mouth before plopping down beside him onto the couch.

"Welcome home, my love." Haruka smiles. Nino's presence always helps put his mind at ease. Even on the day they met, standing in front of Nino felt like basking in the warm rays of an autumn sun.

"Grazie, tesoro. I don't sense our guest?"

"Me neither," Haruka sighs. 6:55 p.m. Sensing the presence and location of another ranked vampire isn't an exact science, but it is a reliable component of their biology. Haruka can sense Nino much more intuitively because they are bonded —not just his location, but his emotional state and well-being. His thoughts too, when they mutually consent to opening their minds to each other. If the distance becomes too great, Haruka can only discern his mortality.

With three minutes left before their scheduled meeting time, he should detect the vampiric aura of their guest approaching. If he is focused, Haruka can sense every ranked vampire within a twenty-five-mile radius—their presence like warm lights speckled against the dark map of his realm.

With regard to this new purebred, he feels nothing on the horizon. It doesn't make any sense.

"Do you think he'll no-show?" Nino asks. "You told me the purebred you sensed in the woods last year smelled like sage. This *has* to be the same creature."

Gael, an associate of the Almeida Clan, had staged an ambush outside Haruka's house in England the previous year. A reckless attempt to steal his *Lore and Lust* manuscript. The first-generation vampire's effort was thwarted, but an unexpected thing happened. A flash of power emanated from the surrounding woods—the unmistakable presence of another purebred.

The incident had been even more strange because there are no purebred vampires left in England. While the entire pureblood population has suffered as a result of the Great Vanishing, purebreds of British descent have become extinct.

The mysterious sage vampire emerged, then quickly disappeared. Gael also disintegrated right before Haruka's eyes.

"I didn't see the purebred in the woods that night," Haruka reasons. "Just sensed them. So I cannot know for certain."

"I wish we could have refused his request. I don't feel good about this at all."

"My love, we discussed this. We cannot outright refuse a request without justification for doing so. Within the expectations of the aristocracy, it is proper to—"

Haruka sucks in a breath. The heavy presence of an old-blooded purebred has suddenly appeared, creating a distinct pressure in the air around them. Nino sits straight, his amber eyes wide. The vampire has materialized from nothing, and yet he is waiting outside their front door.

The bell rings. 7:00 p.m. Bewildered, Haruka stands, his heart beating wildly. How is this possible? What kind of power does this vampire have? The scent of sage drifts through the air, confirming that this is indeed the vampire he sensed in the woods a year ago.

Nino stands beside him, his fingers raking through his hair yet again. Asao appears, rushing past the tearoom to open the front door. The wash of torrential rain and thunder outside breaks the silence before the door shuts again.

When Asao stands in the entryway, he bows in a polite gesture. "My lords, Lajos Almeida of the Almeida Clan." He moves aside, allowing their guest to step into the doorway.

The vampire is ancient with pale flesh, wrinkled and

creased. A hardness is set in his expression. His posture is straight in a tall, thin frame. He's dressed in pristine formal clothing, but his fashion is severely outdated: a deep blue great-coat, waistcoat and white dress shirt tucked into pleated slacks. He taps his cane as he stands there, lifting his sharp chin as if he is a king and they are his menial subjects.

The old creature steps down into the room. Haruka takes a deep breath, then bows at his waist. "Welcome, Lajos Almeida, to Okayama prefecture. I am Haruka Hirano. This is my mate, Nino Bianchi. It is a pleasure to meet you."

Nino bows at his side, his smile kind but without its usual warmth. "Welcome to our home and realm. We're pleased—"

Lajos raises a gloved hand. Nino stops, glancing at Haruka from the corners of his eyes. Lajos's chin lifts even higher, his dark, sharp gaze focused on Haruka underneath bushy eyebrows. "You are of ancient blood. You are the leader of this house? Are you the elder as well?" Despite his frail appearance, the vampire's voice is heavy, weighted with time and authority.

"No," Haruka says, keeping his face even. "My mate is the elder, but we do not operate our household according to such conservative edicts."

Lajos furrows his gray eyebrows. His silver hair is pulled back and gleams against the recess lighting. "So this house has no leader?"

"It has *two* leaders," Haruka says. Without question, this purebred is his elder, and his blood registers as primeval, like Haruka's own. He knows that he should show their guest respect, but their guest should not openly question the operations of his household—especially within the first two minutes of walking through the door.

Smirking, Lajos steps back and toward the sofa opposite them. A small coffee table is set in between. "Two leaders?

That is not possible." He flicks his long coat to the side before sitting down, never breaking eye contact with Haruka.

"And yet, we stand before you." Haruka sits as well, the vein in his temple throbbing as he folds his hands in his lap. The anxiety radiating off of Nino's body beside him is palpable.

Lajos props his cane against the seat cushion beside him. "In any pairing, there is always one stronger and one weaker. One greater and one lesser. It is the role of the lesser to support the stronger."

"I respectfully disagree," says Haruka. "In any pairing, both are strong, but in distinct ways—their talents and support of one another equal in value. You sent us a formal request for introductions. Please disclose the true purpose of your visit with us this evening. How can we assist you?"

At this, Lajos tilts his head back in genuine laughter. The sound of it is boisterous, startling. It irritates Haruka even more.

When Lajos gathers himself, he runs a gloved hand over his head, focusing on Haruka again. "Very sharp. *You*, young male, are the leader of this house. Your speech is bold and resolute. You radiate power and grace, while this male of new-found blood sitting beside you says nothing. Is this not a fascinating introduction? I cannot remember the last time I have been challenged this way. How amusing you are."

"Have you come here seeking amusement?" Haruka asks, his temper reaching a low boil. "To agitate and offend our household?"

*Haru.*

Haruka's eyes flicker to his mate, recognizing the faint call as it echoes in his mind. He opens his senses to receive Nino's thoughts, clear and concise.

*Nothing he says matters. Don't let him upset you. Stay calm.*

Agreeing, he takes a deep breath. He rolls his shoulders, and Nino reaches over to grab his hand. Haruka refocuses on their pompous, uncouth guest that reeks of sage... He won't eat anything with sage again for a very long time.

"Interesting." Lajos tilts his head at Haruka. "Young male, what is your age?"

He speaks through gritted teeth. "One hundred and three."

"Very young... With your mind and power, you could do great things. You should not waste the gifts you have been uniquely blessed with by playing into these soft, contemporary ideals. You have the ability to shift the very foundation of our race. You could rule over all. I can show you how."

For the first time, Haruka is speechless. He hadn't known what to expect tonight, but it was not this. *What the hell is he talking about?*

"Senhor Almeida, why are you here?" Nino asks, cutting to the chase.

"He speaks." Lajos smiles, but his expression is unamused. "Is your renewed bloodline even a century old? Your ancestors are a disgrace for feeding from humans as long as they did. Repulsive."

They both sit, blinking in response to the derogatory comment. Discrimination between purebred bloodlines is irrelevant. Obsolete. Especially not after the Great Vanishing. Purebred blood is purebred blood. Period.

At their silence, Lajos shifts his gaze back to Haruka. "Are you interested in improving our race? Growing our numbers as glorious purebred entities?"

Haruka stares, feeling as if his brain has stalled, or as if he is misunderstanding something. Is this an elaborate hoax? This antiquated creature with his elitist rhetoric and unapologetic arrogance.

"Our race has become bastardized—marred with these first-, second- and third-generation creatures that reek of human blood," Lajos continues. "Purebreds of the past have fornicated with humans to create these lesser vampiric beings. They guzzle both blood and food, like pigs at a trough sucking up all the earth's resources. I have established a solution. A pure and perfect society where we *multiply*. Where we survive on blood alone and remain nocturnal as our ancestors once lived."

Asao enters the room with a tray of tea and rice crackers. He steps up to the small table, then drops the tray against the surface, making the contents spill and shift in a loud clang. He stares at Lajos with his brow furrowed for a long moment before turning and walking out of the room.

Lajos waves a hand. "See? They are a stain on our race. The unfortunate consequence of avarice and perverted curiosities."

Standing from the couch, Haruka gently releases Nino's hand. This stranger has come into his home, insulted his mate, offended his manservant and challenged the moral foundation upon which Haruka stands. Now, he expresses blatant xenophobia toward ranked vampires. Their introductions are finished.

"I do not share in your ideals, nor do I believe I can help you achieve any of your goals. I am sorry that you have wasted your time. I ask that you leave our realm."

Lajos doesn't move. He looks up, blinking his cold eyes as if Haruka hasn't said a word. "I have an associate that tells me you own an interesting collection of research surrounding vampiric bonds. Is this the case?"

"I have asked that you leave our home," Haruka says, unblinking, as Nino stands up beside him. Lajos breathes a laugh.

"Young male," he says, his smile fading, "I do not take kindly to refusals. Perhaps I am spoiled in my old age, but it is not something I am... accustomed to."

"Then I am grateful to assist in your personal development." Haruka nods. "Take your leave. Now."

Lajos stares. The arrogant smile disappears from his wrinkled mouth and his irises flicker back and forth between the two of them. He sighs, eyes closed as he shifts a white-gloved hand up to the center of his forehead to massage with his fingers. "You are quite strong-minded, and thus will take some convincing. I see that now."

He opens his eyes and they're glowing bright, milky white. He flicks his fingers toward them in a lazy motion. Haruka draws back at the odd gesture, but nothing happens.

"*Haru—*"

Haruka whips his head around, meeting Nino's panic-stricken face. He doesn't understand at first, but when he looks down, Nino's body is dissolving from the bottom up. Haruka tenses at the sight of his form misting before his eyes. Panicked, he reaches out to wrap his arms around him, but there is nothing to hold on to. Nino is gone. He'd been standing there warm and solid one moment, but the next, vanished.

Something like a gaping hole opens in Haruka's gut, as if he's been shot through with a cannon ball. He grabs his stomach from the emptiness and pain. The hollow misery. It isn't as if Nino is dead. He can still sense that he's alive. But he's too far away, somewhere indiscernible and beyond Haruka's reach.

His mind burns hot—a thundercloud of rage, confusion and despair gripping him all at once. His eyes alight as he looks at the old vampire sitting on his couch. Haruka releases the heavy weight of his aura with force, thrusting it toward Lajos to subjugate him in totality. He wraps his energy around the decrepit vampire, lifting him from his seated position and tightening the grip of his energy like a large snake suffocating its prey.

But his mental hold on the creature flickers, like something solid within his grip has turned into sand and slips through his fingers. Lajos dissolves in Haruka's grasp, the form of his body rolling and turning into misty nothingness. He is gone.

"I've seen your power, young male."

Haruka looks up, and Lajos is standing in the doorway, calm and with his white eyes glowing like headlights. A sound just beside Haruka shifts his attention. He watches as the cane Lajos walked in with dissolves, then reappears in his hand.

"You are an exceptional creature." Lajos smirks. "But I have lived for centuries and you cannot hold me. You will not be breaking my limbs today—"

"*Return him NOW*—"

"I do not take orders, young male. I give them. You will calm down and politely reconsider my request. Shall we try again in a few days?"

Haruka opens his mouth to speak, but Lajos dissolves. Gone again. The room is silent save for the heavy rainfall outside.

Despair crashes down on Haruka's psyche—violent and painful. Hopeless. An hour ago, his world had been perfect: safe and insulated with the warmth of profound love and security. Now, the world has turned on its head and Nino is gone. Vanished. The gaping hole Haruka feels in his core intensifies, the searing agony and hollowness of it instigating the blind anger flooding his mind.

He curses, and the pressure of his aura explodes from his body. There is a loud boom and the sound of glass breaking. The lights in the room flicker, then die. He drops to his knees from the pain radiating in his body. He gasps, desperate for air as he sits, shrouded in complete darkness.

# SIX

Across the ocean, it's a beautiful morning in Milan. The weather is sunny and mild, and thankfully dry enough to where Cellina is confident that she won't have any surprise hair malfunctions halfway through the day (namely frizz—the cruel and silent aggressor).

She stares at the large, flat calendar covering her desk. It's almost time to leave for her lunch appointment with the new artist she's pursuing. She looks over to her left. The nude, six-inch strappy pumps that she wore into the office lie discarded against the ornate rug covering the marble floor. She sighs. "High heel bullshit."

One day, when she's the sole proprietor of her own small art gallery, she'll never wear high heels. After she's played the game, made the connections and established her name as a credible force in the art world, she'll wear sexy leggings and bright sneakers to work every day. Anyone who takes issue can kindly fuck off.

Her phone rings, disrupting her fantasy of soft hooded sweatshirts and strappy sports bras. Cellina leans forward, glancing at the screen. Giovanni. "Why?" She frowns. He never calls her. Ever—despite knowing each other and being connected their entire lives. Because their fathers were best friends, she spent the bulk of her childhood with the Bianchi siblings. While Cellina adores and has a long history of looking after the younger brother, Nino, Giovanni is... a different circumstance entirely. Complicated.

"Yes?" Cellina answers. Their communications with each other aren't cordial. Not since she was a teenager, anyway. If he's calling, there's a reason. May as well cut to the chase.

"Come to the house," he barks in his husky voice. That's part of the problem with Giovanni. Too male and overflowing with testosterone. Too proud and bullheaded, using his entitled purebred authority to order people around.

"What? Right now?"

"Yes, please," he says. Silence.

*Shit.* Cellina sits back in her chair, dragging her thick, straightened hair past her shoulders. She twists it behind her head as she mentally rearranges her schedule. Reaching for a pencil, she says, "Give me thirty minutes."

"See you soon." He ends the call.

Cellina hits a different number in her phone and brings it back to her ear. She finishes writing on her calendar, then stands to reclaim her heels. They're like a glorified penitentiary for her feet.

"Hi, Gabriella? It's Cellina De Luca... I'm doing well, but I have to apologize to you. Something's come up and I need to reschedule our lunch. How does Friday work for you?"

---

TWENTY-FIVE MINUTES LATER, Cellina knocks on the heavy oak door to Giovanni's office. A long time ago, it was his mother's office. Cellina smiles to herself, remembering the fierce woman with ivory skin and jet-black hair. The little Japanese she knows, she learned from her. In turn, Cellina's mother had gifted both Nino and Giovanni with Swahili.

After hearing Giovanni call out, she steps inside the room. The ceilings are high and arched. Bright recess lighting makes the marble floors and stone walls look creamy and elegant.

Passing the outer sitting area, she walks through the main arch and into the office. Giovanni stands from behind his desk, broad-shouldered and impeccably dressed in a beautiful royal blue suit. His white shirt is crisp, no tie. He never wears ties if he doesn't have to. She remembers as much from when they were young. He used to say that they made him feel like a dog on a leash—a physical representation of his life circumstances.

Stepping forward, Cellina takes a breath, unconsciously inhaling his clean scent. She can never quite put her finger on it. He smells earthy like rosemary, but... mixed with something peppery or spicy. Ginger? He walks around the corner of his desk to sit against the front edge.

She lifts her chin. "Why are you summoning me like the lord of the realm?" This isn't normal. Something is wrong.

"Technically, I am lord of the realm," Giovanni says, his face serious. "I got bad news from Japan."

Cellina's heart rate triples in its intensity. "What happened?"

"Nino is gone."

"*What?*" Cellina's knees weaken, the weight of his words like a wrecking ball to her stomach. She sits down hard against the leather sofa behind her. "Giovanni, what does that mean? How can he be—"

"He vanished. There was some circumstance with a visitor they had, and it sounds like he's done something to him. The situation isn't clear, but we need to keep this to ourselves."

"Oh God," Cellina breathes, bringing her palms to her face. Her heart is shattering. Nino is without doubt the most wonderful creature she has ever known, and yet he's experienced an unacceptable degree of tragedy in his young vampiric life. He was taken advantage of as a child, lost his mother young, and his father is still ill from her absence. Nino had also been isolated growing up—shunned by their society because of his abuse. Modern vampires are genial about a lot of things, but rarely ever sympathetic to emotional wounds or mental health. It is a distinct cultural failing.

The universe had shown Nino mercy in sending him Haruka: a kindhearted vampire and the love of Nino's life. But now, this.

Stress crashes down, her body trembling and her throat tight. Just as the weight of despair overwhelms her, Giovanni is there. She looks up, startled by his solid presence as he sits down atop the coffee table in front of her, legs gaped on either side of her knees. Without a word, he reaches out and wraps a large hand underneath her hair and at the back of her neck. He pulls her forward, bringing their foreheads together. They're so close that their noses touch.

Cellina gasps, her body even more tense from his nearness. They haven't touched each other in more than a century.

A gentle heat washes over her from their physical points of contact. The calming, reassuring influence of his vampiric aura pours out, covering her in a bright haze. Earthy and spiced, the scent eases her racing pulse, causing her to breathe in perfect rhythm with him. Slowly, in and out.

The last time he did this to her—for her—was when she was thirteen. Her younger brother, Cosimo, had read her private journal, then walked around quoting direct lines from it at random. Lines about her private feelings toward Giovanni. She'd been so upset that she'd wanted to drain him. When she started vocally plotting out the logistics of ending his life (because having an organized plan is the key to success), Giovanni surprised her by leaning into her, bumping their foreheads and letting his aura swell and grow. He calmed Cellina that day, giving her peace of mind while inadvertently keeping her little brother alive... not that he deserved it.

Years later, the comforting sensation is the same. But Cellina and Giovanni have changed.

When Giovanni lifts his head, Cellina opens her eyes with heavy lids. His glowing emerald-green irises are staring back at her. "Are you alright?"

"Yeah," Cellina breathes, sitting up straight to escape the weight of his hand against her flesh, the intensity of his vivid eyes. "Thanks. How is Haruka?"

"Not good." Giovanni rubs the back of his neck, his eyes fading and returning to their normal hazel color with flecks of green. "I haven't spoken to him. Everything I told you is second-hand from the all-knowing one."

"Asao." Haruka's manservant. Despite being a third-generation vampire, he has a unique sense of hearing—the trait profound within his family's bloodline to have survived three generations.

"I'm leaving on a flight to Okayama this evening." Giovanni sighs. "Are you coming?"

Cellina sits back against the couch. She's calm now, her mind focused. "Yes. I just need to go back to the office and make some phone calls. Are you okay?"

"I'm alright. I'll feel better once I get there and understand the whole story."

"Agreed. I need to book my flight. Maybe—"

"I bought two plane tickets. If you can be back here by seven, we can leave together."

*Together?* Cellina raises her eyebrow. Why would they

travel together? For the past century, the unspoken rule has been to avoid each other. He made his feelings toward her crystal clear all those years ago. As a result, whenever they meet now, they squabble—petty and bitter.

But today is different. There isn't any space for their trivial grievances and acerbic remarks. They need to work together.

She nods, mentally rearranging her schedule for the next week. In truth, she's grateful that the hassle of booking a flight has been taken off her plate. Why he would extend this kindness to her, she doesn't understand. But she'll take it.

"He has to be okay," she sighs, the image of her sweet friend and his bright amber eyes flashing in her mind. "There's no other option, Giovanni."

He stands from the table. "I know. We'll figure this out."

# SEVEN

After thirty hours of flights, layovers and amicable silence, Cellina and Giovanni arrive at the Kurashiki estate.

They follow behind Haruka's manservant as he guides them down an elegant hardwood hallway, passing sliding doors painted with beautiful sumi-e artwork.

"He's not listening to me," Asao complains, his voice gruff. "He hasn't slept or set foot outside his library in the past forty-eight hours, and he doesn't want to call the police—says they're useless."

He opens a sliding paper door to reveal a breezeway. A warm rush of muggy spring air caresses Cellina's skin. They step outside. She glances over at the grassy, rain-soaked garden and small koi pond as they walk along the veranda. There's a massive Japanese maple tree in the center with rich maroon leaves. Haruka and Nino's home feels like a Zen retreat for spiritual meditation. Peaceful, natural and breathtaking.

"No new developments in two days?" Giovanni asks. "He can only tell that Nino is still alive and nothing else?"

"Yeah," Asao says, opening a door and gesturing for them to

step into another hallway. "He's alive but far away. He can't surmise anything else. I know human police are incompetent in vampire matters, but we should contact that second-gen detective that was working on Ladislao's vanishing. The one in America."

Giovanni shakes his head. "I don't know... I think we should keep this private for now. See if we can handle it on our own."

Cellina agrees. "Everyone has just calmed down from Ladislao's vanishing. This will create a new wave of widespread panic if it gets out. I think I met that detective once when I was in New York. Anika Cuevas. I remember she had very strong opinions."

"And you don't?" Giovanni glances at her, raising his eyebrow.

"This isn't about me, though."

Asao guides them down another short, glossy hardwood hallway. This area of the estate is more compact, like a small residence unto itself—a guest house.

"You should have heard this Lajos asshole," the manservant mutters. "Everything he said was either arrogant or bigoted. I didn't know purebreds like that still existed. Crusty old bastard."

In very old times, purebreds *were* arrogant and bigoted—callous in lording over ranked vampires, using them and putting their own wants and needs above anyone else's. It's one reason why Cellina adores Nino.

Her friend is like the anti-purebred. Innocent, thoughtful and kind. When his mother died, he'd been so distraught that he'd hidden himself away and refused to feed or interact with anyone—as if he'd wanted to die himself. So, at sixteen, Cellina offered to become his feeding source. That hadn't been the original plan, but she's never once regretted her decision... despite the upset it caused between herself and a certain domineering male.

Asao stops in front of a set of double sliding doors. He reaches down and pulls them apart as if manually opening an elevator. There's a library inside, washed with natural but overcast light from the cloudy sky. Cellina glances around. The space would be superb if it wasn't a complete and utter mess.

There are books everywhere—opened, closed, stacked, discarded. Papers and scrolls are spread out all over the tatami flooring. A low table in a corner is covered with old newspapers, some having fallen over the edge.

Amidst all this chaos is Haruka. He wears a traditional robe, his very long hair a mess and shoved away from his face, haphazardly tied behind his head. He flickers his burgundy eyes up at them for a moment before focusing back down on whatever he's reading. He turns a page.

"Haruka—Cellina and Giovanni came to help." Asao waits. Haruka scratches his head, unspeaking and with his eyes still on the book. He turns another page.

At this, Asao practically growls, losing whatever patience he's been holding on to. "You're scared, I get that. But you said Nino is alive, so you can't sit here and internalize everything on your own. These two came to help you and—"

"Help me do *what*?" Haruka looks up, his eyes the pinnacle of stress. They're weighted with dark circles and his complexion is too pale. He looks terrible. "I do not know where Nino is. He has vanished into thin air and I cannot do anything to reverse what has been done. There are no records of this purebred anywhere—where he lives, his ability, his realm, his lineage—nothing!"

He presses his palms to his face, dragging them upward and into his disheveled hair as his speech hastens, frenzied. "And this is my doing—*I* am responsible for protecting my mate. I was overconfident and lazy, and I allowed this miscreant into our home without knowing enough about him and what he was capable of, and now my mate is—"

With a few strides of his long legs, Giovanni closes the distance to reach Haruka. He places a large hand atop his head, and the woodsy, gingery warmth of his aura radiates outward. It settles around them in a soft glow as Giovanni crouches down in front of Haruka. "First, you're going to calm down. Then, we're going to sit in the kitchen and have some coffee—tea, whatever. We're going to talk about this rationally. Understood?"

Cellina walks forward just in time to see Haruka nod underneath Giovanni's palm. After Giovanni stands and releases him, Haruka smooths a hand over his messy hair, clenching his eyes shut. Cellina takes Giovanni's place, lowering herself to rest on her knees in front of him. She frowns, examining his weary expression. "Are you in physical pain?"

He shakes his head, eyes still closed. "It does not matter." He inhales a shaky breath and opens his eyes to meet her gaze. "You both entrusted me with him and I... I have failed you."

Leaning forward, Cellina wraps her arms around his shoulders. "Don't *say* that. He's alive—we'll get him back. Let's go in the kitchen and talk, alright?" She releases him and rises to her feet. "Please? Will you stand?"

She reaches her hands out toward him. After a moment of hesitation, Haruka grasps them, allowing her to help pull him up from the tatami floor. When he's standing, she clasps one of his hands warmly within hers and they all move to leave the library.

"I TOLD my father the name Lajos Almeida, and he recognized it." Giovanni takes a long sip of his coffee as they sit at the kitchen table. The patio doors are cracked open. Cellina can hear the soft drizzle of rain hitting the courtyard pavement like a subtle soundtrack to their conversation.

Haruka stares at his teacup. He hasn't touched it, but the heat of it swirls and dances in the shadowy light. He flicks his eyes up at Giovanni. "In what way?"

"A long time ago—he said maybe two hundred years? Father was young. This was before he'd even met our mother. A vampire with the name Lajos Almeida requested a visit with him, claiming he was doing research.

"Father said he remembered it because he'd never met a purebred with such dogmatic, harsh views on ranked vampires. He said it disturbed him and that Lajos was obviously trying to get a feel for whether they shared the same views. Father didn't —his best friend, Andrea, is Cellina's father, a first-generation male he grew up with in Milan."

The image of Cellina's handsome, dark-haired father flashes in her mind. He and Domenico—Nino and Giovanni's father—had been like brothers until Domenico fell ill and hid himself away. Her father often talks about how much he misses him, but Domenico has been refusing all outside guests for decades.

Giovanni takes another quick sip of his coffee. "Father said the meeting was uncomfortable, so he wrapped things up fast and sent the purebred on his way. He never thought anything else about him."

"Lajos said..." Haruka pauses, thinking. "That he has created a 'pure and perfect' society where there are no ranked vampires. Was he trying to recruit your father at that time?"

Giovanni shrugs. "It's possible. Father said he never heard from him again."

"What Lajos did to Nino," Cellina chimes in, "is how they describe the Vanishing in history books. Do you think Lajos had something to do with the Great Vanishing?"

They all pause, their eyes flickering to one another. Asao huffs from the counter behind them. "Shady old bastard."

"If he was recruiting," says Haruka, his eyes doggedly tired but bright for the first time since they sat at the table, "does this mean that those disappeared vampires still exist somewhere? And that perhaps they volunteered to be part of this new realm?"

"I don't know about volunteering," Asao pipes up again, folding his arms. "Think about Sora Fujihara's father. He was purebred, but happily mated with a first-gen female. I don't think he would have agreed to go to some purist society and abandon his partner and child."

Haruka exhales. "Right... yes. In the historic records detailing those impacted by the Vanishing, there are similar cases of disappeared purebreds who were bonded with ranked vampires—but just a few. If their views were so conservative, they would not have mated with creatures of mixed blood."

Sadness weighs heavy in Cellina's heart. The ranked vampires left behind had all died within a few weeks of their mates disappearing. While it's difficult to survive a mate's death in a bond, it's impossible for a ranked vampire bonded with a purebred. After being conditioned to consume such potent, rich blood, their bodies can't survive without it—like being perilously addicted to a drug.

Giovanni sits back against the chair, bringing his fingers up to massage the center of his forehead. "This shit is unbelievable. Look—Lajos took Nino because he wants *Lore and Lust*, right?"

"Yes," Haruka confirms.

"He told you to calm down and reconsider, so he'll be back."

Asao nods in agreement. "That's what *I* said."

"So when he comes back, we'll demand that he return Nino." Giovanni opens his eyes to look at Haruka. "In exchange, you'll give him the book. Do you have a problem parting with the manuscript?"

"Of *course* not," Haruka breathes, exasperated. "If I could have fathomed that Lajos would go this far, he could have taken the book from the beginning. None of this is necessary—this barbaric and guerrilla style of negotiation. What century are we in? And when he was taken, Nino had not fed from me in a few days. How can someone who proclaims to have such high regard for purebreds simultaneously treat us with such contempt? To separate a bonded couple by force?"

"Hypocrite bastard." Asao scowls. "He gives us old guys a bad name, you know? Get with the damn times."

Giovanni leans with his elbows against the table and focuses on Haruka once more. "Asao said he hasn't informed anyone in your realm about this. What have you been communicating to them? Who's handling Nino's business appointments? And yours?"

Haruka blinks, emotionless. He's looking at Giovanni as if he's a brick wall. "That is the furthest thing from my mind."

"No one," Asao answers. "Everything has just been paused for the past two days. I've made as many calls as I can to apologize, but things are getting suspicious. They can't keep no-showing appointments without an explanation like this. It's social suicide—and they've only been establishing themselves for a year."

Cellina frowns. "Nino has worked so hard to get his Osaka and Kyoto contacts secured and confident in his ability." Every time they talk, he gives her thorough updates about his progress. Nino loves his new work and position. The singular entity that excites him more is the distraught vampire sitting beside her.

Giovanni focuses his sharp eyes on her again. Cellina swallows.

"How much work can you miss?" he asks.

"Work is slow now, but my schedule toward the middle of summer is crazy. It doesn't matter—I'll make it work until Nino is back here and safe."

"I have associates that can handle some of my meetings, but I have to leave in a month to check on Father. I can come back after that if needed. Let's look at their schedules and talk about covering their appointments. Divvy up what we can. What do you think?"

Cellina nods. She wants to help, even if it means working with Giovanni and constantly ignoring the elephant that follows them around like a shared pet. As long as they keep things surface level and focus on the work, it'll be fine. "Let's do it. I'm in."

"We can tell the vamps of your realm that the two of you are busy with an important, confidential project," Giovanni asserts. "We did that with Father in the early days of his illness, when we were keeping it a secret that Mom had starved in the war. Nobody questioned it when I started taking over—for *years*. So that should settle any unrest within your community."

"Sounds good to me." Asao stands from the counter and moves toward the wide doorway. "Let me show you where your rooms are. You two get settled and I'll start dinner."

Giovanni pushes up from the table. Cellina as well, but they both pause. Their eyes trail down to Haruka. He sits hunched with his elbows against the wooden surface, palms rubbing his face. The mug of tea sitting in front of him is cold and full.

Misery. The blackness radiates from him in waves. Cellina has witnessed these raw, visceral emotions from another vampire in her life. She'd been young. When she thinks back to that particular day, the sadness she feels and the burden of it still sit like a rock in her chest.

Cellina looks up at the broad male standing across from her. The male responsible for that weight.

# EIGHT

## SUMMER, 1914

*The ballroom sparkles with glittery chandelier light and joyful energy. Cellina smooths her flowing silk gown the color of champagne, nervous as she adjusts the lace sliding down the curve of her brown shoulder.*

*She looks around the crowded room and at all the fancifully dressed adults. She mumbles, "Where is he?" Sighing, Cellina decides to go sit in the courtyard. The garden at the Bianchi Clan estate is magical at night, with its beautiful marble fountains and ivy-woven gazebos.*

*She steps forward, and two large hands catch her at her waist. Surprised, she flips around. "There you are." She smiles, looking into his bright hazel-green eyes. "Where have you been?" She isn't certain, but it seems like Giovanni has grown at least three inches taller since last summer. At seventeen, he towers over her.*

*He returns her open smile at first, but then narrows his eyes, mischievous as he looks to his left, then right. He bends toward her ear. "Boring business and war talk with the old vamps. I snuck out."*

*Cellina scrunches her nose. "I'll be your accomplice. Garden?"*

*He nods, grabbing her hand and rushing toward the courtyard doors at the back of the room. Cellina squeezes his warm palm in hers. She could take flight from the frenzy of butterflies in her stomach. Just as they reach the double doors, a familiar voice calls out to them.*

*"Sneaking off again, are we?"*

*Giovanni stops dead, causing Cellina to awkwardly crash into his solid back. They both turn to face Giovanni's mother. Her jet-black hair is pinned up, elaborate and adorned with gorgeous flowers. She's chosen to wear a traditional kimono tonight, and she looks incredible: the belle of the ball.*

*"Aren't you supposed to be in the sunroom with your father?" she asks, raising a perfectly shaped eyebrow.*

*"Mother, I was," Giovanni explains. "For the past two hours... I just wanted a little break? Please?"*

*Her stern expression melts, a knowing smile forming in its place. "Hai hai, wakatta wa. Jaa, Otōto mo issho ni tsuretette, ne. Amari osoku naranaide ne."*

*Cellina stretches her mind, remembering everything Giovanni's mother has taught her about her native tongue. She says yes, but they need to take Nino and they have to come back soon. Cellina looks down at Nino. He's adorable in his fancy suit, and he's gotten a little taller, too. He's quiet as he holds his mother's hand. Nino's amber eyes scan the room, as if at any moment something might jump out and grab him.*

*Giovanni sighs. "Sì, Madre, ho capito." He reaches down and grabs Nino's free hand, gently pulling the silent seven-year-old forward. Cellina takes hold of Nino's other hand, and he looks up at her, smiling. The three of them head into the garden.*

*The moon is high and round, brilliant against the dark, star-*

*speckled sky. It's a warm summer night and the balmy heat feels good against Cellina's exposed shoulders.*

"When I'm home, she makes me take him everywhere," Giovanni complains as they walk down the winding path and toward their usual gazebo. Cellina can already hear the fountain through the brush of trees surrounding them. "He's not my kid— he's yours. You *take care* of him."

Cellina laughs and swings Nino's arm, looking down at him. "You like spending time with G, right?"

He nods as they walk forward, but Cellina's smile fades. "Nino, are you having fun tonight?"

"It's okay." He shrugs. Inside, Cellina's heart is strained. Nino isn't related to her by blood, but with the way they've grown up together, he may as well be. In truth, Cellina adores Nino more than her actual younger brother. Cosimo is a little punk, but Nino? He's sweet. Timid. She doesn't know why, but she feels like she needs to look out for him.

"You're going to miss Mom when she goes away to Japan next week, yeah?" Cellina asks. War is calling and so is Nino's grandfather—demanding that his daughter return home to support her clan.

"Yeah..." Nino says, his eyes scanning the walkway ahead of them.

When they round the path, the large fountain comes into view—marble glistening in the moonlight. The water shooting from the elaborate sculpture almost glows. Nino breaks free of their hands and skips toward the fountain. He leans with his palms against the edge to look into the water, then flicks it with his fingers.

"He hardly talks anymore," Cellina observes. "He used to be so talkative and playful—rowdy."

Giovanni rubs the back of his neck, watching his little brother.

"We should have known something was wrong. The change in his behavior was drastic... It's been a year since Mom found out and killed Uncle, but he still acts like a scared little mouse. And with Father and Uncle being identical twins, Nino is terrible with Father now—won't even go near him. I think it hurts his feelings."

When she turns, her dress flows, airy in the subtle nighttime breeze as she moves toward the gazebo. Giovanni follows.

"That's why your parents want you to spend time with him," Cellina reasons, holding the length of her dress as she walks up the stone steps. "I bet they're hoping he'll come out of his shell again if he's around you?"

Cellina sits against the stone bench and Giovanni settles down beside her. He exhales another heavy sigh. "I understand that. But why do I have to do so much? Father drags me to any and every business meeting he has, and Mother always makes me attend social outings. All the while Nino gets to stay home with the maid and play. When I'm finally home, they tell me to spend time with him. I just want something for myself —anything."

He massages his forehead with his long fingers, then runs them into the thick of his honey-brown hair. Giovanni has always been attractive, but within the past year, he's grown up. The soft, childish features that she's always known have sharp-ened—sculpted and strong. He smells wonderful, too. "You're the first son, Giovanni."

He laughs, bitter. "As if I need a reminder."

She reaches over to rest her hand against his on the bench. Registering her touch, he flips his palm up and laces their fingers together. He looks up at her, trepidation in his bright eyes. "Lina?"

"Yes?"

"You'll be sixteen next summer..."

"I will," she says, keeping her face even. But inside, the butterflies are going wild again.

"Have you... thought about who you want as your source? Or who you might offer yourself to for the first time?"

"Not really, it's a year away," Cellina lies. She's been thinking about it since she was twelve. Turning sixteen means that her vampiric flesh has developmentally hardened. No more hand-feeding from someone her parents chose. In a year's time, she can feed like an adult and offer herself to the vampire of her choosing.

In her mind, it's Giovanni. Of course it's him. He's her best friend. They tell each other everything and they have fun together. He looks out for her and she looks out for him—like the time she overheard Antonio being dared to lick Giovanni's cheek when he greeted him at the spring soiree. Giovanni had evaded being treated like a purebred salt lick because of Cellina's valuable insight.

They understand each other—as if they speak the same innate language. It has to be him. There is only him.

But she needs to be modest about this.

"Why?" Cellina asks, ignoring the excited thump of her heart.

"It's a year away, but..." Giovanni says, his gaze cast down. "Would you consider choosing me as your source? What do you think?"

Cellina can't hide her smile as he looks up at her. She raises her eyebrow, teasing. "The future king of Milan is offering himself to me? The scandal."

"Don't call me that." Giovanni frowns. "I hate that—especially from you. That doesn't matter. I—I just want to... be responsible for nourishing you. If that's okay?"

Everyone has been waiting for Giovanni to offer himself to someone. For the past year, since he turned sixteen, he's kept *feeding from the male his parents designated for him. Vampires within their aristocracy young and old are speculating: Will he switch sources? If so, when? The handsome first son of renowned leader Domenico Bianchi—who will have the opportunity to drink his divine, purebred blood?*

And here he is, waiting for her answer. Cellina bites her lip, overjoyed. "I would be honored... and if you find me pleasing, when the time comes, I would like to become your source as well."

Giovanni surprises her when he presses his forehead into hers, the scent of him overwhelming and making her head spin. "I do," he whispers. "I find you very pleasing—so pleasing. You have no idea..."

He lifts his head, but then tilts it and presses his lips to hers in a swift action. Cellina inhales a breath from the wonderful shock of it. He's never done that before. She's wanted him to. Has fantasized about it. But Giovanni is always behaving himself—playful but restrained. The perfect first son.

He pulls away and his eyes shift into bright emerald green as he stares at her. She swallows. The burn behind her own gray eyes ignites in response to him. The very old blood within her churns, triggered by the innate pull between them.

Giovanni reaches up and holds her face with his palm. "I wondered what color your eyes alighted... Silver. Like lightning. It's perfect..."

This time Cellina leans in and places a shy kiss on his full lips. She can't catch her breath as Giovanni smiles and leans forward again.

"Gross."

A small voice makes them pause and shift their attention. Nino is standing on the stone steps, his cute little nose upturned as he watches them. Giovanni growls, and in the blink of an eye, he's off the bench and sweeping his brother up and into his arms.

*Nino screams and laughs as he's lifted into the air. Giovanni maneuvers him so that he's flying through the night sky.*

*The joy of the young vampire echoes through the trees, making Cellina's heart light. Maybe this is the first time in more than a year that she's heard Nino laugh with such cheerfulness. She stands, walking down the steps to join in the laughter of the two vampires she loves.*

# NINE

The rooms in which Cellina and Giovanni are staying share the same veranda. After she's unpacked her things, Cellina slides the paper door open and ventures outside. Sitting down on the hardwood with her legs folded, she breathes the clean, damp air, watching the rain fall over the bamboo-lined garden.

It's dusk. The sky is theatrical—a mix of pink sunset hues and dark-slate rain clouds. Romantic but dreary. Hopeful? She can hear Giovanni pacing back and forth in his room through the thin door, his footfalls heavy against the traditional flooring. He's on the phone, barking in his "King of the Realm" way.

Staring blankly at the rain-soaked landscape, she loses track of time. When the paper door to Giovanni's room slides open, she looks over her shoulder. He's carrying a large leather-bound planner and his smartphone as he sits beside her, his long legs hanging over the edge of the veranda. She shivers. The temperature has dropped.

"Are you cold?" he asks, watching her.

Cellina shakes her head. "I'm alright."

He nods. "Asao gave me their schedules. I've only glanced

at them, but I should probably take Nino's clients while you manage Haruka's responsibilities. They seem more suited to your expertise, but let me know what you prefer."

He opens the tawny leather planner between them, and Cellina scans the pages in silence as Giovanni pounds out text messages on his phone. She reads, but is discreet in lifting her eyes to check his profile. A shadow graces his strong jaw. Giovanni hasn't worn a beard since last year. He's due for a shave. His expression is displeased as he stares into the glow of his phone. He's sitting right beside her, but as always, he feels miles away—like a beautiful husk of the warm, protective vampire she'd once known.

After reading through the planner and considering, Cellina sets her shoulders back. "I agree with you. I'll take over Haruka's responsibilities. I don't have the Japanese to negotiate detailed business contracts, but I think I can get by with social visits and planning some events. This Latin translation project will have to wait, but I'll still go meet the family and let them know Haruka hasn't dropped their request."

"Alright." Giovanni blows out a breath, still typing and focused on his phone. "I'll pick up everything on Nino's end. In about a month I have to go back home. Let's reassess the plan around that time."

"Sounds good." Cellina sighs. "Is there anything else we can do? Haruka seems like he's about to shatter."

"We're here," Giovanni says, looking up at her with empathetic eyes. "All we can do is be together. Haruka has already turned over every book in his library, and I've been as discreet as possible in reaching out to my contacts... Father is a mix between distraught and murderous. But we have to wait. This creature... Lajos will bring Nino back. He has to if he wants the damn book."

*But what if he hurts him? What if he's suffering?* Cellina

wants to ask, but Giovanni doesn't have the answers. No one does. Stressing out won't help anything. "Right," she says, taking a deep breath to calm herself. "We should talk to Asao about securing high-level sources, depending on how long we need to stay?"

Giovanni shakes his head, shifting his attention back down to his phone. "I don't need that. You should ask him for yourself though."

"Um, you can't go a month without feeding."

He looks at her, smirking with his thick lips. "I didn't know you cared."

She frowns. "Like you give a single fuck about whether or not I care."

"Oh, I give a fuck. Several. You can't even imagine the fucks I give."

"Now *that* I agree with. So, what then? Are you planning on bar-hopping to find your next source? I know that's your secret thing—sleeping around and sampling the local goods."

Giovanni scoffs. "That was a long time ago. Over a hundred years ago. I was *eighteen*. Are you going to hold that over my head forever? I can't ever live that down?"

"You can do whatever you want. It has nothing to do with me—"

"It has everything to do with you. And all I wanted was for you to fucking *look* at me. To *acknowledge* me."

His heavy voice echoes through the silence of the rainy garden. Cellina blinks. "What? What the hell are you talking about? You told me—"

"I know what I said, alright? But I—"

There's a knock at Giovanni's door. He turns, and Cellina hears Asao's voice from inside. "I have the table set for dinner."

Giovanni stands, abrupt, then bends to pick up the large planner between them. Cellina gets up, dusting her leggings off as she glances over at him. He avoids her gaze and walks back into his room.

They move toward the kitchen in weighted silence. Cellina is worried about her missing friend and the emotional state of his husband. Now isn't the time to dance with old skeletons from her and Giovanni's closet. That is the absolute last thing she needs right now.

# TEN

Nino opens his eyes and is hit with an overwhelming sense of nausea. His body is like putty, but aches as he flips over against something soft. He groans, his mind in a daze, trying to register his surroundings.

It's sunset. The window in his direct line of vision is filled with orange clouds against a darkening sky. There's also a strange tree... He's never seen anything like it.

"Meu anjo está acordado?"

An unfamiliar voice hovers above him in his hazy state—like a Portuguese-speaking deity. *My angel is awake?* The sound is close. Too close.

He looks over his shoulder, and a male vampire with very long toffee-brown hair is staring at him with pale, oceanic eyes... not quite blue but not green. His face is gaunt as he smiles. He would benefit from having a meal. Or five.

"Look at how gorgeous and golden you are, and this rich, molten aura..." The vampire raises his eyebrow. "Like dipping my cock in warm honey. Uma delícia..."

Nino throws himself off the bed. He hits the hardwood

floor in a heap and his head spins. His perception swirls with vertigo. To make matters worse, there's a distinct hollowness pulsing in his core. Nino arches his neck in a groan, feeling the severe emptiness within himself where there is usually a deep contentment. In combination with the nausea and disorientation, he might crumble altogether.

"Are you okay? I was mostly kidding... na maioria das vezes." The long-haired vampire is leaning over the edge of the bed and looking down at him like a curious child looks at a wounded animal stuck in a well. Nino shifts further away, his body protesting in agony while his eyes water. He pulls himself upright to sit against the wall under the square window.

*Where the hell am I?* One minute he's at home, and the next... His body had started to disappear. Now he's in one piece. But his mind is spinning and the emptiness inside him excruciating—

"Hey, honeycomb. Are you alright? Listen, Esqueleto's vanishing trick leaves you feeling like merda for a day or so... and you slept all day yesterday. Just breathe, okay?"

Nino watches the bony vampire staring back at him from the mattress. *Why were we in bed together? What's going on?*

"My God..." The other vampire slinks off the bed and toward Nino. "You look like you're about to puke. Try and relax—"

As the male reaches out, something inside Nino springs to life. Through the pain, hollowness and confusion, his aura rushes outward. The unknown vampire draws back in haste as Nino's blood-orange essence expands from his body to form a perfect sphere around him. Nino's eyes are wide as he looks at the stranger, his image now tinted sunset by the colored filter of Nino's energy between them.

The thin vampire lifts a hand, hesitant. He presses his palm against the sphere. Nino's chest heaves from anxiety, but the stranger's hand rests flat at least two feet away from his face. The surface is solid.

"Uau! Que lindo! This is incredible, honeycomb... beautiful."

A clicking sound across the small room makes Nino lift his gaze. An old door screeches open. Lajos sweeps inside and moves straight toward him, a tall and young purebred male at his side. Nino narrows his eyes and notices something strange about the younger vampire's appearance. He is emaciated, just like Lajos and the long-haired stranger, but this new male... He's also missing an ear.

The vampire with toffee-brown hair rushes to sit on the bed again, scattering like a large rat as Lajos comes and stands in front of Nino.

"Now then, what is this?" Lajos says, bending to examine the bright sphere. His heart pounding, Nino presses back tighter against the wall. He doesn't know how he's doing this, but he prays that it holds. Lajos rests his palm atop the solid shape. "Hm. There is more to you than meets the eye. Your powerful mate has taught you something."

The long-haired male speaks in Portuguese from the bed. Nino doesn't produce the language well, but his comprehension level is high. "Uncle. It is cruel to separate two bonded purebreds like this."

Lajos runs his hand across the curve of the sphere, focusing, as if it's a complex riddle. "These young, modernized purebreds know nothing of true devotion. I imagine their bond was forced for political means or shallow attraction... The number of attempts it took is probably disgusting."

"A bond is a bond." Long-hair shrugs.

"Incorrect. And as if you care about bonds. Your sexual deviancy is so atrocious I needed to put a stop to it. Disgrace... My brother taught you nothing about modesty and self-worth."

"On the contrary, I feel my self-worth is so valuable that I should be shared with as many creatures—"

"Be *quiet.*" Lajos turns his head, beady eyes focusing on Nino, and switches back to English. "Young male, I realize that perhaps we've gotten off on the wrong foot. With your mate asking me to leave, things escalated rather quickly. My temper does get the better of me at times. I would be remiss in ignoring such a fundamental truth." Lajos blinks, his expression softening as he watches Nino. When Nino remains quiet, he goes on.

"Perhaps we should go to the sitting room and talk? You could tell me a little about this *Lore and Lust* manuscript that your mate possesses, and I can teach you more about my realm and the great things I've achieved here?"

In lieu of responding, Nino shuts his eyes, praying that his aura continues to hold. He doesn't want to go in another room and talk to this strange old creature. He wants to go home.

Nino's eyes fly open again when Lajos slams his hand against the thick surface in a loud bang. "*Yet again* you remain silent! What the hell is *wrong* with you? Where is your pride as a purebred vampire?"

"Please—please just take me back," Nino says, swallowing hard. "If you want to talk, we can do it in my home. You don't need to *do* this. We don't do things this way anymore."

Lajos lifts his creased chin, an arrogant smirk on his thin lips. "Tell me more about the book and I will take you back."

"Take me back first... then we can discuss—"

"I do not take orders from weak, new-found purebreds." His eyes glow bright white in his anger. Nino draws even tighter into the wall but nothing happens. Lajos snarls. "When this shield breaks—and it will—the first thing I'll do is dissolve that useless tongue from your mouth."

The old purebred stands straight, his white eyes burning

out and returning to their darker, hardened state. He turns, the hardwood floor whining under his feet as he walks toward the door. He directs his speech toward the long-haired vampire on the bed. "Make yourself useful for once and watch him. If either of you tries to leave, I promise you won't get very far."

Long-hair nods but remains silent. When Lajos and his tall companion with the missing ear are gone and the door closes, the skinny male turns to Nino. "Listen, if he disappears your tongue, don't worry about it so much, amigo. It will grow back. It's just... painful."

Nino presses his palms against his face, then drags them up to grip his hair. He's terrified and confused, and he wants this hollow, excruciating feeling to subside. *How did this happen?*

Like a timid cat, the male slinks down to the floor again to meet Nino there. He folds his legs just off-center from the protective sphere. "When Esqueleto brought me here last year... I think it's been a year? Eu acho? Anyway, he was so angry—he vanished my *testicles*. Balls and everything."

Meeting the thin purebred's gaze, Nino frowns. "What the hell are you talking about?"

"But they grew back!" he says, cheerful. "Everything—it was slow, and it wasn't pretty... I was like one of those mannequins in the department store. Maybe six months later I was fine? So don't worry. Não se preocupe com isso. I didn't pee the whole time. Turns out we don't need to pee if we're not consuming human food stuff. Who knew?"

"God..." Nino's eyes shut tight as he leans his head back against the wall of his energy. *Is he trying to comfort me?* He feels sick, his body aching in protest of being so far from his mate. He's starved for Haruka in every way.

"Amigo, what is your name?"

Keeping his breathing slow and even, Nino opens his eyes, looking the male in the face and suddenly recognizing him.

He's staring back with his faded turquoise eyes, expectant. Nino doesn't think he can trust him... but given his eagerness to reassure, ignoring him doesn't seem right either.

"It's Nino. You're Ladislao Almeida, aren't you?"

He raises his eyebrows. "You *know* me? I am still recognizable? Ebaaa." He smiles and opens his palms in a grand gesture.

Nino blinks in disbelief. Ladislao is much thinner compared with the images and videos of him in the media. The chiseled features, long hair and olive skin tone are the same. Personality-wise, though, he isn't at all what Nino had expected.

"Where are we?" Nino asks, looking up toward the window and the darkening sky.

"That's a good question. Geography-wise, I have no clue. But I'm pretty certain that this is my tio's realm. His 'perfect purebred society,' or whatever. I've tried to leave this house a couple times during the day, when everyone is sleeping, and, well... I'm still here. There's nothing but dirt and rocks for miles and miles. Tio gets super mad when I try to run, so I've stopped. I like having my testicles attached to my body, you know? He wins."

Nino sighs, exhausted and stressed and really wishing that he would stop bringing that up.

"My tio abuses his power and old blood," Ladislao says. "He doesn't like to kill other purebreds—just teach them lessons so they 'know their place.' É *horrível.*"

"I vanished, but I'm not... I'm here—somewhere. We're not dead." Nino tries to wrap his mind around the situation, needing to make sense out of something.

"Yes, correto. You are not alone. There are many of us here. Can you feel their presence? Try concentrating."

For the first time, Nino turns his focus outward, ignoring the pain and fear reverberating throughout his body. Eyes closed, he breathes in. Ladislao is right. The air around them hums with the energy of purebred vampires. But it's faint... like a gentle electrical current whispering through the atmosphere. He tries to discern their number, but it's difficult. The pulse of energy is too weak. "How many are here?"

"Eu não sei. Sem pistas, amigo. Esqueleto won't let me out of this room, so I can't say. Aside from my failed escapes, I've been stuck in here for a year without food or drinks or sex. No *sex*. Ahh, so boring. Just kill me already."

"Why do you keep calling Lajos 'Skeleton'?"

"Well, look at him—at *me*." Ladislao's seafoam-colored eyes are wide, incredulous. "Everything with my tio is too, too strict. I get blood once every couple days and that's all. You know, there's a myth that we as purebreds don't need to consume food. It's true that we can survive okay without it, but our bodies are *alive*. These things help make us strong."

Nino sits a little straighter within his aura. "Where are all these purebreds I'm sensing? I feel them but... it's distant."

"How about you relax, yes? Do we need this bubble between us?" Ladislao reaches up and knocks against the hard surface. The sound echoes as if he's hitting hollow glass. "I was just kidding earlier... about my cock and the warm honey thing. You are yummy and I'm horny as hell, but I am not your enemy. I respect your bond, I promise."

Nino bites his lip. Part of him worries that if he keeps this up, it'll exhaust him and fizzle out, leaving him defenseless in his already distressed state. He also worries that if he withdraws it, he won't be able to press it outward again. He curses himself for not taking his and Haruka's meditation more seriously.

It's a risk, but he isn't sure how long his body and mind can function while exerting so much energy. He closes his eyes and wills the strength of the sphere back inside him, feeling it fade and dissipate. He'd been warm within his aura, but now the damp, cool and clammy air of the room settles against his skin like a wet blanket. It makes him shiver.

Ladislao smiles. "Much better. You should save your energy. Can you stand? Look out the window above your head."

Ignoring his aching limbs and the hollowed, forlorn sensation in his abdomen, Nino pushes himself up from the floor. He turns, using the sill of the window as leverage to support himself as he takes in the view beyond the glass.

Their position is high, the precipice of a mountain overlooking a vast, desert-like valley with craggy rocks, wild, scattered brush and the most unique trees he's ever seen. They remind him of flipped umbrellas: as if the wind blew them too hard and cast all their branches upright, reaching toward the sky instead of outward and down like most trees. The landscape is alien to him, as if he's on an entirely different planet. The horizon is packed with dark blueish-purple clouds that look like mountains unto themselves, and an orange sunset backlights the broken spaces where he can see the sky. Nothing else is here—no stores, no buildings, no roads or people.

"Look to your right."

Nino jumps at the closeness of Ladislao's voice just at his ear.

"Sorry, sorry." Ladislao holds his hands up in an amicable gesture. "Can you see, just beyond the scatter of trees? Down in the valley waaaay over there..."

Squinting, Nino registers something—squares and rectangles. A large cluster of mud-colored dwellings, darkened and shadowed from the setting sun. If Ladislao hadn't pointed them out, Nino would never have noticed them because they're almost camouflaged within the natural flow of rough terrain. "Is it... some kind of town?"

"A large village, I think? It's where all the purebreds are. They live down there—I see them sometimes at twilight, like tiny specks in this strange place. There's water around us, too. I could smell it in the air when I tried to escape, but I never reached the coast. Maybe this is an island?"

As Nino observes the barren scene through the window, something strikes him. He turns, meeting Ladislao's gaze. "I disappeared from my home... and the news said that you 'vanished.' Is—is this place... Is Lajos responsible for taking all these vampires?"

"Está certo, honeycomb."

Nino frowns. "Please stop calling me that."

"It suits you, celestial creature..." He smiles, batting his eyelashes. "Like a golden angel."

"Should I reform my aura?"

"Ahh, so strict." Ladislao folds his arms, pouting.

# ELEVEN

*I've lost him...*

The rain is still falling heavily on the third day of Nino's absence. Haruka sits on the floor of his library, hunched and staring out the window. The light is gray. His world is dark. Empty. Sorrow eats away at him, eroding and hollowing out his chest. He stares blankly, unmoving, but when he hears Cellina's voice, his eyes shift in her direction.

"Haruka... you should eat something. You didn't eat dinner yesterday either."

He sits up straighter. "I am not hungry."

*I lost him...*

Cellina sits on the floor beside him, folding her legs. Haruka doesn't want to talk. There's nothing to discuss.

But she doesn't talk. She sits beside him on the tatami in silence. They listen to the loud tapping of rain against the roof, breathing in the earthy, damp scent of it mixed with the grassy essence of the flooring.

*I can't lose him... I will not survive this again...*

Haruka rubs his palms against his face. Hopelessness swells

within him, billowing and suffocating like smoke from a forest fire.

"I think when Nino met you... it was love at first sight."

Taking a breath, Haruka lifts his head, glancing at Cellina. Her gray eyes are cast down to the floor and the soft glow of overcast light illuminates her brown skin.

"I remember the first time he told me about you. He said that you were sophisticated and that you smelled really good. I've known Nino since he was a baby, but he'd never talked about another vampire that way. And then he offered himself to you within a couple days of spending time with you. I was *shocked*. He had never offered his blood to anyone before—never even talked about doing it! Did you know you were his first?"

Haruka shakes his head, his mind pushing through the fog and cobwebs of despair to roam back to that time. Those days when his interactions with Nino were so new. Their friendship pure. "No... not initially. I—I was in a dire circumstance, but he offered himself to help me."

Cellina meets his eyes, smiling. "Because he loved you, right from the beginning. He hadn't trusted anyone besides me and his brother for so long, but then he instinctively trusted you. It was beautiful watching my friend bloom and open up with you—in ways he hadn't with anyone else."

She reaches over, taking hold of Haruka's hand as it lies slack against his thigh. She grips his palm. "He told me that being with you felt safe. You were thoughtful, but never treated him strangely because of what happened to him. He said he finally felt normal with you."

"He *is* normal," Haruka says, then pauses. "Well, he is exceptional, but deserving of the same respect and consideration as anyone else."

"You know most vampires don't think like us. What his

uncle did to him is forbidden. His mother killed him, but it's almost like... Nino carried the indignity of it? It wasn't even his fault, but so many vamps in our realm back home rejected and pitied him—like he represented something shameful. It got so bad to where Nino hardly ever left the estate."

Haruka scowls. "*They* are shameful, for harboring misplaced resentment and causing further harm to someone who had already experienced trauma. Narrow-minded idiots..."

"I agree completely." Cellina nods. After a moment, she smiles, tilting her head. "Did you know he can dance really well?"

Haruka blinks and draws back. "I... did not."

"Yup. When he had very hard days after his mom died, I'd blast music in his room and we'd dance. Your hubby has moves."

For the first time in three days, Haruka smiles, thinking that although he has never seen his mate dance, Nino's moves are definitely evident in other areas.

"Hm, what else..." Cellina looks up to the ceiling, thinking. "When he was little, he used to bite into apples and peaches with his fangs and suck all the juice out. He would tell me that he was practicing to be really good at feeding. It was so cute but so weird... Oh! He's also really good at chess and other strategy games."

"I know about this," Haruka admits, amused. "I asked him to play chess with me once. He was reluctant, so I thought his skills were likely novice. But he beat me. When I suggested shōgi, he complained and called it an 'old man's game,' but then he beat me at that as well."

Cellina laughs, a sparkling sound that fills the room. "He *always* wins—against me, Giovanni, my little brother, Cosimo... even Domenico. Nobody can beat him. He's so blasé while he's playing, so you think he's not paying attention. But then you look up and realize you're toast!"

He chuckles with Cellina, his heart warm but still in pieces from the reality of the situation.

"He chose you," Cellina says. "It took Nino a very long time to give himself to someone, and it's only been a year of your bond. I think you two have a long way to go, Haruka. This is just a bump in the road. We'll get through this."

"What if we don't? Cellina, I... I have failed in keeping him safe—"

"You haven't." She squeezes his palm a little tighter. "You had no idea something like this could happen. We were totally caught off guard, but it'll be alright. Have hope."

Sighing, he drops his shoulders. "It is difficult to be optimistic when life has been merciless and cruel in the past."

"But life also gave you Nino."

Haruka nods, the simple statement and the implication behind it undeniable. "Yes."

She scoots a little closer, laying her head against his shoulder and gripping his hand tight. "So we'll get him back. And you don't need to sit here in misery all by yourself. We're here because we're your family. We're going through this together."

When they're silent again, the sound of the heavy downpour rushes to the forefront. Haruka doesn't know what to do. He isn't sure that he trusts life to send him something so good without then ruthlessly snatching it away from him. Hope feels like an indiscernible thing. Something out of focus and far away. But he acknowledges Cellina's warmth and kindness. That much is tangible.

Haruka squeezes her palm back and takes a deep breath, relaxing against the magnolia scent of her mixed in with the rain.

# TWELVE

"So how did you know he was the one? The one you wanted to bond with."

Ladislao sits perched on an old, tufted ottoman at the end of the bed. He's leaning over the chipped brass railing, staring at Nino in the dim candlelight. Everything in the room feels old. Outdated, as if the house were built and decorated sometime in the 1800s and hasn't been touched since. There are light fixtures, but no electricity, and the air around them is dank and cold—the wind howling and rushing outside as soft rain pelts the window.

Nino lies on his back across the top of the bed, palm pressed to his forehead and his eyes closed in concentration. They'd had a stand-off where Nino refused to sit in the bed with Ladislao. The latter conceded (reluctantly and despite many promises that he wouldn't try anything), encouraging Nino to get off the icy, dirty floor.

Sighing, Nino opens his eyes with heavy lids. He stares up at the darkened ceiling, calling Haruka's face to his mind: his warm burgundy eyes, the soft pucker of his lips and the tiny mole just off the bridge of his nose. "His nature sang to me, like... in me and through me. It came to a point where being with him was easier and more natural than being without him. I wanted everything from him, and I'd never felt that way about anyone before."

"Mm, can't say I've ever felt that way... and I've banged a lot of different kinds of creatures—humans and vampires."

Nino shakes his head against the bed, eyes drifting shut.

"But I have fun, you know?" Ladislao says. "In my own ways. Once, I had an affair with a two-hundred-year-old first-gen queen from an aboriginal tribe in Australia. Maybe she was my favorite? And another time, I had a human female who had once been a male, and she—"

A quiet knock at the door makes Nino's eyes flicker open. He sits upright, slow and groaning from the nausea still swirling in his body. Ladislao lifts a hand in reassurance. "No stress, honeycomb, it's just feeding time. Breakfast."

"But it's night."

"The vampires here are nocturnal." Ladislao stands from the ottoman and walks across the creaking floorboards. He cracks the door open, peeking through. After a polite greeting, he opens it wide. A small female vampire with a head full of wild and curly hair enters. She's carrying a fanciful tray in one hand and holding the handle of a firelit lantern in the other. The soft glow of light does little to hedge the darkness within the room.

Nino looks toward the door and notices the tall vampire with the missing ear standing just outside, so he flares the strength of his aura outward to cover himself. The vampire sneers through the crack before turning and shifting out of view.

After setting the tray on a small table, Ladislao takes the

frail female by the hand. Her hesitation is obvious, and she is fearful as he guides her toward Nino.

"Minha amiga, he's okay," Ladislao assures her. "He's kind, like me. And from the outside world."

She's blinking at Nino with large brown eyes. The dim nature of the room makes the light of Nino's aura sparkle and reflect in her irises.

"Nino, can she touch your shield?" Ladislao urges her to stand at the bedside, just beyond the perimeter of his sphere. The girl seems harmless, and Nino knows he's well protected behind his aura, so he nods.

Ladislao guides her hand up. He gently presses her palm flat against the shape. Her eyes widen with astonishment. She sucks in a breath and whips her head toward Ladislao, then to her hand before resting her gaze on Nino.

"She can't speak," Ladislao whispers. "I think my tio or someone did something to her... She's the only purebred I've met here outside of the tall guy with one ear. It took me months to earn her trust, but I think I have it now?"

Looking her over, Nino considers the weak pulse of her purebred aura—the quiet swirl of two separate energies within her. "She's bonded."

"Mm. I think her mate is down in the village." He turns to her. "See? We're not bad people. He's strong, but he won't hurt—"

The three of them jump at a loud banging sound against the door. The small female removes her hand and rushes toward the exit. Before she's there, the one-eared male steps inside, snarling, "*Enough*—Kahla, what's taking you so long? Useless wretch."

As soon as the girl disappears into the dark hallway, the male slams the door shut, rattling the walls. When it's silent,

Nino withdraws his aura and falls back down against the bed in a huff, his energy levels tanking fast.

"I don't know why his ear hasn't regenerated already—it's been over a year now..." Ladislao walks over to the small table, regarding its contents: two glasses filled with liquid.

"She left her lantern. Do you want blood?"

Nino's stomach turns. "Whose blood?" he asks, his voice dry and tired as he lies with his cheek pressed against the silk comforter. *This smells weird...*

"Don't know." Ladislao shrugs. "But it's purebred, so it will help you feel better."

"No thanks."

"You can drink another vampire's blood this way without hurting your bond, amigo. So long as it isn't intimate feeding—"

"I *know* that. I don't want it." Nino sighs, his aching body limp against the bed as he mumbles. "I'd starve first."

Across the room, Ladislao picks one of the glasses up from the tray. "True devotion... My tio is wrong about you and your mate." He lifts the glass to his lips and finishes the entire thing in one long pull.

"Who was that female?" Nino asks when he's done. "Why did you have her touch my aura?"

Ladislao picks the second glass up and holds it in Nino's direction. "Last call?"

"It's all yours."

He lifts the glass and devours it. Nino can't imagine drinking another vampire's blood—under any circumstance. His mate has experienced the deepest betrayal possible within their culture. Nino would never do anything to trigger that feeling within him again. Ever.

When Ladislao is finished, he smacks his lips in a loud, satisfied sound. "I don't know who this is, but they're not bad at all. Very nice to my nature." He places the glass down, then moves back to his seat on the ottoman. "She's been bringing me blood since I arrived a year ago. I think my tio chose her because she's non-verbal, which means she can't talk about me with her other community members... I could be wrong though."

"Are you a secret? And why would she be afraid of me?"

"Because she's young, and maybe... I think some vampires here, they don't know anything about the outside world. She was so skittish and fearful of me at first—for a long time. But after a while, I could see her mind changing. She started smiling at me when I said funny things and she lingered in the room, listening to me talk instead of dropping off the blood and running away. Usually, she doesn't have an escort—the one-eared creepy guy stays pretty close to my tio's side. She was nervous again today, but did you see how she reacted to your aura?"

"She seemed surprised."

Ladislao nods. "It's good for her. This exposure. I've noticed... Aside from my tio, maybe the other vampires here have weak auras? Kahla and One-ear, their energies are so pathetic as purebreds. After being here a year, I feel that mine has faded, too. I think she was surprised at how strong your aura is."

Nino pushes himself upright. "Why is your uncle doing this? Do you know how this started?"

"I know he started this place a little over a hundred and fifty years ago, after he got into a fight with my father. They couldn't agree on how to run the realm in Rio de Janeiro after Grandfather died, but since my father was the elder, he won. My tio decided he'd make his own 'perfect realm' somewhere new."

*Our race has become bastardized—marred with these first-,*

*second- and third-generation creatures that reek of human
blood...*

The harsh words Lajos expressed during his visit to
Kurashiki resurface in Nino's mind. It seems the old vampire
has succeeded in his goal. But to Nino, the result is questionable: faint auras, skittish and non-verbal servants and a one-
eared henchman. Nino has never met purebreds like this. This
realm seems far from perfect.

"Do you think the purebreds like living in this place?"
Nino asks. "Are they happy?"

"Like I said, I haven't spoken to anyone besides Kahla, and
she can't speak to me, so I don't know. But as for me, I would
like to leave as soon as possible. Tio thinks I'll blab about his
society if he lets me go. I don't even know where the heck we
are! So what if I talk—what would I say? Who wants to talk
about this place... Este lugar é um lixo. I want to quickly
forget it."

"Agreed." Nino lays his head back, breathing a deep sigh.
His incisors are throbbing, threatening to elongate on their own
from want of blood. He's hungry and tired, uncomfortable, and
yearns for his mate to fill the excruciating void pulsing in his
abdomen. He shivers from the damp, cold air of the room. It
feels like the faded walls are closing in on him.

"Your condition is not good, honeycomb. When's the last
time you fed?"

Nino considers. This is his third day here. Before that, he
hadn't fed from Haruka in a few days—which isn't like them,
but things had gotten busy with Nino staying overnight in
Osaka for business. "Almost a week."

"Nada de bom. Your skin is looking gray. Are you cold?
Should we cuddle?"

"No."

"I can warm you up. I'm a little bony right now, but it could help?"

Nino closes his eyes again, concentrating on his inner nature and insulating himself with his own warmth. As the glow of it radiates, he thinks about his home—his and Haruka's nest and the peace, love and security they've built there.

"I want to meet your mate."

At the sound of Ladislao's voice, Nino's concentration breaks, but he keeps his eyes closed. Silent.

"I want to see this person that inspires such fidelity within you. So much so that I can't even sit on the bed with you... This dirty velvet thing, ah! Tão desconfortável! Eu não gosto..."

Recognizing the pout in his voice, Nino bites back a grin. "You can sit on the bed—but stay at the foot, please."

HOURS LATER, Nino's breathing is shallow. Faint. He lies motionless on his side. When he runs his tongue along his teeth, his incisors have sharpened of their own accord.

He needs to feed. His skin is dry—his insides too, as if he's been lying out in the sun and all the life and nutrients are being siphoned from his body. Moving even an inch sends shock-waves of pain through Nino's core and limbs.

"Ei, honeycomb, you need to drink the blood later tonight—you won't last like this." Despite Nino's request, Ladislao is sitting just behind him and against the headboard, his long fingers flittering and stroking Nino's hair. "You have to think of your mate. His survival is rooted in yours, amigo." Even speaking takes energy that Nino can't afford to expend.

Loud footfalls in the hallway make Ladislao jump up from his relaxed position. By the time the door swings open, he's back on the ottoman at the end of the large bed. Using all the energy he can muster, Nino flares his aura outward. It's weaker now—he can feel it. But it'll still hold.

The footsteps draw closer as he lies with his cheek flat against the comforter.

"Time to go home."

Nino lifts, slow, cautious. Lajos is standing over him, his black eyes emotionless. He lifts his cane and taps the glassy surface of Nino's essence. His smile is eerie. "I cannot return you if you remain shielded from me, now can I?" The tall vampire with one ear walks up to stand just beside Lajos, his thin, pointed face cast in shadows.

Nino flicks his eyes toward Ladislao at the end of the bed, who then offers a slight shrug. The tension is thick in the silence, with everyone staring at Nino inside his bright orb.

"Well?" Lajos asks. "It is not my intention to keep you here. Not without your mate, anyway…"

Heart racing, pulse throbbing in his ears, Nino swallows. *I have to get back home…* He can't survive much longer in this state. He doesn't have a choice. Breathing in, he unfurls and withdraws the power of his aura, but the second it dissolves around him, the old vampire's hand darts out, his fingers gripping Nino's chin hard.

"*Ah—*"

Lajos's eyes glow bright white as his face contorts in anger. Before Nino can process what's happening, a hot, bubbling sensation swells within his mouth—as if it's full of baking soda, vinegar and fire. He inhales from the discomfort and the space is unexpectedly hollow. Empty and bewildering. He tries to swallow but coughs, his chest rattling as he gags from the loss of something fundamental. Lajos removes his fingers from Nino's face and an intense pressure pounds against his chest, knocking him back so that he tumbles off the opposite side of the bed.

"*Tio*, this is too much—"

"Keep your mouth shut or you're next."

Nino is coughing, choking and trying to breathe through the pain of the surprise attack. He rolls onto his back against the icy floor. When he opens his eyes, the one-eared vampire is menacing and towering over him. Nino lifts his arms, but there's another intense slam against his ribs.

Then there's nothing. Blackness and silence as his body goes limp.

# THIRTEEN

*Personality, problem-solving, behaviors and emotions... judg-
ment. Speech? No—not this. Body movement... motor strip?*

Haruka pushes his current book aside and picks up a heavy
clinical anatomy reference. He flips to the index and scans with
his finger as he sits crouched on the floor.

He doesn't know what time it is. It doesn't matter. It's dark.

*Motor strip—primary motor cortex... controls voluntary
movement, speech, swallowing. The thalamus relays sensory and
motor signals to the cerebral cortex... cerebral cortex. Higher
intellectual functions... Perhaps—*

He tosses the book away in a lazy motion, then lifts to grab
another reference, flipping to the back once more. Haruka's
head snaps up as he senses the vaguest hum of energy, like elec-
trodes shifting in the atmosphere of the room. He stands
upright, slow and with every muscle in his body tensing. On
instinct, his eyes alight against the darkness.

The intruder materializes in the center of the room, his thin
body solidifying from a misty wave of atoms and silver parti-

cles. It is Lajos, wearing the same dark, formal and outdated clothing. He taps his cane against the tatami and flashes an arrogant smile. "Have you reconsidered, young male?"

"Return my mate." Haruka stares, trembling. Burning fury and desperation swirl within his mind, chaotic. Being at this cruel creature's mercy... He *hates* it. "Return him now and you can have the manuscript."

Lajos raises an eyebrow. "Both you and your mate insist on negotiating with me. Is this how things are done in the modern age? Quid pro quo and diplomatic conversations—"

"*Enough talking.*" Haruka takes a breath, seconds from shattering. "Return him, take the book, leave us."

Lajos stares at him for what feels like an eternity before his white eyes finally alight. "This arrangement suits me. Consider yourself fortunate that I do not teach you a lesson about respecting your elders."

The energy in the room shifts again, silvery atoms waving and gathering in the air of the space between them. Nino's body forms, then drops hard against the tatami. He groans, his eyes clenched as a bright sphere of blood-orange light flashes, growing and radiating around him. Haruka rushes forward, smoothly passing through the warmth of the shape and dropping to his knees to cradle Nino's head against his thighs.

"You insufferable little twit," Lajos snarls, his gaze focused on Nino. He addresses Haruka. "*Where is the manuscript?*"

Haruka holds Nino's head. He is gray and in a great deal of pain. The bronzed glow of his skin tone is diluted and ashen, the texture of it flaking and dry. Haruka answers while examining his mate. "The table behind you."

Nino's chest is heaving, his face clenched in distress. Haruka runs his fingers into the top of his hair, then holds Nino's cheek. "My love, you need to feed." He presses his palm against his mate's mouth to urge him, but he surprises

Haruka when he shifts his head away, shaking him off before coughing and choking in violent spasms. "Why?" Haruka asks, the relief he felt from having Nino in his arms morphing into anxiety.

A loud, sharp tap of something hitting glass makes Haruka look up. Lajos is standing over them, his cane resting on top of the sphere. Haruka blinks. *It's solid?* He hasn't taught Nino to manipulate his aura to this extent. He has never even seen Nino create this shape of his own volition.

"The fact is"—Lajos grins—"your exquisite youth combined with your ancient blood and powerful aura impresses me. Are you certain that you would not be interested in visiting my realm?"

"Leave our home. Never return. If you do, you will regret it."

Lajos laughs. "Is that a threat, young male—"

"It is a promise."

"Hm... you have challenged me, negotiated with me and now threatened me. I have not been this entertained in almost two centuries. I'm certain that we will meet again."

Before another word is spoken, the bright light within the old vampire's eyes flashes. He disappears. The putrid scent of sage lingers in his absence. Haruka refocuses on his mate. "Nino, *please* feed, you must—"

The energy around them fizzles out as Nino's head falls to the side against Haruka's lap. When the door to the library slides open, Asao is there with Cellina close behind.

"We need to go to the hospital." Haruka stands, wrapping the power of his essence around Nino as he cradles him against his body, lifting and carrying him. The two are engulfed in a fiery glow. "Please bring the car to the front."

Cellina rushes forward, observing Nino's anguished expression as they move. "What's wrong? Is he alright?"

"I don't know," Haruka says, careful in moving through the doorway. "He won't feed and he hasn't spoken."

---

ASAO MAKES the drive to the hospital in Himeji in half the time it would normally take. At four in the morning, the roads are clear.

Sora Fujihara had told Haruka about a human doctor in Himeji that specializes in vampire health and medicine. The doctor has just recently moved to Japan. Already, very low-ranked vampires within their realm visit him on a regular basis to receive donated blood bags for feeding and other medical or psychological purposes.

Nino is almost catatonic when they reach the hospital. Haruka had tried to feed him during the car ride, but he refused over and over, elevating Haruka's internal distress. The nurses attend to him as soon as they arrive, setting him up in a room and withdrawing Haruka's blood for an IV drip.

After Nino is stable and the physician examines him, a nurse directs Haruka into a nearby office to discuss his mate's condition. Asao remains in the hospital room, but Cellina insists on joining Haruka to hear the prognosis.

They sit together in the doctor's office now, waiting. Haruka's hands are clasped in his lap. He takes a deep breath and closes his eyes.

"You look exhausted." Cellina's voice cuts through the silence, soft, almost a whisper. "When Giovanni gets here from Osaka, we can sit with Nino. You should try to get some sleep. You gave a lot of blood and Asao said you haven't eaten anything in days."

Haruka smiles weakly. "I am fine. Thank you for your concern."

Cellina sighs. "Haruka, listen—"

The door to the office swings open and shuts. The doctor makes his way behind the desk. He is average height with warm brown eyes behind modern, black-framed glasses. His hair is light brown but with golden highlights, the subtle wave of it cleanly swept back from his face.

"Good morning." The doctor offers a polite bow and smiles. His white teeth are straight and gleaming. "I'm Doctor Davies. The nurse told me that you're mated with Nino Bianchi, but... are you legally responsible for him?"

"I am," Haruka confirms.

"Great. Nice to meet you, Mr. Hirano. And... this is?" He tilts his head toward Cellina.

"This is Cellina De Luca. She has my consent to attend the consultation. She is not fluent in Japanese, so please speak in simple expressions."

The doctor nods, but his demeanor reads stiff. Uncomfortable, somehow. Sora had told Haruka good things about him as a medical professional, but the subtle tension radiating from the doctor is unsettling.

"Right, I understand." Doctor Davies rolls his shoulders. "I —I have to give you the legal speech first. Himeji Prefectural Hospital does not explicitly specialize in vampire biology. However, we do not discriminate based on race, biology, gender, color, ethnicity or religious beliefs. The results I'm giving you today have been assessed and derived by licensed and professional human doctors who possess a limited understanding of vampire biology. In no way are these doctors proficient in the infinite complexities associated with a vampire's genetic makeup, and are subject to scrutiny. Do you both accept the conditions under which I give my prognosis?"

"I do," Haruka and Cellina say at once.

"Alright. Great... I hate saying all that." Doctor Davies

smiles. He takes a breath and continues in simple Japanese. "It makes me seem incompetent—but I'm not! I've studied vampire biology for more than twenty years... which is nothing compared with your lifetime, I guess... but, anyway..."

The doctor rolls his shoulders again, turning toward his computer. Haruka raises an eyebrow. *Are humans always this nervous?*

Something is odd about him. However, this circumstance is unusual. Ranked vampires almost never need doctors, and purebreds are arguably the healthiest beings on the planet. Given time, their bodies heal themselves. But with Nino refusing to feed, Haruka had decided to play it safe and bring him to a medical professional for help.

"Nino is stable. I'm confident he'll make a full recovery—so rest assured there." The doctor clicks and moves his computer mouse as he speaks, a white glare from the screen flashing against his glasses. "But there are a few things happening, one being very odd. First, he was severely underfed. With the IV drip, that will be addressed within the next twenty-four hours.

"The second thing is some of his ribs are broken, as if they've been damaged by blunt trauma—perhaps someone used an object or kicked him? His organs are bruised, but nothing is pierced. This will heal itself within a month or two... maybe a month, since you're both purebred? Healing tends to be even faster with your biology."

Closing his eyes, Haruka stifles a flare of unfiltered rage. Lajos not only abducted his mate but caused him physical harm. The realization creates a fire in Haruka, urging him to hunt the decrepit vampire down and—

When Cellina's hand rests on top of his own, he opens his eyes. Her bright gray irises are focused on him, blinking. The doctor is also staring, his hands hovering in place over the keyboard. Haruka's eyes are alighted. He takes a deep breath. "My apologies."

"It... it's okay," Doctor Davies says, his brow furrowed. "Should I continue?"

"Please."

He nods. "Right... The last thing is very strange. I've never seen anything like it." Doctor Davies turns the large screen so that Cellina and Haruka can see. There is a black-and-white X-ray scan. The doctor points. "This is the cavity of Nino's mouth. Do you see this big, empty space? This is where his tongue should be. It's just... not there. It doesn't exist! There's no trauma—no evidence of it being removed. It's very strange."

Haruka takes another deep breath, quelling the silent fury within.

"Is this why he wouldn't feed?" Cellina asks.

"He can't," the doctor says. "You need your tongue to control the flow of liquid and saliva, to guide food down into your throat to swallow. Without it he would struggle. Did... did he have a tongue before?"

Silence.

Cellina balks. "Are you kidding?"

"*Yes*," Haruka assures the doctor.

"Of course—stupid question, very sorry." Doctor Davies sits up straighter and smiles. "It will regenerate. I'll be honest with you, vampiric regeneration is a very painful and slow process. Depending on the body part and the blood quality of the feeding source, it could take anywhere from two months to a year."

Nodding, Haruka mentally prepares himself for the long road ahead. "He will need to use this IV drip and have my blood drawn until his tongue has regenerated?"

"Yes, that's right. It won't be fun for him, but again, since you're both purebreds, I imagine the process will be on the shorter end. His ribs should heal pretty fast, too. Your mate will be back to normal within a few months."

"That is a relief," Haruka breathes. None of the details matter. As long as Nino will be safe and healthy again, all is well. They can deal with the particulars together.

"You'll need to take it slow." Doctor Davies turns his screen forward, then clicks with his mouse before giving them his full attention. "He'll need a lot of blood as he heals, but you can't starve yourself feeding him. So take it little by little. I would also recommend you restrain from rigorous physical activity while he heals... Maybe avoid pulling his aura? Or nature? Are the two interchangeable? In all my studies I've never been clear on that."

"Fundamentally, they are one and the same, but a vampire's aura is the physical, outward manifestation of their internal nature," Haruka explains.

Doctor Davies nods, his caramel-colored eyes bright behind his glasses. "Right. Got it. Makes perfect sense. Thank you for that. I'd like to have a follow-up appointment in two months to check on your progress, maybe even give you both the green light to resume your normal activities. How does that sound?"

"Understood. Thank you, Doctor Davies."

Cellina sighs. "Thank you, Doctor."

"It's my pleasure—honor, really." He grins. "Stop by the nurse's station at the end of the hall. Sora should be there. She'll schedule the follow-up. We'll also need to have your blood drawn each week for the IV—"

"Is there someone who can make house calls?" Haruka asks, not wanting to traverse back and forth to Himeji for the next two months or so.

"Um, sure..." Doctor Davies scratches the back of his head. "I'll look into that for you. We'll get something figured out."

"And..." Haruka smiles, charming. "Do you have any

recommendations for books or resources that focus on the phys-iology of the frontal and parietal lobes of the brain? Something that outlines precise details?"

Doctor Davies pauses. His brow lifts above his black glasses. "Ah... I'll see what I can do?"

# FOURTEEN

Haruka hates the smell of hospitals. He is sensitive to odors, and the barrage of human blood and harsh cleaning products gives him a headache. He sits beside Nino on the bed. The benefit of this is twofold—he is closer in proximity to his mate, and the unique scent of Nino helps to drown out the other distasteful scents surrounding him.

Nino is out cold, lying on his back and tucked underneath the sheets with his chest rising and falling. The doctor said he needs much sleep as part of his recovery. Haruka slides and tangles his fingers into the coppery length atop his head. It is soft but weighted down from days of being unwashed.

There is a thick dusting of coppery-golden hair tracing his jawline, chin and upper lip. Nino hates his facial hair and shaves it clean every day, but Haruka smiles, looking down at him. He likes it. His husband looks like a youthful, gingery lumberjack. He needs some flannel.

The door to the hospital room slides open and Giovanni is there. Stylish in a dark trench coat over his dress shirt and slacks, he has just arrived from managing Nino's business dealings in Osaka. Cellina and Asao sit together at a small table off to the side near an open window. His manservant is teaching her how to play karuta.

"What's the prognosis?" Giovanni walks to the opposite side of the bed, looking down at his sleeping brother.

"He is underfed." Haruka sighs. "His ribs are damaged and his tongue is missing."

Giovanni flickers his hazel-green eyes over to him, frowning. "What was that last part?"

"Lajos vanished his tongue and assaulted him." Haruka shakes his head, resentment churning thick within his heart. If he even *sees* Lajos again, he will strangle him and put an end to his repulsive life. Period.

"What a fucking maniac—What purpose did any of that serve?" The green behind Giovanni's eyes flashes a little brighter. He takes a deep breath and runs his palm down his face. "Has he been awake enough to tell you anything?"

"No. Earlier, he opened his eyes for about five seconds, but only said 'Hi' to me with his inner voice and smiled before falling asleep again."

"Well, that's a good sign, I guess. What happened to the old man?"

"He disappeared again," Haruka grumbles. The situation is unnerving. A callous, malevolent creature is roaming free and with full knowledge of their location. He can appear at will and without warning, capable of vanishing either or both of them at any time of the day or night.

Stress pounds between Haruka's ears—the utter lack of control within this circumstance creates stiff tension all throughout his body. How can he ever go on as he was? Blasé and wildly unprepared for a sudden attack. Lazy and overconfident in his ability. Nothing will ever be the same. From this day forward, he'll do whatever it takes to protect his mate.

"This old creep's ability is terrifying," Cellina professes. "You ancient-blooded vamps and your bizarre powers... To use his ability like this in the modern age is crazy. If Haruka decided to bend other vampires to his will, who could realistically stop him?"

Asao laughs, boisterous. "He's waaay too introverted for that."

Haruka nods in agreement. "From a personal standpoint, that sounds like a nightmare."

Nino rouses underneath Haruka's palm, opening his eyes with heavy lids. He looks exhausted—still too pale. He stretches his body and flinches from the pain. Giovanni steps closer, frowning. "Why does his mouth look full like that? Because his tongue is gone?"

"No," Haruka says. He slides his hand down Nino's face, then presses his thumb against his soft lips. Nino opens, letting him slip it inside to drag his top lip up. Sharp white teeth gleam, protruding from his mate's gums. "His incisors won't retract because he was close to being starved and needed to feed. The doctor said his body should adjust to the IV drip of my blood within twenty-four hours. They will return to normal soon."

Stepping forward, Giovanni places a large hand atop Nino's head. "You can't walk around with your fangs hanging out, kiddo. It's uncivilized. What will the neighbors think?"

Nino snorts in a faint sound, but then it escalates into violent coughing and choking. Haruka lifts, anxious as he places both of his hands against Nino's cheeks. "*Breathe*, my love. Open your mouth."

Obedient, Nino opens his fanged mouth and draws in a deep breath, his chest heaving up and down. He repeats this action until his body relaxes and he regains control. Haruka frowns, snapping his head toward Giovanni. "Don't make him laugh!"

Giovanni shrugs, grinning. "It's better to keep our spirits up."

While still holding his face with one palm, Haruka leans down and caresses his nose against Nino's fuzzy cheek. "Welcome home."

Nino's voice is groggy in his mind, soft. *Thanks... I missed you. It was painful.*

"I missed *you*. You're safe now."

*I know.*

"I will never let this happen again. Where did he take you?"

*I... don't know. Somewhere with desert mountains... and an old house. Ladislao was there.*

"Almeida? From Rio de Janeiro?"

Nino smirks, lazy. *Tesoro, what other Ladislao is there?*

"Of course." Haruka leans in once more, kissing the tip of his nose. "Who did this to you?"

His mate gasps in a deep yawn, his lids growing heavier and his eyes like narrow slits. *Lajos... just before he brought me back...* Nino's eyes are shut, his breathing shallow. Haruka caresses his thumb against the bristly hair of his cheek, lulling him to sleep.

"What did he say?" Giovanni asks.

"That he was in an old house somewhere surrounded by desert and mountains. Ladislao was there."

"Almeida? From Brazil?"

Haruka glares. "Did you not just hear me say that?"

"I couldn't hear his responses!"

"So including Nino," Cellina says thoughtfully, "that's two vampires we know for sure Lajos is responsible for vanishing."

"Are you telling me that a singular vampire is responsible

for the Vanishing?" Giovanni asks. "That this one crazy-ass old man pulled off the greatest upset of our culture's history?"

The silence in the room is stiff as they look at each other. Haruka glances down, taking Nino's limp hand into his own and entwining their fingers. Despite being asleep, Nino grips his palm.

Cellina stands from the table and stretches her arms over her head. The moment she moves, Giovanni's gaze follows her like a hawk eyeing its prey. She rolls her shoulders underneath her hooded sweatshirt. "I need coffee if we're going to unpack the aristocracy's greatest mysteries. How many am I bringing back?"

"I would like a cup," Haruka says. "Thank you, Cellina."

"Me too... please," Giovanni admits.

Asao stands from the table as well. "I'll go with you. I need to move around." Giovanni's head turns, scanning her as she saunters toward the door. Cellina is a beautiful female with smooth, cinnamon-brown skin and thick, curly hair. Even dressed in casual clothes and with her curls stacked and messy atop her head, an undeniable allure and confidence radiates from her.

When she's gone, Giovanni relaxes his shoulders as if he'd been waiting for something—a fight? When it doesn't come, he exhales and moves to take the place she'd occupied at the table. He looks down at the playing cards there and pokes them with his fingers.

"Did you think she would refuse to get you coffee?" Haruka asks. Nino's eyes are closed. He's sleeping again.

"Maybe," Giovanni says, turning his head to glance out the bright window. "I have to go home in a month to take care of some things, but I'll be back as soon as I can."

"Asao has secured a source for Cellina. Would you like him to arrange one for yourself? We are more than happy to accommodate you."

"No. I'm alright."

Haruka turns to face Giovanni. He is not one to push, but having a second starving Bianchi within his household is undesirable. "Giovanni, you should not go a month without feeding."

His brother-in-law's gaze shifts toward him. "I'm feeding. I have bags."

"Bags?" Haruka cringes. "Why would you choose to feed this way?" Haruka has fed from bags in his past, when he was avoiding intimacy and being indebted to other vampires. It had served the intended purpose, but the practice was abysmal. Stale. Feeding fresh from the warmth of a living, breathing creature—especially one that you love... There is nothing better. Nothing.

Giovanni folds his arms. He stares down at the karuta cards atop the table for a long minute. Just as Haruka opens his mouth again, Giovanni speaks. "I don't choose to feed this way. I have to, to help keep our father alive. I'm my father's source, so my feeding source impacts his well-being. It's too risky to feed from just anyone."

Haruka's mouth is still open as Giovanni's confession sinks in. He blinks and closes it, processing. "This... this is how your father survives without his mate?"

"Yes. My blood is a combination of my father's and mother's blood. The biology he receives from me helps to nourish the part of him that suffers from the loss of my mother. He doesn't feed directly though. We're not complete fucking weirdos."

*Unbelievable...* Haruka stares out the window, considering. When his mother died, there had been talk. He wasn't supposed to be listening, but he'd been eavesdropping, as children do. He'd noticed his father, Hayato, getting weaker, day by day. So Haruka had taken to quietly following him around. Just to be near him and watch over him, knowing that their time together was finite.

In a hushed conversation, Asao had asked if Hayato might try feeding from Haruka. He'd refused. It was the first and singular time he'd seen his father display anger toward Asao. Haruka still remembers his words as if it were yesterday...

*I will not sacrifice my son's entire life to cling to some deficient, hapless version of my own.*

Given the opportunity, Haruka would have done anything to save his father—to keep him alive and with him. Even if it meant a questionable quality of life for both of them. His father made his choice, gifting Haruka with free will and loneliness in exchange.

Giovanni's father, Domenico, made a different choice.

"You cannot feed of your own free will?" Haruka asks, refocusing on Giovanni. "And you cannot form a bond?"

Haruka waits, the silence stretching out between them before Giovanni answers.

"Nope."

Familiar voices approach the closed door. Giovanni looks up at him, serious. "You don't repeat *any* of this."

"Does Nino know about this?"

Giovanni scoffs. "Of course he knows."

"Cellina?"

"No."

The door slides open and Asao walks in first with a tray full of coffee cups. Cellina follows behind. Giovanni stands from the seat, says "Thanks" as he takes a cup from Asao's tray, then moves toward the armchair in the opposite corner of the room. He sips the coffee, but his eyes keep darting over to Cellina.

# FIFTEEN

## SUMMER, 1915

*This is not how Cellina had envisioned her sixteenth birthday.*

*She follows the maidservant down the long hallway. This in and of itself is unsettling. At what point did Cellina start needing an escort to see him?*

*The estate is quiet. Cold. The warmth she usually feels here —the energy, liveliness and laughter—is gone. Everything is muted now, as if all the vivid color has been sucked out of a beautiful painting.*

*The maidservant knocks on the door. "Your grace, Miss Cellina De Luca is here to see you."*

*She has been announced like a stranger. Cellina steps into the formal room stuffed with antique furniture, old family portraits and heavy, dusty drapes. They used to make fun of this room: the drawing room. In name alone it sounds dramatic—this place where all the older vampires talk about boring, serious things. Things she and her dear friend have no interest in.*

*Giovanni is standing at a window, his tall frame washed in the gray light of the overcast sky. The rain pelts the glass and drizzles down the window like teardrops. He doesn't turn as she* walks forward. He doesn't smile, move across the room to meet her or grab her hands like normal. Instead, he stands like a statue, staring through the glass.

"G..." Cellina's voice is small in the vast silence of the large room. She hates it.

"What do you want?"

She stops, setting her shoulders back. He knows. Of course he does. But this reaction... she never anticipated. She thought he'd understand. How could he not? "I—Can we please talk? About Nino—"

"No."

When he faces her, Cellina draws back. The anger and mistrust in his eyes are like an arrow to her chest. She shakes her head, taking a step forward. It doesn't need to be like this. Things will be okay after a while. She just needs a little time to help Nino stabilize. "Giovanni, I had to—"

"Right," he laughs, turning away from her. The sound is bitter, ugly and full of contempt. "You had to. Is this what you wanted all along? Were you just using me—"

"Don't be disgusting—that's disgusting!" Cellina says, her voice rising. Is he insinuating what she thinks? "Nino is like my little brother. You know that. You know me. He wouldn't feed from anyone. Everyone's been trying for two weeks. How could you even suggest—"

"Why you? Of all creatures, why the hell does it have to be you?" He stares hard, eyes like daggers. The sound of the rain litters the silence. She opens her mouth to speak, but he shakes his head.

"Get out." His expression crumbles, his eyes watering. "Leave. I don't want you here—I don't want to see your face anymore. You made your fucking choice."

# JUNE
(PRESENT DAY)

# SIXTEEN

*The corpus callosum traverses the longitudinal fissure... here.* Haruka holds the model brain upside down, narrowing his eyes as he uses a black marker to designate the critical site. *The cerebral mantle is above the corpus callosum. This area. Perhaps these gyri... near this sulcus?*

A heavy knock against the open bedroom door breaks his concentration. He looks up and Giovanni is in the doorway. He's dressed in tailored slacks and a patterned dress shirt, his suit jacket folded over his arm. He glances at Haruka on the floor as he walks toward the bed.

"You stayed up all night again, didn't you?" Giovanni asks.

Haruka shrugs. "What time is it now?"

"Four thirty in the morning. I have a meeting at eight in Osaka, and then I'll meet Cellina in Kyoto at three to go over next week's schedule. I'll be back here around ten tonight."

"Thank you, Giovanni." With his legs folded, Haruka leans his head back against the wall.

"You alright, kiddo?" Giovanni says. From his position on

the floor, Haruka can see that Giovanni's hand is resting atop Nino's head. His mate nods against the pillow.

"You look better today," the broad vampire continues, "but your husband looks like shit. He's staying up all night and not eating—like some old-school fucking vampire. Should I drag a coffin in here for him to sleep in? Is he going to start hanging upside down in the damn closet?"

Nino squirms in bed and grabs his ribs, wheezing in what Haruka understands as painful laughter. Haruka frowns. The more time he spends with Nino's older brother, the more apparent his dual personality becomes. He is one part charming diplomat and one part embittered antagonist—one half or the other capable of surfacing at any given moment.

"The four contracts you secured are stable," Giovanni explains. "Good-quality clients—they seem serious about making the changes you recommended and are flexible. Nice work. I have a meeting for a new prospect today. I could get you more leads, but you just want five at a time, right?"

Nino nods again under his brother's palm. Giovanni steps back from the bed. "Alright. I'll wrap that up before I go home to see about Father. My blood supply is getting low." Giovanni turns and walks in long strides toward the bedroom door. He looks over his shoulder just before leaving. "*Eat* something— and take a damn nap. What good is all this studying going to do if Lajos shows up and you pass out from exhaustion?"

Haruka sets the model brain down in his lap, considering. "Your personality is not unlike a two-headed snake's."

Giovanni smirks. "But a king cobra, right? Not one of those wimpy garden snakes. I'll be back later."

When he's gone, Haruka rolls his eyes and lifts the plastic model. Giovanni might be older, but he is out of line. *Walking around* my *house and barking orders...* He wonders how he ended up being the youngest vampire among his intimate circle of peers.

Nino rustles against the bed, sluggish and maneuvering to remove the IV drip from his arm. Haruka sets his plastic brain down and stands from the floor with urgency, stepping over the mess of books, papers and markers spread around him.

He moves to Nino's arm. "Good morning, my love—I will take care of this. Is it finished?" He looks up and pinches the clear plastic bag. No blood. Sora will be back on Sunday as per their usual appointment to draw more blood and create new bags. Each time, Haruka's body needs the full week to recover.

Falling into his routine, he takes the sterile gauze from the bedside table tray and presses the soft material to Nino's skin at the insertion site. Meticulous, he pulls the cannula out of his arm, discards it and unhooks the empty IV bag.

"Did you sleep well?" Haruka asks, tossing the bag into the trash. "I tried not to disturb you—"

*Feed.*

Nino's groggy voice registers in Haruka's head. He is grateful that they can communicate this way, but he misses the sound of his healthy, physical voice.

His tasks completed, Haruka shifts toward the end of the bed at Nino's feet, kneeling there and taking hold of his mate's ankle. "I will." He smiles. "How are you feeling?" Haruka lifts his leg and Nino complies, allowing him to bend his knee toward his chest in a slow stretch.

*I'm okay. Why aren't you eating food? You love eating.*

"Solidarity. And there is too much to do." He gently rolls his hip in its socket, deepening the stretch. After a moment, he straightens Nino's leg, then sets his foot against the mattress. He moves to stretch the opposite leg. "Nino, how long has Giovanni been feeding your father?"

*Since right after Mom died... maybe 1915? Or sixteen? I'm still amazed he told you.*

Haruka holds Nino's bent knee toward his chest, then rolls it. Learning that Giovanni is solely responsible for providing their father's nourishment had been shocking, and it has also answered other long-standing questions in Haruka's mind.

Losing a mate is detrimental to the surviving member of a bond—their complex biology having grown dependent upon a bespoke source of nourishment. Haruka had wondered how Domenico, a purebred vampire, has survived this long without his mate. Consuming his son's blood provides the nourishment necessary to survive. It is a controversial choice, so it's no wonder the family prefers to keep it secret.

It also explains why Giovanni—a renowned and attractive purebred realm leader—has remained unbonded. Mixing another, outside vampire's biology with his own could cause devastating results for the father in his precarious circumstance.

"Who is Giovanni's source?" Haruka asks, straightening Nino's leg.

*One of our cousins—my uncle's daughter. So the family bloodline within G stays consistent. Nobody feeds directly. Father employs a small staff of medical professionals to help draw and bag everyone's blood. Did he mention that?*

"He did. In less detail."

*I don't think G has fed from another vampire in an intimate way since he was a teenager. I remember there was a time... for a short while, maybe a month? It wasn't long after Mom died, but G went kind of wild. He wasn't home much and I barely saw him. Then Father got worse in his sickness and he screamed at G one night. I was little but I remember it was scary as hell—how mad he was. That was the end of that. G has been on the straight and narrow path ever since.*

"Will he always be held to this strict circumstance?" Haruka asks. He has never felt sympathetic toward Giovanni, nor has he ever heard the dynamic male complain. Not once. But knowing the entire circumstances, it is overwhelming.

Overseeing a bustling aristocracy alone, constantly addressing the needs and whimsies of other ranked vampires, being responsible for the vitality of his father while unable to feed and satisfy his own inherent needs... and now, Giovanni is also managing his brother's realm while he recovers.

*I don't know. We don't talk about any of it. I know, deep down, G resents me for a lot of reasons, so I just leave it alone. Our relationship is much better since I bonded with you though. That's been nice.*

Haruka smiles. "I am pleased that I have brought some relief to this complex situation." He lifts Nino's ankle, then kisses the arch of his bare foot. Nino grins, his honeyed skin shifting into a warm, rosy color.

*If... if G were allowed to bond and feed...*

"He would undoubtedly choose Cellina?" Haruka interrupts. "If she is present, his gaze follows her. His respect and desire for her are obvious."

*To everyone but her. They had an argument forever ago and refuse to call a truce. I can't imagine him mating with anyone else—especially not another male. I think he would eat him alive.*

"Yes, when other males are involved, your brother becomes 'alpha' in even the most unnecessary circumstances." Like sitting at the head of Haruka's kitchen table, making everyone around him default to Italian or walking around and barking out uncouth, unsolicited opinions. Haruka shakes his head.

*Tesoro, will you please feed from me? You need to feed.*

Haruka stands from the bed. "How about we shower? I will

help you bathe, and perhaps at some point during the process, I will feed."

Nino's face brightens. *Yeah? Will you pull my aura? While we're in the shower?*

"No," Haruka admonishes. "I cannot feed deeply from you. The doctor said we should not engage in such rigorous activities until he clears us."

Groaning, Nino slides down further against the bed and turns his head away. Haruka laughs, standing by his side. "Am I not still capable of pouring very pleasant emotions into you?"

Nino flips his head back, his amber eyes frowning. *Tease.*

Haruka huffs in a clipped laugh. He leans down to grip Nino's chin with his fingers. "Open, please."

Hesitating, Nino shifts his gaze, then opens his mouth. Haruka examines him. Things are much improved from a month ago. He stands straight, gratified. "I am grateful that the speech pathologist is coming next week. I miss hearing your natural voice."

*I know. Can you help me shave again? Lifting my arms for too long is still painful.*

"Of course."

Careful, Nino sits straight, moving himself to the edge of the bed. During Sora's last visit, she reported that his ribs have fused, but that his body will be tender and achy for a little while longer. Haruka holds his hands out and bends at the knees. Once Nino grips his hands, Haruka slides his palms down Nino's arms to hold his elbows, firm and just as Sora taught him. Nino adjusts his weight, planting his feet on the floor. He counts, then lifts Nino from the bed to stand.

Nino groans, his face pained. *This is such bullshit.*

Haruka stands behind, holding his waist and guiding him to the master bathroom. "It is incredible to me that you conjured such a powerful defensive shield. I have never manipulated my energy in that way."

*You taught me how to focus and create that shape. Who knows what he would have done to me if I hadn't learned that.* Nino yawns, trembling as they move. Communicating like this for too long mentally exhausts him. Haruka needs to get him showered and back in bed as soon as possible.

*Haru?*

"Yes, my love."

*I keep thinking about that place... and Ladislao. He didn't want to be there. Shouldn't we try to help? Or at least tell someone?*

"From what you've told me, this issue sounds like a family matter. In addition, Lajos's realm has been established for almost two centuries. At this point, many of the vampires within that society were born there. It is not our place to kick a beehive, and you are still healing from our first encounter with him."

Nino sighs. *You're right...*

Sensing his discontent, Haruka adds, "Can we revisit this topic once you are healed?"

*Okay, sure... Will you please eat today? G is right, you've lost a lot of weight. And when was the last time you slept?*

In the bathroom, Haruka unties Nino's robe, then slides the material over his honeyed shoulders to maneuver it from his body. "I will eat today—"

*Promise me.* Nino's beautiful eyes are serious as he stares.

Haruka places a swift kiss on his mouth. "I promise. Enough about me. Let's finish this so you can return to bed. The doctor said that sleep is the best way for your body to regenerate quickly. I will watch over you and keep you safe."

# SEVENTEEN

Cellina rests against her hip on the tatami floor of the traditional restaurant, her arms folded atop the low table. The small building is situated along the Kamogawa river, streaming and sparkling in the sunlight. She's seated beside a large, open window overlooking the downtown area of central Kyoto. The rain has stopped and the weather is glorious—a pristine, early summer day with white, fluffy clouds scattered across the blue sky.

Detecting his gingery scent, Cellina sits up straight and looks toward the entrance. A minute later he's there. He smiles at the hostess and bows. Impeccably dressed as always, and his honey-brown waves are longer now, but pulled back to the nape of his neck in a neat style.

At the table, he nods in greeting. Cellina returns the gesture, distracted by the way the sunlight catches the green flecks in his eyes like flashes of emerald stone. Giovanni makes himself comfortable across from her as the waitress grins above them. She registers as vampiric in nature—maybe third-gen?

"Is there anything I can get you to start?"

He looks at Cellina. "Did you already order?"

"Just two iced coffees and a cake for myself."

"Dessert first." Giovanni offers a little half-smile, as if the choice has jogged something in his memory. He looks up at the waitress. "The iced coffee is fine for now, thank you."

"You're very welcome... Are you Nino Bianchi's brother?"

Giovanni's countenance shifts, oozing purebred charm as he smiles brighter. "I am."

"Nino works with my brother in Osaka—Daiki Izumi," she explains. "He told me you've been helping him and how awesome you are. Thank you for saving the family business." She offers a deep, reverent bow.

Giovanni lifts his square jawline, his eyes thoughtful. "Your brother is a hard-working vampire with a lot of creative ideas. It's my pleasure to support my kin in any way—particularly with entrepreneurial aspirations. The business will thrive in time."

She bows again, bubbling with enthusiasm. "Thank you—when things are up and running, I want to go back home and work. I'm looking forward to it. I—I'll go check on your coffees! Please excuse me."

"Thank you." He nods. When the young waitress shuffles away, Giovanni's entire demeanor drops as he lays his scheduler on the table. He reminds Cellina of a helium balloon deflating. The shift is drastic, and the more time they spend together, the more she notices the hard lines forming in his chiseled face.

He opens the book with one hand, then presses his fingers to the center of his forehead with the other. "I have to fly home next weekend. I'm wrapping up a new restaurant contract this week, then I have follow-up meetings scheduled with three of Nino's clients before I leave. His newest client is having some sort of centennial celebration next Friday night in Osaka, so I think I can squeeze that in before my flight in the morning. What's happening with the social visits in Okayama? How's planning going for Tanabata?"

"It's going well," Cellina reports, just as the waitress returns and sets their coffees and her cake on the table. "I'm working with the temple to schedule renovations, and managing the food vendors. The Shōwa Clan handles all the details for the decoration competition, so I'm leaving that in their hands. But they know to reach out if they need me. I'm having fun covering for Haruka. Everyone is so nice. I love planning events and talking to new vampires—my Japanese is getting better, too."

"That's good, I'm glad you're enjoying yourself. If I can get all of Nino's clients settled, Asao said I may not need to come back. That works, because I have to fly to Paris and Germany while I'm at home, but we'll play it by ear."

He looks down to scribble dates in his calendar. Cellina shakes her head. She considers herself a productive, professional person. Having aspirations to manage her own gallery in the future means she's always studying and working, networking and schmoozing. But this purebred's schedule is insane. "Giovanni, when do you just breathe?"

He looks up at her, a deep frown etched in his forehead. "Breathe? What does that mean?"

"Take a break. Relax."

He scoffs. "When I'm asleep."

She watches him write things into his calendar, erase, then re-write. Everything about him is tense. Uptight and strained. Who is this male sitting in front of her? What happened to the playfully defiant and sweet vampire that she'd once considered her best friend? They had their falling out so long ago, but the ramifications of it are still present between them even now.

What have the years done to Giovanni? It feels like time

has ravaged him—worn him down to this gruff, bitter state like a weathered stone in sand.

"Why don't I go to the centennial celebration on Nino's behalf next Friday, since it's the night before your flight home?" Cellina asks. "You can go back to the Kurashiki estate and rest."

He shakes his head, still writing. "I'll already be in the area. It doesn't make sense for you to go all the way there. Don't worry about it. I'll just change my flight to leave from Kansai International."

Cellina takes a sip of her iced coffee, letting the cool, sweet liquid settle her nerves. She takes a deep breath. "Then... do you want me to come with you? I can meet you in Osaka and we can go together? If you don't mind... Two reps at a social event are always better than one."

Giovanni freezes, meeting her eyes. "You're willing to attend a social engagement... with me? *Together?*"

*That should* be my *line.* Nervous, she smooths her hair up to her oversized, curly bun. With all this humidity in Japan, every day is curly-bun day. "Yes... if you're comfortable with me being there?"

Dropping his pencil, he sits up straight, massaging the back of his neck. "Of course." An awkward silence hangs listless between them until he says, "It's always better with you there."

"Always?" Cellina frowns. "Always since when?"

"Since we were kids. Like when my father would trap me in those boring-ass conversations about agricultural trade and exports, or national annual growth rates. Having you there... Sneaking away with you made it better. It gave me something to look forward to."

"I... thought about that recently," Cellina admits. "The summer parties at your family's estate were the best. The food —and I loved roaming the gardens at night. It was like magic." She relaxes her shoulders. They haven't talked like this in forever: calm, casual and without some explicit purpose or underlying hostility. It's nice... like dipping her toes into a warm bath.

"Yeah." Giovanni nods. "We spent a lot of time out there. Do you remember how we used to tell Nino and Cosimo that we were going to play hide-and-seek, then they'd run off somewhere and we'd go sit by the fountain and talk?"

Cellina laughs. "We got away with that for a long time before Cosimo figured it out. He was so upset. Nino didn't even care, did he?"

"Nope." Giovanni smiles. "He used to go climb that old peach tree near the gazebo—the one by that hedge of rose bushes? The gardener would find shriveled-up peaches and their pits around the bottom of the tree the next day and make a big fuss about them destroying his lawn equipment."

"I recently told Haruka about that silly habit." Cellina laughs. "And Nino was always hiding in that area with the rose bushes. God, he was such a little loner... Cosimo tried his damndest to get Nino to open up to him after they came of age."

"By that time, Cos was so desperate to fuck him and feed from him that it made Nino uncomfortable."

"He was *so* into Nino," Cellina admits. "He came on way too strong."

Giovanni smirks in a laugh, folding his arms across his broad chest. "Thank God for Haruka."

"I love Nino like he's my own little brother—probably more. But yes, thank God for Haruka. Nino was always good though, you know? He never once tested my boundaries and always fed from my hand. He also let me expose him to nineties American R&B and TV shows when I was going through that phase."

"Hm. Everyone in our estate was exposed to it by proxy."

"And you're all very welcome." Cellina sticks her chin out. Giovanni smiles.

A comfortable pause settles over them as the sunlight shifts behind a cloud. They're talking to each other. Amicably. Reminiscing about the good times and when their lives were simpler. Cellina can almost smell the summery, smoky but sweet aroma of cypress trees floating through the balmy night air of the garden. She can almost hear the white noise of the marble fountain, its fresh water spouting in the distance.

Her mood dampens, melancholy settling in her heart. She looks up at the vampire sitting across from her, meeting his lovely but unfamiliar eyes. "What happened to us?"

He takes a deep breath, his chest rising and falling. "Everything changed."

It did. Without question. Cellina considers. *Maybe it's time to talk this through?*

"I didn't make that choice to hurt you, Giovanni. That was never my intention."

"I know that," he says, his gaze cast down. "I couldn't understand it at the time—my juvenile vampire mind couldn't process it."

"A lot happened back then," Cellina says, taking a moment to steel herself. She's spent so many years wrestling with the mess of complex emotions resulting from that time—frustration, indignation, regret and deep sorrow for her friend. She wanted to be there for him when things were difficult, but he didn't want her there. He told her to go away, so she did.

But now...

"So... you're not angry with me anymore?" she asks. "You don't hate me?"

"I *never* hated you. I could never feel that way about you."

"I'm sorry if I hurt you. I don't regret my decision, but... we made a promise and I broke it."

"You made the right choice." Giovanni closes his eyes, bringing his fingers up to massage the space between his brows. "You saved Nino's life. He needed you more than I did—and I did some stupid things back then."

"We were young," Cellina says, letting the moment wash over her. Relief. The freedom of it long overdue. This unfortunate circumstance of Nino's abduction brought them here—in Kyoto together and at this table, forcing them to sit down and acknowledge the elephant. To tackle and push it from in between them.

Feeling comfortable enough to put both feet in the water, Cellina grins. "I will admit that when I offered myself to Nino, I didn't think I'd be feeding him for the next one hundred and four years."

"You fed him for a long fucking time."

Cellina laughs, covering her face with her palms. "So damn long—why was it so long? I thought he'd come of age at twenty-one and find someone."

"Nope," Giovanni says. "You enabled him. We both did in different ways."

"I think... I just wanted to protect him, you know? The vamps in our society were being such shitheads, I felt like I had to compensate... God." Cellina shakes her head and picks up her dessert fork. She takes a bite of her cake, sighing as the fluffy, buttery and sweet texture engulfs her senses.

"What is that?" Giovanni asks, eyeing her plate as he takes a sip of his coffee.

"It's called Castella. It's from Portugal originally, but you know how the Japanese like to take things and put their own spin on it. One of the families I visited gave me some and now I'm hooked. Do you want to try it?"

Giovanni's full lips curve into a surprised grin. "Sure."

Cellina cuts a piece of the cake with her fork and holds it

out to him. Maybe they won't ever be as close as they were. So much time has been lost between them and they're very different vampires now. No longer kids sneaking out of boring, adult conversations to roam around moonlit summer gardens.

*They* are the boring adults now. Totally changed. Grown up and experienced much of life in absence of each other. But this—an open conversation, a moment of warm recollection and laughter. It's a nice beginning. A true cease-fire.

Giovanni leans forward, opening his mouth to take the small chunk of cake. Not thinking, Cellina watches him, mesmerized by his beautiful lips wrapping around her fork then slowly pulling the dessert off the utensil. He flashes a rogue look, his vivid eyes shining. "See something you like?"

"Shut up." She frowns, brushing off the mild embarrassment. "I was just thinking... it would be nice if we could be friends again."

He raises a golden-brown eyebrow. "Were we just friends before?"

"Of course we were."

"I remember it a little differently," he says, bringing the iced coffee to his mouth.

Cellina narrows her eyes and leans forward. "Then it'll be nice for us to be friends for the *first* time, apparently." At this, Giovanni laughs, the frown lines in his forehead easing and giving way to mirth.

*His damn mouth,* Cellina thinks. *That's changed over the years, for sure.*

Among other things.

# EIGHTEEN

Chaos. It's the first word that springs to mind the moment Cellina steps off the train that drops her into the concrete maze of Osaka station the following week. It's Friday evening. She navigates the thick current of people, feeling as if she's inside one of those intricate underground ant farms.

Following the signs toward Sakurabashi Gate, she weaves her way through, keeping with the intense flow of the crowd. From her peripheral vision, she observes the shiny allure of clean-looking, brightly lit convenience stores and souvenir shops filled with pretty objects: handmade bags patterned with vibrant Japanese textiles and colorful bento boxes neatly stacked under artificial cherry blossom trees.

Stepping out of the revolving doors, Cellina sucks in a breath. The air is balmy and hazy and smells of a city—exhaust fumes, cement high-rises, rubber and paved roads. Neon signs in both kanji she can't read and English she can flash atop tall buildings. First impression: Osaka feels gritty. Busier and rougher around the edges than Kyoto and Okayama. The latter two cities are more like a charming, gentle aunt who bakes cookies while Osaka is a rowdy uncle who drinks too much.

Cellina stops, trying to discern Giovanni through the urban haze with her innate senses. A second later he's there, his fingertips gentle as he touches her waist.

"Hey," he says.

"Hi." She smiles, happy to see a familiar face amidst the overwhelming foreignness of her surroundings. His suit looks black... or is it very dark blue? His shirt underneath reminds her of sangria and his tie is soft and satiny in a darker shade of the same color.

Cellina snickers. They match. It wasn't intentional, of course, but she's wearing her breezy navy blue jersey dress with fluttery sleeves and a plunge neckline. The train ride from Okayama is two hours, and she knew this particular dress would travel well and keep her comfortable in the summer humidity. Her strappy burnt-orange heels offer nothing as far as comfort, but they look amazing with the dress. She'll deal with the consequences of prioritizing fashion over the general health and well-being of her feet later.

"The car is this way." He nods his head to the right, stepping in the same direction. He flips his hand open in a casual gesture. Without thinking, she slides her palm into his, clasping his fingers as he guides her. The gentle contact makes something like electricity shimmer up her arm and to her chest. Her heart pulses and skips.

When they're in the back seat of a black town car, she takes a deep breath. The space is a cool shelter compared with the frenetic heat and tenacity of the city outside.

"You look wonderful," Giovanni says, focusing on her before looking down at his smartphone. The blue-white glow of the device illuminates his sculpted features in the dusky evening light.

"Thanks, you too." And he smells wonderful. Clean, gingery and perfectly male. His purebred aura radiates from him, subtle but filling the vehicle. In a meager effort to distract herself, Cellina looks out the window, watching the bright lights, tall buildings and throngs of people zip by.

"This is nice." He slips his phone into the inside pocket of his jacket and focuses on her.

"What is?"

"Going to an aristocracy event together... sitting here." He grins. "You not ignoring me."

Cellina raises her eyebrow, haughty. "I was under the impression that we were ignoring each other."

"Nope. I never ignored you. Not once."

"You're playing innocent now?" Cellina asks. "Like you didn't tell me to go away and that you didn't want to look at me ever again."

"I regretted saying that the minute you walked away."

Cellina frowns. "How was I supposed to know that? Why didn't you say something?"

Giovanni shrugs. "Because you were ignoring me—stone cold. Like I didn't even exist if we were in the same room together."

"That's my superpower. I was just doing what my realm leader told me to do."

"Your superpower sucks." Giovanni smirks, adjusting his back against the seat. "Is that what we are now, Lina? Realm leader and dutiful subject? You're coming with me tonight as part of some aristocratic obligation?"

"No. I'm here because... I wanted to support you, and Haruka and Nino. Because I want the two of us to be friends like we used to be."

Giovanni scoffs in the dim light. "There's that word again."

"What then, Giovanni? What do you want us to be?"

He turns his head to meet her gaze. The intensity behind his hazel-green irises makes Cellina inhale and sit up straighter. Her body temperature rises as the silence stretches on. His eyes flicker down, taking her in before he faces forward again. "What I want and what I can have are two very different things."

"My lord, my lady, we're here," the driver announces.

She blows out a breath as Giovanni exits the car. *What the hell does that mean?* He's a purebred vampire—realm leader over one of the most prosperous and dense communities of vampires in Europe. In general, he can have and do whatever he pleases, and no one can understand why Giovanni still hasn't bonded after all this time. There are some rumors and speculations, but nobody knows the reason.

Wanting any moment of escape she could manage, Cellina had undone her shoes upon getting into the vehicle. She bends down, rushing to secure the ribbon on her left foot as Giovanni opens the car door.

"One second, please," she says, finishing up the left foot and shifting her long legs out the door so she has more room to do the right shoe. Before she can bend down, Giovanni crouches in front of her, taking hold of her foot in his large hand and examining the shoe. Cellina shakes her head in protest. "I'll do it—"

"It's fine." Giovanni focuses, fitting her heel into the suede shoe and tying the laces at her ankle. "Your neckline is low. I don't want our driver getting a view he doesn't deserve."

When Cellina looks up, the driver is absolutely staring at her chest. Not speaking Italian, he doesn't understand Giovanni's declaration. But when his gaze meets Cellina's, he smiles, awkward, before turning and walking away. Cellina breathes a laugh. "Are you protecting my virtue now?"

"I'm shielding your exquisite body from wayward onlookers," he says, securing the bow.

"My knight in shining armor." Cellina smirks. "Why are you wearing a tie? You hate ties." He would complain about them when they were young—when his parents had formal parties and made him wear them. The maidservant who helped dress him always tied it too tight. Stifling him. As soon as they were in the garden and away from the adults, Cellina would untie it for him, roll it up and stuff it in a hedge, her adolescent theory being the less ties he owned, the less likely he'd be made to wear one.

He stands, then holds his hand out to her. "This isn't my aristocracy, so I should follow formal protocols. I'm happy you remember something about me."

"Oh please." Cellina rolls her eyes, smiling as she steps into him and pinches the soft, smooth material between her fingers. "You said they made you feel, quote, 'Like a damn dog on a leash.' At least you picked a pretty leash tonight. This color is wonderful."

When he doesn't answer, she looks up. His vivid eyes are unreadable as he stares down at her. He huffs out a warm, gingery breath and pulls his mouth into a little grin. "Thanks."

Cellina steps back and brushes the flowy fabric of her dress, the heat of her nature bubbling at her spine. *Cool it with the close encounters, Lina.*

This is how it always was with him. Whenever they were close, her nature would flip and writhe around within her, pulling her toward his solidity and warmth. His roguish, playful nature and rebellious spirit. His honesty and sincere consideration of the vampires around him. Even now, he's managing his little brother's realm—didn't hesitate one moment to rearrange his already insane schedule to be here for both Haruka and Nino when they needed him.

Giovanni is always like this: outward focused. Adhering to his parent's wishes, supporting Nino through his abuse, calming her through her silly fits of rage over her brother. He is the rock upon which everyone leans and stands. Dependable.

Maybe to a fault.

She doesn't know anything about his private life anymore, but she hopes he enjoys himself of his own accord. Somewhere between the appointments, social gatherings, business deals, responsibilities and crises. He should have fun and escape, at least sometimes. Like they used to when they were kids.

———————

NO ONE PARTIES quite like a four-hundred-year-old female vampire in Japan. There'd been heartfelt speeches and raucous laughter, high-end liquor and fresh seafood. At one point, she'd been gathered up in other vampires' arms, then lifted, crowd-surfing style, and tossed into the air.

Reaching four hundred is an impressive feat in their culture, and the elder female had been spry and sharp with no outward signs of her biology breaking down and turning into dust. Absolutely worthy of a rock star–style celebration.

Cellina appreciates the cultural experience—even being showered with compliments and flirtatious remarks from vampires twice her age. Throughout, Giovanni had been the perfect purebred. He had one glass of wine the whole night. He smiled and laughed on cue, offered serious business insight to those who wanted it and showed concern and empathy where appropriate.

He is diplomacy at its finest. A well-oiled machine of civility and grace.

The moment they climb back into the town car to drop Cellina at the station, Giovanni pulls at his tie, then sits back against the seat and closes his eyes, breathing. She smiles. *The diplomacy robot is recharging.*

"Hey," she says after giving him a long moment of silence.

"Yes?" he answers, eyes still closed.

"Have you ever had okonomiyaki, Osaka style? I hear it's the best."

He turns his head. "Are you hungry? We just ate all that damn food."

She shrugs. "I didn't eat much because of all the chitchat. And we're here. We should try it." She leans forward, deciding to put her growing Japanese-language skills to good use. "Sumi-masen, oishii okonomiyaki no resutoran wa doko desu ka? Osusume no mise wa?"

"I know a place," the driver says. "Best spot for okonomiyaki and takoyaki in all of Osaka. It's in Namba. We're not too far. They have good beer too."

Cellina grins at Giovanni. He looks at his watch. "You might miss the last train?"

"It's okay," she says. "You have a room. I can sleep on the couch or get another room."

"You are *not* sleeping on a couch." He frowns. "Are you sure?"

"Positive." She narrows her eyes. "Let's go have late-night fried things and beer. I want to enjoy Osaka."

And they do. The driver takes them to a small, locally owned shop in the bustling Namba area. The street is hectic, crowded, with buildings donning neon signs that glow in sharp colors against the black sky. Up a narrow flight of stairs and into a warm, hazy room, they're greeted by a busy human chef and two waitstaff who mildly balk at their vampiric natures. They fry the Japanese-style savory "pancakes" at the large griddle on their private table, the heat, smoke and smells swirling all around them. Giovanni ditches his jacket, loosens his shirt collar, and they drink cold beer. He laughs a lot—they both do, reminiscing more about their younger days and filling in the gaps of their long separation.

When the griddle has been turned off and wayward bits of cold noodle, fish flakes and squid remain on their plates, Cellina sits back, relaxed. "How do you have fun and unwind these days? Just out of curiosity."

He frowns as he looks at her, his eyes glossy from the lamp hanging over their table. "What is this word? Fun?"

"Stop it."

"Tonight aside, I haven't had 'fun' since the early 1900s—"

"Ah... was it when you went on your famous sexcapade?"

They pause. Giovanni frowns. "Is *that* what you call it?"

"Mmhm." Cellina nods, grinning. "Your great sexploration. Your youthful foray into sexdom."

"No." Giovanni picks up his beer and brings it to his lips. "It wasn't then."

"We just... shut each other out." Cellina sighs, staring at the messy griddle. "I wanted to talk things through with you— maybe come up with a plan together? But I had no idea you'd react that way. I was so angry and disappointed, even if you'd tried to talk to me, I probably wouldn't have listened."

Giovanni places his beer on the table and takes a deep breath. "Nineteen fifteen was the worst year of my life—and every day... every year after has been the same. Numb."

"Nineteen fifteen..." Cellina considers. "I turned sixteen that year. That was also the year your mother starved in the war and Domenico got sick... I started feeding Nino. The sexcapade—"

"*And* I lost you," Giovanni adds. "The only vampire in my life that has ever cared about my well-being. I did that shit to get your attention—in my idiotic eighteen-year-old head I was trying to make you jealous. My father ended up screaming at me about that and saying the vilest shit he's ever said to me. It feels like everything went to hell that year and never recovered."

*It worked.* Little did he know, he'd been successful. His actions back then had made her jealous and very angry, fueling her superpower to maximum strength. She shakes her head. "Giovanni, I'm not the only person who cares about you. Vampires in our aristocracy and across Europe adore you. Your father cares for sure. Nino, too."

He sneers. "I'm a civil servant to all of them—someone who handles their fucking problems."

Cellina disagrees, but she won't argue with him about a touchy subject like this. "Well... you and I are talking now, at least? I just wish we could have talked about what happened sooner."

"I'm glad we're talking about it, period." Giovanni looks down into his empty glass and twists it against the table with his fingers. "I didn't think we ever would."

Cellina nods as she stretches her arms up, yawning. The driver had been right. The food was delicious.

"Are you tired?" Giovanni asks.

"Are you?" Cellina smiles. "Don't worry about me. You're the one with a flight to catch in a few hours. Should we go back to the hotel so you can get some sleep?"

He considers for a moment, still twisting his beer. He meets her gaze. "No. If you're up for it, let's walk around—maybe find something sweet? They have something called taiyaki. It's a hot pancake shaped like a fish and stuffed with custard or red bean... sometimes other things. You might like it. We could split one?"

"Hell yeah I'll like it—we'll see about this splitting business." Another stuffed-pancake situation? Cellina's mouth is already watering. Tonight feels like a challenge: how much delicious food can she stuff into her body. "I might need to buy a new wardrobe by the end of this trip." She smiles in jest. "It'll be worth it though."

"Doesn't matter," he says. "You'll always be you—someone I can drop the 'purebred leader' bullshit around. You've never subscribed to it and have always treated me like a normal, feeling person and not just someone who could do something for you. You live by your *own* rules and it's mesmerizing to me. I admire that in you, and I wish I could..."

Giovanni pauses, staring down at his empty beer glass. Blood rushes to Cellina's cheeks and she takes a breath, willing her nature inside to stop flipping around before her eyes alight and embarrass her in the middle of this restaurant.

He shakes his head, smiling when he meets her eyes. "Will you walk with me? Let's stay out all night... just one night. I'll sleep on the plane."

She looks up at him, controlling her bubbling insides. *Uncomfortable shoes and oppressive body images be damned.*

"Yes. I'm in."

# NINETEEN

A couple weeks later, Nino focuses on his phone, watching the gray bubbles of the impending text from Cellina float in the bright white glow of the screen.

[I don't know, I'm pretty sure he's flirting with me.]

Nino smiles, typing his response. He hits send.

[Not to downplay your obvious attractiveness, but I think that's Jun's resting personality?]

[He's so charming. An excellent date, and he's wearing this killer like… pearl-white suit. I've never seen anything like it.]

Nino scoffs, typing his response.

[Don't tell G that.]

[Yeah whatever. I'll see you tomorrow morning.]

[Ciao bella.]

Slowly, Nino sits up in bed. He's tired of lying around, tired of being in pain. His ribs and organs have recovered, but this tongue-regeneration business is absolute hell. His entire mouth throbs and burns—the sensation reverberating in his jaw and sending tremors throughout his skull. It makes him immobile sometimes. Dizzy and nauseous.

At the moment, a breakthrough is occurring. The fiery tingles of regrowth are still present, but not all-consuming. He looks at the space across from the foot of the bed. His mate's sprawling nest of books, papers and notes, markers and plastic model brains is enclosed within a messy half-circle. Haruka always describes his research methods as "organized chaos." Having observed him for more than a month, Nino now understands.

The maker of the nest is missing. He looks out the patio doors, and the crescent moon is high, casting their natural hot spring area in soft white light. The massive cherry blossom trees are flowerless and full of rich green leaves. He stands from the bed, then exits the room in search of his doting mate.

Predictably, he's in the library. Nino slides the double doors shut behind him. Haruka sits in the floor with his legs folded, but he's asleep—a large book open and settled within the concave of his folded legs. Haruka's chin rests down against his chest, his breathing silent and deep.

Relaxing on his knees in front of him, Nino reaches out to hold and lift Haruka's chin with his fingertips. He doesn't rouse at all. Nino smiles. Haruka has been unbelievable in taking care of him. He knew his mate to be patient and loving, but the level of benevolence, selflessness and tenderness he's exhibited has been indescribable.

With his mate's sleeping face lifted, Nino tilts his head and places a soft kiss against his lips. Haruka inhales, his unfocused eyes flickering open. He blinks, confused. His deep voice is thick with exhaustion. "I'm sorry, what—"

*Why are you sorry?*

Haruka takes another deep breath, looking around the room. "I fell asleep. What—what time is it?"

*Almost ten thirty at night. Don't sleep like this. Come to bed.*

"I'm fine." Haruka yawns. "I am awake now." He rubs his hand against the back of his neck and beneath his heavy, disheveled bun. The bags underneath Haruka's eyes are prominent. His features, usually lean and elegant, appear sharp and gaunt. In tending to Nino, Haruka has let his own health and body fall to ruin.

Nino leans forward and kisses the corner of his mouth. He pulls away, and Haruka's eyes are focused on his lips. When they flicker up to Nino's irises, the hesitation there is obvious.

*I miss you, tesoro...*

He misses the satisfaction of being entwined with his naked body. His earthy, rosy aura enveloping him in a bright haze of passion when they make love. The delicious taste of his cool flesh and blood in his mouth. Nino is sick of feeding through an IV and tired of lying in bed. Tired of being hindered.

He cherishes their intimacy. It gives him confidence, and Haruka always encourages his actions. He wants to explore and dig deeper with his mate, truly understanding how to fulfill him and reach new heights together.

Haruka sighs, eyes closed. "My love, the doctor said we should wait at least two months."

*But I want you right now.*

He leans into him again and Haruka drops his jaw, exhaling a weighted moan as he slides his fingers against the back of Nino's overgrown hair. But a moment later, he pulls away from the kiss, a timid smile on his lips.

"You should be in bed. "

Frustration bubbles up inside Nino, tightening his chest. He blows out a breath to squelch it and rests his forehead against Haruka's shoulder. *Then come with me? Don't stay in here alone all night again.*

"It is better if I keep watch here so that I do not disturb your rest—"

*No.* Nino turns his head, rubbing his face within the concave of Haruka's neck. He reaches down and takes hold of his hand against the tatami. *Just—come with me and try to relax, alright? I'll sleep better if you're next to me anyway. And I want you to sleep at night, too. You need to try.*

Haruka's shoulders rise and fall in a sigh. Nino can feel him conflicted, paranoid and painfully anxious. The emotions are strong, but shrouded deep within him. Quiet, like a darkened sky over black ocean waves just before a terrible storm.

"I—I cannot sleep knowing that we are vulnerable to Lajos and any potential assault. I will walk you back to the room, but then I'll keep watch—"

*He might not ever come back here.*

"And yet, he could return at any second."

"Haru..." Nino lifts, staring into his mate's eyes. "Pl-*please*."

His mate sits frozen, his gaze softening. "You spoke to me."

*I speak to you all the time.*

"Yes, but hearing your physical voice..." Haruka shakes his head, his eyes glassy in the dim light. "I have missed it so much." He leans forward, wrapping his arms around Nino's shoulders. He can feel the subtle relief washing through Haruka, easing just a small bit of the thick tension.

"Come... t-to bed. With me." Nino sits back from the hug, waiting. Despite having a tongue in his mouth his entire life, losing it for almost two months has been more impactful than he could have ever imagined. Even now, it feels bulky—awkward and making him trip over his words.

Haruka nods, standing upright and urging Nino to his feet as well. They walk hand in hand as they move through the silent hallways and toward their bedroom. When they're inside and lying against the firm mattress, Nino tries to relax, but it's impossible. Haruka rests on his back, unmoving beside him. He's excruciatingly tense—taut like an overstretched rubber band and seconds from snapping.

Turning on his side, Nino faces him. Haruka is staring up at the ceiling, barely even blinking. Nino reaches and takes hold of his wrist. *Please sleep?*

"I'm not tired..." He turns his head against the pillow to meet Nino's eyes. "But I sincerely wish that you would. It is paramount for your healing."

Nino sighs, gruff in adjusting against his pillow. He hates this: Haruka wearing himself thin, the constant paranoia and this obsession with protecting him from some unknown event. Everything has changed because of Lajos—the healthy flow and peace of their everyday lives ruined. He's starting to feel like a child on punishment for something that wasn't his fault.

To make matters worse, the burning tingles of regeneration flare up within his jaws once more. He closes his eyes and groans from the familiar torture. Haruka turns on his side and into Nino, wrapping him up in his arms and holding him through the worst of the pain.

# TWENTY

"Good morning, your grace." Junichi smiles, sitting at the table with Asao and holding a steaming cup of coffee.

Haruka draws closer, squinting from the flood of bright morning light filling the kitchen. Confused, he scratches his head. "I thought you were traveling in Europe until August?"

"I was, but plans change. Giovanni is back home and Cellina is leaving this weekend, yes?"

"Yes... Our outstanding responsibilities are settled for now, so I feel there is no tangible reason for them to stay."

"Right. And how's Nino recovering?" Junichi asks.

"He is excellent—sleeping, presently." Haruka sits in the open chair at the head of the table, shielding his eyes from the light. It's intense, lately. "His ribs are healed and he started working with a speech pathologist last week. This week, we will begin feeding therapy. Sora is coming today to draw my blood. But why did you shorten your trip? You always enjoy your business excursions to Europe."

"Is the light bothering your eyes?" Junichi tilts his head. "You seem distressed by it."

Haruka reaches up and rubs with his fingertips. His irises are burning—but not in the usual way when they alight. This is different. "I do not know why, but they seem irritated at the moment."

"They look irritated. Asao told me you're not sleeping at night... that you haven't in over a month and you have a habit of passing out somewhere in the house during the day."

"Did he?" Haruka drops his hands, narrowing his eyes at his manservant. Asao stares forward, ignoring him while he drinks.

"Haruka..." Junichi probes. "If you become nocturnal—"

"I am not."

"*Yes*, you are," Asao interjects, frowning. "You already are, Haruka. It's a problem."

"If you're nocturnal," Junichi continues, "we *all* have to become nocturnal—do you understand that? Even if you don't mandate it, our natures will follow your lead by instinct, because your essence is like a beacon to us. It's old and power-ful, and it impacts us. If we want to meet with you or conduct business with you, but you're only awake at night, then guess what? We have to be, too."

Haruka shakes his head. His eyes are burning and it feels as if his brain is swimming in murky water. "No—I do not want this community to change its practices."

"Then why aren't you sleeping?" Junichi asks.

"I... I cannot. Not right now."

"Why?" Asao presses.

Leaning with his elbows on the table, Haruka places his palms against his irritated eyes, shielding them from the light. "Because Lajos is nocturnal. Nino's attacker walks at night. How can I sleep and leave us both defenseless against him?"

"Didn't you verbally rescind his invitation into our home?"

Asao asks. "He can't come inside anymore. You don't need to do this."

"*It's not enough!*" Haruka pauses from the outburst, taking a breath. "He can still use his power to vanish us, even if he is not inside the house. As long as he knows we are here, we are vulnerable and I cannot... I can't sleep knowing this. I will not."

"So, why not let Cellina and Giovanni stay to help?" Junichi asks.

"Because they have already done more than enough for us. I refuse to burden them any more than I already have. I can handle this."

Silence falls over the warm space of the kitchen. Haruka rubs his eyes. The inflammation there is growing unbearable.

"How long will this go on?" Junichi asks. "This practice of living in fear and paranoia?"

"I don't know," Haruka says, his throat tightening from the anxiety and cutting off his breathing. Everything—the stress, shock and uncertainty of the past month—it all crashes down on his psyche. "I have lost much in my life, Junichi. I lost my parents very young, and I lost my first mate and a child. I almost lost Nino and it scares me to death. If I lose him... I'm finished. There's nothing else for me in this life."

Haruka clenches his eyes shut, the fear deep within him rising to the surface and spilling over. His eyes water and he wipes the tears away with his fingertips. "I was too complacent, too relaxed. I... I will do whatever it takes to protect the vampire I love and our home. If this means becoming nocturnal, then so be it. But I do not wish for your lives to be uprooted by my actions. I do not want to make things difficult for my community. I am sorry."

"You don't need to be sorry," Junichi says. "But I don't like that all of our lives are being shifted because of this vile vampire. You're giving him a lot of power, Haruka."

"I don't know what else to do."

Asao exhales a groan and runs his palms against his face. "Going to the bank and grocery shopping are going to be a real bitch."

Junichi laughs. "You crabby old man—that's all you're worried about right now?"

"No more high school baseball games, or afternoon karuta matches at the local rec center. And think about vamps whose businesses thrive in the daytime hours, or how the trains stop running at two in the morning—travel and accessibility are going to be shit. Night buses for everyone!"

"Mm." Junichi shakes his head. "Fuck the night bus, I'm not doing that."

Asao laughs. "*Vampires on the Night Bus* sounds like some cheap horror film—"

The doorbell rings and Asao stands to leave. When he's gone, Haruka squints at the suave peanut-brown vampire beside him. "Did Asao tell you to come back home to talk to me?"

"Asao is not the boss of me. I make my own decisions."

"He's your elder."

"Doesn't matter. After my father died, I stopped listening to my elders. Evil bastard ruined it for all of 'em."

Haruka scoffs, unconvinced. Junichi will be one hundred and thirty this fall. Haruka outranks him, but the dynamic of their relationship is comfortable—not rigid in their culture's traditional, hierarchical manner. It's nice.

"Thank you, Jun. For listening, and for keeping my circumstance secret... for as long as possible, anyway."

"You're welcome." Junichi smiles, watching Haruka from the corner of his eyes. "That's what friends are for. Should I start making you new clothes since you're rail thin now? My dark, ethereal muse is becoming skeletal, so I need to adjust my aesthetic?"

"Ethereal?" Haruka turns his nose up, but then looks down at his baggy sweater, his loose pants with his belt augmented by a self-made hole to draw it in tighter. "Is it so bad?"

"It's not *good*. Why aren't you eating?"

"Solidarity. But I eat sometimes... I am busy."

"Doesn't Nino get a feeding tube for nutrition *and* a blood IV? Plus, your mate is a little more toned than you, Haruka. He can handle the weight loss better. You, on the other hand, need to eat more than 'sometimes,' my dear friend."

Haruka shrugs. "We have always been taught that as pure-breds, we do not need to consume food to survive."

"Right. You can walk around looking like Nosferatu in a wig if you want to, but you'd be better off with some meat on your bones."

Asao reappears in the doorway and Haruka is surprised when a casually dressed Doctor Davies is standing beside him. He bows at the waist as he holds the handles of a large bag within his fists. Haruka turns to Junichi, the moment shocking him. He whispers, "There is a human in my house."

"Who is this?" Junichi sits forward, whispering back with his black eyes wide. "He's exquisite..."

Stepping into the kitchen, the doctor nods his head. The action is stiff. "Good morning, Mr. Hirano. I—well... Sora had a double shift yesterday and you had asked me about medical books. So I decided to make the house call since I'm off on Sundays. I tried contacting you directly but—but your phone was off."

Haruka has no idea where his phone is. He can't even remember the last time he's seen or used it. "Please call me Haruka, and thank you for making a personal visit. Doctor

Davies, this is Junichi Takayama. He is a close friend. Junichi, Doctor Davies."

Doctor Davies bows. "It's a pleasure to meet you."

"Likewise." Junichi smiles. "Is this your first time being in a house full of high-level vampires?"

The doctor relaxes his shoulders and scratches the back of his thick ombre hair. The color reminds Haruka of a lion's mane. He lifts his eyebrows behind his glasses. "Is it obvious?"

"Very." Junichi sits back, examining him. "But don't worry. We won't bite... before a first date, anyway. Do you have dinner plans tonight?"

Doctor Davies blinks. "Ex-excuse me?"

Haruka holds his hand up, shaking his head. "I apologize for my friend's facetious rhetoric. Nino is in the bedroom—Asao will guide you there—and thank you for the books. That was very kind of you."

Doctor Davies narrows his eyes toward Junichi, but then adjusts and softens his expression. He smiles toward Haruka. "It's... my pleasure. I'll need to draw your blood for the new IV today as well. I'll examine Nino first, then let you know when I'm ready. Haruka... are you doing okay? You look a little—"

"I am fine, Doctor. Thank you for your concern."

The doctor nods politely before Asao guides him out of the kitchen. Haruka whips his head toward Junichi when they're gone. "What are you doing? He's Nino's doctor."

"*Why* are you cockblocking me? And why does he smell like that?" Junichi points at the empty doorway. "Do you not notice how incredible he smells? Is he human?"

Haruka blinks, frowning. He has never heard the term "cockblocking" before, but given the context and Junichi's demeanor he can easily understand. "I admit that he is oddly appealing to my nature. But he reads as human."

"I know humans." Junichi folds his arms. "They smell like

dirt. He does *not* smell like dirt, and he's stunning. He's at my mother's hospital with Sora? Damn... maybe I feel sick, too?"

Junichi forces a shallow cough, the sound unnatural and awkward. Haruka purses his lips in a frown. "Please do not harass my mate's doctor."

"I make no promises." Junichi grins. "Do you think he likes males? Humans are very particular about that."

———

THIRTY MINUTES LATER, Doctor Davies has finished examining Nino and drawn bags of Haruka's blood for the upcoming week.

With Nino lying behind him, Haruka unrolls the sleeves of his sweater while seated on the edge of the mattress. "He says that the regeneration process is, quote, 'like earthquakes and hellfire' in his mouth."

The doctor smiles. "Well, yes, that sounds about right—I did say it wouldn't be easy. But everything is progressing as it should. Hopefully the hellfire rages on and burns out soon?" At Haruka's silence, the doctor pauses from packing his bag and looks up. Nino's face is flat as he shakes his head.

Haruka grins. "He says, 'Is he joking about this right now?' There was also an expletive that I don't care to repeat."

"N-no, not at all. Sorry about that."

The doorbell rings, surprising Haruka. They aren't expecting anyone else today. But within a few minutes, he can hear the pitter-patter of small feet, the whisper of excited voices. He sits up straighter, his heart light.

"Behave, please, or we won't do this again," Sora cautions as they enter the doorway. Shion and Amon are at her sides, their hands gripped in hers and their faces full of wonder. This is the first time they have ever visited the estate.

"Haru-sama!" Amon shouts, then bolts from Sora's grip. She calls after him but it's no use. He bounds, then slams into Haruka as he sits with his legs gaped on the bed. He wraps his arms around Haruka's waist in a tight hug, his face pressed into his sweater.

Haruka grips Amon's head in his palms and pulls his gaze up, smiling. "Well, hello."

"Hi!"

"Amon, Mom said *don't* run," Shion scolds from beside her mother. Amon turns his head and sticks his tongue out before snuggling into Haruka's stomach again.

"Hi, Sora." Doctor Davies blinks. "I told you I'd take care of things today?"

"I know, I know," she says. "But I wanted to surprise Haruka since it's been rough the past several weeks. And I forgot that I promised the little ones I'd bring them with me this week so, you know... they don't understand the concept of 'Mommy worked a thirty-hour shift so the trip you were looking forward to for three weeks is cancelled.'"

"Ah, well, fair enough." The doctor grins. "Should I come next week, too?"

As they talk, Haruka pulls Amon up from his vise-like position around his waist and sits him against his thighs. When he's settled, he looks up at Haruka with bright brown eyes. "Can I show you something?" he whispers.

"Yes." Haruka nods, whispering in turn. "But first, I think we should apologize for not listening to Mom, shouldn't we?"

Amon turns his head toward Sora and nods in a polite bow. "Momma, I'm sorry."

Sora smiles in acknowledgment. "Thank you, sweetie—but *listen* next time." She narrows her eyes, then turns back toward the doctor.

Haruka pats Amon against his back. "And can we also

properly greet Nino-sama?" Amon turns his head and dips it in a hasty bow.

"Hello, Nino-sama!"

"Hel-hello..."

Amon flips back, looking up at Haruka. "Can I show you now, *please*?"

"Of course, what is it?"

He digs into his jacket pocket and pulls out a complex-looking object. Holding it within his small hands, Amon flips the toy around as he speaks. "It's nanoblocks. It's a shark, see? And it can open and close its mouth—*chomp chomp chomp*." Amon grips the shark's jaw with his fingers, demonstrating and holding it up a little too close to Haruka's face.

"It's wonderful." Haruka chuckles, leaning back. "Did you build this by yourself?"

"No, Dad helped. It took a long time—ah! Can we please do one together? Next time you come visit?"

"I love this idea. What animal should we choose?"

"Hmm, you pick."

Haruka contemplates, scratching his head. Truly, he has no clue as to what this line of toys has available—

*There's a pig, a parakeet, kangaroo... a fox and all manner of Pokémon.*

Haruka meets Nino's eyes and his mate is watching him. He has his phone in his hands, a gentle smile on his lips. Haruka grins. *Thank you, my love.*

*You're welcome...*

Confident, Haruka looks down at Amon. "I think I would like to do a Pokémon."

"Yeah!" Amon brightens. "Which one is your favorite?"

*For fuck's sake, Haru. You couldn't pick the pig? Or one of the other three you recognized?*

Haruka bites his lips, discreetly eying his mate. *What the hell is a Pokémon?*

*Unbelievable—*

"Nino-sama?"

Shion is at Nino's side. She places her hands against his exposed arm, affectionately rubbing him there. "Are you okay?"

Nino nods, briefly flickering his eyes toward Haruka before answering, his words slow and careful. "Yes. Th-thank you... for asking..."

"Please feel all better soon," says Shion. "Then you can come over with Haru-sama, and me and Dad will make mochi!"

"I'll help too!" Amon frowns.

Shion sighs. "Amon will help, too."

Nino smiles, hesitating, but then lays his hand on top of hers as it rests against his arm. "Okay, s-sounds good."

JULY

# TWENTY-ONE

"On a scale of one to ten, how drunk was I last night?" Mia groans and lays her head back, careful not to spill her coffee on the plush couch. She runs a hand into her long wavy hair. It's still the off-season, so of course, it's dyed. Something like a rich plum tint shines against the deep walnut of her natural color. "Ten being like, totally shit-faced and falling down... I don't remember falling down, though? Wait—is that worse?"

"Oh God."

"I should *not* have drunk that much rum."

Cellina takes a sip of her own coffee and smiles. "You shouldn't have drunk that much, no, you didn't fall down, and maybe an eight? If I'm being nice."

"Dammit. Was I embarrassing? I feel like I did something embarrassing, like blatantly spitting on people while I was talking. I spit when I'm drunk—I think my glands become hyper liquified."

"You were fine." Cellina laughs. "Gross. Just forget about it."

"The stupid pressure gets to me, you know? Too many ranked vamps concentrated in a small place. I *hate* it."

They both attended a society event the previous evening. The Moretti Clan—a family of first-generation vampires prominent in the art world—held their annual summer soiree. Everyone who is anyone attends. The evening is a staple within the Milan aristocracy.

"My parents keep pressuring me to bond and find a mate—like the shit is easy," Mia whines. "Can't they just be proud of me for who I am? For what I've achieved?"

Cellina smiles at her friend. "You've been a prima ballerina for La Scalla for the past fifty years—of course they're proud of you. They just want tiny vampires to cuddle sooner rather than later."

Mia folds her arms. "Then *they* should pop out some more."

"Uh, you know they can't. Your parents are well over two hundred. That ship has sailed."

"Listen, can you and I just... *try* bonding, and then find a donor?" Mia bats her eyes. "We've known each other forever and we're comfortable. We could do whatever we wanted, you know? Without the antiquated gender roles and hierarchy bullshit. It could be the perfect relationship."

Cellina stands from the couch and walks to the large window, stretching her legs. She looks out over the gray, dreary buildings of the city underneath the cloudy skyline—the sharp pillars of the Duomo like ornate upright daggers in the distance. Heavy raindrops pelt against the glass and stream down. "Mia, I love you and all, but I'm not committing to taking care of your drunk ass for the rest of my life. We already talked about this."

"I know, but I don't drink as much as I used to! I'm getting better. It's only bad like this off-season... and we know how to have fun together, yeah? Even though it's been a while..." Mia winks in a smile. Cellina frowns.

"You got a lot of attention last night—as usual," Mia goes on, smirking. "Just swatting them off like flies. Why is it that the vampire who doesn't want the attention gets a shit ton? Meanwhile, I'm flashing my fangs and can't even get a date. You're finally finished with school and papers and internships, you have an amazing position at Pinacoteca di Brera... So when will we start opening ourselves to dating?"

"I still have things I want to accomplish—there's a long road ahead."

"Okay..." Mia nods. "But you can do those things and be with the right vampire... Apparently that vampire is not *me*, but whatever. Someone?"

Cellina moves back toward the couch with her coffee. "Romantic relationships take a lot of work and attention— people are needy and co-dependent. I don't have time to coddle someone. Nor do I want to."

In truth, she's still recovering from coddling her best friend for most of his life. Worn out from being Nino's feeding source for more than a century. The last thing she wants right now is to take on another ward. Being the vampire she is—forthright and ambitious—it would inevitably end up that way.

Unless she found someone more like herself? Someone who would be a *true* partner as opposed to a third leg she'd need to drag along and mother.

Mia sits up from the couch in a jolt, sniffing the air in a dramatic gesture and lifting her chin. Her pale blue eyes are wide. "Smells like Giovanni."

"Yeah." Cellina raises an eyebrow. "This is his usual day and time to visit with my father."

Grabbing her purse in a tizzy, Mia rummages through and pulls a compact mirror out. "Why the hell didn't you warn me

—Shit. *Shit.*" She runs her fingers through to fluff and accentuate her shiny waves, then hastily grabs her lipstick and applies it. Cherry red.

Cellina's mouth is agape. "Are you serious right now?"

"Are *you* serious?" Mia frowns, replacing the cap on her lipstick and puckering. "Giovanni is purebred and hot. Nobody can figure out why he won't choose a mate. I don't get it either, but when he's ready, I'll be standing in line."

"Giovanni is too busy to mate," Cellina reasons. "He's always running around all over the place. Doesn't it seem a little crazy? Like he's wearing himself too thin?"

Mia freezes and stares at Cellina as if she's just declared something stupidly obvious, like water is wet. Her friend shrugs. "He's realm leader. It's his job."

"But still... I know what it's like to be busy and driven, but there has to be some balance."

"I don't know." Mia stuffs her compact and lipstick back into her purse. "All I know is, there's one Bianchi left on the market. Nino is cute, right? Like sweet and unassuming. Giovanni is a *fucking man.*" Mia grunts and flexes her arms to emphasize her point.

Cellina falls back into the couch, laughing. "What is he again? One more time, I missed it—"

"Shut up." Mia grins. "You know what I mean. He's all broad and tall with those gorgeous greenish eyes, and he takes care of all the shit. That's my ideal—take care of me. Look after my drunk ass."

Cellina is laughing so hard she can barely catch her breath. "Giovanni does *not* have time to take care of your drunk ass."

"You don't know that." Mia reaches over and smacks Cellina's hip, playful. "He might have a few extra hours to spare. At night... in his bedroom."

There's a soft knock on the door to the study. It opens and

Giovanni is there. He's more casual than normal in dark blue jeans and a light beige sweater with his sleeves pushed up over his honeyed forearms. His golden-brown hair is cut short now, the length trimmed and cleanly swept back from his chiseled face.

Mia stands up like a rocket, surprising Cellina as she stares from the couch. Her friend bows, polite. Prissy. "Good afternoon, your grace—it's such a pleasure to see you here."

Giovanni smiles as he walks forward, game face on. "Hello, Mia. Cellina." He's carrying a small pink box with a neat string handle. It's about the size of a half-loaf of bread. "Did you both enjoy the soiree yesterday evening?"

"It was delightful, your grace." Mia bats her eyelashes, sitting back down on the couch as if she were a swan. Cellina places her palm against her face, amazed as Mia continues. "You looked very handsome in your suit—but truly, you look incredible in anything... or maybe in nothing?" Mia lifts one shoulder, flirtatious. Cellina covers her face with both palms.

"Thank you for the compliment." Giovanni grins, humble. "I'm looking forward to your performance in *Giselle* in the fall season. Have rehearsals already started?"

"Well I—" There's a beeping sound from Mia's purse and she curses underneath her breath. She takes her phone out and turns off the alarm. "Actually, rehearsals start next week. But I need to get going—hair appointment. My apologies, your grace. It was an absolute pleasure seeing you."

Mia stands, then bends and kisses Cellina on both cheeks before rushing past Giovanni and out the door. After she shuts it, he turns to look at Cellina. "Is she drunk?"

Cellina laughs. "Not at the moment, no."

"Mm." Giovanni frowns. "That's rare..."

Unfolding her leg from its tucked position beneath her, she

points her toes at the small box he's carrying "And what is this?"

"There's a Japanese bakery near Porta Nuova. I was in the area for a social visit this morning, so I stopped by." Cellina sits upright, folding her legging-clad limbs against the couch and accepting the box with both hands as he gives it to her. He groans in a sigh and sits on the floor, his back against the couch just beside her.

She unties the string, then lifts the flap. Inside sits a moist and buttery-smelling Castella cake. She breathes a little squeal. "Thank you."

"You're welcome. Is Mia still your source?"

"These days. For better or worse." Cellina examines the cake. It isn't a single slice like she'd always received in vampires' houses or at cafés when she was in Japan. It is a small cake unto itself. She'll need more coffee.

"She's been your friend for a long time," Giovanni says thoughtfully, the lines in his forehead crinkling. "Does her blood taste different when she drinks too much?"

"It's not too bad. If she knows I'm going to feed, she cleans up her act for at least twenty-four hours prior. Giovanni, who's your source? I know your parents originally chose Dante, but he's mated now... Is it Sergio?" The image of Giovanni's equally mannish and charismatic friend flashes in her mind.

"Absolutely not." Giovanni frowns even harder.

Cellina tilts her head. "I thought he was your friend?"

"He is... kind of." Giovanni sighs. "It's hard to consider vampires as friends when you're purebred. They always want shit from you. I talked to Haruka about it once and he agreed. He said his entire life had been spent focusing on what everyone else around him wanted and needed until he isolated himself in England. Apparently, Nino was the first genuine friend he'd ever made... but then they started fucking each other, so I'm not even sure if that counts."

"It *counts*." Cellina laughs. "God... Junichi is his genuine friend now?"

"They definitely can't fuck."

Rolling her eyes, Cellina shakes her head. "Nino called me yesterday morning and said that Haru is still a ball of tension and not sleeping. So of course, Nino is stressed the hell out. I don't know how long they can function like this."

"I offered to come back and help, but Haruka insists that they're fine. I don't know, but something has to give."

Cellina nods in agreement. When Giovanni doesn't say anything else, she lifts her chin. "So back to you—who do you feed from? You haven't answered me."

His chest rises and falls in a deep breath, the furrow in his brow somehow deepening. But his voice is light, teasing. "I don't feed from anyone, Cellina."

She pauses, processing the words. "What does that mean?"

"It means what I said."

"Whose blood do you drink in order to sustain your body?"

Giovanni smirks. "My cousin's."

She sits straight, thinking. "This... has to do with your father, doesn't it? Are you feeding him?" She looks down at his side profile, waiting. Her heart is heavy in her chest and her breathing clipped. It's unfair to put so much weight and responsibility on one vampire.

"Yes," he says. "But that information is confidential. Please don't repeat it."

She sits back and sighs, running her fingers into the thick of her curly hair. She closes her eyes.

"It's fine, Lina," he assures her. She opens her eyes, and his head is turned to the side. "This is my life. I'm the first son, remember? It's just how it is—how it'll always be. I accept it."

Cellina leans forward, serious. "I don't accept it. It's too much." She laces her fingers into the back of his soft hair, then uses her other hand to massage his forehead. "And these lines— stop frowning so much. God, Giovanni, you didn't used to have these lines."

"I'm old now—"

"No. You're not. We're young. Your damn face is just scrunched up all the time."

She continues rubbing at the lines in his forehead, as if she can erase them by sheer will alone. Her other hand grips the back of his head. "When's the last time you physically fed from another vampire?"

"Dante. The sexcapade."

"*Dante* was your last true feed? Damn... that was over a hundred years ago." The sensation of feeding—the intimacy of breaking through another vampire's flesh and experiencing the rush of their blood in your mouth—is an innate need. Maybe even more so for purebreds. To deny someone this primal right feels harsh. Almost cruel. She never knew Domenico to be a cruel vampire. In fact, he was always the exact opposite when it came to Nino.

After a moment, she tilts his head back against the couch, playful in tugging his hair. "How's that?" she asks, leaning over his face and noticing the gentle shadow of a beard already forming against his jawline.

"What are you doing, exactly?"

"Massaging the lines out of your damn forehead."

"Is this a sympathy massage?" He closes his eyes, flashing straight white teeth in a grin.

"No. This is an 'I'm worried about my friend' massage."

"That word again." He opens his eyes, slow, and Cellina's breath catches. His irises are glowing emerald green and haunting. He stares up at her unashamed. It calls to her, making her nature deep within her warm and restless. It's as if a fire burns in her belly, in between her thighs and up her spine, her own eyes threatening to glow to life.

Panicked and in need of a distraction, she reaches over with her free hand and flips the lid of the cake box open. She pinches a large piece of the soft texture with her fingers, then holds the chunk over Giovanni's mouth. "Open."

Obedient, he parts his lips. She places the bite inside, but Giovanni closes his lips around her fingers before she removes them. Without thinking, she slides her damp finger into her mouth, cleaning the crumbs. "Better? Less stressed?"

"*Worse.*" He lifts his head, shaking it. "You and this damn cake." He draws his tall body up from the floor, and Cellina stretches her leg to kick his hip.

"I'm trying to get you to relax—"

Giovanni turns on a dime and catches her ankle in his large palm. He tugs, making Cellina gasp as she slides down, slouching into the bend of the couch cushions. He leans over her, his smoldering emerald eyes staring as he speaks through clenched teeth.

"You're not helping."

# TWENTY-TWO

Nino flips onto his side as he lies in bed, the restlessness like a deep ache in his bones. He can't sleep at all now. It's getting worse.

Haruka is lying still beside him on his back. The moonlight from the patio doors silhouettes his shadowed frame like silver.

Nino frowns. "Haru." He waits. His mate doesn't move, doesn't speak. Eyes closed. Annoyed, Nino reaches out and pinches high on his side and just underneath his rib cage. Haruka jumps in shock, wincing and scooting away.

"Are you *pretending* to sleep right now?" Nino sits up, disbelieving. "Do you forget that we're biologically connected? You can't fake anything with me."

He groans, rubbing and nursing his side where Nino pinched him. Nino scoffs, smiling. "I can't believe you."

Haruka peeks over his shoulder. "Just... if I go to the library, perhaps I won't disturb you there?"

"That doesn't matter. It's late. You can't keep doing this, Haru. It's not just about me—or even us. We're upsetting the pulse and energy of our entire realm. Every vampire is impacted by it."

Haruka shifts to his opposite side so that he faces Nino. He looks up from the pillow. "I... I know this, but *you* are my priority. My only wish is that you are safe and healthy—no matter the cost."

"So, it's okay for you to ruin and starve yourself in the name of my health and safety, and I'm supposed to be fine with that? Do you think this doesn't go both ways?"

"I am not 'starving' myself," Haruka gripes, then sighs as he tumbles flat on his back once more. He closes his eyes. Nino stares down at him with his mouth pursed. After a moment, Haruka opens one eye, grinning. "Such pressure."

Nino leans over toward his nightstand drawer, opens it, then grabs the bottle of liquid from inside. When he pops the cap open with his thumb, Haruka blinks both eyes open from the distinct sound. The usual look of concern rests in his brow. "Nino, it has not quite been two months. The doc—"

"If you say the phrase 'the doctor said' to me one more time, Haruka, I swear to God."

Haruka stares up at him, biting his tongue. Nino goes on. "I feel great, okay? It'll be two months in three more days. Would you stop telling me 'no'? May I *please* touch you?"

"Of—of course. I simply wanted to make sure you were restored to your optimum health. It was not my intention to be difficult."

Leaning, Nino slides his palm underneath Haruka's thigh. "Knees up. It's not that you're being difficult." Haruka does as he's told, and Nino sits upright and settles himself between his gaped thighs. "You're the most thorough, amazing and handsome caretaker I could ever ask for... but a tad strict."

Haruka lifts his head from the pillow, brows drawn together in protest. "If the doc... If the medical professional suggests that we do something, it is wise to follow his recommendations. Especially if *ah—*"

Nino moves swiftly, dropping the bottle and crawling his fingers underneath Haruka's robe like spiders to tickle the bend of his waist. Haruka squirms in protest, reaching to grab Nino's hands while biting back laughter.

"*Nino, sto—*"

"I see what you did there, smartass." Nino wrestles and teases, but Haruka clamps down tight on his wrists, chuckling as he catches his breath.

Nino pauses, looking down at Haruka lying against the bed. The bags underneath his eyes are noticeable even in the moonlit room. His fatigued appearance: his bony face and sharp collarbone... the deep-rooted anxiety Nino feels pulsing within him. Haruka tries to stifle it, but it seeps out, manifesting in his inability to properly sleep, eat and relax.

"I think this is the first time you've laughed in two months."

"That isn't true..." Haruka inhales, relaxing his shoulders.

"You need to sleep."

"I cannot."

"Can't or won't?"

Haruka doesn't answer but releases his wrists. Nino caresses his palms against his mate's hips, soft and gliding across his cool skin. "I think... I want to indulge in you a little, since it's been a while. Can I try something different? Are you with me?"

Haruka smiles. "Always."

"Will you talk to me while we do this?"

Now, Haruka tenses, raising a dark brow in suspicion. "It depends..."

"Let's keep it simple. I'll ask questions, and you can tell me yes or no?"

He lifts his chin, his relief obvious. "*Yes.*"

Nino shakes his head, stifling a laugh. "I just want you to try and relax. Can we take off your robe?" Haruka sits up from the bed, and Nino helps to remove his robe from around his shoulders, unwrapping it from the length of his body. When he's naked, Haruka plops back down against the pillow in a huff, exhaling and adjusting his spine with his eyes closed. Nino scans his rail-thin frame, thinking he has a lot of work to do in the coming weeks.

Lifting so that he's on all fours and hovering above Haruka's face, Nino takes hold of his chin. Haruka opens his eyes and their mutual gaze locks in a weighted moment before Nino shifts higher, leaning down to kiss his forehead. "Can I start here?" he whispers, placing another kiss just between his eyebrows.

"Yes."

Nino moves to the tip of Haruka's nose, grazing the smooth, curved shape with his lips. He slides his palm up one side of Haruka's face and leans in to kiss just underneath his eye, wishing he had the power to make the heavy bags there magically disappear. When Haruka's lids flicker closed, Nino brushes his lips against the delicate skin of one lid, and then the other, thinking about how much he loves the vivid color of this creature's eyes. The infinite range of expression layered within them, and how looking into the depths of his gaze makes his heart race.

He lifts, watching. Haruka's lids are heavy as he opens them. His tongue slides out over his bottom lip before he parts them in quiet anticipation. But when Nino leans down, he kisses one corner of Haruka's mouth, then the other. He kisses underneath his bottom lip and just at his chin, teasing and avoiding direct contact with his lips altogether.

Haruka exhales a heavy sigh, stretching his neck against the pillow as Nino moves underneath to kiss his throat, following the exquisite line there and sensing the pulse of his rosy blood flowing underneath his skin.

He caresses one finger along the hard edge of his collarbone. "Can I kiss you here?"

"Yes," Haruka breathes.

While he shifts low to trace the bone with his tongue, he slides his hand down his mate's chest, feeling Haruka's nipple tickling the center of his palm. Nino adjusts his hand, circling the hardness of it with his thumb.

"What about here?" He moves lower, caressing down Haruka's torso as he kisses the center of his chest. His mate is silent, breathing heavy in the stillness of the room and his body writhing against the dark bedsheets and underneath Nino's hands. Holding Haruka's hips, Nino dips down to lick the flat concave of his stomach. He smiles against Haruka's skin when his belly tightens and shudders from his tongue dipping into his navel.

Slowly, Nino sits straight, drawing one of Haruka's legs up from the bed. His mate clenches the sheets in tight fists on either side of his hips while he watches Nino's movements.

"Are we okay?" Nino asks, holding Haruka's bent leg in front of him. He lifts it higher, stretching his hip and kissing the thin, soft skin behind his knee. As he does this, he glides his free hand down and along the flesh of Haruka's inner thigh, tracing with his fingertips.

"*Yes,*" Haruka says, his eyes morphing and glowing like a fiery sunset.

Nino kisses his calf, then rests his face against Haruka's skin to follow the swell of muscle toward his foot. He laps his tongue within the dip of his Achilles tendon, then kisses his heel. "Every time you stretched my legs when I was on bedrest, I always wished we were naked."

"I know," Haruka groans, breathless. "You were quite vocal about it."

"One day you kissed the bottom of my foot—like it was no big deal. It surprised me..." Nino mimics Haruka's action, first resting his nose against the warm arch of his mate's foot, then tilting his head and littering the curve with soft kisses.

Haruka's chest rises and falls as he stares. "I love every part of you."

"And I, you." Nino smiles, his fingertips still gliding up and down the inside of Haruka's thigh. "May I have this part of you? Can I try?" he asks, holding his foot steady.

"Yes," Haruka says. He relaxes the tension in his leg as Nino dips down, teasing his foot and toes with his mouth. While he licks, sucks and kisses, he delicately strokes the inside of Haruka's thigh as if it were a stringed instrument—something elegant, like a harp or koto.

"Nino..."

At the sound of his mate's raspy voice, Nino stops, pulling up from the swell of Haruka's toe. "Yeah?"

His glowing eyes are eager under furrowed brows. "Please..."

Nino drops his leg, but surprises Haruka when he leans down to take hold of his wrists. He gently pulls, urging his mate upright so that he's in a sitting position with his legs gaped wide, knees bent. When he's close, Nino presses their foreheads together. "Please *what*, tesoro?"

His head tilted, eyes half closed, Haruka stretches up to meet Nino's mouth. He whispers, "Enough..."

Their lips touch in a swift graze before Nino pulls back, lifting his hands to hold Haruka's face. He stares down into his glowing eyes. "Tell me what you want."

Haruka closes his parted lips, blinking. His eyes shift to the side before meeting Nino's gaze once more. "I... I want *you*."

In a smooth motion, he grabs the liquid that Nino had set aside, then lifts to his knees. Placing the small bottle in Nino's hand, he grabs his wrist and pulls him up toward the top of the bed. Haruka adjusts so that his back is facing Nino, reaches behind and tugs him into his spine. When Haruka turns his head, his hair tickles Nino's face. "I want you."

Nestling against his ear, Nino wraps his arms around Haruka's body. He whispers against his skin, "You don't need to want me, Haruka. You have me. I'm already yours."

Nino revels in the feel of his mate's cool flesh and nakedness underneath his hands, holding him tight. He litters Haruka's shoulder with kisses. "And you're mine?" Nino asks, sliding one hand down to rest flat against his stomach. Haruka arches into Nino's groin, leaning his head back to rest on his shoulder.

"Forever."

He unwraps Haruka's body, but only for a moment to swiftly lather his fingers and crawl them down and between his soft flesh. Nino keeps hold of his belly and kisses his upper back while easing two fingers inside. Haruka relaxes, gripping the headboard and pushing back to encourage him.

"I want to try something." Nino swallows, his body stiff with arousal.

"Mm," Haruka breathes.

Focusing, Nino closes his eyes. The warm energy deep within him swirls. He channels it, making it flow like hot honey up his core, through his veins and down the sinews of his arm. When it reaches his fingertips inside his mate, he presses it outward, soft, like candlelight. Faint and with just enough heat.

"*God*—" Haruka sucks in a breath, then exhales a deep moan through parted lips.

"Does it hurt? Should I stop—"

"*No*... n-no. I'm—it's..." Haruka pants and swallows, chest rising and falling underneath Nino's palm as he holds him.

"Panther, are you sure?"

Haruka blows out a breath. "Yes, don't... please don't stop."

Nino focuses, manifesting the gentle glow of his energy through his fingertips again. Haruka tenses and huffs, but Nino trusts in his assurance and doesn't stop this time. Knowing his mate's body even better than his own, he twists and rubs his warm fingertips within his inner walls, stroking just the right spot. A soft moan escapes Haruka's lips, and Nino has never heard him make this sound before: something like pleasure and purring smooshed into a singular, luscious expression.

He practically melts in Nino's embrace when he spills over in ecstasy. His rosy aura fills the bedroom, wild and free like an ancient, mythical creature. Nino whispers against his ear. "Are we good?"

Haruka is trembling in his arms, his eyes closed. "*So good...*"

Removing his fingers, Nino hooks his thumb into the waist of his pajama pants. He pulls the soft material down to free himself, grips his shaft with a slick palm and gradually guides himself inside. Haruka meets Nino's intention, arching into the friction and wetness of their joined bodies. His mate's skin is always cool to the touch, but inside is delectable heat: warm, tight and perfect.

Instead of rolling his hips, Nino pauses. Everything within him is threatening to overflow—Haruka's smell and the soft sounds of his pleasure, the feel of his body submitting to him, his aura all around him.

Realizing their lack of movement, Haruka turns his head. "What is it?"

Nino moans in a sigh, enjoying the stillness of him within his embrace and his body warmly wrapped around his shaft. He brushes his nose along the curve of Haruka's neck. "Ti amo molto."

"I love *you*," Haruka says, amusement in his deep voice. "Why... have we stopped?"

"Because I want you to come first and I was too close to the edge."

Haruka chuckles warm and deep. "It does not matter." He smiles, lifting a hand and running his fingers into Nino's hair at the back of his head. He turns just enough to where Nino can catch his mouth in a lazy kiss.

"It matters to me," Nino whispers against his lips. "You like it when I feed from you while I'm inside you."

Haruka's body stiffens, his eyes wide. Nino can practically feel the flush of shame radiating off his mate's skin.

"Why are you embarrassed?" Nino prods, smiling. "I just notice you come really hard if I do that."

"I..." Haruka turns his head away, taking a breath. He squirms but Nino holds him tighter.

"Technically, it's just another yes or no question." Nino kisses the back of his neck, softly, just at the center. "Do you want me to bite you?"

His mate's voice is quiet, just above a whisper. "Yes..."

Nino reaches up and unravels Haruka's hair from its tie, letting the length of it fall and spill down his back. He runs his fingers into it, gripping and pulling Haruka's head to the side before he bites down into his flesh.

Haruka tenses underneath his mouth, but Nino pulls, feeding to indulge his mate's intrinsic nature—to fulfill and stir his emotions. He pours his affection and gratitude into him, wanting to offer at least some notion of how much he means to Nino and how deeply he loves him.

While he feeds, he rolls his hips, rhythmic and thrusting, until Haruka spasms, groaning as the climax overtakes him. The sound of his voice and the feel of him unraveling within his arms push Nino over the edge. He allows himself to let go, his own body shivering from the satisfying rush of release as he holds Haruka tight.

When they've mutually relaxed from the exquisite high, Nino disconnects their bodies, grabs Haruka by his waist and pulls him from the headboard. Gently, he guides him to lie against the mattress. Haruka's eyes are closed, his long dark hair wild, as if he's been caught in a violent storm.

Breathless, Nino glances at the headboard. "We made a mess." He crawls forward, stretching the length of his body and then resting his weight on top of him—into the damp, rosy and sex-infused scent of him.

He kisses Haruka underneath his chin as he whispers, "I'll take care of it in the morning. Sleep, panther."

Haruka is already passed out, his breathing slow and even. Nino shifts so that he lies against his side. He closes his eyes, and soon, he joins him.

---

THE FOLLOWING morning is muggy and hot. Cicadas are buzzing loudly outside, their mating calls reverberating within the hallways of the estate as Nino walks. He readjusts his summer robe, tying the belt tighter. He needs coffee.

Running his fingers through freshly washed hair, he steps into the kitchen. "Hey, Jun."

"Good morning." The charming vampire is sitting at the kitchen table in his usual seat near the open patio doors. He waves a deep blue half-shell fan near his face. The color of the fan matches the large traditional pattern printed on his white button-down. Junichi is nothing if not stylish, his choices always bold, unapologetic in nature.

"I thought you were coming later. Why are you here so early?"

"I like to spend time with my favorite purebred couple." Junichi grins. "Being in your presence melts my old, jaded heart." He places a hand on his chest, dramatic. Nino chuckles.

"Jun, you're *not* old."

He bats his dark eyelashes. "I'm older than the two of you. Where is his highness?"

"Sleeping."

Junichi stops fanning, his onyx eyes wide. "Through the whole night?"

"Yes." Nino fills his coffee cup to the brim. He needs a bigger mug. Maybe two.

"Well, that's amazing news. Maybe things will get back to normal? I hear the local elementary school has been having a hell of a time. None of the little ones have been sleeping at night for the past month. You know their natures are very sensitive to him."

"Really?" Nino sits down at the table across from Junichi. "I mean, I definitely feel the unrest, but I'm with him all the time."

Junichi leans with his elbow on the table, cradling his chin in his palm. "We all feel it. Sora said the twins haven't slept at night in two weeks. Between that and her strenuous hospital shifts, she said she might drop them off here if Haruka doesn't stop this—see how much he enjoys them when they're bouncing off the walls at three in the morning."

Nino takes a long sip of his coffee. When he's finished, he sighs, relaxing his shoulders. "He does like them a lot..." The image of an excitable Amon showing off his toy shark while sitting on Haruka's knees flashes in Nino's mind. He'd watched the gentle interaction, awestruck. Something within his mate had brightened—like a dense fog lifting or a locked chest opening. Haruka had been so content and singularly focused on the small boy, as if everyone else in the room had ceased to exist.

"Do you like kids, Nino?"

"I don't know... I don't dislike them. I haven't ever given them much thought. Honestly, I didn't know if I'd ever be bonded. Thinking about anything past that seemed pointless."

"Well, seeing as you've reached this milestone, maybe it's time to start thinking about what else you might want?"

"Hm... maybe. Do you want kids someday, Jun?"

"*Hell* no."

"Mail call." Asao walks into the kitchen, a small stack of letters in one hand and a delivery box the size of large book in the other. Nino beams, excited as he stands from the table to relieve his manservant of the package. He takes it over to the counter.

Junichi smiles. "Hey, old coot—"

"*Watch* it." Asao points, grinning.

"How do you feel about some little vampires running around here in the future? More monsters for you to take care of."

Asao shrugs. "It'd be fine. Haruka wanted that when he was little, anyway."

Nino stops unpacking the shipping box, blinking up at Asao. "He did?"

"Yeah. He made a pitiful little declaration right after his father died. He said that when he bonded with Yuna, he wanted to have a big family. He's an only child, you know? So with Aika and Hayato passing, it left him pretty damn lonely. But Yuna didn't want any part of that so... end of story. He's never brought it up again—at least not to me?"

Both Asao and Junichi look at Nino, making him swallow hard. "He hasn't said anything to me either."

"Where is he, anyway?" Asao asks.

"Sleeping, apparently," Junichi answers. "You want to go out for coffee? Since I'm here..."

"Sure." Asao nods. "He slept the whole night?"

"Yes." Nino pulls a second, smaller, elegantly wrapped box from the package. "He won't be nocturnal for much longer. We'll get this fixed, somehow. He's been so intense and stressed lately. I don't want 'the threat of Lajos' dictating the rest of our damn lives."

"Agreed." Junichi nods. "Have you thought any more about reporting what you know to the detective? Could help ease some of the pressure, knowing a professional is on the case?"

"I want to." Nino sighs. "I need to talk to Haru about it." Between his own regeneration challenges and his mate's general distress, Nino had pushed the subject aside. How can they help solve someone else's problems when their own household is under duress? As of last night though, maybe they've finally taken a firm step in the right direction? Just an inch closer to getting back to their normal lives.

*Maybe I should try bringing it up again?*

# TWENTY-THREE

Haruka bolts upright in bed, eyes wide. Daylight. He sucks in a deep breath as if he'd been dead—the rush of oxygen in his lungs bringing him back to life. Fear washes over his body as he whips his head to the side.

"Everything is fine."

Nino is freshly showered beside him, sitting in his navy yukata with his back against the headboard. He's reading something. "I'm right here."

Exhaling, Haruka falls back hard against the bed. His entire body feels like pudding, or something else soft and without discernable form. He's still completely naked and tangled up in the bed sheets as a result of last night's encounter. Locating and putting on his robe feels like an insurmountable task. He groans and rolls toward Nino, scooting himself so that his head rests on his firm thigh. He snuggles against him and wraps his arms around Nino's waist. His voice is raspy and full of sleep. "Good morning."

"Hello, gorgeous. How are you feeling?"

Haruka stops, taking inventory. He needs a shower and his

legs are numb. "Like... mush."

Nino snorts, laughing. "Good. You've been disturbingly tense for the past two months. Turns out you just needed to be thoroughly fucked."

At this, Haruka stiffens. He burrows his flushed face into the soft bend of Nino's hip, his voice muffled. "I'm not sure what that says about me..."

"Well, it's definitely not the *only* thing you need." Nino runs his fingers against his scalp. "But you enjoy sex. There's nothing wrong with that, Haru."

"I enjoy *you*." Haruka lifts his head, blinking up at him. "The sex is a bonus."

"I enjoy you, too." Nino lazily combs through the length of his hair, pulling and untangling the long strands. Haruka closes his eyes, calm as he rests against the warmth and firmness of Nino's lap. He takes a deep breath, inhaling the woodsy and sweet essence of him. This singular moment... It is the most tranquil Haruka has felt in months.

"Tesoro?"

"Mm?"

"I have something for you."

Haruka drags himself upright, the thick weight of his hair falling and covering his bare shoulders. "For me? Why?"

"Remember on our anniversary, I told you I had something else for you? It's here..." Nino leans, grabbing a brown gift box from atop the nightstand. It is the size of a large book and tied with a red silk ribbon.

Haruka accepts the offering with both hands, placing it in his lap. He unravels the bow, then removes the box top. He separates the crisp white tissue paper inside to reveal a very neat-looking journal. His heart beats faster as he reads the embossed title.

"I backed up and reprinted *Lore and Lust*." Nino wiggles

his coppery brows. "I started working on it right after we bonded last year. It was crazy to me that you just had one hard copy of something so important to your family legacy."

Haruka lifts the condensed version of his clan's research from the box. It's bound in the same tawny leather, but sleeker and newer. He flips through the pages, and the typeface is also clean and organized—even more so than the data in the original version.

Nino bites his lip. "I reorganized the entries a bit... It's set up by section, then by time frame, and then again by couple ranking and last alphabetically. Now, you can see bonding patterns and make comparisons. There's an index too."

Flipping back to the index, Haruka stares in awe, scanning the list of first names and last initials. Nino has even addressed the privacy matter Haruka had been concerned about. It is incredible that he's mated to someone with such impressive organizational skills. Haruka isn't sure if he has a singular organizational skill within his entire being.

The box shifts in his lap and Haruka looks down. Something slid across the bottom. He reaches into the mess of tissue paper and pulls out a small USB.

"I put all the data in a spreadsheet too," Nino explains. "You can manipulate it any way you want, depending on what you're looking for."

Haruka sets the book and USB back down in the box, then places his gift aside. He leans forward, wrapping his arms around his infinitely thoughtful and clever mate. "I cannot believe you did this alone—and within a year!"

"You know I work fast. Plus, late nights and long train rides back and forth to Kyoto gave me lots of time." Nino hugs Haruka at his waist, pulling him closer. "It needed to be done. I know Lajos took the original, but at least the information is still in your hands?"

"You are phenomenal," Haruka whispers, lifting from the warm embrace and cradling Nino's head in his hands. "Exceptional. Brilliant..." He leans, lips already parted when he meets Nino's mouth. Nino reciprocates, and Haruka opens his mouth wider, sliding his tongue against his mate's and sighing from the taste of his cinnamon-and-coffee-infused flavor.

When Haruka pulls away, Nino's honeyed complexion is flushed and his smile bright. "With this new tongue, you're technically my first kiss!"

Haruka rises to his knees, climbing onto Nino's lap while still gripping his head. He leans down, ravenous in taking his mouth again, growling from want of him and plunging his tongue into Nino's wet warmth.

Nino rests his palms against his naked hips, but he startles Haruka when he pulls away from the affection. Nino swallows, his face pained. "I really... *really* don't want to stop this."

"Why would you?" Haruka smirks, gripping his mate's coppery hair in a fist and playfully yanking his head back. He raises an eyebrow. "You would deny me?"

"I would never," Nino sighs, closing his eyes. "But... I think we're overdue to talk about some things..."

"Such as?"

Nino takes a deep breath. "Maybe you should get dressed first? We can go sit in the kitchen and—"

Something in the atmosphere shifts and Haruka freezes. He looks down at his mate beneath him and his amber eyes are wide with alert. Haruka moves with the speed and intensity of a tornado, jumping up from Nino's lap, grabbing his robe at the end of the bed and wrapping his body up. Without a word, he moves toward the door of the bedroom with Nino close at his heels.

The sensation is unmistakable and the scent of sage hangs in the air like a toxic gas. Nino's abductor has returned.

# TWENTY-FOUR

Two things Cellina hates—working on Sundays and being ignored. Having both occur in the same instance is turning her mood sour. Very quickly.

She peeks inside her father's office. The cool, gingery scent remains despite its owner having disappeared. Andrea is sitting in his weathered armchair. His office is the singular place that her mother hasn't redecorated to flow in rhythm with modern aesthetics. It looks like something from the 1980s—her father's favorite decade. She blames him for her own fascination with American television shows and music spanning that time.

When he meets her gaze, there's warmth in his sparkling gray eyes: the eyes Cellina has inherited from him. He looks handsome, having recently trimmed his thick salt-and-pepper curls. He smiles, the affection radiating from him like a haze. "Caffettino."

*My little coffee.* Cellina shakes her head. When she's two hundred he'll still be calling her that. "Hey, Papà—E' andato via Giovanni?"

"Sì, sei arrabbiata?" Her father casts his gaze back down to the newspaper he's holding. Where does he even find newspapers nowadays?

"No, I'm not mad, but I told him to wait one second." Cellina sits across from him, on the old leather couch. She glances at the mahogany shelves behind his desk, overstuffed with books on real-estate law. On the coffee table between them, there's a small pink cake box with a business card on top. "I just needed to change clothes," she says.

"Giovanni is a very busy vampire." He closes and folds his newspaper, offering his full attention. "He told me to apologize on his behalf."

Grumbling, Cellina folds her arms. "He could have waited a damn minute." Maybe she's being paranoid, but it's starting to feel as if he's avoiding her. They're supposed to be rebuilding their friendship—burying the hatchet, or however the saying goes.

"Go easy on him, darling. He's having a difficult time right now. Rest assured, he thinks highly of you."

"I'm not worried about him thinking highly of me." Cellina frowns. "We made amends, so he can tell me if something is bothering him. He *used* to. I know that was a long time ago... But I don't know. It would be nice if he felt comfortable with me again."

Andrea folds his ankle over his knee and relaxes back. "He told me that you know about his feeding situation now. Sounds to me like he's confiding in you in earnest."

"*You* knew?" Cellina's eyes widen. "He told you about it?"

"He did, a long time ago. And I'm glad. Giovanni carries a lot of responsibility on his shoulders—admirably. But everyone needs an outlet. He's not a machine."

"I'm glad he confides in you." Cellina leans forward and toward the small box. She grins. "Is this mine?"

"It is. I told him you were complaining about finding a new

art conservator in the coming weeks. He has a client who works with a freelance artist that might be looking for a full-time position. That's their card on top. It's just a lead."

Cellina picks the card up, turning it over in her fingers. "Realm leader at his best."

"He's well connected." Andrea shrugs. Cellina opens the cake box and grins. Castella.

"Huh. The cake has changed?" her father asks.

"What are you talking about?"

He smiles, playful. "Now I'm going to reveal more secrets—but since you two are getting along, maybe it's okay? Do you remember when I was working on the Castiglione project?"

"Not really."

"Darling, you were knee-deep in graduate school—maybe the first year?"

"Oh yes, yes. I remember that particular hell."

"Right." Her father grins. "You were having a rough time, so every Friday after my client meeting, a box of bakery-fresh tiramisu would magically appear on the kitchen counter?"

Cellina beams. That had been the one bright spot each week in a very dark and stressful time in her pursuit of higher education and a new career. "I remember. I would invite Mia over and we'd have it together with coffee. It was the highlight of my week back then."

"Well, I hate to seem like a fraud... but Giovanni bought that for you. Every week. He always asked about you, and I told him you were having a difficult time. He is well aware of your sweet tooth, so he wanted to help. Of course, I was sworn to secrecy."

"Oh give me a break—seriously?" Cellina sits back against the couch, her heart beating warm in her chest. But she's also annoyed. "It's too much."

Andrea laughs. "He's stuck between a rock and a hard place, but he finds joy where he can?"

Cellina pouts, thinking about how upset she'd been with him. For *decades*. Anytime they'd crossed paths, she ignored him and treated him coldly, thinking he preferred things that way. Meanwhile, he was being unfair and buying her secret cakes. He was supposed to be mad at her, too. That's how it works when two people fight. Does he not understand that?

He'd shut her out, gone on a rampage around town and drunk from and fornicated with any vampire he could find. All this when he was supposed to be feeding from and (ideally) fornicating with her. How much time have they wasted? She wishes they could have resolved this sooner. If he didn't hate her, and if he regretted what he said... She understands that he's in a difficult situation, but he should have said something.

"How's Nino doing?" her father asks. "Is he all better after his accident?"

"Yes, he's doing great." Cellina smiles, shrinking a little on the inside. As a general rule, she tells her parents everything. But with this, she's been sworn to secrecy. No need to cause alarm where it isn't due.

When she'd left a month ago, the situation was somewhat under control (notwithstanding Haruka's unrealistic resolve to handle everything on his own—a common thread among pure-bred males, apparently).

With any luck, they'll never see or hear from Lajos again.

---

LATER THAT EVENING, Cellina walks into a bicentennial event for a member of the Milan aristocracy. It's a late-night garden party, with tiny white lights twinkling overhead and candles burning along the cobblestone paths to set a *Midsummer Night's Dream* kind of mood.

Before leaving the museum, she'd ditched her blouse underneath her suit jacket for a sexy lace bustier, which matches her black, high-waisted tuxedo pants to a tee. It's humid tonight, so the hair is pulled up into a bun, as sleek as she could manage. Hopefully the oversized earrings distract from the unruly situation atop her head.

She sees her friend Matteo among the crowd, standing alone by a tall table. Cellina tips across the cobblestones in her high heels to reach him. When she's there, he kisses both of her cheeks in a warm greeting.

"Queen."

"Hey, handsome."

He takes her hand and lifts it above her head, urging her to turn in a full circle. She complies and he shakes his head. "Honey, you look fuckin' *hot*. Those skinny model bitches I do makeup for don't have anything on you. Gorgeous. And this cleave. Yas."

"Thanks, dear. I like this blazer." Cellina pinches his burgundy satin lapel. The rest of the fabric subtly glitters underneath the soft lighting like a sparkling red wine.

"Dolce, honey, don't touch." Matteo purses his lips and swats her hand away. "Is our drunken ballerina coming?"

"Oh man." Cellina bites back a laugh. "Mia had practice all day today, so I doubt it. And she's only drunk in the off-season."

"You're just naïve. That thing is *always* drunk. It's her natural state of being now, like a damn fish swimming in the sea —*Oh my*." Matteo grabs his chest in a dramatic gesture. "His highness has arrived."

Cellina lifts to her toes, stretching her neck. She smelled him when she walked in, but she wasn't sure if Giovanni was already in attendance or just arriving.

"I swear to God..." Matteo sighs, his shoulders falling. "I'd drop to my knees and eat his ass right now if he'd let me."

"You are at *maximum* capacity." Cellina holds her palm up, her eyes wide. "*Calm down.* Not appropriate."

"He's too perfect and fucking gorgeous," Matteo goes on, narrowing his eyes. "He probably bites his toenails, or he likes to be pissed on when he's having sex—some unexpected, freaky shit... I'll do it if he wants—"

"Matteo, *stop*." Cellina laughs.

Matteo lifts his chin, a charismatic smile plastered on his lips. He raises his beautifully arched brow. "He's making a beeline over here, and I doubt it's because of *my* second-gen ass."

A moment later, Giovanni is in front of them. Classic black suit, crisp white shirt, no tie. His hazel-green eyes shine and his charming game face is in action, the frown lines barely noticeable.

"Good evening, your grace." Matteo offers a smooth, shallow bow from his waist. Cellina never calls him by formal titles. Never bows either. The thought of doing so is weird, but she figures what the hell? She'll give it a try in present company.

Cellina nods. "Your grace." Giovanni's expression shifts into a look of disgust as he draws back, like she called him something offensive. The mask has slipped, but he quickly takes a breath.

"Good evening. Are you both enjoying the party?"

"Little Miss Lina just arrived, but I've been here a minute." Her friend smiles, his voice playful. "I need another drink. Would you like one, your grace? I'll get it for you."

"Thank you, Matteo," Giovanni says. "Scotch on the rocks, please."

Matteo nods as he raises his eyebrow toward Cellina. "Amaretto sour?"

"Thanks, dear." Cellina lifts her shoulder, flirty.

"Don't talk about me while I'm gone—unless it's about how incredible I am." He winks as he turns and walks toward the bar. Giovanni's brows drop into the usual frown.

"*Do not* bow at me or call me that."

Cellina scrunches her nose. "Is that an official order as my realm leader?"

"I hate it—especially from you." He takes a deep breath, running his large hand into the back of his honey-brown waves.

"I hate that you left without speaking to me on Sunday," Cellina counters. "What the hell, G? That's two weeks in a row. Are you upset that I kicked you that Sunday? Was my head massage offensive?" She smirks, trying to ease the odd tension growing between them.

He takes another deep breath, but as he does so, his eyes flicker, shameless as he scans the length of her body. Top to bottom, then back up again. Cellina shifts her stance, suddenly more aware of his raw masculine energy and feeling the usual spark in her stomach and between her legs.

"You look very nice," he says, his voice low.

"Thanks..." She clears her throat, focusing. "What's with you? You were fine a couple weeks ago, when we were in Japan. Now you're being... Is this *shy*? What are you doing?"

"There was a barrier between us before," he says, looking away. "But you keep lowering it. It's different now."

"Isn't that a good thing?"

"For some vampires... in most circumstances. Probably." Giovanni turns his broad body to the side and stretches his neck, looking for Matteo. As if standing alone with her is somehow uncomfortable.

Cellina glares. "What does that mean?"

"It means what I said."

"Why are you acting like this?"

"I'm not acting like anything."

"Great, so you're going to just repeat and deflect everything I say—"

"Because I *want* you, Cellina. But I can't have you."

The silence lingers as he stares at her with his intense eyes. "And it's *not* a joke," he says. "It's not funny and it's not cute. I accept my awful prison of a life, but when you flirt with me and put your hands on me, it fucks with my resolve. It messes with my head."

Cellina watches him, recognizing the pain and frustration in his face. "Maybe..." She blinks, considering. "Your resolve needs to be fucked with? Maybe you should stop being your family's martyr."

Giovanni draws back, his expression shifting to something between confusion and insult. Matteo returns, handing out drinks as he holds a small silver tray. Giovanni takes his glass, nods in thanks and walks away from them as if in a hurry to escape.

Matteo stares after him with his mouth gaped open. "Um... *what?*" He turns and looks at Cellina. "Where is he going? I haven't even offered to do nasty things to him yet! Did you insult our king?"

"No," Cellina sighs, pulling her drink to her lips. "I told him the truth."

# TWENTY-FIVE

Nino has never seen this expression on his mate before: pure rage tinted with lethal conviction. The tenderness and vulnerability he's grown accustomed to have all but disappeared as they walk down the hallway and toward the outdoor garden at the center of the estate.

Nino runs trembling fingers into his hair. "Why the hell is he back?"

"Because despicable creatures like this *always* come back. Once they acquire one thing, they inevitably want more."

Haruka opens the outer door to the breezeway, then steps onto the veranda, purpose in his long strides. Nino follows behind, fear almost crippling him. He doesn't want Haruka to be taken from him, nor does he have any desire to return to that strange and barren place with Ladislao as a lurid roommate.

"Maybe if we stay inside, we'll be safe—"

"*No.* He may be capable of pinpointing our locations. This ends now."

They stand together, watching the still garden cast in a gray summertime haze from the cloud cover. It's humid and the air is thick and smells of impending rain. Lajos steps out from behind the large maple tree centered in the lawn. Pale and wiry, his movement is graceful, as if floating beside the dark, glassy surface of the koi pond.

Nino flares his protective aura outward, the skill much easier to invoke compared with the first time he'd discovered the ability.

"This power..." Lajos rests his cane against the grass and stands before them, his wrinkled, thin face shifting into a smirk. "The two of you should consider joining in my endeavors. Your combined blood and natures would produce exquisite offspring. I could help arrange it for you? The result would be a wonderful addition to the gene pool of my community."

Nino stifles a dry heave. Lajos makes having children sound like some scientific experiment—something clinical and unfeeling. Plus, Nino still hasn't broached this subject with his mate. It feels all wrong: having this callous vampire talk to them about a topic so weighted and unaddressed within their private communication. None of this is his business.

Lajos waits. No one speaks. Nino glances at Haruka and he's perfectly calm. The rage is dispelled, but his eyes are like daggers as he focuses on the decrepit purebred.

"Consider it." Lajos lifts his chin at their silence. "You could do much good for the future of our kin. Which brings me to the purpose of my visit. The manuscript you gifted me is excellent. I wonder if we could discuss your findings in more detail? I have learned much about purebred biology while over-seeing my realm—the extremes to which we can survive and flourish are remarkable! Perhaps we could exchange stories and work together to reestablish a pure vampire race?"

*Exchange stories and work together? He's fucking insane...* When Nino swallows, the sound is loud in his ears. Haruka doesn't move, but his eyes brighten. Instead of the deep sunset color of their shared genealogy, his mate's irises burn bright crimson.

Lajos grins as if amused by something. "Need I remind you that you cannot subjugate me with your impressive essence, young male. My powers are—"

Haruka brings his arm up and flicks his fingers toward Lajos in a swift motion, as if he is ridding them of water. Lajos gasps loudly, shocked as he falls straight back onto the grass, like a tree that's been chopped down. Haruka steps off the veranda and moves to stand over the old vampire's body. The silvery mist of Lajos's power trembles and stirs at his feet, but Haruka holds a palm out over his head, then clenches his fist tight.

Lajos screams, the sound blood-curdling and echoing through the air. He brings his wrinkled palms up to his temples, holding his head as he cries in agony. Haruka speaks out, his deep voice loud and forceful over the old vampire's screeching.

"I distinctly warned you that if you *ever* came back here, you would regret it. How dare you return here and converse with us? As if you have not threatened me and caused unforgivable harm to my mate!"

Haruka opens his palm again, then clenches it shut. Lajos twists against the grass, his screams turning into unintelligible whines. Haruka moves his hand down until it hovers over the old vampire's neck. He pinches the air with his fingers and Lajos writhes and chokes, the wheezing sound from his vocal chords a clear indication that his throat is being shut.

"Haru, stop—that's enough!" Nino steps down from the hardwood of the veranda and toward his mate.

"*Why?*" Haruka's burning red eyes are full of malice as he watches the old vampire. When he speaks, Nino can see that his incisors have sharpened into sleek daggers. "He deserves much more than this for what he's put us through." He moves his open palm down further until it hovers over Lajos's chest. Nino reaches out, taking hold of Haruka's face with his palms. When his husband's terrifying gaze meets his own, Nino takes a deep breath.

"Don't kill him because of me. I—I don't want to watch someone I love do that in front of me again."

The anger in Haruka's expression softens, melting like thawed ice. His glowing eyes shift back to their normal wine color. The dark and frightening creature disappears.

"I don't want that, alright?" Nino says, stepping into Haruka and embracing him. "Do you hear me?"

"Yes." Haruka nods against his ear, wrapping his arms around Nino's waist. "I hear you—I understand."

Nino closes his eyes, still trembling with unease. The entire scene had thrown him back to when he was six years old and his mother discovered his uncle feeding from him in his room. With no hesitation, no questions asked, she'd ripped his throat out.

"I don't need another graphic and violent memory in my head," Nino whispers against his ear. "Can we please try contacting that detective so she can handle this?"

"We can, of course..." Haruka lifts his head from the hug and they both glance down at the twitching old vampire at their feet. His eyes are blank, transfixed on the cloudy sky.

"What did you do to him?" Nino asks. "Is he in a coma?"

"Perhaps. I made some educated guesses with regard to his frontal lobe. I knew I had one chance to get this right. It appears I was successful..." Haruka looks into his eyes. "Have I upset you? I apologize—"

"No, tesoro. I'm fine. You're perfect. I just want to talk to the detective and tell her what I know. I feel like it's important and we've put it off long enough."

Haruka sighs, scratching the back of his head as he looks

down at Lajos. "I do not wish to attract attention to ourselves with this matter. Maybe we can request some discretion? Somehow..."

"I agree. I'll ask G if he has any connections to her—I'll bet he does. What should we do with him in the meantime? Should we call the local police?"

"I doubt they are equipped to manage such a vile creature." Haruka grabs Nino's hand, urging him toward the house. "Leave him for now. He is fortunate to be alive."

---

THE RAIN IS frantic and drizzling in every direction by the afternoon, which means Nino still feels damp even though he's walking underneath an awning.

Displeased with keeping Lajos as a lawn ornament, Asao made Haruka use his aura to move him. His mate refuses to allow the decrepit vampire inside their home—even incapacitated—so they've opted for dumping him at the very back of the compound, underneath the large, open enclosure of the kyudojo.

Haruka's father, Hayato Hirano, was a skilled archer and used the space long ago. Haruka, having failed to adopt an interest in archery (or in any sport or exercise whatsoever), never uses the expansive, professional-quality building.

Nino pulls the heavy door to the kyudojo open, the smell of polished cedar and straw wafting against his face. He kicks his outdoor shoes off before stepping up onto the clean flooring. Nino walks toward the open front of the building, where Haruka is sitting with Lajos. As he approaches, he hears his mate's voice.

"If you move in *any* capacity, I will end you."

Lajos's voice is a raspy whisper, barely perceptible even in the silent, drizzling atmosphere. "Y-you... would... kill... a fell-fellow purebred?"

"One that captures and violently assaults my mate? That threatens the peace of our existence? Without question."

Nino walks onto the large, open deck. Lajos is unmoving on the glossy wooden floor, lying in a heap. Haruka sits with his arms folded on a cedar bench that runs along the back wall. Past Lajos's body, his view overlooks the stretch of green lawn that runs up against the target bank at the opposite end of the range.

When he's beside his mate, Nino addresses him within his mind. *I thought we talked about this. You're not going to kill him.*

*Of course, but he* doesn't know that.

Nino shakes his head, sitting down beside him. *Have you ever killed anyone before?*

*I have not.*

*Then let's not start.*

Lajos groans, and Haruka whips his head forward, eyes flashing bright as he unfolds one arm and flicks his fingers at the old vampire's head. Lajos screams, the sound echoing across the open space. His body jerks. Then nothing. Silence.

"*Haruka—*"

"My love, he is fine. He is an ancient creature. It would take much more than this for me to end his sordid life." He reaches over and grabs Nino's hand, entwining their fingers. "You have asked that I spare him, so I would never go against your wishes. Never."

Nino inhales a deep breath and blows it out, easing the tension in his chest.

"I thought I'd caused severe damage to his frontal lobe last night," Haruka goes on, "but he was able to speak to me just now. I must have missed something fundamental to his speech production... Infuriating."

"What did you do to him? Why did you need to study so much?"

"It's complicated," Haruka sighs. "Typically, I cover my victim in my essence first to subjugate them, then target specific areas of their anatomy that I have studied—bones, muscles, joints, ligaments and so on. It is a two-step process, and as such, there is a lag in my efficiency. Lajos was at an advantage, having witnessed my ability in England last year. As soon as he sensed my aura covering him, he could vanish himself to evade me. I have never come across a vampire with such an ability, so I needed to strategize and surprise him."

"Hit him hard and fast?"

"Yes," Haruka says, "but with precision. I have never studied the brain in such detail—just a general, overarching comprehension. Knowing exactly where I needed to strike Lajos was paramount. The brain is infinitely complex, and even with my research, understanding the origin of his power within his mind was difficult. So I made suppositions."

"You supposed correctly." Nino smiles. "You're amazing. My hero."

Haruka leans in, pressing a soft peck on his lips. "Any goodness in me is a direct reflection of you."

Nino's smile broadens, the inevitable warmth rushing to his cheeks. "Charmer..."

"Did you speak with Giovanni?"

"Oh yeah—shit!" Nino blinks. "He got ahold of the detective and she's planning to catch the next flight out. She also said she'll have the local police take him into custody, so we don't have to sit here and watch him until she arrives. I'll honestly feel better when he's not underneath our noses like this anymore... and maybe I can finally start working again soon."

"Should we consider your permanently working from within the estate? There are many methods for conducting business remotely now. You do not need to travel so far, and your clients could come here if needed."

"I... I don't know why I would need to do that?"

"To ensure your safety."

"Well, technically... I was vanished while I was at home, so—"

"That will *never* happen again. I will do everything in my power to make certain."

"Haru..." Nino sighs, rubbing his palm against his forehead and wondering if they'll ever get back to normal, or if this constant state of paranoia is their new standard of living. *God, I hope not...*

"You hope not, what?" Haruka asks.

Nino's eyes widen. "You heard that? I—I wasn't trying to communicate to you directly..."

"I did. I sense that you're upset about something?"

"No, well... I'm alright..." Nino runs his fingers into the top of his hair, but his mate eyes him suspiciously.

# TWENTY-SIX

It took Detective Anika Cuevas a full week to arrive in Kurashiki from New York. Haruka had needed to visit the local police station once to check on Lajos. The old vampire had roused, but this time his speech was incoherent and his movements jerky. He was groaning and lying on the floor—more of a nuisance to the station staff than an actual threat.

"Alright, so tell me more about this place—where you vanished to." Detective Cuevas sits in the front tearoom of the estate, perched on the edge of the small couch opposite Nino and Haruka. She is full figured in her sharp gray suit, a blue-striped button-down shirt underneath. Her soft features are complemented by the short, curly haircut framing her face.

"I was in an old house, inside a dark and cold room with a window," Nino explains. "It was furnished, but there wasn't any electricity. Ladislao was there, like I said earlier, and when I looked out the window, there were craggy mountains all around. We were really high up and the landscape was barren —like a desert."

"Well, that could be anywhere," the detective says. "Anything more specific? Something to help us pinpoint exactly where you were?"

Nino sighs, scratching his head. "I... Ladislao said he could smell water around when he'd tried to escape before. It could be an island? I don't—ah! There were weird trees scattered around, too. I'd never seen anything like them before. They looked like... umbrellas? But flipped upside down." Nino gestures with his hands to emphasize the shape. "The branches reached up toward the sky instead of out or down like most trees."

The detective pulls her phone out from the bag at her side. She mumbles as she focuses on the screen, her thumbs moving at rapid speed. "Trees that look like upside-down umbrellas..." She swipes up with her index finger, her blueish-brown eyes scanning. A moment later, the detective turns her phone toward Nino, handing it to him. *"The World's Most Magnificent Trees.* See anything familiar?"

Taking the phone, Nino scrolls while Haruka leans in beside him. Nino's eyes widen at a particular tree and he points. "This one. It says 'Dragon's Blood Tree'... in Yemen. Was I in Yemen?"

He hands the phone back to her and she reads the screen, scrolling once more. "Bingo. This tree only grows in a place called Socotra, which is also an island. We've got a solid location, gentlemen... Damn. I've been working this case for a whole year and my first major break hinges on a fucking tree."

Haruka chuckles. "We have handed you the smoking gun, so to speak."

Detective Cuevas narrows her eyes. "I do solid detective work, alright? But it usually consists of much more than correctly utilizing Internet search engines. Anyway, this is a strong lead. We'll follow through with this and see where it takes us."

"How will you keep Lajos incapacitated?" Haruka asks.

"Lower-level blood source," the detective says. "If we have him feed from a first-gen vamp, that should stifle his powers pretty damn well, since he's old blood."

"Agreed." Haruka knows from personal experience how impactful first-generation blood can be to an old-blooded purebred's health.

"Tell me this." The detective sits straight, her gaze serious. "Why did he abduct you in the first place? What is the root of all this?"

Haruka shifts his eyes to his mate, apprehensive.

*I think we can tell her. It's safe, Haru.*

Nodding, Haruka takes a breath. "My clan has established a collection of data surrounding vampiric bonds. It goes back almost five centuries, and thus helps to create meaning and insight with regard to mating."

"Sounds interesting..." Detective Cuevas says thoughtfully. "And nerdy. So Lajos wanted this book?"

"Correct. He abducted Nino and demanded the book as ransom. How he learned about it, we are uncertain. But there is a connection between us and a former manservant from his clan."

"Is this book so important?" she asks. "It sounds impressive but... it's just a book, right? Is it made of gold and rubies and shit?"

"No. In truth, I was also taken aback by Lajos's drastic actions regarding my family's research. However, based on everything else we know about him, it seems as if radical actions are his modus operandi."

"And you think this creature is responsible for the Great Vanishing?" Detective Cuevas asks. "That he's got all these disappeared vampires in some mud-hut village within the mountains of Socotra?"

"I'm pretty sure," Nino confirms. "But I couldn't tell how many there were. It was hard to sense their distinct numbers."

"Crazy... we thought they all died, didn't we?" the detective says. "Do you think he took all the British purebreds, too? Could this also be the answer to that mystery?"

"We cannot be certain, but it is possible," Haruka says. When he and Nino met a little more than a year ago in England, they were the only two purebred vampires in the entire country. Purebreds of English descent have been extinct for almost two hundred years.

Or so they have been led to believe.

Detective Cuevas stands from the sofa, pulling her bag up onto her shoulder. "Alright, we'll have Lajos transported to New York within the week, so he'll be out of your hair. I'll keep you up to speed on our progress with the search."

"I do not think that will be necessary."

"What?" The detective frowns.

*Tesoro...*

*My love, as I said before, I do not wish to interfere with this creature's realm.*

*But if these vampires need help, we should help them.*

*We cannot know that for certain. Perhaps they are content—*

"Hello?" The detective blinks. "Is something happening right now?"

Asao speaks as he walks into the room and toward the low table laden with cups of green tea. "They have this awkward habit of talking about things in front of people, but inside their heads."

Haruka straightens, clearing his throat. "My apologies. Yes, please keep us abreast of the situation."

"Thanks." She nods. "I'll try to get more answers out of Lajos, too... once his brain heals a little. If we need your help locating his realm, I'll let you know."

His eyes wide, Haruka recoils. "Locating his realm? In *Socotra?*"

"Apparently," the detective says, lifting her chin. "Sorry to ask you to leave your swanky estate. Think of it as your civic duty to the safety and well-being of our vampiric society—or maybe an adventure?"

Haruka sits back and folds his arms, thoroughly hating the sound of both of those things.

*You know, you're pretty damn sexy when you pout... Makes me want to bite you.*

Despite his frustration, Haruka smiles, chuckling. *You can. Later.*

The detective frowns. "Why are you laughing?"

"They're doing it again," Asao explains, clearing the table.

# AUGUST

# TWENTY-SEVEN

The gallery opening for the new artist Cellina has contracted is in full swing on a windy summer evening. The musicians are in place, the food is beautifully presented, the art is showcased with the perfect lighting and the patrons and donors are pouring in through the doors. Cellina's hard work is paying off and everyone seems to be pleased with the results.

Everyone except for the prick artist.

He's complained and raised hell about a myriad of insignificant things. The latest being that the brand of water bottles she'd chosen don't match up with his refined standards, nor are they "reflective of the quality of his art."

*They're fucking water bottles.*

And they're expensive water bottles—glass, recycled and eco-friendly, for God's sake. The artist has even complained to Cellina's director. She's just walked out of an impromptu "emergency meeting" where she was berated by the artist for not meeting his petty demands. She storms through the gallery, weaving in and out of the amazing crowd of people that she's procured.

Her mind is white with rage when someone steps in front of her, causing her to crash into them. It's like she's hit a brick wall. She looks up and Giovanni is there, smiling down at her. His brow shifts into a look of concern. "What's wrong with you?"

She shakes her head and lifts her palm. *"Not now."* She hasn't even seen him in two weeks, since he walked away from her at the Midsummer Night's party. He's been avoiding her altogether now, so why the hell is he even here? She moves around him and heads straight to her office in the upper corridor, away from the main hall and festivities.

Cellina enters the darkened space and doesn't bother turning the lights on. She's pacing and rubbing her forehead in disbelief. *How can this pompous asshole be so ungrateful?*

She knew this artist back when no one had heard of him. While she was still in school, she'd been the one to help him achieve his major break within the Milan art scene. But he's changed. It's inconceivable how disloyal and shallow people become when given a little success.

On top of tonight's meeting, her director has told her that they will meet tomorrow as well. Apparently, they need to clarify "artist expectations" for gallery openings going forward. *"My ass*—donor support has increased by twenty percent since I took over the programming."

Cellina grumbles in frustration as her office door creaks open. She pauses, watching in the darkness. Giovanni peeks his head around the corner. He steps inside, loosening his tie and smiling. "Hey..."

"I said *not* right now."

Walking forward, her heel catches on the throw rug covering the marble floor. She reaches down and unties the straps at her ankles before throwing the shoes across the room one at a time. "Stupid high heel *bullshit.*"

"Lina—your guests will be looking for you. You need to calm down."

She meets his gaze, her eyes wild as she points. "Don't you dare come in here fucking telling me what to do. I'm done with *all* of this shit."

Giovanni crosses the room, his long legs carrying him into the intimacy of her personal space within seconds. Startled from his sudden movement, Cellina backs away. She hits the wall beside her desk and looks up at him. "What the *hell*—"

He places his large hands against her jawline and presses their foreheads together. Immediately, she's grounded by his soothing, gingery warmth. It slows her heart rate, making her inhale and exhale his spicy scent as her eyes close. Soon, her breathing is in rhythm with his. She unwinds, allowing the peaceful sensation to wash over her.

They stand together for a long moment before Giovanni pulls his head up. Cellina opens her eyes. He's staring back at her through glowing irises.

"Listen," he says. "This event is fantastic, and you've worked too hard to let it be ruined by some shithead artist. I saw him come out of the room behind you, and he was acting like a little bitch and making a fuss. But you have to stay calm in these situations."

Cellina leans back, relaxing her head against the wall. Giovanni's hand drifts down to the small of her waist. "And you look incredible, by the way. You always do..."

His hand is heavy against her body—against the soft, silky material of her mustard-colored dress. She loves this dress. The hem flows and moves when she walks, the capped sleeves and neckline fit her bust perfectly. It makes her feel exquisite.

Lifting her chin, she meets Giovanni's emerald eyes. "Thank you. I like this suit. You wore a tie tonight?"

He sighs. "I hate ties."

"I know you do." Cellina reaches up to his neck, maneuvering her fingers around the knot to loosen it. She unravels the silky material, amazed at how much calmer she feels. "Don't do things you hate. Tonight isn't so formal anyway."

He stands still, unspeaking, as she pulls and slides the tie from his neck altogether, then tosses it onto her desk nearby. Giovanni's breathing is deep and his Adam's apple bobs in his throat. She unfastens the first two buttons of his collar and separates the shirt. "Better?"

He clenches his eyes shut, shaking his head in a tight smile. "*No.*"

Cellina grips his shirt collar and urges him down toward her. She lifts her chin to meet his mouth, softly brushing their lips. The warmth of his breath catches, hesitating just before he leans into her, fully pressing their mouths together as he grips her waist.

She parts her lips. His tongue is warm and sweet as it touches hers, and he tastes just like he smells—gingery and smoky, like hot chai or some other spiced and earthy concoction. Wanting more of him, she tilts her head and lifts to her toes, wrapping her arms around his broad shoulders to press tighter into his body.

When Giovanni slides his hands down to her hips, Cellina decides she wants all of him. Or whatever he's willing to give her. Right now, in this quiet office, hidden away from society and responsibility. She pulls away from the kiss, leaning her back into the wall. The silver glow of her own eyes alights as he watches her with his smoldering irises. He chases her, resting against her forehead. His voice is husky and deep when he speaks. "You smell so damn good to me—*everything* about you is just... Your nature sings to me."

He exhales a heavy sigh, lifting from her and rubbing his large palm down his handsome face and closing his eyes.

Cellina watches him, her mind calm and resolute. "You want me."

Giovanni scoffs, amusement in his voice. "Understatement."

"I want you, too. Right now."

Blinking, he meets her eyes. "Here?"

"Should we wait another century?"

He pauses, staring, before he shakes his head. His face is mesmerized as he stares down at her. "No... we shouldn't." Giovanni pulls the silky material of her dress upward with his fingertips, the sensation tickling her skin. His large palms are warm against her naked thighs, sliding upward in a slow, intentional movement.

The way he touches her feels cautious, as if he's an explorer carefully searching for something. She waits in anticipation of his discovery, enjoying the feel of his hands on her bare skin.

Giovanni reaches her hips underneath her dress and pauses, his smile wicked. He drags his palms up her soft curves, then grips her naked ass. "Are you serious?"

"I never wear underwear." Cellina grins. "I hate it."

"Good God," he breathes. "Never?"

She lifts her chin to place a swift peck on his mouth. Kissing his full lips and having his hands on her flesh is wonderful—a deep and gratifying experience that her body has been yearning for. "You can test it going forward. You have consent."

"Going forward..." Hesitation washes over his expression, but Cellina leans into him and kisses him again, wanting to redirect him from whatever path his mind is spiraling down. He responds to the kiss, groaning and hungry. She gasps when he breaks the affection to bend down and grip her thighs. He lifts, smooth, like the weight of her is nothing. The soft material of her dress slips higher up her thighs as she spreads her legs wider, her back pressed into the wall.

When she's steady with her arms over Giovanni's shoulders, he uses one hand to reach in between them. He traces his fingers up the inside of her thigh, the delicate sensation making her toes curl. Reaching his target, he touches in between her legs with his fingertips. Gentle but assured. The raw intimacy and contact make her inhale and shift her hips forward, chasing his fingers.

*Finally...*

It's taken more than a hundred years but they're here. The innate longing she's always felt for him—the unyielding, warm thing sitting stagnate and deep in her nature—it can be fed and gratified at last.

He rubs his fingers against her flesh, teasing and making her breath shorter as he leans in to kiss her again. She moans when he presses his thick fingers inside, moving them slowly in and out to stretch her. Cellina lifts her head and arches her neck. Her body is hot, as if it's on fire, and she can't wait to have him inside her. Not just his fingers but Giovanni. This frustrating male that she's been wanting since she knew how to want another creature.

When he removes his fingers, she sighs from the loss of it. His knuckles brush her flesh while he unfastens his pants to free himself. Running her fingers into his soft golden-brown hair, she settles against the wall, wrapping her legs around him and staring into his eyes. "You made me wait a long time for you."

One corner of Giovanni's full lips quirks up in a smile. "I didn't even think you wanted me." The moment she feels the warmth of his shaft touching her body, she sucks in a breath. Giovanni exhales as he guides himself into her. "I thought you hated me."

Cellina relaxes her body around his shaft, welcoming it. She shifts her hips forward, urging the fullness and heat of him deeper, her entire body prickling with ecstasy. "I could say the same thing."

The movement of his hips is slow, languid, as he grips the meat of her thigh with one hand. He moves his free hand up the curve of her body until his palm reaches her breast. He squeezes and Cellina exhales from pleasure, but he covers her mouth in another ravenous kiss—enticing and teasing her body in multiple ways. He lifts his head, and his voice is quiet but heavy with lust. "You... were the *only* good thing about my life. I could never hate you."

Giovanni supports her weight with his broad frame, moving his hand between them once more. He caresses her flesh with his fingers as he rocks into her. She closes her eyes and meets his rhythm, using the wall as leverage to shift her hips forward and into his firm body. Something primal springs to life within her.

Whenever she's with him, her nature twists and writhes in response to him. Even when they were young. After their fight, she ignored it. Refused to acknowledge any feelings she held for him. Now, everything stirs, threatening to expand and overtake her.

The heat of climax simmers low in her belly. She sinks down and spreads her thighs wider, wanting him deeper inside. He feels thick and strong, and the gingery sent of him is growing more intense, making her head spin and her eyes burn bright. He leans in, kissing her with a ferocity she's never known just as the pressure within spills over. She moans against his mouth, the fizzy warmth and liberation of the orgasm racing up her spine and making her shiver all over.

Giovanni groans as he holds her. Soon, she feels his release warm as it spills inside. Laying her head back against the wall,

Cellina closes her eyes, reveling in the feel of him—in the heat and scent of his body. She's fantasized about this in secret for years, over and over. But the reality is wild. More innately satisfying than she could have anticipated.

He opens his beautiful green eyes and she smiles. She's thinking of something funny and snarky to say, but he tilts his head and bends into her. Before she can blink, he bites her neck, high and just below her ear. Her eyes widen in shock as he pulls hard at her flesh. Cellina gasps. The emotion she feels from him is intense—an overwhelming sense of desire and love. Naked, sincere adoration and want. Desperate need.

His sentiments are beautiful as they fill her, but something in it makes her heart ache. Hopelessness? As if this moment and the inherent satisfaction he feels within it are fleeting. Something he may never experience again.

He wraps his arms around her waist, holding her tight against his body as he feeds. He pulls hard again and Cellina takes a deep breath, grounding herself so that his intense emotions don't overtake her—so they don't reduce her to a blubbering pile of mush and tears.

Cellina laces her fingers against the back of his head. "Giovanni."

He pulls his head up from her neck with a jolt. Giovanni's incisors are still elongated, his green eyes bewildered. His expression is a mix of confusion and worry, as if he's just been awakened after being hypnotized. He rubs his palm down his face. "I'm so sorry—*shit*. God. Cellina, I—"

She leans in and kisses the tip of his nose. She moves to his cheek, then the corner of his mouth before meeting his lips. When Cellina pulls up, she whispers, staring into his distressed eyes, "It's okay, Giovanni. You're okay."

# TWENTY-EIGHT

Nino marvels as they fly in the small commuter plane, the Arabian Sea magnificent and vivid beneath them in their descent toward Socotra Island. The coastline is the most striking gradient of blue, turquoise and green he's ever seen. It reminds him of a precious gemstone hidden deep within a cave: raw malachite or fluorite.

The jagged cliffs loom in the backdrop, imposing. Immovable like strict barriers—titans drawn up from the earth and reaching toward the sky. They make him feel insignificant. His one hundred and fourteen years as a creature of this earth are nothing next to the millennia and fortitude of these mountains.

After twenty hours of travel, they land in Hadibu to meet Detective Cuevas. She and her third-gen deputy, Marcus, are their escort from the airport, driving them in an old white minibus toward the town they'll be staying in before traveling to Lajos's house in the mountains.

Within a few weeks, the detective had discovered the location, but it was abandoned. Not a single purebred could be found—in the house, or within the mud-brick village Nino had seen in the distance. Knowing that purebreds have a sharp sense of awareness, the detective asked that Nino and Haruka join them in Socotra to assist in the case.

The ride into town is rough, dusty and jostling against the road. Nino doesn't bother looking over at his house cat of a mate, afraid of what he might see: eyes like daggers that read "I had to leave the comfort of my library for this? A nauseating ride in a toy bus?"

It's basically what he's thinking. Lately, when Haruka is displeased, his thoughts resonate loud in Nino's head, whether he wants them to or not. Something about them sharing mind space for the past two months and while Nino's tongue was regenerating has made communicating this way easier than ever before. Whether this is good or bad, Nino isn't certain.

"Another monsoon is rolling in," Detective Cuevas shouts over the noise of the road, the loud hum of the vehicle's engine. "We'll wait it out tonight, then take a helicopter tomorrow when the weather clears."

The deputy turns a corner a little harder than necessary, making Nino grip the metal bar above him, but not before slamming into Haruka's shoulder.

"Sorry about that." Marcus raises a hand from the steering wheel.

Now, he does look over at his mate. Haruka is healthy again. After a few weeks of intentional TLC under Nino's supervision (which included a series of homecooked meals, some pretty intense sexual encounters and, consequently, several nights of deep sleep), the dark circles are gone, his features elegant and glowing once more.

Also, his hair is short—the shortest Nino has ever seen it. He'd gotten it cut just before leaving. The young, lounging ukiyo-e feudal lord is gone, replaced by an intellectual university student who takes his research too seriously.

At present, Haruka's expression is dead serious. His eyes are clenched shut. Nino shifts his gaze ahead. "How long is the helicopter ride to get to Lajos's house?" he asks.

"About an hour," the detective yells. "It's deep in the Hajhir mountains. We can't drive there. Any other method would take days of travel."

*God help me.*

Nino blinks toward his mate. *Sorry, Haru...*

"This is it," Detective Cuevas announces.

The vehicle slows, still bumping along the wide path that weaves through the village. Nino looks out the window. The sun is low with thick gray clouds hovering in the west.

Their surroundings are stark—colorless except for the singular spectrum of beige to dirt brown. The occasional pastel green of an awning. Hadibu is like a small town born in the middle of a desert wilderness. Most of the structures are packed together, flat and low. Some are dirty and partially destroyed, others are intact but with rock debris or litter scattered along the gravel in front of them. Clothes, blankets and household wares adorn the entrance of one structure they pass. Another, a small herd of goats.

The van stops in front of a squat square house with a large crack in the stone steps leading to the entrance.

"Your accommodations for the evening, my lords." Detective Cuevas turns, smirking at them from the front passenger seat. Having traveled light, they grab their respective bags and head inside. The stone construction of the outside continues within the interior. It's a single room with no pictures or decorations, only the most basic necessities: a twin-sized bed with a quilt, a wash basin, a chair. A naked light bulb hangs overhead, and a door in the back corner leads to a narrow bathroom with a toilet and shower.

"At least there's hot water?" the detective says. She lifts her chin, snide. "There's a kind of crappy hotel down the road, but they had a pipe burst yesterday, so this is the best we've got under short notice. You rich, upper-crust purebreds probably aren't used to dumpy places like this. My apologies for your discomfort."

Haruka is bent and rummaging through his bag against the bed, but he stands straight, eyeing the detective. "Why do you insult these people's way of living in your attempt to mock us?"

The detective scoffs. "Please. You know what I mean—"

"I do not. Our accommodations are modest but adequate. The people of this town may live a different lifestyle than ours, but your judgment is insensitive."

"Seriously?" she pushes back. "You're going to stand here and act like their lifestyles are just 'different' from yours? You live in a beautiful, sprawling estate in one of the wealthiest countries in the world and want for nothing—living life happy dappy. Meanwhile, these people are penniless, starving and living in squalor."

"What is your intent behind this declaration?" Haruka asks. "What should we do?"

The detective starts, frowning. "I—I don't know... *donate* or something."

"We do. To numerous causes. What else?"

"Look. I know you can't just swoop in and save a whole country, alright? I'm just saying that these people are probably suffering. It's not just about 'lifestyles.'"

"In my experience, misery and suffering exist in many forms, and contentment can be found in the humblest of circumstances. I feel that the true danger lies in making shallow comparisons and broad assumptions."

She turns toward the door, sneering. "Right. I guess I haven't lived long enough yet in my meager second-gen life to reach such high levels of enlightenment. I'll be back in the morning, my lords." She offers a shallow bow, then leaves.

"What the hell is *her* problem?" Nino frowns. "Why is she so bitter toward us? Should I tell her that even though I lived in a fancy house, I was being abused? That my mom died when I was eight and my entire community ostracized me—like I was a stain on society? Is my suffering invalid because I grew up in a 'sprawling estate'?"

"Ignore her. Whatever issue she has, it is within herself." When Haruka sits on the bed, it squeaks in a loud whine. He stretches his hand out, a gentle smile gracing his lips.

Understanding, Nino walks toward him. He meets the gesture, sliding his palm within his mate's and moving to stand in between Haruka's gaped legs. Outside, the wind is already howling, gaining momentum all around them like loud whispers.

Nino takes a deep breath, then sighs. "Thank you for doing this."

"Are you uncomfortable? Being so close to your place of captivity?"

"Not really... The detective made me feel anxious just now, but I'm alright. Shit... I'm looking forward to taking you back to Milan and then Trentino after we're done here. I think we're way overdue for some peace."

Haruka brings the back of Nino's hand to his mouth, placing a soft kiss against his knuckles. "Let's concentrate and work together tomorrow so that we can leave as soon as possible? I do not wish to bear the brunt of her misplaced resentment for any longer than necessary."

"Sounds good," Nino breathes. He looks past his mate and at the narrow bed. "I call big spoon tonight."

THE BIRD'S-EYE view of the ocean is now replaced with mountains—rolling and cavernous as far as Nino can see. Sharp peaks and low valleys covered with dirt and dust. Dragon's Blood trees stretch upward with their inverted roots and vegetation grows wild but sparse between cracks and cliffs. When Lajos's house comes into view, Nino's heart pounds. His pulse beats in his ears over the loud chop of the helicopter's propeller.

A large white Victorian-style house stands atop the mountain—completely out of place in this vast, alien wilderness. The design is two-story and asymmetrical with rounded rooftops and towers. Somehow, the drama of its appearance emphasizes the odd juxtaposition of its location, like a nun at a basement rave who is also wearing a sequined habit.

As the helicopter draws closer in its descent, the house is in serious decay: chipped paint and damaged shutters. The roof is dilapidated, even caved in over one small section toward the back. There's no movement anywhere out here. No vampires, people or animals. Just the large, misplaced house in ruins.

They touch down on a generous spread of flat rock beneath the house. The helicopter operator remains seated while the detective, Marcus, Haruka and Nino make their exit. When Nino steps onto the mountain, he shivers. The temperature is low from the altitude, much lower than in the village where they stayed overnight.

"I warned you, didn't I?" Detective Cuevas chides as Nino bristles from the chill. "I'm surprised you purebreds even get cold."

"We are not infallible," Haruka says coolly, his hands tucked within the pockets of his long wool navy blue coat. "If you prick us, do we not bleed for five seconds?"

The detective snorts. "Funny."

"How are we supposed to get up there?" Nino asks, rubbing his hands together before sticking them in the pockets of his hooded bomber jacket. His unease is low grade but threatening to boil. The sooner they start moving, the better.

"There's a path around the side with steps leading up to the front. The house is in pretty bad shape, so we should be careful. Follow me, please." Both the detective and her deputy are wearing large red backpacks, which they adjust and grip as they move forward, leading the way.

Rocks crunch and slide underneath their feet. The path climbs higher and higher, the wind picking up and whipping everyone's hair and coats as they move. This trail has been manually carved out, because soon, they're walking through a stone corridor with towering walls on either side of them. Nino likens the sensation to being in a wind tunnel, the sound of it loud as it rushes past his ears. When the breeze quiets, he looks over his shoulder at Haruka.

*Do you feel this?*

Haruka flicks his irises up to meet his gaze, resolute. *Yes. There are other purebreds here.*

The wind sweeps violently again, making Nino swallow hard. *But where? I can feel the hum of their energy, but it's almost... muffled?*

"Look."

Both Nino and Haruka pause. The tunnel opens to a wide cliff with the landscape below stretching on for miles, seemingly endless.

Detective Cuevas points toward the west. "You can see the mud-brick houses in the distance. We went down there before, but like I told you when I called, it was deserted—not a singular vampire in sight. Very eerie and dank. No electricity or plumbing or anything. It felt like something out of the Stone Ages."

A winding trail of jagged steps looms before them. Detective Cuevas leads the ascent. "Almost there, gentlemen."

Nino moves forward, but his chest is strained. This place is isolated—far away from anyone or anything familiar—and the strangeness of it weighs heavy in his mind. It's as if they've come to the very ends of the earth, and the realization unsettles him.

*What the hell was I thinking? What if the helicopter stops running and we're stuck here... What if there's something waiting for us in the house? What will we—*

Haruka steps up beside him, crawling his fingers into Nino's pocket to remove and grasp his hand. *We'll be fine. This will be over soon.*

He inhales a deep breath and blows it out, taking comfort in the warmth and surety of Haruka's hand gripping his own.

When the house stands before them, it appears even more derelict up close. The glass is missing from some windows and cracked like a spider's web in others. The ones that are intact are dirty: filmy with dried mud, dust and raindrop stains.

"How did he get this house all the way out here?" Marcus asks.

"I don't know, but it looks like he couldn't afford the upkeep after it was built," Detective Cuevas observes. "It's damn near ready to be demolished."

When they're at the front door and on the rickety wooden porch, Detective Cuevas grabs the knob. She pushes, but it doesn't budge. "Weird... this was open when we came before." She turns to her deputy. "Did you lock this?"

"I don't know how the heck I would do that without a key..."

She narrows her eyes. "Strange."

"If I may?" Haruka asks, stepping forward.

"Of course." The detective shifts aside, watching as Haruka's eyes glow to life. He places his fingertips against the tarnished brass plate of the keyhole. Nino can sense his mate's energy moving and interacting with the lock, examining it to understand its inner workings. A moment later there's a loud click. Haruka wraps his long fingers around the knob, then pushes the door open, effortless.

"Very nice," Detective Cuevas remarks. "I also could have had my deputy break it down."

"We all have our methods."

"I suppose so," she says, stepping past him and into the house. "Sorry about yesterday, by the way... going off the fucking rails like that. Lajos is still refusing to feed, but he's improved enough to where he can shout xenophobic bullshit about ranked vampires in broken speech patterns all day and night. Maybe I've let him get to me. Didn't mean to take it out on you—and of course I know that money doesn't equal happiness."

"Apology accepted." Haruka grins. "Although, you should know that most purebred wealth is tied up in very old property and land ownership. We do not have money to burn."

Detective Cuevas reaches up to scratch her curly head. "I had no idea. You know, Lajos... That old nutcase is belittling and refusing *first-gen* blood. By all accounts, first-gen vampire blood is *good* for your average purebred. He won't even acknowledge me when I try to talk to him—like I'm a peasant."

"Not all purebreds hold such immoral and dogmatic views," Haruka offers.

"Right... I get it."

The inside of the house is somber and drab—dusky from the overcast light outdoors. With every step, the floors creak and whine, protesting all movement.

When they reach an empty drawing room covered in faded gold velvet damask wallpaper, the detective turns to them. "Alright, does either of you sense anything?"

"Yeah." Nino nods. "From the second we landed."

"Okay... so speak up about it, maybe?"

"The source is uncertain," says Haruka. "The purebreds here have not vanished a second time, as you had suggested. Their energy is present, but the sensation is very weak... similar to a low frequency."

Nino paces the large and dirty ornate rug with his hands in his jacket pockets. Inside the house feels even colder than outside. "It feels blocked by something—like a wall or a barrier. We can't tell where it's centered."

"Well, already, it was worth bringing you here. My deputy and I couldn't sense squat. Shall we split up? Roam the house a bit and see if you can get some clarification?"

They agree. The detective and Marcus head upstairs while Nino and Haruka remain on the ground floor. They wander through the drawing room, down a dark, narrow hallway, and end up in a large kitchen space.

As with the rest of the house, it's cold here, darkened from the partly cloudy sky outside. The white appliances are like props from the 1950s and are backed by mint-green tiling on the walls. Haruka tries a light switch upon entering, but it doesn't work.

"This is so confusing." Nino wanders past a large island counter in the center of the room and toward a small window. "I feel the hum of purebred energy, but... it isn't sharp like the normal sensation." Despite the setting, the view through the glass is breathtaking. The mountain range meets a blueish-orange skyline filled with stormy clouds.

"Stand still," Haruka says. Nino turns to meet his gaze, but then does as instructed. Unmoving and with their eyes locked, the gentle reverberation of energy Nino feels pulses. It swells, not all around him like it usually would—free-flowing through the air. No. The hum is... moving up through the soles of his feet, triggering his awareness as if the purebreds are somehow part of the earth. Or *in* the earth.

Nino's eyes widen as he inhales. "They're underground—"

"Someone is coming."

They both turn their heads toward a wooden door at the opposite end of the kitchen. It looks like the opening to a pantry or closet, but a dim pulse of purebred energy is growing and closing in from behind it. Haruka moves closer to stand at Nino's side, never taking his eyes off the closed door. The silence of the room is palpable, so when the door slowly creaks open, Nino's spine stiffens and his eyes alight.

The door bangs open wide and a thick stream of yellow-green light darts out and straight toward them. Nino conjures the sphere of his aura to cover them just as the light makes contact and ricochets off the surface, hitting and shattering the glass window at his side. In the same moment, the crimson haze of his mate's essence unfurls, stretching out toward the darkened door like a thick viper. It grabs hold of something—someone—because the room is immediately filled with a blood-curdling scream. Torturous and loud, it overwhelms Nino's senses. He slams his palms to his ears as he maintains the protective bubble around them.

Haruka's energy draws inward, carrying with it a frozen figure from the shadowed door. He's floating, arms and legs straight. His eyes are wide as he screams.

When he's closer, Nino recognizes him as the one-eared purebred from his captivity. Lajos's sidekick is thin, disheveled and horrified. His clothes are soiled and ragged. Nino turns to his mate, focusing through the ruckus. *What are you doing to him?*

*Nothing. I am just holding him still!*

*Try letting him go—*

*He attacked us, unprovoked.*

*I know, but he can't do anything if I hold this shape.*

Nodding, Haruka unwraps his aura from the male's body, making him stumble onto the floor. They both stare at him from behind Nino's sunset-colored shield. The vampire stops screaming. He looks up at them in an uncertain moment, terror planted on his face. But then he scrambles, tripping and running back toward the darkened doorway from which he came.

# TWENTY-NINE

"They're here," Nino explains. "Underneath the house."

"Like, in a basement?" Detective Cuevas frowns.

"We are not certain," Haruka says, his arms folded as he leans with the small of his back against the kitchen counter. "The pulse of energy we feel is underneath our feet, but the sensation is muffled. Likely, they are far beneath the surface— much more so than a shallow basement."

"So that awful screaming we heard... The guy just ran away?" the deputy asks.

"Yes," Haruka confirms. "I did nothing to harm him."

The detective shakes her head. "It sounded like you were literally murdering him."

"I was not. I only held him still because he attacked us without warning." Haruka exhales, bringing his fingers to the bridge of his nose. *What the hell is this place?*

The geography, desolation and remoteness of this realm are jarring enough, but seeing that purebred—an emaciated and ragged creature with his bulging eyes and shallow cheeks— screaming and scattering away like an oversized cockroach...

Haruka has met a diverse assortment of purebreds in his travels. From different cultures, ethnic and indigenous backgrounds, varying social-economic statuses and ranging in all ages. He has never seen a purebred like this: existing in such a horrific, malnourished and terrified state.

"Well?" the detective says, walking toward the door where the purebred retreated. "Are we following or what?"

"We've come this far." Haruka shrugs. He looks up to see Nino staring out the window. The apprehension set in his expression is heavy—his anxiety rolling all throughout his tensed body. Haruka pushes up from the counter and takes a few steps forward to meet him. When he's standing in front of him, he lifts both hands, running his fingers into the back of Nino's hair to cradle his head. Haruka pulls him close so that their foreheads touch. Nino closes his eyes.

*You do not need to do this,* Haruka assures him. *I can go with the detective, and you can remain here with Marcus?*

Nino lifts to look into Haruka's eyes. "I can help protect you with our aura. It's better if we're together, right? Offense and defense."

"I agree." Haruka rubs his fingertips against his scalp, rustling his coppery waves. "But it is your choice."

Tilting his head, Nino leans into him, his lips parted but his eyes open. Haruka drops his jaw to receive the swift kiss, reveling in the unexpected heat and sweet-smoky flavor of his mate's mouth and tongue. Nino sighs and raises his head, his gaze heavy with affection. "I have to go with you—I'll just be worried otherwise. But thank you for giving me that option."

"Of course," says Haruka, lowering his hands and grasping both of Nino's between their bodies. "Shall we?"

"Mm." Nino nods.

When Haruka turns, the detective is staring at them, her

mouth agape. "Well damn, that was... quite the display. I thought I might have to turn a hose on you two."

Haruka scoffs, holding one of Nino's hands as he walks forward. "I would be impressed at your resourcefulness in finding one in this godforsaken place."

---

AS HARUKA HAD SUSPECTED, the descent into the space underneath Lajos's house runs deep. A narrow set of stone steps was revealed when they opened the kitchen door, the path leading into the depth and darkness of the mountain. There are no lights or torches lit with fire along the cold stone walls, just blackness. Thankfully, the detective and her deputy brought many emergency supplies in their backpacks, including two flashlights.

"Even purebreds can't see in the dark, right?" Marcus asks, trailing behind Haruka to bring up the rear. "I've never met any purebreds until the two of you... and Lajos."

"Same," Detective Cuevas calls from the front. "Only seen the more famous and flashy ones on TV. We have an aristocracy in New York, but... our realm leaders don't interact much with vamps under first-gen status. It seems like the purebreds overseeing aristocracies in other countries maintain a much stronger sense of community."

"To answer your question, the way we *see* is based in feeling and sensing another vampire's energy," Haruka says, following the path and stepping down, deeper and deeper into the clammy earth. "Our vampiric natures and abilities as purebreds are rooted in attracting prey for feeding, or partners for sex and mating. But we have since evolved with the modernization and civility of society. Feeding and mating are no longer a purebred's sole objective in life."

"You think?" the detective asks. "Ladislao is pretty famous for being focused on feeding and sex."

"Well... *most* modern purebreds?"

"That guy..." Nino says contemplatively. "The one who attacked us... His energy came at us like a laser beam. It didn't do anything to my aura, but it surprised me."

"Yes," Haruka agrees. "The impact was rather weak."

When Detective Cuevas stops, everyone behind her halts. She shines her flashlight further down the steps. "Thank God. The path is flat a little further ahead. I didn't think I was claustrophobic, but this place is suffocating me. What are your purebred vibes telling you?"

"That there are many creatures down here," Haruka says. "The map of my consciousness is lit with multiple faint energies."

The detective moves faster, demanding that the others fall into step behind her. Soon, they reach a flat, cavernous space. It is large—how large, Haruka can't discern due to its dark nature. But he can feel the vastness of it. The cool breeze whisks against his cheeks and the damp, muddy smell is surprisingly clean as he breathes.

Without warning, Nino swells the weight of his red-orange essence outward so that it covers the four of them. The detective jumps from the sensation, unaccustomed to being directly impacted by a purebred's aura. She stiffens, turning on Nino. "Wh—*What the hell* are you doing? A little warning next time you decide to whip your energy out?"

"There wasn't any time!"

"We are surrounded," Haruka announces.

Lights in every color of the rainbow shower them, fierce and unyielding—some like long arrows or darts, others like spears or bullets. If this wasn't some sort of full-frontal attack, it might be a pleasant display. But Nino's aura holds firm, the energies bouncing and shattering against the glassy surface of the sphere. Haruka steps up behind him, ignoring the ruckus and placing his palms on his shoulders. "Is this hurting you in any way?"

Nino shakes his head, glancing around. "No. It's a little tingly, but I'm fine."

Haruka squeezes his shoulders, reassuring as the barrage continues. Glowing streaks of yellow and purple, varying shades of green and some blues fly through the air like festival fireworks against a nighttime sky. Haruka addresses his mate. "Should I stop this?"

"I, for one, would appreciate it if you *did*," the detective snarks. "Are these creatures freakishly weak, or are you two freakishly strong? It's like they're throwing electric rainbow sprinkles at us!"

Nino turns his head, eyeing him. "Maybe yes? I don't know how long they plan to do this and it's not getting us anywhere. We just need to talk."

Haruka steps around him and moves to pass the barrier of Nino's protective aura. Nino reaches out, his voice panicked. "Wait! Haru, *don't—*"

When Haruka steps outside, the warm energy around him lingers—pulling and reforming around his body in a bright, fiery glow. He pauses and looks back. He is encapsulated in his own protective aura, autonomous but identical to the one enclosing Nino, Marcus and Detective Cuevas.

Nino blinks, standing straight with his hand still outstretched toward him. "Okay, wow... Are you doing this?"

"I am not," Haruka confirms. "This is your power but initiated within me."

"Alright... so that's a thing I can do."

Grinning, Haruka moves forward and near what he perceives as the center of the large space. The bright lights of purebred energy are still assaulting him within the darkness as he lifts his hands, breathing and allowing the power within himself to unfurl and fan out toward the energy sources surrounding him. His eyes alighted, it pours bright red, moving with intention and glowing within the cave.

Voices cry out, but having learned his lesson, he focuses to promptly silence them. Haruka pulls his energy back into himself, dragging his victims with it. They're hefty, like a fisherman hauling a crowded net from the water and onto a ship's deck.

Fifteen—twenty... then more and more bodies float through the darkness and toward him like glowing red orbs. He arranges the still figures in multiple rows so that they rest on the ground before him, sitting upright. He walks among the crowd, eyes scanning. There are at least fifty creatures here altogether and they look skeletal—hollowed cheeks, long, bony limbs and bug eyes. Somehow, they are even worse off than their companion from earlier in the kitchen. Their clothes are like rags, insufficient in covering their pale bodies.

Haruka shakes his head in disbelief at the wasted, depressing sight of them. *Is this a perfect purebred society?* He chooses one of the vampires at random. A female. He isn't sure what language these creatures speak, but he defaults to English. His deep voice echoes in the cavern. "Why do you attack us when we have done nothing to provoke or harm you? We come to you in peace."

Lifting a hand, Haruka removes his hold on her mouth. The scrawny female stares up at him, her face twisted in rage. "*Intruders!* Powerful monsters from the outside world! Demons! *Where* is our leader? *What have you done—*"

With a flick of his fingers, Haruka reseals her mouth shut. He sighs. "That was pointless."

"Tesoro, let's ask someone about Ladislao—if he's still

here?" Nino stands at his side, his nearness causes the two bubbles to brighten then merge back into one entity.

Nodding, Haruka looks around. The vampires on either side of the female read just as hostile, their brows furrowed tightly and their eyes filled with unwarranted hate as they stare up at him. Glancing a little further back, he eyes a young male with a dark, scabby gash across his bony forehead. His eyes are much less hostile than the others'. Taking a chance, Haruka lifts his hand and removes the hold on his mouth. The male inhales a sharp gasp but doesn't scream.

"We are not here to harm you. Can you please tell us if the vampire called Ladislao is here?"

The young male nods, his eyes wide and his raspy voice quiet. "He is."

"If I release you, would you bring him here? Then, I promise that we will gladly leave your society and I, for one, will never return."

"Yes," the young vampire whispers. Haruka releases him. The male pauses, placing his hands against his half-exposed chest. Checking himself. He looks up at Haruka, then stands and nods. "One moment... my lord." The young vampire runs off, disappearing down a dark tunnel.

Haruka turns to face his comrades, rolling his shoulders. "Your move, Detective."

The glow of both Haruka's and Nino's auras lights her distraught features as Detective Cuevas steps forward. "Look at them. Purebreds. The state of them down here. My God. This is horrific."

"And they're fighting us," Marcus offers, stepping up beside the detective. "They're defending their home. Are *we* in the wrong, here?"

Nino looks at Haruka. "What should we do about this?"

"We have to get them out of here, of course." The detective

gestures. "This is awful—they need *food* and sunlight and accommodations. They're down here living and looking like ancient horror-movie vampires. It's unbelievable that Lajos has done this to them, and for almost two hundred years!"

"You may wish to rescue them," Haruka says, "but it is possible that they do not want to be liberated."

"What?" Detective Cuevas balks. "You're insane! Why on earth—"

Haruka holds a hand up, then chooses a vampire at random, removing his hold on their mouth.

The male spits, but it lands just in front of their protective sphere. "Get out! Intruders! *Devils*—" Haruka seals his mouth again. He does this with another vampire, who offers similar rhetoric, then another, until Haruka has tested several vampires. He turns to the detective. "Does this help you to understand?"

"I can't believe this..." She stares. "They... they just need to *see*. We can teach them."

"Forcefully removing them from the only environment and world they have known may create more harm than good. We will become the intruders and demons they already believe us to be."

Haruka looks to his side. Through the darkness, he senses the male who initiated the attack in the kitchen. He steps away from Nino, and again the light and strength of his mate's aura reform independently around him.

*Haru, what are you doing?*

*One moment.*

Within a few steps, he's standing before the male, examining him. The red-orange light surrounding Haruka brightens his features in the darkness. Strangely, he is missing an ear. He waves his hand and removes the hold on his mouth. "Are you the acting leader of this realm?"

The vampire shifts his eyes up but doesn't speak. His stare is cold, menacing. Haruka is about to repeat himself when yellow light warms and shines in the male's eyes. Something in it is slightly green, like jaundice or unripened bananas. In the next second, the thin vampire opens his mouth wide and the yellowish light fills the cavern of his fanged mouth. Haruka steps back in shock, but it's too late. The beam of light rushes from his mouth, making direct impact with Haruka's shield. The cavern booms loud in echo and confusion. The ground shakes and the distinct sound of rocks falling and sliding fills Haruka's ears.

Dust hovers in the darkness like fog. As the dirt settles, he hears Nino calling out to him from a few feet away. Haruka examines himself and takes a breath—checking his hands, chest and limbs. He moves slowly, stepping over the rubble and across the cave floor to rejoin his mate. When he's there, Nino grasps his hand tightly, his voice strained. "What the *fuck*—Are you okay?"

"I think... I am unharmed," Haruka reassures him, his body trembling from shock. "Are you?"

Nino nods, leaning and wrapping his arms around his shoulders. Haruka glances over to where he was standing. The vampires he's holding captive within his aura are also untouched, frozen in place among the rocks and debris. But the vampire with one ear lies on his back several feet away. No movement other than his chest barely rising and falling. The ground beneath him is scorched, concave.

"It... it ricocheted," Marcus says calmly, but then his voice escalates. "That idiot blasted himself in the face! You guys can breathe your auras? Like—like friggin' vampire *dragons*?"

"Some of us, it seems." Haruka rolls his shoulders as Nino releases him from their embrace, but they re-link their hands. Nino frowns and pulls Haruka close.

"Would you stop wandering around down here? Don't walk away from me anymore."

"I apologize, I—"

Everyone's attention shifts at the sound of footfalls approaching. The young vampire with the gash appears first, followed by another thin vampire with very long hair. He pauses, but then beams, white teeth flashing with his arms outstretched.

"Honeycomb! Ebaaa, you came to rescue me—I *knew* you would." He moves through the crowd of frozen vampires to reach them. When he's standing just outside their protective bubble, he throws his arms around the curve of the large sphere, resting his cheek against the surface and grinning. "I had faith in you this whole time—my beautiful golden angel." He closes his eyes.

*Honeycomb?* Haruka turns to his mate, a prickly feeling stirring inside him and making him frown. "Why is he addressing you in such an affectionate manner?"

"Whatever this is that I'm sensing from you, please stop it. I can't control this creature or what he says. It's just how he is."

The dark map of Haruka's awareness changes, the number of dim lights he first sensed suddenly multiplying, as if blinking into existence. One hundred, no, two... then it doubles again, more and more as warm spots of energy brighten in his mind. His pulse quickens as they draw closer toward them, slow but steady. It feels as if they've disturbed an ant hill and all of the creatures are now descending upon them.

"Haru... do you feel this?" Nino is panicked at his side, his mind frenzied as he takes a step back to shift the position of the bubble. Ladislao trips forward from Nino's movement, surprised as he opens his eyes.

"There are too many," Haruka says. He takes a deep breath.

Nino's aura is strong enough to fend off fifty purebreds... but hundreds of them?

Ladislao stands straight, looking at them with his head cocked to the side as if confused. But then he follows their gaze toward the darkness. When he turns back to them, he's smiling. "Ah—they're awake from all the ruckus. Don't worry about them! It's okay, it's okay. They won't fight, trust me. They're just curious about you."

It's dark, but Haruka can see and feel them crowding in the wide opening at the opposite end of the cavern, the bright light of his and Nino's aura giving them subtle shape. Hundreds of purebreds: skeletal and drooping with bulging eyes and rags for clothes. Cave dwellers from an ancient time living cut off from the modern world.

Haruka stares as if in a trance, disbelieving this inexplicable situation. He's only shaken when Ladislao knocks upside the solid surface of Nino's aura.

"Olá—my beautiful saviors, can we go upstairs now? I would really like to get the hell out of this cavern, but I want to talk a little first. Is that alright?" Ladislao moves without waiting for their response. He walks around the sphere and straight toward the stairs leading back to the surface. Not knowing what else to do, Nino, Haruka, Detective Cuevas and Marcus all turn and follow his lead.

When they reach the stairs, Haruka looks back one last time, watching the sea of zombie-like purebreds watching him in turn. When he's out of sight, he releases his hold on the army that assaulted them. Thankfully, no one follows.

# THIRTY

"Você é tão bonito como... like a demon prince and an angel."

Nino bumps Haruka's shoulder beside him. *See? He says whatever he wants.*

They're sitting in a shadowy tearoom just off the kitchen. There are two antique-style couches, a small bistro table covered in a dusty tablecloth and heavy velvet curtains hanging from a tall window. Detective Cuevas is hovering behind Nino and Haruka as they face Ladislao on the opposite couch. Marcus is in the kitchen, keeping watch for any movement even though Ladislao has assured them that, quote, "maybe nobody will come."

Wrapped in a gray emergency blanket from the detective's backpack, Ladislao stands from the faded velvet couch. He bows deep from his waist, the gesture emphasized by his long, dirty toffee-brown hair cascading forward. "It is my sincere honor to meet you, my beloved prince. Thank you for rescuing me—"

"Sente-se, por favor," Haruka assures him, his palm lifted. "Não seja tão formal."

Ladislao blinks up from his bow, his eyes bright. "You speak my native tongue? Ahh, incredible. I understand your devotion now, honeycomb. I would follow this sexy, ancient-blooded creature into the fires of hell... these ruby-red eyes and dark hair..."

When Haruka lifts his fingers to the bridge of his nose, Nino senses that it's time to get down to business. "What happened? Why were you down there? When I was here, everyone was still living in that village."

Ladislao plops back down onto the couch. A small puff of dust swirls out in a cloud, hovering around his hips. "Correct. After my tio wasn't around for about two days, some kind of emergency plan went into action and everyone was moved underground. The one-eared guy has been a nervous mess trying to manage everyone. I think he's terrified of the responsibility."

"Your *tio* is in prison in New York," Detective Cuevas says from behind them. Nino turns, and her arms are folded, her chin lifted in contest.

"Good." Ladislao focuses on the detective. "That's where he should be. You're pretty."

Detective Cuevas starts. "Is that important right now?"

"For me it is." Ladislao bites his lip. "Delicious and soft, full-figured female—are you second-gen?"

The detective unfolds her arms and shifts her footing, her face upset but flushed in bright red. "I—Excuse me, but can you *focus?*"

"I can't." Ladislao shrugs. "You are definitely second-gen. Every second-gen vampire I meet is a little grumpy like this— because you are the middle children of the aristocracy, no?"

Gasping, the detective draws back, her face fixed for a rant, but Haruka cuts her off.

"Why has your uncle done this?" he asks. "Why has he

stolen these creatures and forced them to exist in such... wretchedness? Do they not know that their lives are unnatural? Are they blind to their environment?"

The detective scoffs. "Funny. You scolded me yesterday about judging people who live in poverty."

"No." Haruka shakes his head. "This is different. These vampires are unknowingly enslaved. These purebreds are—"

"Brainwashed."

The three of them look at Ladislao. He goes on. "They don't know any better. My tio has trained them to think that this is how a purebred should be living. With nothing. Only drinking blood. Only mating and reproducing. He allows them to know languages and math and science. Some trade skills for building and construction. They're smart about these kinds of things, which is weird... but that's it! He tells them that the outside world is evil, and that they would be miserable if they tried to leave."

"And they believe him?" Haruka asks. "What about the ones whom he originally took in the Vanishing? They would know better—that the outside world has much more to offer than this."

"I don't know everything, dark prince, but—"

"*Do not* call me that."

Ladislao tilts his head, blinking. "But it suits you?" Nino snickers as Ladislao continues. "Like I said, I don't know the whole story, but I met a very old purebred after they made me move down to the cave. Isaac. He was the first British purebred I ever met—"

"There are British purebreds down there?" The detective is leaning with her palms wrapped around the ornate wooden molding of the seat back, her eyes wide.

"No, amiga. He died last week, and he was the only one

here. He and his wife came in the original Vanishing. They volunteered to come here! Can you believe it?

"He said at the time, there were terrible clan wars across England, and many of the vampires were doing drastic things to survive and preserve their bloodlines. He said he didn't like the direction that his people were going in—some of the choices they were making. So he chose Lajos. He said his mate died in child labor here many years ago, and that he has always wanted to leave but couldn't. My tio wouldn't let him go. I told him, 'Isaac, you are the *last* British purebred on the planet!' He said I was wrong. He said, 'You can't see my people, but they're there.' He told me they were hidden in plain sight... Honestly, that creeped me out and I didn't sleep for two nights after he said that... down there in that freezing cave."

Ladislao shivers his body in a dramatic gesture. "Like a ghost story... Are the British purebreds ghosts?"

Haruka sits back against the dusty seat, folding his arms. Nino can feel the wheels of his mind turning over and dissecting the information Ladislao has given him. Nino turns, meeting Ladislao's aqua-tinged eyes. "So... some of the vampires down there want to leave?"

He shrugs underneath his blanket. "Maybe? I think they're scared. And some believe my tio's claim that the outside world is so terrible. You met his minions in the cave—the diehards. They will protect this place until my tio returns, even if he never does. But we should ask if anyone wants to leave. I think it would be nice to offer?"

"I was thinking the same thing," Detective Cuevas says. "Haruka mentioned that some might not want to leave, and after hearing this, well... we shouldn't force anyone to do anything drastic. Maybe we can ask now, then try again in a few months? Find a way to keep an eye on them?"

Ladislao lifts his eyebrow toward the detective in a pointed look. "Meu amor, our minds are already connected. It means when our bodies join, it will be explosive!"

"It's been a while since you've gotten laid, hasn't it?" the detective asks.

"Oh God, *so long*." Ladislao rubs his bony hands against his face, stressed. "It's painful."

"I still do not understand *why*," Haruka says, his gaze focused on the low coffee table. "The extent to which he has gone to hide this poorly maintained place, why—"

"Offspring, my prince," Ladislao says. "He wanted to make more purebreds. This whole setup... The main goal is to increase the number of purebreds in the world. And he has— not without casualties, of course. Isaac told me at the beginning, there were about five hundred purebreds here. Now, there are over one thousand."

"A *thousand* of them are stuck down there?" the detective exclaims.

"Yes, I counted a little, but got tired and stopped around there." Ladislao nods. "Some are so weak, it's hard to sense them—they can't even regenerate well. And you know, in our culture, purebred babies are becoming more and more rare, which means the race is slowly dying out.

"My tio hated that, and seeing purebreds mixing with lower-ranked vampires, or even purebreds creating weak bonds with other purebreds, to the point where they can't even reproduce because their energies are so out of whack. So he made this place to do population control and to study how to make stronger vampire bonds. That's what he fought with my father about. They couldn't see eye to eye."

"Huh, I guess your nerdy sex book would be the perfect thing to help him with that?" the detective chides. "I wonder where it is... He wouldn't tell us, of course. But it must be here, somewhere?"

"We all know this about our culture, and that the lack of purebred children is a genuine problem... but to go to these lengths." Haruka exhales a breath, his dark brows drawn together. The frustration Nino feels inside of his mate is stirring his own heart. Confusion, disgust, sadness, and quietly, tucked somewhere very, very deep, there's something else. Something Nino is capable of noticing because he's seen Haruka interact with Sora's twins. Because Asao exposed something about him and gave Nino a small glimpse into his past.

Haruka abruptly looks up, his wine eyes concerned. "What is it? Why are you—"

"Nothing." Nino shakes his head, his heart in his throat.

"Ahh *crap*, someone's coming, someone's coming!" When Marcus yells from the kitchen, Nino realizes he senses multiple energies approaching from deep beneath the surface. He and Haruka stand and move toward the kitchen, walking swiftly with their long legs. The detective follows and Ladislao shouts from behind.

"I said don't worry! It's okay, they won't hurt you. They're too weak."

Marcus is backed away from the door and standing at the far end of the kitchen, his eyes wide. Haruka steps inside first, and Nino stands beside him. They wait in silence, feeling the approach of timid purebred energies. *Three... four... and a half?* Nino is about to flare his aura out, but Ladislao steps up and slaps his hand against his shoulder, making Nino jump.

"Ei, relaxa—you don't need to do that, amigo." He grins, then walks toward the door. He opens it and waits. Soon, he lifts his hands in a warm gesture. "Ebaaa, you decided! I hoped you would. Come, come—meet my friends. Honeycomb and his dark prince."

Ladislao steps aside. A small female vampire with wild,

curly black hair emerges from the darkness. She's holding hands with another female that has tawny-brown skin and very straight black hair, heavy and thick. The latter is holding hands with a third vampire. A very small one—no older than five. Her pale eyes are darting all around in wonder as the female with straight hair picks her up and sets the child against her hip.

Nino recognizes the one with curly hair. It's Kahla, the female who touched his aura and brought blood into the room during his captivity. The next vampire to emerge from the darkness is a male with sandy-brown hair and a scabbed scar across his forehead. He's holding hands with a blonde female, but unlike the first couple to emerge, their essences are not bonded.

Beaming, Ladislao turns to Nino and Haruka. "See! Some will want to leave this place. Let's go back down and ask, just to make sure? My tio's minions are weaklings. Maybe they won't fight you again now that they've seen it's useless."

*Haru, is that okay with you?* Nino eyes his mate, waiting. When Haruka meets his gaze, he offers a warm smile.

*Of course.*

# THIRTY-ONE

By the time they arrive in Milan, Haruka is exhausted. The trip from Yemen to Italy was long, and prior to that, discussing the logistics of transporting the refugee purebreds was also daunting.

In the end, twenty-seven vampires wished to leave the island. To start, they'll be routed to New York. There, the detective will begin the work of creating formalized IDs, establishing any remaining family connections and starting the long road of acclimating them to the concepts of food, warm shelter and water.

With Haruka and Nino's assistance, the detective also wishes to convince other trustworthy purebred leaders to adopt refugees into their realms. That way, the newly free vampires can receive more thorough rehabilitation, as well as guidance in being introduced to modern society, humans and ranked vampires.

Ladislao had left his realm in Rio de Janeiro in much turmoil after acting out and attracting his uncle's attention, so the long-haired purebred insisted that Haruka and Nino adopt Kahla and her family when the detective finishes processing them in New York. They agreed. They also volunteered to rehab and shelter the young fighter and his female companion.

The trip was tumultuous, and Haruka had not wanted to participate in the excursion. But in the end, he is glad to have helped, and his Historian mind is eager to document the cultural insight and experience for future generations.

When they step outside Milan International Airport, it is nighttime. A car from the Bianchi estate is waiting at the designated meeting place. Nino greets the manservant from the estate and helps him with the bags as Haruka climbs into the back seat. Giovanni is there.

Haruka pauses, taking notice of the subtle shift in his scent. Nino's brother and Cellina are getting along very well. He smiles. "Hello, Giovanni."

"Hello, dark prince."

Haruka rolls his eyes. Clearly, his mate has already updated Giovanni on the details of their journey. He scoots toward the other side of the seat as Nino climbs in behind him. His mate sits down and closes the door, but then whips his head around to face his brother, amber eyes wide. "Wha—*what the hell* is going on?"

Giovanni sits back, irritation in his voice. "How about 'Hey, G, how's it going? Thanks for picking us up.'"

"*Why* do you smell like Cellina? Did you feed from her? She let you feed from her?" Nino's voice is high-pitched and incredulous. He's looking at Giovanni with something like disgust. Haruka interjects, calm.

"Perhaps the two of you intend to bond?"

"No," Nino says, the volume of his voice increasing. "Y-you *can't—*"

Giovanni puts his hand up, his face flat. "Nino, you need to fucking calm down."

"If you fed from Cellina—then what about Father? Do I need to start feeding him now? *Can* I? Does he know about this?"

Haruka senses that Giovanni is trying to stay calm, but his patience is dissipating. "Nino. Stop. Yelling."

"I—I don't want to feed Father." Nino ignores his brother, his eyes bewildered. "I don't even live here, how could I—Did you think this through? What about—"

"You selfish, ungrateful *little shit*."

The force of emotion behind Giovanni's words makes Nino pause and draw back. The insult isn't directed at Haruka, but his chest is tight from the sudden disquiet.

"God forbid you have to do something—*anything* for our family," Giovanni says, his heavy voice booming in the small space. "If everyone isn't bending over backward to cater to your self-absorbed ass—"

"That's not true." Nino sits up straighter. "I... I'm not—"

"I just got back from helping you for *two fucking months* in Japan. Running your damn realm and managing your clients. Anytime you need something, I help you. You call me at ungodly hours with questions and I answer. I've never asked you to do a damn thing your entire life, and all you do is take take take from me like everyone else and do whatever the hell you want. Must be nice."

Nino clenches the edge of the back seat with his hands as he stares at his brother. "G, I don't... I'm *not*—"

"Just shut up," Giovanni spits, rubbing his temple with his eyes closed. "You know how much I care about Cellina. I finally make some headway with her, and you're yelling and whining at me about yourself and how it impacts you. *And* you kept her tied up as your own personal feeding source for a century. Fuck you. I'll figure this out on my own—I always do. Nobody needs you to do a damn thing."

The rest of the car ride to the estate is silent. Haruka can feel the stress and tension radiating off his mate's body as Nino stares down at his smartphone. Although the delivery was a bit hostile, he agrees with Giovanni. Nino should not have reacted that way.

As soon as they pull up to the main outer gate of the Bianchi estate, Nino pushes the back door open. There is another car waiting on the street, and Haruka starts, confused. "Where are you going?"

"To talk to Lina." Nino closes the door without another word and moves toward the second vehicle. A moment later, it drives off and down the dark lane.

"Probably to bad-mouth me." Giovanni shakes his head. "He's going to tell Mommy that I yelled at him. I'm letting you off here."

"You're not coming in?" Haruka asks. The excursion to Socotra is starting to feel like the more relaxing trip.

"No. I'm staying at a human-owned hotel in the business district. I need to figure out what the hell I'm doing before my father finds out. I can't go home yet." Giovanni rubs his hand up his face and into his thick wavy hair. He blows out a deep breath.

"How do you anticipate your father reacting?"

"Not good," Giovanni says, massaging the top of his head with his eyes closed. "My father is sweet as fucking pie to Nino, but he's a strict bastard toward me. I disobeyed him *once* and he screamed at me and scared the shit out of me. Been on my best behavior ever since. Until now."

Haruka nods, understanding the situation. "You hold much resentment toward Nino, but perhaps your communication needs... tempering?"

Giovanni drops his hand. His face flat. "I know, alright? Yelling doesn't help, but I'm fucking *tired*. He does whatever the hell he wants—always has. But I can't ever do shit. The one time I have something good for myself, the first thing out of his mouth is 'What about me?' I'm over it."

"What will you do about Cellina? Do the two of you wish to create a bond?"

"I don't know." Giovanni sighs. "Cellina knows my circumstance. Her mother and father already know how I feel about her, but I don't... I don't think I can. Bonding isn't an option for me."

Haruka folds his arms, considering. Bonding is an innate birthright to *every* ranked vampire. It feels unfair that something so essential should be denied. Especially considering that there is a particular vampire that Giovanni finds himself drawn to—which is a rare circumstance in and of itself.

Then again, sacrificing the health and potential vitality of his father for his own personal desires... The situation is difficult.

"There must be a sensible resolution here," says Haruka. "One in which we all work together? My bloodline is very old and profoundly co-mingled with your brother's. Cellina is first-gen but... the purebred half of her bloodline feels ancient as well. Your father's diet has been strict, but we won't know until we try? And I know that I am biased, but Nino can be very self-less and thoughtful."

"He can be," Giovanni admits. "With other vampires. Not with me. He avoids our father and uses me as a substitute. He's been doing it since Mom died. I know that all this stems from our uncle abusing him, and I know I've enabled him because of that, but I'm *not* his fucking dad. Nino is a grown-ass bonded vampire now. He still expects me to take care of everything for him and then I do. I'm sick of this bullshit cycle. Enough already."

"Nonetheless," Haruka counters, "the situation is complex and he values your opinion. I imagine that your words tonight have struck him deeply."

"Good." Giovanni lifts his chin. "Little punk. He asked for it."

# THIRTY-TWO

When Nino rings the doorbell to the high-rise apartment where the De Luca family lives on the top floor, Cellina's younger brother answers... which is awkward.

Cosimo always acts as if Nino should have bonded with him—as if there was some unspoken understanding between them. Except Nino doesn't understand at all. Yes, they grew up together, and they were sexually intimate a few times (the encounters stressful and finicky), but Nino has never once given Cosimo any inclination that he wanted to mate with him or offer his blood.

Nino keeps the stiff conversation short. He's had enough tension-filled discussions tonight to last him the rest of his life. He knocks when he reaches Cellina's bedroom, but there's no answer. He turns the knob and peeks his head inside.

It's dark. She's lying in bed, unmoving. "Lina?" Nino whispers. Still no response. He walks over to the bed and sits along the side. He looks down at her. Something is off. Her normally rich, coffee-brown skin seems gray and the texture is rough. Nino touches her shoulder, panic rising in his chest. "Cellina?"

Her eyes flicker open. Instead of the haunting steel gray he's accustomed to, they're pale, almost white. She looks at him and gasps, scooting away. "N-Nino? What the hell?"

"I told you I was flying in today."

"Yeah, but you didn't say you were coming here? Good Lord, you scared me." She places her palm against her chest and takes a deep breath.

"Lina, why do you look like this?"

"I—I'm... well..." She attempts to smooth her coily, curly bedhead down with no luck. She lifts her chin. "I'm thinking."

"About what?" Nino asks. "You need to feed. Who did this to you? Did Giovanni do this?"

Her face falls flat as she purses her lips. "Listen, Giovanni didn't 'do' anything to harm me, alright? Fix your tone."

"Sorry."

"Yes, he fed from me... and it was intense," Cellina goes on, pulling the length of her hair to one side. "But we decided that I shouldn't feed from him until he talks to his father. I told him I would feed from my source, but..."

"But?"

"I don't know..." Cellina sighs. "I don't want to. He fed from me, and it was glorious. Now it's like my insides are all twisted up and throwing a tantrum."

Nino understands. There had been a time when Haruka was feeding from him but Nino couldn't have his blood in return. He accepted the circumstance at the time, but the intense yearning for Haruka's blood had been maddening—sometimes keeping him awake at night.

"We decided," Cellina goes on. "But I just want *him*. So I'm thinking."

"Did you tell G this?"

Cellina shakes her head. "Giovanni has so much on his

plate already. I'm not going to add an extra layer of shit for him to deal with."

Nino reaches out and holds Cellina's shoulders, looking her dead in her translucent eyes. "Any layer of shit *you* have to offer, Giovanni will gladly accept. Tell him. Don't worry about Father. We... we can figure that out later. You need to feed."

"Yeah, I do. I feel like I'm drying up from the inside out. It's not fun. Why are you here? What's wrong?"

Dropping his hands, Nino sits straight. He runs his fingers into the top of his hair. "Why do you think something is wrong?"

"Because you show up in the middle of the night as soon as your plane lands, and you're running your hand through your hair. What is it?"

"It's nothing. I—I wanted you to know that I think it's great that you and G are getting along so well. I want the two of you to be happy. He loves you."

"I know." Cellina smiles and shrugs. "He's a good male. He needs to stop hurling himself on the family sword though."

"Yeah... I'm going to try and help with that."

"I agree with that choice." Cellina looks at him. "I think we've given you space to grow and heal? And Haruka is wonderful support."

Nino nods. "You have. He is. I'm sorry if I fed from you for too long. If I was a burden."

"No." Cellina smiles. "You were never a burden. You blossomed later than I expected, but that's okay. Everyone has their own timing in doing things. You needed someone who made you feel comfortable and that you trusted. He was worth the wait, yes?"

"Definitely." Nino smiles and nods. "Absolutely. When are you going to call G?"

Cellina shrugs, settling herself back down in the bed. "I'll text him tomorrow. I need to sleep."

"Text him *now*."

She yawns. "It's fine."

Nino frowns. It isn't fine. Within a moment, she's asleep again. He pulls his phone out of his pocket, hands shaking. Taking a deep breath, he maneuvers to the messaging app.

[Where are you?]

He sits, waiting. It feels like an eternity, the way his nerves are jumbled up in his stomach, replaying the tense conversation in the car. A few minutes later, his phone buzzes.

[Why.]

[Are you at home?]

[No.]

[Can you send me the address to where you are? Please?]

If he focuses hard enough, Nino can sense and find his brother organically. But this is the easiest and fastest method, and it saves him from stalking around half the night like some creepy fictional vampire character.

Nino stands from the bed and moves toward the door, his temples pounding from anxiety. By the time he's back down on the street and stepping into his taxi, the address to the hotel where Giovanni is staying has popped up on his phone screen.

STANDING outside Giovanni's hotel room, Nino's heart thumps in his chest.

He knocks on the door and waits. At least two minutes later, the door swings open and Giovanni is standing there. He's still dressed in casual clothes, his wavy hair shining underneath recess lighting. He's also wearing eyeglasses with a modern brown frame that suits his chiseled face.

Nino blinks, caught off guard. "Since when do you wear glasses?"

"The light from the computer screen bothers my eyes and this helps."

"Huh, Haruka says the same thing about his smartphone... maybe I should get him a pair? I bet he'd look good in glasses..."

"Nino, what do you want?"

"Can I come in... please?"

Giovanni glares in a moment of pause, then sighs. He steps back and Nino walks inside.

There are papers organized into piles everywhere. His work laptop is open on a desk near the darkened window, and there are takeout containers on the coffee table in front of the sofa. Aside from the organized clutter, the suite is nice.

Nino steps over his brother's bag and a stack of papers. "It looks like your office threw up in here..."

"It's difficult to be organized in an unfamiliar space." Giovanni walks toward the desk in the corner, then sits in front of his laptop.

Plopping down on the couch, Nino turns, folding one leg against the cushions and adjusting his body so that he can see his brother. "So... when are you going to tell Father?"

Giovanni concentrates on the glowing computer screen. "I don't know."

"I saw Cellina."

"Right." His brother stares at the monitor. Typing. Not paying Nino any attention.

"G, I apologize for the way I reacted in the car. I'm *sorry*— and I don't mean to be selfish... I don't." Nino swallows hard, waiting. He knows that he's played the role of innocent bystander for most of his life, never offering to help Giovanni with difficult aristocracy situations, or to assist in feeding their father. No one asked for his help, so he always shrugged and kept to himself. Did his own thing.

"Fine," is all Giovanni offers, still focused on his computer.

"Tell Father tomorrow," Nino urges. "Haru says he's willing to help, too. I can try to take over the feeding. We know a good doctor who can do the blood draws in Japan—we'd just need to figure out reliable shipping if Father responds well."

Giovanni stops typing and rubs his temple. "Just calm down, alright? I told you I'll figure everything out—"

"We have to do things quickly," says Nino. "You need to go and see Lina. She hasn't fed from her source, so she's at home lying in her bed, mummifying."

"What?" Giovanni scrunches his face.

"She doesn't want to feed from her source. She wants to feed from *you*, but like you, she's being all nonchalant about the circumstance. Meanwhile she's starving herself. So you need to go over there right now. Then let's talk to Father tomorrow morning."

"*Dammit.*" Giovanni frowns, standing from his desk. "Why wouldn't she tell me this?"

Nino shakes his head, blinking. "You're both too stubborn and self-sufficient. It's okay to tell people that you need help... or be honest about what you want."

Giovanni snatches the glasses from his face and rubs his eyes. Nino smiles, timid. "You're both amazing. Like a vampire power couple... a vampower couple." His smile drops and he mumbles, "That's so cheesy."

"Are you trying to butter me up now?"

"No. I'm being honest. You'll be great together. This has been a long time coming. I'm sorry I got in the way."

Giovanni rolls his eyes. "Alright, give it a rest." He moves across the room and grabs his jacket off the back of the couch.

"Are you going to her now?"

"Yes." Giovanni pats the back of his dark jeans pocket, distracted as he looks around the room.

"Good." Nino watches him.

His brother moves to the desk, then grabs the key card and his wallet before walking across the room once more. "Close the door behind you when you leave."

Nino nods. "I will... I love you."

When Giovanni is at the door, he swings it open. He doesn't look back, but his voice is clear. "I love you, too."

Nino flops down backward against the couch the moment he's gone, feeling a small sense of relief from the tension clogging his chest. He pulls his phone from his pocket, lifting it overhead as he sends a quick message.

[G is on his way to see Lina. I'll be back home shortly. We're okay.]

A moment later, his mate responds.

[Good. See you soon. xx]

Nino grins and scrunches his nose, his heart suddenly light.

[Be naked. xxxxxxx]

# THIRTY-THREE

*Ginger... and oak.*

Cellina inhales, smiling as she lies half asleep in bed, warmth and shadow covering her like a wonderful, comforting blanket. It gives her a sense of peace and calm. Security.

A soft kiss on her cheek makes her eyes flicker open. Giovanni is there—handsome, broad and silent as he leans over her body. He's resting on his elbows above her and sitting on the side of the bed. Cellina grins. "Luce dei miei occhi."

"Perché non mi hai chiamato?" he says, his brow furrowed. She reaches up, rubbing her fingertips against his forehead.

*Why didn't you call me?* "Stop frowning," she scolds, groggy. "You frown too much... like a... very sexy Shar Pei."

He takes hold of her wrist, his eyes serious. "Don't ever do this. If you need anything from me, tell me. I love you more than you can imagine—whatever you need, I'll give it to you. Do you understand?"

Ignoring the rush of heat flooding her cheeks, she snarks, "Is that an official mandate? As my realm leader."

"Feed." He sits straight, tugging her upright with him.

"What about Domenico?" She rubs her eyes, wondering how utterly insane she must look with her hair standing up all over the place and her dry-ass skin. She makes a weak attempt to quell her frizzy curls. It's pointless.

He cups her face with his large palm. The warmth of his touch sends sparks down her neck and all throughout her body. She closes her eyes, indulging.

"Don't worry about that right now," Giovanni pleads, his husky voice quiet in the darkness. "Just feed."

Cellina opens her eyes and stares into his chiseled face. "What if I feed from you and we bond. It happened to Haruka and Nino. First time."

Giovanni shakes his head. "They're weird."

Laughing, she brings her palms up, rubbing her face and feeling her skin flake. "*Not* weird. It's romantic."

"It's weird," Giovanni says, a smile behind his voice.

Cellina considers for a moment, then nods and places her fingertips to the center of his chest, urging him to lie down against the bed. Understanding, Giovanni kicks off his shoes, then brings his legs up. He rests on his back and Cellina crawls forward to straddle his hips. She settles down and immediately feels the distinct hardness of Giovanni's shaft through his jeans.

She rests her palms at his waist, then slides her hands underneath his cotton shirt to feel the warmth of his toned, naked abdomen. "But what if I have you a second time before I feed from you? What then?" she asks.

Giovanni lifts his hips, adjusting his arousal underneath her. He brings his large hands to her waist, then slides them down to cup the curve of her naked ass underneath her oversized nightshirt. "You can feed first, then have me a second time." He smiles, then furrows his brow. "You really never wear underwear?"

"Especially not to bed. Only sociopaths wear underwear to bed."

"That's... not true."

Cellina laughs, devilish in urging his shirt up until he grabs the hem. He lifts his torso and yanks it over his head. Giovanni's muscled body is beautiful in the moonlight and she is mesmerized by him: the scent of him and the devotion in his words and actions.

He's always giving of himself. It's his character and moral foundation. Who he is as a well-groomed purebred vampire. If she can, she wants to give something to him for once. Something innate and good that she alone can give.

"Can I pull your aura?" she asks.

He swallows hard, his throat bobbing as he caresses his fingertips up and down her thighs. "You can do whatever you want with me. I feel like this is a dream that I'm going to wake up from any minute."

She leans down, stretching the length of her body to press her chest into his. He sighs a deep, throaty sound as she rests her elbows on either side of his head, her face just above his. "It's not a dream," she whispers. "I love you, Giovanni Bianchi."

His hands move up her spine, exposing her naked backside to the coolness of the night air in the room. "You love me..." He grins, innocent, almost childlike.

"Yeah," she says. "And I missed you. Very much."

Leaning into his neck, she licks his skin to taste him first. Warm and spicy. Delicious. Her eyes glow to life as she bites down into him, the rush of his blood on her tongue peppery and complex. More fulfilling than any other vampire she's ever tasted.

His blood is like a drug, euphoric as it goes straight to her head. She moans as one large hand holds her shoulder blade and the other grips her ass. She pulls hard at his flesh, sensing the deep, innate barrier of Giovanni's purebred aura. Cellina has never released a purebred vampire's aura before, but she knows it takes mental focus and emotional determination. Two things she is well equipped with.

Steadying herself against his hips, she braces her hands above his head. Cellina focuses her mind on the selfless and strong male underneath her and sucks as hard as she can. She thinks about how long she's wanted him—to touch him, comfort him and make him smile. To let him know he doesn't have to handle everything alone, that she'll stand by him. That they can stand by each other.

Giovanni's body arches, his grip tightening. She pulls hard once more and he breathes, cursing. The rush and power of his aura releasing is stunning: a wild haze of vivid green light. She sits upright as it surrounds them, her heart dancing in her chest. Cellina closes her eyes, enjoying the fierce, shimmering energy as it swirls and pulses like a sandstorm of crushed emeralds.

After a moment, the intense sensation dissipates. They're both silent—only the sound of Giovanni's labored breathing underneath her straddle litters the quiet. He brings his palms to his face, covering a broad smile. "*Holy fucking shit.*"

Cellina brushes her wild hair back, then works to unfasten his pants. "Nice job for a first try, right?"

"Whatever my father says or does to me tomorrow, it's worth it."

She lifts herself and tugs at his waist to urge his pants down. "Let's make it count?"

SOMETHING ABOUT THE NIGHT, being alone together in the darkened vacuum of Cellina's room, just the two of them... It makes them confident. Fearless.

In the morning, Cellina wakes first. She is shrouded within the embrace of a rather large, naked, muscled and gingery-smelling male. Giovanni's skin is warm but soft—the fuzzy golden-brown hairs of his firm body tickling hers from top to bottom. His chest is pressed into the length of her spine. His groin at her ass and his thick legs tangled with hers.

To be clear, it is glorious: this man-blanket situation. If she'd realized the goodness of it sooner, maybe she would have tried to purchase one online.

His hold is secure, but she wiggles and turns herself in his grasp. He adjusts, feeling her intention and helping her face him. When she does, his eyes are still closed. Cellina examines him—the way the sunlight reveals the subtle shadow accumulating on his square jaw, how it highlights the golden undertones of his messy brown hair. His forehead is smooth, his face relaxed in a way she hasn't seen since they were very young.

"Smettila di fissarmi."

Cellina stifles a laugh. Giovanni's voice is low and thick with sleep. His eyes are still closed, but a warm smile forms on his lips. *Stop staring.*

"I've been ignoring you for decades." Cellina grins, nuzzling into him. "I need to make up for lost time."

"You keep looking at me so hard, I'm scared you're going to change your mind about this."

She reaches up and pinches his nose shut, making him open his eyes and draw his head back in a startled snort. "Now that I have your full attention," she says, "don't be stupid. I won't change my mind. Ever."

He leans into her once more, pulling her even tighter into his warmth and rubbing his lips against her forehead. "Please don't change your mind," he whispers. He kisses the line down her nose, so soft and tender that it gives Cellina a rush of goosebumps across her skin. When he hovers over her lips, brushing his full ones over hers, he says, "My heart couldn't take it."

She lifts her chin, kissing him hard—with everything. He meets her tenacity, shifting so that he's on top of her with his weight resting on her chest, belly and hips. He's heavy and divine, hard and thick between her gaped thighs. Giovanni lifts from the kiss, his eyes glowing green magnificence. Regal. "May I feed again?"

Cellina breathes a laugh, wrapping her palms against the small of his back. "You're just going to town now?"

"Might as well..." He gives a weak shrug. He smiles, but something shadowed crosses his expression. "Don't know when or if I can ever do this again. Please?"

"Of course you can." Cellina moves her arms up, sliding her fingers into his hair. "Try not to be so disheartened. We'll talk to Domenico together, alright? We'll figure this out."

He nods as he leans into her, his eyes focused on her as if she's his first and last meal. His only hope. Cellina draws her knees up to cradle Giovanni's heavy body and he licks her neck. At the same time he sinks his teeth into her, he slides his large palm down the side of her body, settling it in the curve of her waist and stroking his thumb against her skin.

Cellina breathes as he takes, closing her eyes. Before when he fed, the thoughts were loving but desperate—wild with hunger and need. Now, his mind feels calm. There's gratitude flowing within her, lovingly swirled with something more. Reverence? It makes Cellina's heart warm and her skin tingle.

She relaxes, opening her mind and body to him completely. At that moment, a deep wave rocks her entire psyche. It's dizzying, as if she's been struck with a severe case of vertigo. He pulls up from her neck, and before she can gather her senses, the cool rush of her nature expands within her, making her eyes shine bright silver.

Giovanni's weight on top of her stiffens—the rich emerald-green haze of his aura intensifying around them. The pleasing scent of him consumes her as it grips her frame, but Cellina's own nature fans out like starlight. She's never seen her own unique aura manifest outside her body like this. As a first-gen, she has purebred blood within her, but she's incapable of wielding and manipulating it as purebreds sometimes do.

Her essence melts into Giovanni's—the image of it reminding her of a lava lamp. Slow, graceful and hypnotic before it bursts and shimmers. It pours into the emerald haze, intense and silvery before the fusion of their two auras cocoons their bodies.

The moment is dazzling, but lasts just a few seconds. The light dissipates, taking refuge in both their bodies as if by osmosis. Her nature is settling within her, but it's warm and melty throughout her core. Different somehow. Reassuring. Even stronger. And something about Giovanni... The feel and scent of him are there, too. Inside of her.

Giovanni lifts up from her body, his eyes still glowing bright and his face a mix of just about every emotion possible. His mind is a complete mess: joy, relief, fear, intense guilt, worry. Somehow, she feels all of it.

Cellina places her hands on either side of her mate's face and takes a deep breath. "We definitely need to speak with your father. Now."

# THIRTY-FOUR

*Two times...* Cellina ponders. *Not as "weird" as Nino and Haruka, but still pretty damn good.* It isn't a competition, but something about the ease with which their bond has formed gives her confidence.

Standing beside Giovanni now in front of his father, she needs that assurance.

Giovanni is holding her hand so tight that if Cellina doesn't match his grip, he might crush it. The anxiety rolls off his broad shoulders above her. He's staring straight forward: no game face. This face reads terrified. More like, "Please don't scream at me and try to take this away from me." Not that Domenico could take her away from him at this point. Not without endangering both of their lives.

Domenico and Cellina's father could be brothers, except Giovanni's father is taller, burlier and more headstrong. When he was younger and healthier, he reminded Cellina of a very handsome gladiator, or maybe an Italian Viking, if such a thing could have existed. He's older now—his thick wavy hair is silver and his physique still imposing but less brawny as he sits upright in bed.

He stares at the two of them with faded hazel eyes, but there isn't anger there. He's silent, considering something in the bright golden rays of sunlight filling the intimate room. Giovanni's body is trembling beside her. She adjusts their hands so that their fingers are entwined, then grips his palm even tighter.

At Giovanni's silence, she smiles and bows her head. "Good morning, your grace. It's good to see you again."

Domenico frowns and purses his thick lips. "Cellina—do not call me 'your grace.' I know it has been many years since we last met, but you insult me with formalities... Besides, we are family now, it seems." His frown breaks into a gentle smile. Cellina considers this a very positive sign. But when Domenico looks at Giovanni, his expression hardens. "You have bonded with this beautiful young vampire. Yet you did not discuss this with me—this intention nor your desire."

Giovanni runs his free palm down his face and takes a breath. "I apologize, Father."

"I heard of this first from Andrea through a phone call a couple months ago," Domenico goes on. "I wondered when you would disclose this to me, the deep affection you've secretly harbored for his daughter. You relay every aspect of business and society to me—even detailed updates on your brother. But you confide in Andrea when it comes to your own private matters?"

There is rebuke in his tone, but Domenico seems less angry and more hurt by his eldest son's secrecy. Giovanni rubs his forehead again and lowers his face. "I'm sorry—"

"I was *waiting*, Giovanni. This is a critical decision that you should discuss with me—your biological father. Now you stand before me, bonded. It is inconceivable to me." He sighs and closes his eyes. "Is this why you have not come home the past four days? To further conceal this from me? To delude me as if I were a fool?"

Cellina looks up at her silent mate. Giovanni's eyes are still downcast. He's like a wall standing beside her. An unsteady wall, teetering on the brink of collapse and steeling itself for the impact of a wrecking ball.

"Come here." Domenico's words are resolute. Giovanni peels his hand from hers and moves toward the large bed. Cellina takes a step forward, but stops herself. She brings her palms up to her cheeks, her stomach in knots. They hadn't known they'd bond the second time he fed.

Or maybe deep down, they had? Cellina hasn't read *Lore and Lust*, Haruka's infamous manuscript on forming vampiric bonds. Deep within her nature, though, she isn't surprised. She knew it wouldn't take very long for their energies to click, to latch on to each other in a metaphysical embrace and inter-weave their bloodlines for life.

Giovanni sinks to his knees at Domenico's bedside. Normally, his square shoulders are back, proud with his broad chest forward. Now, they're rounded and his head is lowered. Domenico looks down at him. "When your mother starved and died in the war, half of *me* died. This is the nature of bonds, and it is unusual that I have lived so long without her. With the equilibrium of my nature so ruined."

Domenico lifts a large hand and places it atop Giovanni's golden-brown head. His son's shoulders flinch from the contact, but he remains still.

"This severe imbalance within me..." Domenico sighs, his eyes softening. "Has manifested itself through my actions with you and your brother. I have known for a long time. But I... I did not know how I should resolve it. How to right my wrongs. I have been... very harsh toward you. Strict in demanding and requiring much of you—to the point where you are so fearful to tell me that you are in love with Andrea's daughter, and that you wished to form a bond with her."

Domenico takes another deep breath, but this time, a hint of a smile forms on his mouth. He rubs his thick fingers against the top of his son's head. "You have chosen well, and I am not angry with you. I am sorry that I have brought our relationship to such a state as this. You have sacrificed much to sustain our realm... and me. I am grateful. Congratulations on your union. May it be blessed."

Cellina's heart is in her throat when Domenico lifts his gaze to focus on her. "When I should expect grandchildren, please tell me in advance? Do not hide this from me."

Nodding, Cellina steps up to the bed. She looks down at Giovanni and there are tears streaming down his face. He clenches his eyes shut as Cellina meets him on the floor, sinking to her knees. She wraps her arms around Giovanni's shoulders to bring his head into her chest. He leans into her, shuddering from scattered breaths and quiet sobs as she rests her chin against the top of his soft hair.

She meets Domenico's eyes. "You'll be the first to know, we promise." She turns her face into her mate's hair and kisses him, holding him tighter.

"My youngest and his mate came to me very late last night," Domenico says. "They wish to try giving me their blood. I have agreed, but the process will need to be slow. Gradual. Can you accept this?"

"Of course." Cellina smiles. "I know my father would love to visit with you, too. He misses your friendship—especially, quote, 'beating you in chess.'"

"Ha." Domenico throws his head back, a bright smile on his face. "I lie on my death bed and your father spreads insipid lies. That old hound wishes he could beat me."

"You should put him in his place." Cellina flashes her most

innocent face, batting her eyes. Domenico stares at her, shaking his head in a slow motion.

"My son, you have bonded with a cunning and beautiful female. I should expect nothing less from Andrea and Saida's offspring. God help you."

# THIRTY-FIVE

The moment Haruka passes through the doorway to the bright sunroom, Cellina stands, blinking her round gray eyes. Her dark auburn hair is twisted in an intricate bun atop her head, and she wears a beautiful mint-green dress that flutters when she walks. Cellina always reminds Haruka of a lovely butterfly... that could bite you if provoked.

She reaches out toward him as they draw closer, urging him to do the same. When their palms are clasped, she smiles in awe as she looks him over. "You cut all your long hair off—you look so handsome." She stretches her neck and Haruka bends down. She kisses him on both cheeks. "The long hair was beautiful," she says, beaming, "but this is more modern... fresh! Now you both have the sexy boy-next-door vibe."

"You looked like a woman." Giovanni sits with his arms folded at the head of the table. He raises his eyebrow in a smirk.

"I don't think so." Cellina tilts her head, considering. "If anything, he presented even more gender ambiguous with the long hair. Very gorgeous either way."

"And so what?" Nino frowns at his brother. "What difference does it make?"

"*Relax.*" Giovanni stares, his face flat. "It was just an observation."

Haruka rolls his eyes. Unsolicited opinions, as usual. *Pompous creature.*

Without warning, Nino laughs as he sits at the table. "I heard that."

"You heard what?" Giovanni asks. Nino shrugs, his eyebrows lifted in innocence. Giovanni grumbles, "Don't talk shit about me in your heads in front of me. I don't like that."

"I said that you are pompous, which is true." Haruka sits down and scoots his chair up to the table. "How was the talk with Domenico this morning?"

Giovanni leans with his elbow on the table and points with his finger. "*And* good-looking. Don't forget that part."

"The talk went well, Haruka." Cellina waves her hand in front of her mate to dismiss him. Giovanni sits back, snickering to himself. He is obviously in high spirits. Cellina grins. "He's already asking us about grandchildren."

The tension in Nino's body skyrockets, so much so that it catches Haruka off guard, making his own body tense in response. He turns to his mate, bewildered. "What is wrong? Why—"

"*Nothing.*" Nino shakes his head, then runs his fingers into the top of his scalp. An unmistakable sign that it is definitely not nothing. "I'm fine. Sorry, Haru." He takes a deep breath, but Haruka watches him, trying to read and understand his internal anxiety.

"Nino mentioned something about taking on some of these Socotra refugees," Giovanni says. "If we do this, we need to develop a plan for integrating them into society. We can't just dump them into an apartment and expect them to thrive. There's a lot they need to learn—a lot of hand-holding."

"I agree." Haruka sits back, sighing. "They are already educated in math, science and languages, so that is one obstacle we do not need to be concerned with. Helping them adapt to the social-emotional aspects of dwelling in a modern society will be the true challenge."

Cellina leans forward, folding her arms against the table. "Should we consider which realm leaders we'd want to be involved first, then have them help with developing a program?"

"I like that." Giovanni nods. "But we should limit it. We don't want too many chefs in the kitchen—or for this to become some weird political issue. What kinds of powers do these vampires have?"

"With the ones we're accepting, Kahla is non-verbal because Lajos did something to her voice," Nino explains. "But her mate told me that Kahla's voice was very persuasive. Her aura's manifested power was in her speech. Her mate—her name is Mai—she can manipulate her aura in shapes as an extension of her body. She showed me by making her essence into the shape of these giant blue and glittery bat wings. She can even fly."

"Good God." Giovanni frowns. "Flying vampires... Have you unleashed a bunch of freaks into our society?"

"Rude," Cellina scolds. "Those purebreds have been enslaved for almost two centuries."

Nino scowls at his brother. "I think all they want now is to live somewhere peaceful and to have freedom. They won't form an alliance and turn into the X-Men." Nino twists in his chair and looks at Haruka. "Do you know who the X-Men are?"

Haruka nods, but in truth, he has no clue. He isn't in the mood for a digression into trivial human pop culture. Nino laughs. "You're lying to me right now, but I'm going to let it slide."

"We'll figure out the details for the refugee plan later," Giovanni asserts. "Let's talk about feeding Father. He needs a bag at least twice a week—if all is well and he's stable, which has been the case for a couple decades now. The best option is to create as many bags in advance as possible. I checked the reserve and there are twenty-six bags of my blood in there. That gives us a little over three months to get ahead of the curve and figure out this new situation."

Giovanni takes a breath, rubbing his large hand against the back of his head. "Before we test your blood, I'm going to try feeding him with my blood interlaced with Lina's—"

"No." Nino sits up, his body tense again. "I said I'm doing it! Stop trying to do everything when I'm willing to help—"

"It's okay, Nino," Cellina chimes in. "It's all experimental, and it would be best if we could share the task. It'll make it easier on everyone."

"And it'll still be a hell of a lot better for me than it was," Giovanni says. "Trust me."

Acquiesced, Nino sits back in his chair. He exhales a heavy breath and shifts his eyes away. Haruka reaches over to grab his hand, and Nino laces their fingers together underneath the table. He squeezes Nino's palm tight.

---

AFTER HAVING LUNCH TOGETHER, Haruka trails behind Nino as they walk to the western building of the estate. Haruka smiles, reminded of a time when he and Nino were simply friends.

Back then, he would follow Nino up to his room, similar to this. But their relationship had been so careful in those days.

Innocent and sincere. They politely stifled their true feelings for each other—the mounting sense of desire, love and need for something more. The emotional intimacy between them grew and bloomed, to a point where everything inside of them demanded the physical.

Being with Nino, touching him, kissing him, tasting and breathing him... It is fundamental now. Haruka cannot imagine his life any other way—nor would he want to.

When they're upstairs in the master bedroom, Nino kicks off his shoes then plops down onto the bed to lie on his side. He's been quiet since lunch, and he was quiet last night when he returned home, too.

Haruka pushes the door closed with a soft click, then moves toward the bed. He removes his shoes as well before climbing up and resting on his hands and knees, hovering over his mate. "May I claim the position of big spoon?"

Nino snickers through his nose, his eyes closed. "You may."

After a little shifting and adjusting, Nino is warmly encapsulated against the curve of Haruka's chest and body, his arms wrapped tight around his waist. The light filtering into the bedroom is white and clean. The vivid green leaves of a tree outside the window bounce and sway in the gentle breeze. It's quiet. Haruka can hear the muffled birdsong outside the glass, as well as his mate's slow breathing within his embrace.

But he feels Nino's emotions stirring. His mind is frustrated, chaotic. Haruka waits, holding him until Nino's voice registers soft in the silence.

"I don't want to be selfish."

Haruka lowers his head, nuzzling him against the nape of his neck. "You are not."

"But G still thinks I am—I... I don't want to be that person anymore. I'm trying not to be. I'm *trying*."

He feels Nino quiver and curl into himself, so Haruka

curves to envelope him, holding him tight. "You are not selfish. You have experienced serious trauma within your family environment, which has rightfully led to your apprehension in being involved with these household matters. Your relationship with your brother is intricate. But you are both changing as a result of your new circumstances. This will lead to inevitable growing pains between you. It is natural."

"I know. I know, but... I'm not a child. He yelled at me like I was still a prepubescent vampire! What is it about me that makes people treat me that way? My whole life has been like this—my uncle taking advantage of me—"

"Nino, what your uncle did to you has *nothing* to do with your own behavior or personality. Do not assume any blame for his grotesque actions."

"Alright, I... I get that. I do. Even still, my mom hauling off and killing him to protect me... Father not giving me any kind of boundaries, and G and Cellina dragging me along and holding my hand..." Nino shifts, turning in Haruka's embrace so that he's facing him directly. His amber eyes are glassy. Distraught. "And you, too..."

"Me?" Haruka blinks, his chest tight.

"Yeah," Nino says. "When we go home, I need to start working again. Out in Osaka. In Kyoto. Spending the night away sometimes if needed or coming back on the last train. I enjoy going out for work and meeting people. I can't keep staying in the house because you want to babysit me, Haru. It feels like I've been knocked back ten steps because of fucking Lajos and his vanishing me and the injuries. We need to get back to our regular lives—before all this happened." Nino stares into his eyes, unwavering in the bright light of the room.

"I—" Haruka swallows hard. The stress, fear and uncertainty swelling and overpowering him at the mere thought of Nino being off somewhere and far away from him. Outside of his reach, helpless and unknowing. He shifts his eyes away, but Nino reaches up, placing his warm palms against Haruka's face to hold his gaze.

"No one is going to hurt me or take me away from you again. Tesoro, you don't need to be afraid like this. You keep trying to hide it from me, but you can't hide *anything* from me. I can feel it too and it's suffocating—this dread deep inside you. *Please* stop worrying like this."

Just before the onslaught of buried emotions overtakes Haruka, he feels the warmth of their shared aura swell from within. Outside of him and all around him, Nino is manipulating it, calling it forward to comfort him like only he can. Nino snakes his arms around Haruka's neck to pull him in tight. The oak and cinnamon of him combined with the heat of their aura soothes Haruka and slows his breathing. He reaches out to hold Nino around his waist and pull him even closer. Breathing.

"When Lajos took you away from me, I was..." Haruka takes another short breath, allowing their aura to calm him. "My world became nothing. It was terrifying and I—I *cannot* lose you—"

"You won't."

"But I *have*, Nino. I have lost much in the past. If this happens to me again, I don't know... I will not live on without you—"

Nino leans in, his eyes closed as he places the softest kiss against Haruka's lips. "You won't need to. That was the past. This situation is totally new for you. Plus, I can protect myself now, right?"

Exhaling, Haruka rests against his forehead, his eyes closed. "Yes."

"I protected both of us in Socotra—from a full-on attack with fifty-something purebreds *and* a cave-in! I showed you that I can do that, so you don't need to be paranoid like this anymore. We're safe now. And I'll focus and learn even more when we meditate. Let's start our lives again..."

Nino lowers his head, nestling his face into the small hollow between Haruka's neck and the comforter, making him lift his chin. He rests, wrapped securely against Haruka's body, their legs entwined. He can feel the slow rise and fall of Nino's chest as they lie still in the sunlight.

Haruka traces his fingers along Nino's lower back, enjoying the feel of him in the silence. In this perfect, peaceful moment. "I asked to be the big spoon with the intent of comforting you— in the end, you consoled me."

Muffled against his neck, Nino's voice registers half asleep. "We console each other. You forget that as easily as you can read and sense me, I can do the same for you. It goes both ways, panther."

"It does..." Haruka sighs, closing his eyes.

"You also wanted to be the big spoon because you like cuddling up against my ass and smelling my neck."

Haruka opens his eyes, grinning. "I do."

# THIRTY-SIX

Two weeks later, Cellina pushes the weight of her thick curls behind her shoulders as she steps inside the restaurant. It glows with warm candlelight and old romance, busy in its location just off a cobblestoned street within the Brera district. She looks around the crowded room and at all the prominent vampires celebrating the restaurant's opening. She mumbles to herself, "Where is he?"

Giovanni is here. She can feel him. Not just externally—like a static electric current caressing her skin—but inside as well. The power and strength of his blood swirl within her, pulling her toward him as if they're magnets. When he's close, it feels like he's everywhere, all around her. It's magnificent.

She flips around on instinct just as his large hands grip the small of her waist. He's handsome in his dark suit, his eyes sparkling with affection. No creases whatsoever in his forehead. Without a word, he leans down. She wraps him up in her arms and lifts to her toes to meet Giovanni's mouth, parting her lips for him. He kisses her once, fully and sensually, as he holds her, then lifts his head. His voice is low and husky. "Amore della mia vita."

*Love of my life.* She smiles. "When did you get here?"

He holds her a little tighter and she stifles a squeal from the pleasure of being pressed against his muscled body. "Ten minutes ago—but I was stuck outside. Boring business stuff with Esposito."

A waiter walks around the fancy oak desk and gives a little bow. "My lady, my lord, this way, please."

Giovanni unwraps her body, but she reaches down and holds his hand as she follows the waiter. Cellina tries to ignore the blatant stares as they move through the restaurant. They've announced their bond and are doing formal social visits, but the news is still fresh. Aside from a few envious remarks, the aristocracy at large is very positive about their union. Everyone is looking forward to the wedding ceremony they'll have next year in the spring.

"Esposito runs the software company out of Hamburg, right?" Cellina asks as they walk. "He's looking for a new lead front-end developer?"

"Right," Giovanni confirms. "And they have the programming deal with the Fischer Corporation that depends on it."

The waiter guides them to a table in the middle of the floor. Cellina feels like she's in a fishbowl as Giovanni pulls her chair out, but this is her life now. She holds her head high as she sits, smoothing the fitted material of her black dress hugging her curves. Giovanni sits beside her and the waiter hands them menus.

"Thank you." She smiles, then opens and glances at the contents. "And Paul Fischer is the youngest son who's getting married in January—I already have the date on my calendar. He's leading the project on the client side, if I remember correctly?"

When Giovanni doesn't say anything, Cellina blinks up at him. He's staring at her, mesmerized. "You are incredible. And stunning."

"Why thank you." Cellina winks.

"I can't believe how quickly you're memorizing and learning all this banal bullshit I have to endure every day. You act like you're really into it—"

"I'm not acting, Giovanni. I *am* into it. Because I'm into you and our society and helping. It's interesting to me, learning about and being privy to all these different facets of business and the aristocracy. It's exciting."

Picking up his menu, Giovanni's face reads skeptical. His broad shoulders rise and fall in a deep breath. "Exciting? I wish I shared your enthusiasm. I'm in a perpetual functional state of exhaustion."

"I think it's a huge relief that Domenico is responding well to our mixed blood, and Nino and Haruka's. One less thing to be stressed about."

He sits back hard in his seat, shaking his head. "*Huge* relief. God. All these years I've had to suffer alone. And listen to this —the doctor called me an hour ago and said he thinks Father's biology is being *healed* from this mix of all of us. Something about the combination of me, Nino and our mates is making him stronger than he's been in decades. Can you believe this shit? Fuck me."

"Just focus on the positive." Cellina smirks as he lifts his menu to read. She watches him in silence. Since they've bonded, he's unquestionably more relaxed—the frown lines in his forehead almost invisible. It's nearing the end of the busy season for the art gallery and Cellina is a little worn down herself.

"G."

"Yes, beautiful."

"Have you ever been on vacation?"

He looks up from the menu. "What's that?"

"Stop..."

"How did you pronounce it again? Vay-kay-shon?" Giovanni laughs, setting his menu down. "I know what a vacation is, but I might as well not."

"Okay..." Cellina folds her arms against the table, leaning in. "What's your dream vacation?"

"Tanzania."

Cellina narrows her eyes, suspicious. "Are you sucking up to me right now?"

"No." Giovanni laughs. "When we were kids, you would go to your aunt's estate in Zanzibar for a month every winter, right?"

"Yes, of course."

"When you came back, you painted this vivid fucking picture of the white sandy beach and the turquoise sea just outside her property. The exotic birds and palm trees. So I always wanted to go there and see it for myself."

Cellina blinks, impressed. "Huh. You remember that?"

"I remember everything about you. I remember the first time you came to the house with your hair straightened in the late thirties. I remember overhearing you telling Nino about how much you loved Boyz II Men and Guy in the nineties, so I bought both albums and ended up loving that shit, too. I remember you dated that little second-gen prick Carlos Russo in the early 2000s that owns that popular seafood restaurant in Navigli. To this day I won't set foot in his restaurant and he has no idea why."

"The first two were sweet." Cellina smiles, shaking her head. "But the last one was petty as hell."

"*I'm* petty as hell." Giovanni frowns in a kind of smile. "Fuck him. He's lucky to be alive."

They both laugh, but Cellina composes herself when the waiter returns to take their drink orders. When he leaves, she turns back to Giovanni, amused. "So you kept track of all the vampires I've dated and have covertly held grudges against them? Was this some kind of romantic gesture? I would prefer roses."

"Yes and no." Giovanni grins, rubbing the back of his neck. "I was just jealous. And overthinking. Lying in bed at night—because that's the only time I've ever had to myself—stressed about you bonding with some loser who was beneath you, and how I could put on a happy face, attend your wedding and congratulate you without throwing myself off the nearest skyscraper immediately after. But with you feeding Nino for a century, I knew you couldn't offer your blood to anyone else while he was still leeching off you."

"Not leeching," Cellina scolds, even though Giovanni is somewhat right. That had been a constant point of contention throughout her dating life. It'd been difficult to explain: "Sorry, I can't offer my blood because I'm my best friend's source. No, we're not romantically involved. No, we're not bonding. He's emotionally traumatized and I just have to support him. That alright with you?" Her relationships never lasted very long, but she'd never been too attached to anyone, either.

That is, except for the male sitting beside her. He always lingered in the back corner of her mind and heart. She ignored it for years—ignored *him*. He was always there though, occupying space.

Giovanni folds his arms. "I suppose in a way, he ended up helping me. I'll never say it though... little cockblocking bloodsucker."

"You being rude to Nino is getting old—what did you do to make him show up on my doorstep in the middle of the night a few weeks ago?"

He pauses, the guilt written all over his face. "He didn't say anything?"

"No, he didn't. I could tell he was upset, but he told me he supported us and that I should call you. I didn't, but an hour later you showed up on my doorstep anyway. Spill it."

Giovanni exhales a deep breath and looks away, keeping his mouth shut. Cellina smirks. "You don't want to tell me because you *know* you did wrong."

"Not wrong. But maybe... harsh."

"Listen, Nino is doing fantastic, right? He's not latched to my hip anymore or hiding in your estate. He's bonded with an incredible creature who adores him and would do anything for him. He has his own business and contacts in a new realm, and you even admitted that you were impressed with what he's established for himself. He went all the way to Yemen to help rescue enslaved vampires and solve a long-standing cultural mystery! Will you cut him some slack? You totally yelled at him, I know it. He's not a kid—if you just talk, he'll listen to you."

"I *know*. I won't do it again."

"Tell him he's doing a good job—he'll really appreciate that from you."

"I *do*... sometimes. It was just a bad moment."

"Right. Listen. With all the stress and drama lately, we need a vacation. Nino and Haru have the right idea. I'm taking you to Tanzania."

The light in Giovanni's hazel-green eyes flickers. An innocent smile spreads across his face. "Yeah?"

"Yeah. Maybe we can adjust our schedules and go this December? We'll call it a honeymoon for our bonding. Or we can wait until after our official wedding in spring next year?"

"The sooner the better." He grins. "God, I cannot fucking wait. A *vacation*." His eyes shift straight ahead and Cellina follows his gaze. A small woman with caramel-colored skin and lustrous black hair is walking toward their table. They both stand in greeting. Cellina reaches out to shake her hand, thrilled as she introduces herself.

Armeena Khan is the successful owner of a contemporary art gallery in Madrid. She's visiting Milan for the weekend but joining them for dinner at Giovanni's personal request. If anyone can give insight with regard to owning a thriving art gallery in a major metropolis, it is this woman.

# THIRTY-SEVEN

Nino blinks his eyes open—the heat of the morning sun streams in through the window, warming his face. He turns his head against the pillow, looking at the view beyond the glass. The sky is a bright, pristine shade of blue, and the rugged mountains surrounding the cabin stand majestic and vast.

He takes a deep breath to suck in the clean air. Haruka must have opened the window when he got out of bed, because the room is filled with the scent of summery forests all around them—green earth and sunshine.

"Today," Nino says to himself. "We have to talk about this..."

The universe keeps showing him something. Multiple times now, and even here in Trentino. Instead of taking the bull by the horns, Nino is still falling back into his childish way of thinking.

*If Haru doesn't say anything... then maybe I should mind my own business? Maybe he'll talk about it when he's ready?*

But Nino knows better. They've been bonded more than a year, and he's learned many things about his mate. One of which is his surprising reluctance to tell Nino what he wants. With simple things, there's no issue. Coffee or tea. Shower or a bath (or both). Easy. In matters of diplomacy, too, or in circumstances where his authority is needed, Haruka is easily outspoken—eloquent in his expression. Masterful and confident.

When it comes to his deeper desires, the quiet things he enjoys, hopes for, prefers or holds close to his heart... he's like a sealed armoire. Nino understands some things because of his own intentional deductions—paying close attention to Haruka's actions, his responses, his inner emotions, or taking note of the things he doesn't say.

Today marks a week in Trentino together. One more week left. For the most part, they've isolated themselves in natural, splendid bliss. Yesterday, Nino took Haruka into the charming town of Andalo. The vampire population is small there, with no official purebred leader, which means no formalized meetings or rigid expectations. It's perfect.

When they went into a coffee shop, Nino sat at a table and watched his mate in awe as Haruka stood in line. A young third-gen male stood behind him with whom Nino assumed to be his son. The father struggled to keep the little vampire from reaching out and grabbing at Haruka's legs, so the father picked him up. In that moment, Nino recalled Junichi's insight about vampire children being sensitive to Haruka's old blood.

Haruka had looked over his shoulder at the boy and father. He nodded at first, polite in recognizing the unrest of the child. Soon, they were chatting. As the child continued to reach and twist in his father's grasp, Haruka lifted his arms and smiled. The little male jumped into his embrace as his father apologized. Haruka held the boy and rocked him, both of them content as he continued his conversation with the father.

The entire scene had struck Nino yet again—just as it had

with Sora's children before. Each time, it feels as if a heavy curtain has been unexpectedly drawn back on a play he thought he knew by heart and he's witnessing a secret exchange —a meaningful but hidden act that he'd never fathomed.

When Haruka returned to the table, the curtain had fallen back into place. The production he knew and loved was moving forward as usual, the secret thing he'd witnessed like a phantom within his imagination.

Nino sits upright in the bed and rolls his shoulders before throwing his legs over the edge of the mattress. When he brought up the topic of kids the first time, he did it the wrong way. He knows Haruka dislikes reminiscing about his former mate, but Nino couldn't bring himself to ask the *right* question. He'd been too uncertain of his own thoughts on the topic.

He stands from the bed and walks toward the door, comfortable in his nakedness. He moves straight through the cozy cabin and outside to the front porch. It's still early morning and the rays of the sun beat down, showering everything in crisp golden light.

Shielding his eyes with his palm, he looks out over the lake: clear and glittering like flecks of silver as it mirrors the surrounding mountains and trees. Just off to the side and near the shoreline, he sees his mate floating on his back in the aqua-tinged water.

Nino bounds off the porch and runs toward Haruka. When his feet hit the edge of the lake, the water sparkles and splashes loud in the vastness. It's already warm out and the cool wetness is refreshing against his skin.

Just before he dives in, Haruka pulls himself upright. Nino glides underneath the glassy surface, propelling forward with his arms and blowing out bubbles through his nose. His instincts guide him toward the goal and soon he breaks the surface once more and swims freestyle to close the remaining distance. He lifts his head from the water as he approaches. Haruka is watching him, peaceful.

"Good morn—"

The moment he's within reach, Nino thrusts his body out of the water, then places his palms on Haruka's shoulders to drive him beneath the surface. When they're both underwater, Nino wraps his long legs around Haruka's waist. He embraces his shoulders, dragging his mate down even deeper.

The warmth of their shared aura flares out, surrounding them. Haruka drags them both back up toward the glimmering sunlight. When they surface, he gasps in a deep breath and shakes the water from his head. "What the *hell* are you doing?"

"Playing." Nino grins, smoothing wet hair back with one hand as he keeps himself wrapped tight against his husband. "This is what they do in movies—"

"Send their mates to the hospital to get their lungs pumped? This is what they do? Create expensive medical bills?"

"Not exactly," Nino says, squeezing him tighter. He kisses his forehead. "It's just fun, tesoro. Playful."

Haruka raises his eyebrow. "Fun?"

Slowly, Nino's body unlatches from Haruka's, but not of his own accord. He's being manipulated off Haruka and upward. Then up some more. Nino blinks, his body immovable as he rises higher and higher. At first, he's amazed, taking in his new perspective of the placid, shimmering lake, the breathtaking mountains and surrounding forest. The sunlight makes all the colors vivid, as if everything is dialed up ten more notches than usual.

He rises even higher. Nino's heart beats harder in his chest. He calls out, "Haru... what are you doing?" Nino narrows his eyes to view the small features of his mate's face far below. Haruka is smiling a little too hard.

"Having fun," his voice echoes.

"You're *not* going to drop me from this high up."

Haruka grins.

"*Haru*—"

The sensation is like being in a bubble that unexpectedly bursts, or if the invisible floor beneath him has dropped out. Nino gasps as his body free-falls down toward the surface. Just as he mentally prepares himself for impact, his body freezes again, graceful and bouncing in mid-air. He's paused a foot above the surface, getting just a moment to catch his breath before the bubble pops again. He tumbles into the water.

When he's reoriented, he swims over to Haruka again, this time breaking the surface just in front of him. Nino wipes his face. "That was like a rollercoaster. You have this devilish streak in you that catches me off guard. It's kind of sexy though —I like it."

"This is 'fun,' is it not?" Haruka smirks, flicking water at Nino with his fingertips.

Nino draws back, scrunching his face. "Smartass." He inhales a deep breath and stiffens his body so that he dips below the surface. Underneath, he opens his eyes, watching Haruka's long, creamy frame twist within the shiny turquoise lake, trying to move away from him. Nino grabs the back of Haruka's knees on his way up, pulling him into his body.

Above the surface, Nino shakes his head free of water. He grips and lifts Haruka against him, wrapping his arms underneath his ass so that his thighs are gapped open at Nino's hips. Haruka holds onto his shoulders, apprehension set in his burgundy eyes. "I do not want water in my lungs, Nino. It is extremely uncomfortable."

Nino embraces him tight, holding him still against his body. The water stops stirring and is calm. The summer birdsong echoes through the surrounding forest. He stares into his mate's face, serious. "Would I ever cause you harm?"

Haruka raises his eyebrow as he looks down at him. "Perhaps not intentionally."

"You think I would hurt you by accident? Like a stupid kid?"

His mate's teasing expression drops like a sack of potatoes. "No—I... Of course not. I thought we were being playful. You said *playful*." Haruka brings his palms up to Nino's face, then leans in and kisses him. The heat in Nino's chest cools and relaxes. He takes a deep breath.

"Why are you upset, my love?" Haruka asks. "There is no need. I have had water in my lungs before from an unfortunate bathtub incident, and it is not painful. It just... sucks?" Haruka blinks, then frowns as if he's uncertain about something distasteful he's just tried.

Nino shakes his head. "It feels weird when you use slang. What kind of bathtub incident?"

"I agree. And the incident is not important. Are we okay? My comment was not to be taken in a serious context. Of course I know you would never harm me." Haruka kisses him again, even slower this time—licking Nino's bottom lip and nipping it between his own, soft and teasing.

"We're more than okay." Nino smiles, caressing his hand up the small of Haruka's slick back underneath the water. He feels like an idiot. Taking his own insecurities out on his mate and making things confusing. *And I was totally acting like a child...*

"You were not," Haruka assures him. "I love your playful and effervescent nature. It is who you are—"

"Please don't dip into my head right now." Nino grins, staring up at the elegant vampire wrapped around his body. "Jesus, we can hear each other without even trying. I think we've been doing this too much..."

He makes a firm decision. After everything he's been through in the past few months, after what he's realized from Giovanni and Cellina, and what he's witnessed in those quiet moments of Haruka unknowingly revealing a hidden part of himself, Nino has an answer to the question he's been avoiding. It's time to address it head on.

"Is this bad?" Haruka asks, concern lingering in his evocative eyes. "If I am not in your head then I don't know exactly what's wrong."

"Can we go inside? I want to talk to you about something."

# THIRTY-EIGHT

Having showered first, Haruka sits on the couch in the front room of the cabin, arms folded tight against his chest and his knee bouncing like a paddleball on a string.

He'd showered *first*. As in, they had showered separately, because Nino said he didn't want them to get distracted. At what point has their intimacy become a "distraction"? Nino's temperament had shifted while they were in the lake together. Haruka usually feels confident in knowing his mate—in understanding his unspoken emotions and discerning his general state of mind.

The shift happened without warning, and then he asked that Haruka stop intentionally reading his mind. They've been openly communicating their thoughts for months, ever since Nino couldn't speak. It isn't an all-seeing technique: the mind encompasses infinite layers of consciousness and they can't read every single thought verbatim. But in cutting it off, Haruka feels as if he's relinquished his flashlight and is now stumbling around in a pitch-black room.

The rich scent of coffee drifts from the kitchen and intermingles with the summery pine smell of the forests. Soon, Nino walks into the front room, two steaming mugs in his hands. "Here." He hands one to Haruka. He accepts the offering as Nino makes himself comfortable at his side.

Haruka doesn't drink but turns his head. "Nino, what is wrong? Your behavior has been unusual since we were in the lake. I apologized for my comment—"

"Nothing is wrong." Nino meets his gaze. "I just... I want us to have a conversation. It's important."

"Okay..."

Nino shifts his body so that he's facing Haruka, one leg folded against the couch while the other hangs down. He holds his coffee cup in the gap of his thighs. "I noticed something... about you. You change a little. Whenever there's a kid around. It's like..."

Haruka looks down as Nino shifts his coffee cup to one hand. He clenches his free hand into a fist. "I'm not saying this in a bad way—at all. But it's like you're always like this." He grips his fist a little tighter. "Then, when a kid shows up..." Nino opens his hand, his palm flat and his fingers spread. "Something inside you opens up. I had no idea that thing was even there—that there was something... closed off? Or locked away like that within you. You don't even think about it actively. Like, it's an innate response. Do you realize this?"

Nino's amber eyes are serious as he watches him, waiting. Haruka shakes his head, still trying to ignore the tension in his stomach. "No. I don't."

Taking a deep breath, Nino cradles his coffee cup in both hands once more. "Haru, do you want kids?"

Haruka's throat tightens. He doesn't want to go through this a second time. This conversation. This disagreement. The first time was very painful and unexpected: a long, difficult discussion that, in the end, left him feeling as if his heart were broken in some invisible but significant way. Like hairline fractures that cut all the way through and deep into the center. He has noticed how stressed Nino becomes every time someone even mentions the subject of children—how tense he is at this moment, trying to talk about it.

Haruka smiles. It is best to quickly wrap this up so that they can continue with their peaceful vacation. He doesn't want to think about this.

"My love, I have no expectation to have children in my lifetime." Haruka breathes out. "It is not something that you should feel stressed or anxious about." He reaches down and takes hold of Nino's hand, hoping to have put his mate's concerns to rest.

Nino's head bobs in the silence as he stares down at his cup. "I hear you, but... you didn't answer my question."

Haruka inhales and exhales another deep breath. *Why is he pushing this?* "It is not something I think about."

"Okay, Haru, but I'm asking you to think about it." Nino looks up again, meeting his eyes. "I know... I understand that this is a sensitive topic for you. That you had a bad experience and situation with Yuna—but I'm *not* Yuna. So I think... you should give me a fair chance. I want you to be honest with me, like this is the first time you've ever had this conversation."

*The first time?* Haruka shifts his gaze toward the window and the bright blue sky. What had he been like the first time he told Yuna that he wanted children? Young, overly optimistic and hopeful. Naïve. Who was that vampire? Haruka wouldn't recognize him if he were somehow standing before him.

"Guardami, caro." Nino reaches up to hold his chin in his fingertips, bringing Haruka's gaze back toward him. *Look at me.* Nino's voice is calm as he continues. "Do you want kids?"

"Do you?" Haruka asks.

Dropping his hand, Nino takes a deep breath. "I'm open to

it. I didn't grow up dreaming about having kids someday. But...
I love you, and I want to experience *everything* with you. If it's
something you want, then I want it, too. I think it would be
incredible to do that together—to bring some new little purebreds into the world and watch over them... raise them. I
wonder what it would be like?"

Haruka lowers his head, gripping the handle of his coffee
cup tighter as Nino's words swell inside him like something
warm and reassuring. Like liquid, pouring throughout and
fusing the broken places, filling the empty gaps. Nino leans
down, catching his attention. He lifts his brows. "So? Do you?"

"Yes..." Haruka nods. "I do. Someday."

Nino's face brightens, shifting into a warm smile that
makes his amber eyes sparkle. "Right. Thank you for telling me
what you want. For being honest with me. Maybe, when we're
ready, we can ask Doctor Davies about the surrogacy process?
He seems like he studies hard about all things vampire
culture."

"The... the process itself is not difficult," Haruka says. "The
true challenge is finding someone who is a compatible surrogate
for the requesting couple. In the case of purebred vampires, the
pregnancy itself is five months."

Grinning, Nino brings his coffee cup to his lips. "You know
about this already?"

Haruka shrugs. "I read a lot... and as realm leader, I should
know about this topic at least somewhat, so that I can offer
advice when needed."

"Well, then I should know more, too," Nino says. "How
would we understand our compatibility with the right female?"

"Through bloodlines. We should not request a surrogate
that is ranked well below our bloodline, or whose blood is older
than mine—or newer than yours. Ideally, her lineage would fall
someplace within the spectrum of ours."

While Nino nods, Haruka takes a sip of his coffee. It's room temperature now, which is the worst.

"So with male couples," Nino begins, "one provides the... seed?"

"Biological sample, yes." Haruka smiles.

"And the other feeds the female surrogate throughout the pregnancy, right?"

"Yes, but through medical extraction so that the bond remains undamaged." Haruka leans down to place his coffee cup on the oak table in front of them. "In this way, the genetic makeup of the offspring is richly grounded in the requesting couple's lineage. That is why the surrogate should be as innocuous as possible. If her bloodline were older than mine, her biology would be dominant over mine within the child. If she were first-gen or second-gen, the child would be imbalanced. It is the same with female couplings. Although while one can serve as carrier to the growing child, the male surrogate sample should still be as benign as possible."

Nino sits back against the couch and folds his arms. Haruka's eyes flicker down, taking in the contoured definition in his honeyed bicep. "So we'd need an unbonded purebred female with a semi-old bloodline," Nino says. "That may not be easy."

"Finding an organic match is difficult, but not impossible. We have much time, and we... we could repeat the process as often as we wanted, so there's no rush. Do you truly wish to do this with me? To grow our family someday?"

Nino reaches down and grasps his hand, then looks into his eyes. "I already told you, *yes*. I want to do everything with you —if you wanted to swim with sharks, I'd probably do that, too." Nino leans in and places a quick kiss on his mouth, but Haruka blinks, bewildered.

"Th—that won't be necessary."

Laughing, Nino stands, grabbing Haruka's lukewarm coffee

cup from his grasp. "I'll reheat this," he says, walking toward the kitchen. He looks over his shoulder, grinning. "I think we should start giving each other privacy with our thoughts again. It just feels like the healthy thing to do?"

Haruka slides down into the couch, frowning. "But I enjoy knowing your mind. You are generally easy for me to read and—"

"Boundaries, please. We can do it sometimes, but not always. I can talk now, so back to normal?"

"Fine..." Still slouching, Haruka shifts his face toward the window again, allowing the bright morning light to wash over his skin. The heat of it matches the quiet sensation flooding his heart and body.

For the first time in a very long while, he allows himself to imagine the prospect of a cozy nest humming with small creatures—or at least one? A boy or a girl, maybe with warm, honeyed skin and innocent amber eyes.

SEPTEMBER

# THIRTY-NINE

"Lajos is dead."

Nino balks, blinking with the phone to his ear. "What?"

"Well," the detective says, "he's *almost* dead. But he's dead to me, so..."

"You can't just declare that someone is dead when they're not."

"Meh. He's on his way. He's still refusing to feed with the first-gen blood we're offering him. We've had him locked up in here since June. That's three months he's gone without feeding. He's just lying in the cell bed. He doesn't bother moving and his pulse is weak. There's no reason for him to do this. But if he'd rather die than drink blood that's, quote, 'beneath him,' then I say go right on ahead and die. One less racist, classist bastard in the world."

"Jesus." Nino frowns, rubbing his fingers into the top of his head.

"Anyway, I wish I was calling to tell you that, but the reason I'm actually calling is because we found your nerd sex book. *Lore and Lust.*"

A little spark of glee races up Nino's spine. Haruka will be happy to hear this news. "That's great! Where was it?"

"We lingered in Socotra for a while after the two of you scampered off—ended up going back to the house and down underneath again. One of the vamps in that purebred army fired at us with their rainbow-colored laser beam. It ended up leaving my deputy with an awful gash in his upper arm. When we were there with the two of you, those lights seemed like kid's toys—some kind of cute joke. In reality that shit was *really* dangerous. We were able to calm them down, though. We asked about the book and someone brought it to us. Also convinced ten more vampires to leave that place. All in all it was a successful trip."

"That was brave of you to go back down there unarmed," Nino says.

"I'm a brave chick, what can I say? I estimate it'll take us at least six months to get all the refugees properly documented before they choose their next, more permanent realm. We're going to have therapists come in and work with them during that time."

"That sounds smart." Nino nods. "We're still planning the rehabilitation program on our end, but we have a list of international realm leaders we'd like to bring into this project."

"Perfect. I'll keep you updated on our progress here, and I'll have the book shipped out soon. How do you feel about having the female couple and young guy discharged early as a test run? If any weird shit goes down, you two could certainly handle it... being freakishly strong and all."

"Ah... maybe? I'll have to talk to Haru about it first. Can we get back to you?"

"Of course—let me know. And thanks for all your help. We couldn't have found them without you."

As Nino finishes his phone call, he hears voices approaching. Asao and Junichi turn the corner into the narrow hallway just as he's hanging up the receiver. "You're back early. How was yakitori?"

"Busy," Junichi grumbles. "I would rather not go on Friday nights, but the old coot insists. Then he 'forgets' his wallet."

"Two beef tongue skewers for the price of one on Fridays!" Asao shrugs as if no further explanation is needed. "And I got this next round—we're not finished. I booked a table for us at my friend's izakaya downtown, so we won't even need to wait."

The two vampires move into the kitchen, but a thought pops into Nino's mind. "Hey, Jun—did you ever return those books to Doctor Davies? Since you go to the hospital often, I asked Asao to pack them up for you while we were in Yemen."

Junichi lifts his dark eyebrow, his black irises shining in the evening light. "Not too often... but yes, I'm taking care of it. Slowly."

Nino breathes a laugh. "What does *that* mean?"

"It means Casanova is on the prowl," Asao says, slapping Junichi's shoulder. The tall vampire winces, but frowns in a kind of smile.

---

AFTER SEEING Asao and Junichi off, Nino wanders the quiet halls in search of his husband. Not that Haruka is ever difficult to find. The compound is sprawling in its design but somehow intimate, comfortable. A short walk down a hardwood hallway, a right turn and a sliding paper door lead him outside to the veranda near the library.

It's twilight. The weather is perfect and the elegant garden is drenched in dusky shadows. It's a calm late-summer evening with crickets chirping in soft, cheerful chorus all around. The quiet breeze is laced with the hint of autumn's cool approach.

Haruka is stretched out on the veranda in his yukata, a messy pile of books and an empty wine glass near his head as he reads. Essentially, in his element. The soft, rosy coolness of his vampiric nature hovers around him in a haze, comfortably resting outward.

Sitting upright, his smile is peaceful as he meets Nino's eyes. "Who was on the phone?"

"The detective." Nino sits down beside him so that his legs hang over the edge of the veranda. "They found your book."

As suspected, Haruka's wine-colored eyes widen with joy. "This is wonderful news."

"I think so. She said she'll have it shipped to us soon. She also wants us to think about having our refugees come sooner than the others as a kind of trial run?"

"We can discuss it tomorrow." He waves his hand, dismissive. "However, I do look forward to having the book in my possession once more..." Haruka's irises flicker down to Nino's robe. "Is this new?"

"Yes," Nino confirms. "Jun made it for me while we were gone." The material of the summer robe is a rich burgundy color with a traditional Japanese wave pattern stitched in navy blue. The color of the fabric reminds Nino of Haruka's eyes.

"Mi piace. Ti voglio bene." Smiling, Haruka kisses him, lingering against his mouth in an expectant gesture.

*I like it. I love you.* Nino grins against the kiss, pressing into him before lifting his head again. "What are you reading?"

Haruka glances at his open book. "*Cien Sonetos de Amor.*"

"Sonnets?" Nino rubs his hand down his face, a weak attempt to stifle his amusement. "You're in a mood. Now who's the romantic?"

"Is this a bad thing?" Haruka lifts himself with his palms flat against the veranda before sliding off the edge. With his feet on the ground, he moves to stand in between Nino's thighs.

"No..." Nino says, aroused by his mate's rosy scent and nearness. Haruka unties Nino's belt, the action making his stomach clench. He takes a deep breath to calm himself. "I'm glad that you're so happy lately."

"Lately?" Haruka pouts, separating the material of the robe and exposing Nino's naked body to the comfortable nighttime air. He leans into Nino's face, his deep voice seductive and low. "Am I not typically happy?"

"You are..." Nino swallows as Haruka slides his palms along his thighs to spread them wider. "But not professing your love for me in Italian and reading Chilean love sonnets happy. We've for sure reached a new level of contentment."

Haruka laughs from his throat, low and bubbly the way Nino loves, as he lifts his chin and presses their mouths together. Nino laces his fingers into Haruka's short hair, tilting his head and intensifying the affection.

He indulges in his mate. To Nino, Haruka is the most delicious and satisfying thing he has ever consumed. From the first moment they locked eyes in his bar, everything about this vampire has always called to him. Now, the feeling is rooted, essential in the same way a plant needs sunlight to grow, or how fire needs oxygen to thrive.

Nino inhales when Haruka breaks the kiss and moves down his body. His mate's actions are slow, kissing Nino's jawline, then down his Adam's apple to the top of his chest and collarbone. Haruka squats down. Nino's stomach tightens when he kisses him there and flickers his tongue inside his belly button. He moves even lower, gripping his hardness and playfully licking the tip before sliding the length of Nino into his mouth.

Haruka moans in satisfaction as he takes him in deeper— the sound and subtle vibration of it combined with the wetness of his tongue makes Nino's entire body tremble with heat and ecstasy. He lays his head back, clenching his eyes shut to the night sky.

The moment Haruka grips and squeezes the heavy skin underneath his shaft, the climax takes firm hold of Nino's body. It rushes all throughout him like hot lava: tingling down his legs, up his spine and to his brain. He calls out Haruka's name, gasping as he spills over from release.

When Haruka lifts his head and opens his eyes, they're glowing in deep sunset. His gaze focused, he wraps his arms around Nino's hips, shifts forward and tilts his head to bite into his abdomen. Nino watches, his fingers gripping the back of Haruka's head as he feeds to satisfy his needs. The swell of his mate's emotions pulses within him—gratitude and pure delight. The vulnerability of it makes Nino's heart race and his breath catch.

Haruka's milky almond skin is flushed when he stands. He looks radiant in the shadowy twilight: contented and healthy. Finally at peace.

Nino slides off the veranda, but grabs his mate's hand as he moves to lie against the soft grass of the garden below them. Haruka blinks in confusion at first, then allows Nino to drag him down to the ground. Nino relaxes on his back, staring up at the darkened sky as Haruka settles down next to him. His mate lies on his side, resting on an elbow and looking at Nino with affection in his vintage-wine eyes.

"So happy..." Nino whispers, watching him. The sheer peacefulness radiating from him is incredible—a drastic (and welcomed) shift from his disposition a couple months ago. "Haru, if you wanted kids, why didn't you just tell me?"

# FORTY

Nino is staring up at Haruka with bright amber eyes. The soft, emergent moonlight above makes his honeyed skin glow. His mate is dazzling both inside and out, the heartfelt question hanging between them.

Considering, Haruka looks away. "I was not keeping this from you. I had not thought about having children in decades. After... When my bond with Yuna broke, I thought I would be alone forever. I thought, 'This is life's way of telling me that I am meant to be isolated. It is my fate.' I had accepted that truth. But when we became friends... then lovers, and our bond triggered so easily... I was astonished—"

"You *freaked out*." Nino laughs.

Haruka's face falls flat. He pokes Nino's side, making his mate's body jerk as he continues laughing.

"Yes," Haruka admits. "Will I never be pardoned for this?"

"No way." Nino shakes his head. "It was great. Because even though you were stressed, you tried so hard to pull yourself together and you held my hand. I'll never forget that."

Haruka smiles, self-deprecating. He appreciates Nino's

positive point of view on a shameful moment in their history. He reaches down, and Nino closes his eyes when Haruka runs his fingertips along his jaw.

"Once I came to my senses," Haruka continues, "I felt eternally grateful for you. I never fathomed meeting you—or having this second chance. To *not* live my life alone, but to spend it with a vampire so warm and affectionate. So loving and kind. How could I want or ask for anything more, when you are exceedingly above my expectations for my life?"

Whatever Nino saw—this behavior that he described in Trentino—Haruka was unaware of it. Just as the thought of being mated again had been sealed in a box and tucked away until being with Nino ripped it open, the thought of having a family was the same. It wasn't an option, so he'd buried it deep down and ignored it.

Nino takes hold of Haruka's hand, bringing his palm to his mouth and placing a kiss there. "Tesoro, it's healthy to hope for things—to like certain things or want things. You don't have to be complacent and just accept what life hands you. You can push for what you want, or at least express it?" Nino chuckles, lifting his gaze to the sky. "That would make things easier for me, so I don't have to Sherlock Holmes everything out of you... Do you know who—"

"*Of course* I know who Sherlock Holmes is."

"Right." Nino nods against the soft grass. "Literary reference. Did you know there are Sherlock Holmes movies? And there was a popular TV show, too."

"They could not possibly live up to the intricate, masterful writings of Sir Arthur Conan Doyle."

"They're not bad," Nino says. He adjusts his grip on their hands, then pulls Haruka over until he hovers above Nino's body. Understanding the hint, Haruka lifts himself to straddle him, then lies flat, settling his hips square against his mate. He rests with his elbows on either side of Nino's coppery head.

"So let's take inventory." Nino smiles, adjusting underneath Haruka's weight. "You like Sir Arthur Conan Doyle, you don't like dystopia novels—I noticed that a few months ago."

"I do not," Haruka confirms. "Self-help books are also objectionable. *You* like contemporary films and television shows —especially those set within the sci-fi genre—"

"Right, right. This isn't about me, because I tell you what I like and want, and I'm easy to read, remember? This is about decoding Haruka." Nino artfully tugs at the side of Haruka's belt. Haruka lifts, allowing his husband to untie it.

When Nino parts the cotton robe, Haruka sucks in a breath at the night air caressing his naked skin. "Decoding..." Haruka smiles. "Am I an enigma?"

"Sometimes," Nino breathes, sliding his warm hands down Haruka's sides until they rest at the small of his back underneath his robe. "But if I pay attention, I can figure you out." He urges Haruka back down, pressing his fingertips into his spine. Haruka sighs from the warmth of Nino's frame underneath him. From their naked bodies wonderfully aligned and pressed together.

"I've also noticed..." Nino slides his hands down, cupping his ass firmly with both hands. "That you have a preference when we make love."

Haruka spreads his thighs and shifts his hips against Nino's body, wanting to feel and move against him. He is helpless to it, as if his nature within him desperately needs it. Requires it. He leans down into Nino, shaking his head and rubbing their noses together. "I don't," Haruka breathes. He brushes their lips, his body temperature rising as one of Nino's hands slides lower and between his cheeks.

Nino breaks the feathery kiss, his full lips shifting into a smile as he opens his eyes. "You *do*." His fingers are playful in spreading Haruka's flesh, and when Nino uses one finger to caress the soft skin of his opening, Haruka gasps and rocks his hips back, chasing the sensation.

"Tesoro, your reaction is different... stronger when we make love a certain way." Nino caresses his sensitive skin with his fingers while he grips his cheek with his free hand. Haruka feels as if a fire is burning in his groin and lower spine, and Nino's teasing only makes him ache and writhe.

He tries to breathe, but his heart is beating like a rabbit's. "No, I... I love everything we do—"

Nino lifts his hips, shifting Haruka up a little higher, just right against his body as he continues teasing him with his fingers. "I know," Nino says. "But you have a preference. Can you please say it to me? What you really like..."

Haruka swallows hard, his chest tight from both yearning and anxiety. "You are much more... liberated in voicing your sexual preferences than I am."

"Is that bad?" Nino raises his hips once more, sliding his fingers in between their bellies and dragging his digits along their damp flesh.

"*No*—of course not. I am just... unaccustomed to it."

"You and Yuna never talked to each other about what you liked?"

"Never. And... if you notice what I like, why do I need to say it?" The sensation of Nino's wet fingertips against his body derails him from his thoughts. Haruka moans, relaxing himself as Nino presses them inside.

"Because I want to hear it," Nino says, lifting his head to lick and suck Haruka's bottom lip between his own as he moves his fingers deeper. "Knowing what turns you on gives me confidence—and I don't want you to feel ashamed to tell me what you like or want to try..."

Haruka's body trembles with want, with desperate need of his mate and their completion.

"*Ah—*"

Nino pulses his energy inside, the sensation like fizzy heat radiating from his slick fingers. Haruka is breathless as Nino's energy intensifies. When the low embers of pleasure finally spiral outward into a blaze of ecstasy, he stretches his spine, letting the bliss of climax wash over him—surrendering to what Nino is giving him.

He breathes through it: inhaling the scent of grass and trees swirled with the cinnamon notes of Nino's essence. It makes Haruka's head foggy.

Removing his fingers, Nino grips his body and rolls, delicate in shifting Haruka onto his back against the grass. Nino straddles him, but as he leans down, he slides his fingers through the damp of Haruka's release against his abdomen, then reaches down to grip and stroke his own shaft.

Haruka shifts his tailbone down and lifts his knees. He is blissful, watching his honeyed mate through hazy eyes. This love. These feelings that Nino cultivates inside of him: honesty and freedom, hope and promise. Haruka never imagined this was possible. That the cold darkness of his life could be changed and painted with such color and joy. That he would feel so alive.

Nino hovers above him, his amber gaze soft. "Say it, Haru," he whispers. "Please?"

He closes his eyes as Nino's palms rest against his hips. He waits for Haruka's response, patient as he caresses him. Haruka takes a deep breath, pushing through the block he feels in his chest. "I—" Haruka swallows, self-conscious. He brings his palm to his forehead. "I like... I prefer... you. Inside me."

Nino lowers his hips, pressing his damp tip to the outside of Haruka's body. "Tesoro, relax for me."

Haruka blows out a breath, easing the strain in his body after the confession. He shifts his hips upward, still breathing to relax himself but wanting to meet Nino's body. Wanting him inside. His mate lowers his hips, but not enough to push through. Not enough to break the intimate barrier.

"Thank you for telling me..." Nino smiles, leaning down and kissing the mole on the bridge of Haruka's nose. When he pulls back, his tone is gentle but serious. "Can we try to be more open and talk about these things going forward, so I don't have to guess all the time?"

Staring into his mate's eyes, Haruka nods in earnest. "I'll try," he breathes.

Nino slowly guides himself into his body, and a wave of relief and satisfaction washes over Haruka from head to toe. He closes his eyes and arches his neck in a groan, loving the feel of him. Wanting him deeper.

Nino keeps his body low and still, allowing Haruka to independently roll his hips up and into him, over and over again as he holds the small of Nino's back. Already, he feels the second climax bubbling in his groin like a pot of hot water, so close to boiling over. Through the thick haze of lust, he hears Nino's voice. "How do I feel inside you?"

He licks and bites his bottom lip, his body shaking. So close. "Full," he breathes. "*Perfect.*"

Something in his response triggers Nino into movement. He presses his hips down, driving Haruka's body back into the lush grass as he thrusts and rocks. Haruka lifts his knees to cradle him—the passion behind Nino's movement sends a flash of heat up Haruka's spine. Soon, he groans in pleasure, his deep voice echoing in the vastness of the starry sky above him.

He grips his mate's strong back underneath his robe, holding him tight as the climax subsides. Haruka sighs in pleasure when he feels Nino's sculpted body tense in his arms—the heat of his release pouring out like something delicious and intimate inside of him.

Haruka rolls his hips once more, reveling in the weight of him and the wetness of their bodies. Nino dips his head into the nape of Haruka's neck and bites down. He feeds and Haruka's eyelids grow heavy—his body relaxed and profoundly satiated.

By the time Nino is finished, Haruka can barely keep his eyes open. As always, his mate smiles, genuine and handsome. "I also notice... that if I do a good job of making love to you, you fall asleep right after."

Haruka frowns, but it feels weak. Without true conviction. He's too warm and too comfortable lying half naked in the grass. The image of his mate hovering over him and set against the starry sky is too dreamlike. "It's—" Haruka yawns, the sensation rattling his chest. "Embarrassing."

Nino laughs, the sound like a gentle echo far away from his conscious mind. "It's not," he says. "I love it—that you trust me enough to be vulnerable and let go like this. Shall I carry his lordship to the bedchamber? Is this context appropriate for such an act?"

"No." Haruka breathes deep, unable to keep his eyelids open. "I... I'll walk..." But then there is nothing. Just blackness, deep contentment and calm.

When Haruka flickers his eyes open again, morning light and a cool breeze are pouring in through the open patio doors. He is warmly tucked into his bed, the love of his life nestled against his chest and sleeping in his arms.

# EPILOGUE

"Everything was very... bright. There was so much color?"

Mai tilts her head, her dark eyes perplexed, as if she isn't certain that she's expressing herself correctly. Her tawny-brown skin is clear and rich—much healthier compared with the first time they saw her in Lajos's mansion two months ago. "And the smells were abundant—offensive. Here, it is better. Still strange but... not overpowering."

Nino nods in understanding. Even without the experience of being isolated in a desert wilderness his entire life, he can easily agree that the smells in New York are probably overwhelming.

"Being around so many humans is strange," Mai declares. "Their smell is also unpleasant."

At this, Kahla bobs her head in agreement with her mate. Their daughter, Aleyna, sits quietly in her lap, her small hands smoothly caressing and twisting the kokeshi doll that Haruka and Nino gifted her upon their arrival to the Kurashiki estate. Her light brown eyes keep darting back and forth between the intricately designed wooden toy in her palms and Haruka and Nino across from her.

"As purebreds, humans are not an appropriate feeding source," Haruka states, "hence their displeasing scent. But you will grow accustomed to their presence. Eventually, their essence will almost disappear within your awareness—like background noise."

Mai tilts her head again, her very straight, long dark hair shifting to the side like a silk blanket. "Background noise... What is this expression—" She stops, turning her head and meeting her mate's intense gaze in silence. Nino narrows his eyes, but then Mai nods in understanding. "Yes—yes, background noise. I look forward to this situation. My awareness of them is uncomfortable now. These humans..."

Given Kahla's inability to produce verbal speech, she and Mai communicate telepathically. It's the same ability that Nino and Haruka have, but Nino has never witnessed anyone else doing this besides himself and his mate. Seeing it from a new perspective, he agrees with Asao. It's very weird.

"Does the presence of all these new vampires help to offset your discomfort with humans?" Nino asks.

"The lesser vampires—" Mai stops again, blinking. Beside her, Kahla shakes her curly head, and Mai nods. "No. My apologies. Ranked vampires?"

"Yes," Nino confirms. "We call them 'ranked' vampires."

"Of course. Their smell is confusing. They have the blood of our origins but... with water mixed in? Dirt?" Mai offers, raising her slim eyebrow. Kahla shakes her head in something like disapproval.

"You'll grow accustomed to it over time," Nino says. "We'll be here to support you through it. Do you like the accommodations we've established for you?"

Kahla nods, her smile bright. She lifts her hands out and

around her daughter on her lap to make several gestures. Nino glances at his mate beside him. Haruka reciprocates her signals with a series of swift movements in response, his hands shifting in a fluid motion. When he's finished, Kahla's smile is even livelier.

"They are very pleased," Haruka translates for Nino. "Particularly with the bathtub and the water temperature."

"We were not given these comforts in our realm—clean accommodations, hot water or warm clothing. Academics were *always* the priority. Lord Almeida would say, 'An uneducated purebred is a disgrace to all purebreds.' He valued books and scholars over shelter and provisions. Many nights were so cold, my skin would split and peel because our regeneration was very slow…

"And this new form of communication! We did not learn this on the island—the use of hands and physical gestures. Lord Almeida took her voice, so I often speak for my mate. However, it is nice… that she can speak for herself in this way."

Haruka sits back, folding his arms. "There is a recognized system of Arabic Sign Language that might be beneficial to learn if you ever want to return to Kahla's home country. I am not familiar with its intricacies. I am only acquainted with Japanese Sign Language because of my casual studies in various linguistics."

"Your grace, the fact that you can understand even the smallest gesture is much more than we've ever experienced," Mai says, shifting to the edge of her seat. "Kahla is very… thrilled to communicate with you directly. You cannot imagine how challenging—hopeless it has been. The disrespect we received from other vampires in our realm because of her disability. Because of what Lord Almeida did to her. They ostracized her, and they were also jealous of her because she was allowed to visit the mansion. It was an abysmal life. But meeting you—both of you, as realm leaders—it is a breath of fresh air we did not know existed."

Kahla reaches around her daughter once more to make a quick series of hand gestures. When she finishes, Haruka surprises Nino by taking hold of his hand. "She said that when she met you, your aura was powerful, but warm. And there was kindness in your eyes even though you were afraid." Haruka smiles, his wine irises full of affection. Nino bites back a grin, feeling the rush of heat threatening to flood his cheeks.

"Do you think... that my mate's voice can regenerate? Living this transformed life?"

"It is possible," Haruka says, still staring at Nino. He shifts his gaze away to address Mai. "Even if it does not, we will do our best to ensure your comfort and prosperity within our realm. We welcome you and hope that you will enjoy your life here."

"We're still developing our rehabilitation plans for you," Nino adds. "But we'll have a few of our ranked vampires come to your place and assist with your everyday needs—for example, learning to grocery shop, cooking, cleaning and other tasks associated with running a modern household. This way you'll learn basic routines and also become acclimated to the presence and existence of ranked vampires. Aozora Nanba is the principal of the local elementary school. We'll schedule a time for you to meet with her as well. Little by little."

The two females nod in agreement, and Kahla reaches over to grasp Mai's hand. Mai takes a breath. "We are ready for this new existence. We look forward to it."

When Mai, Kahla and Aleyna have left the estate, Nino and Haruka sit on the small couch in the quiet tearoom, reflecting.

"That went pretty well for a first meeting?" Nino says.

"Mm." Haruka nods, letting go of Nino's hand and folding

his arms. "The fact that they adhered to our request to relax and settle into their new space for the first week was already a positive sign. This meeting confirms my impression of their peaceful intent."

"Kahla is a descendant of that famous family in Lebanon that vanished. The Arslan Clan?"

"Yes. Detective Cuevas offered to send them to her realm of origin if they wished, but she chose to come here instead—because she trusts *you* and wants to be under your realm and leadership."

"*Our* realm and leadership." Nino smiles, chagrinned. "I read in the report from the detective that Mai wants to visit the American Southwest to find her native tribe—once they're fully adapted to modern living. They found out she still has family in Arizona."

"We should support her in that endeavor when the time is right."

"Agreed. I meant to tell you that when Sydney arrives next week, he'll be alone. The female he left Socotra with has decided to stay in New York. Apparently being off the island and living together has been challenging."

"Whatever works best for them." Haruka shrugs. "They are not bonded, so if they wish to explore this new life independent of each other, they should be free to do so."

"I think so, too." A gentle silence settles over the room, the scent of leftover tea and salty rice crackers wafting from the tray on the low table just in front of them. Nino checks his watch. 3:46 p.m. He looks at his mate. "Hey, panther."

"Yes?"

"We're alone in the house... probably for the next fifteen minutes before Asao gets back from dropping everyone off."

"So?"

"So..." Nino turns and pushes his mate so that he falls to

the couch. He climbs over him, grabbing the back of Haruka's knee and pulling so that his legs are gaped and he rests on his back. He kneels in between his knees, grinning. "Someone tends to be a little more open with me when Asao isn't in the house and potentially listening."

Haruka shakes his head, frowning but unsuccessful in hiding his amusement. "Not here... It's too close to the front door and—"

Nino is swift in sliding his palm against the inside of Haruka's thigh and firmly gripping his shaft through his pants. Nino caresses him, and Haruka's chest heaves in a shortened breath.

"Here. Just a quickie..." Nino leans down, whispering and brushing their lips together. He can feel Haruka's soft, rosy breaths puffing out cool against his mouth. "We're alone, tesoro... What do I have my hand on?" Nino gives him another firm squeeze for good measure, rubbing their noses. He lifts his face, waiting.

Slowly, Haruka opens his burgundy eyes, his expression flat and his rich, creamy voice resolute. "My cock."

Everything inside Nino—his blood, his nature and energy—rushes down to his groin like fire, his heart rate skyrocketing. But he holds it together and takes a breath. "And what should I do with it?"

Haruka lifts his arms, sliding his long fingers against the back of Nino's head to hold him close. "You can undo my pants and touch me." He lifts his chin, licking Nino's lips with a quick flicker of his tongue. "Or put it in your mouth."

"Holy *shit*." Nino sits upright, shaking his head. He runs his palms down his face. "He said it... Shit. I might come from this alone. God..."

Haruka huffs in a clipped laugh as he lies beneath him. "This is ridiculous."

"It's not."

"You have been pushing me to say these things for *months.*"

"I—I know. But... I don't think I was mentally prepared... I didn't know it'd hit me this hard..."

Nino jumps slightly when Haruka shifts and sits up straight. His mate places his palm against Nino's chest to urge him backward, turning the tables. When Haruka is settled between his thighs, he caresses his pointer finger across Nino's lips. "How hard, exactly?" he asks, his brow lifted. Nino parts his lips, taking Haruka's finger into his mouth, letting it slide against his tongue.

While Nino sucks, Haruka shifts against his groin, slow and intentionally rocking so that their bodies align in just the right spot through their clothes. Haruka grinds and Nino moans in utter, perfect satisfaction. He sighs, his body inches away from release as he snakes his hands underneath Haruka's shirt to feel his cool skin beneath his palms, encouraging his movement.

But Haruka stops dead. Confused, Nino's eyes fly open.

"God help me..." His mate slips his finger from within Nino's mouth and places his palm flat against his face. A second later, the front door swings open. They're frozen in their intimate position as Asao passes by the tearoom. He doesn't stop, but glances inside as he strolls by. "Left the grocery list on the counter."

Haruka shifts to move but Nino reaches up and holds his hips, shaking his head with a nervous smile. Within another moment, Asao walks back toward the front door. Just before exiting, he calls out to them, "Don't make a mess in the tearoom."

"Ugh." Haruka drops his shoulders, crumbling as the humiliation rolls from him in waves. Nino sits up, snickering and wrapping his arms around his mate's waist.

"We can keep going—we just have to clean up our mess!"

"Absolutely not." Haruka exhales, his palm plastered to his face. Nino reaches up and grabs his wrist to pull it down. Haruka's eyes shift, reluctant in meeting his gaze.

Nino lifts his chin beneath him, smiling sweetly. "Thank you for giving me that. It was hot."

Haruka rolls his eyes, smirking. "You're welcome." He leans down to meet Nino's mouth. The kiss is gentle, just a peck at first. But Nino keeps his chin lifted and Haruka dips down into him once more, lingering, teasing. He tilts his head for a new angle against Nino's mouth, moving slowly and sliding his tongue inside as he breathes into Nino.

When he lifts his head, Haruka's voice is quiet. "Bedroom?"

"Mm." Nino grins. "We're not stopping again. I don't care who walks in."

-The Middle-

PREVIEW

Lore and Lust book 3: *The Awakening*

# JUNICHI

*I'm too close to home for this shit. I shouldn't be doing this.*

Walking down the long hallway, I can smell the doctor already. It's faint, but still strong enough to cut through the abundance of antiseptic and bleach, latex gloves, scratchy cotton gowns and all the other typical hospital smells assaulting my senses.

Humans are humans. I like them. I've had a bunch and they're pretty much all the same. But something about this doctor stirs me. Ever since I laid eyes on him, something's been nagging me, and I need to know why the hell.

My father would kill me. Literally. If he knew about the things I've done... the things I want to do right now to this inexplicable doctor. He'd rather see me dead than fraternizing with humans and low-level vamps—recklessly jeopardizing the one half of my "elite, purebred Takayama bloodline."

Lucky for me, though, the old bastard is dead. Now all I have to do is manage my constant, addictive desire to feed from my evil-harpy purebred source. I have my father to thank for that bullshit. For attaching me to a monster, thinking I would bond with it.

I should not be doing this.

Moving down the hallway, I turn the corner and see that the doctor's office door is open. Two weeks I've been flirting with this male. No tangible progress made. If anything, he's getting a little agitated, which, in and of itself, is intriguing—the slow evaporation of some politically correct mask he's been wearing.

It's confusing, because Doctor Davies hasn't told me to fuck off, either. Hasn't said he's engaged or doesn't like men. Hasn't tried to call security... not that calling security would solve anything. The doctor isn't saying yes but he isn't saying no, either. He's told me he's busy, but it's not like he's *always* busy. He has to eat at some point, so why not with me?

This is going to sound arrogant, but he's a challenge and I find that a little exciting. I haven't had someone brush me off like this in a long while—if ever. At a hundred and thirty years old, not much excites me anymore.

I'm carrying a singular textbook in my hand—which is ridiculous, but I have a point. I grip the doorframe with my free hand and peek inside the office. Doctor Davies is reading something at his desk. There's a window behind him and the bright morning sunlight is pouring over his back. He looks like a damn angel. His scent is just as sweet and heavenly.

I walk into the room, then sit in one of the two chairs in front of his desk. I smile and speak in polite Japanese. "Good morning, Doctor J. Davies." I place the textbook at the edge of his desk. Waiting.

The doctor keeps his gaze focused on the file in front of him. "Please bring back all of my books next time?"

"If I do that, I won't have a reason to visit you." I sit back, bringing my leg up to cross my ankle at my knee. "Just think of me as a bespoke delivery man—returning your precious books one at a time."

The doctor breathes a laugh and rolls his eyes, pulling his glasses from his face. He has a nice smile. His warm skin tone reminds me of buttermilk.

"See?" I smile, watching him. "I make you laugh. Tell me your first name and have dinner with me." I could easily find his name. Easily. But where's the fun in that?

Doctor Davies looks up at me, staring. His eyes are chestnut brown and shaped like sideways raindrops. He doesn't speak. Angelic and expressionless. I look at the ambiguous name placard on his desk. It reads *Doctor J. Davies, M.D.*

"Is it... John?" I ask.

"No."

"Jeremy."

"No."

"Juan? Juan-José? Juan-Manuel?"

"What?"

"I could look it up online." I fold my arms. "Or ask someone. But it would be much more personable and meaningful to our story if you told me yourself."

The doctor shakes his head. "It's not online. We don't have a story."

"We could." I smile. "'Once upon a time, I asked Doctor Davies to dinner and he said yes. Little did he know, it was only the beginning.'"

At this, the doctor inhales a deep breath and blows it out. The action makes his subtle scent waft out at me. I blink my eyes, trying to ignore how lovely it smells. So fucking weird.

"How can you just waltz in here every week?" he asks. "This isn't a coffee shop. Why are you hounding me?"

Seriously? I'm staring at this bewildered male with deep

golden-blonde hair framed in bright sunlight. "You're beautiful," I say.

He blinks and draws back in his chair, looking off to the side as if I couldn't have been talking to him. As if there was some secret third person in the room that I'd missed.

"And obviously intelligent," I go on. "Driven. Why *wouldn't* I be 'hounding' you? I'd be a fool not to. So have dinner with me... Is my maleness distasteful to you? Is that it?"

"No—I..." The doctor reaches up and scratches his head, mistrust coloring his eyes. "You want sex, right? I'm human, so you couldn't possibly want to feed from me. You're too high level. So if we have sex, you'll feel satisfied and move on?"

Dios mío. Now *I* draw back. What the hell? Where is the fun in cutting to the chase like this? The best part of a new romantic partner is the seduction—and I'm *good* at that part. Why is he fucking it up? "Doctor J., this isn't a hostage negotiation. It's just dinner. Does dinner equate to sex in your world? Is it squeezed in between the appetizers and main course? Between the bread rolls and the salad? Sounds kinky. Messy."

He watches me for another moment like he's struggling with something. I'm thinking I should just pull the plug on this. Clearly, he isn't interested, so I should get up and leave.

The doctor takes a deep breath and slides his handsome glasses back onto his face. "Come to my house next Friday. I'm on call, but I'll be home after seven."

"Your house?" I ask, my eyebrow raised. "Are you *making* me dinner then?"

"Sure, that's what I'm doing."

"Doctor Davies. Why are you trying so hard to deflect my sincere advances?"

He blinks at me as if I've asked him a stupid question. "I'm human. You're a ranked vampire and I don't understand what you want from me. And I'm *busy*. I'm a full-time doctor. How many times—Should I say it in another language?"

We've been speaking in polite Japanese, but I feel wicked. "Sure. Say it in English."

"Because I'm too busy for your puffed-up vampire *bullshit*."

Silence. Not a single sound in the room and I'm speechless. He said the phrase perfectly, nuanced with an airy British accent. I unfold my leg and lean forward, as if doing so will help me discern something deeper.

Who is this human? Why does he smell like this, and why does he vaguely resonate within my nature? Pulling me toward him as if a fishing line is hooked into my navel.

I shake my head. This is not part of the seduction, but I can't help myself. I respond in English, narrowing my eyes. "What are you?"

Doctor Davies straightens his back and blinks. Expressionless. "Boku wa isha desu."

*I'm a doctor.* The intercom buzzes. The doctor presses a button and speaks into it, telling his nurse he's on the way. When the phone clicks off, he stands, somewhat frantic. "*Shit.*" Again, perfect English as he whirls around to grab his brown leather backpack from the floor behind his desk. He weaves his arms through the straps, checks his watch and moves toward the door.

I turn, dumbfounded. "You're not going to give me your cell number or address? Your *first name*?"

He glances over his shoulder as he moves. "Ask Sora at the nurse's desk." Then he's gone. Only the subtle and sweet scent of him remains.

"Why the fuck is he being so weird?" It's not like I'm asking him to do my business taxes or help me move into a third-floor apartment without an elevator. It's just dinner, dammit.

I sigh, standing and walking out of the office and down the hall toward Sora at the nurse's station. When I'm there, she smiles, setting her elbows against the low desk and cradling her chin in her palms.

"Hello, Jun."

Pretty female. She's bonded, of course. But she wears these red cat-eye glasses that complement her narrow face. "Hey, Sora. How are you? Kids alright?"

"I'm great. The kids are with their father. God save him. Are you here on official business? Or are you returning another book?"

"Returning books *is* official business, so I'm not sure what you mean." I fold my arms and lean against the high counter, grinning. "Can you please give me Doctor J.'s address? He'd rather I ship the books to his home."

"Right." Sora smirks, pushing her glasses up her nose. She sits straight, her fingers tapping in a rapid motion against her keyboard as she focuses on the monitor. "You don't mind humans at all, do you, Junichi?"

She's asked the question casually, but the insinuation is heavy. I keep my response innocuous. Last thing I need is rumors spreading around the aristocracy. "I encounter and work with humans on a regular basis—both here and abroad. I'm accustomed to them."

"Doctor J. is sweet—and he's weirdly cute. For a human." She grabs a sticky note and pen, writing down the address. "He was an excellent hire for the hospital—you should be pleased. He's very popular with the low-level vamps that come in to see him. I think being around higher-ranked vamps like us makes him nervous for some reason. It's been three months since he started, but he's still prickly with me sometimes."

I raise my eyebrow. "You call him Doctor J. as well? I keep asking but he won't tell me his name."

Sora looks up at me, blinking her dark brown eyes. "That's his name, Junichi. It's spelled *J-A-E*, as in the Korean iteration. Doctor Jae Davies."

I rub my palm into the top of my head and scoff. I've been calling this heinous male by his name the entire time. For *two weeks* he said nothing.

Incredible. This curious, delicious little doctor. Despite myself, I'm genuinely looking forward to seeing him again next week. It's been a very long time since I looked forward to something.

---

*Thank you for reading!*
*The third book in the Lore and Lust series,*
The Awakening, *will be released in the Fall of 2021.*

# LOVE, MAGIC AND MISFORTUNE

A new adult romance filled with whimsical, peculiar and magical things.

Violet Ainsworth is a fierce woman, but she also falls out of trees. She twists her ankle missing shallow steps and jams her fingers simply reaching for doorknobs.

Jasper Laurent, her best friend, completely disappeared from her life for fifteen years. The confusion and secrecy of it still hovers in Violet's mind like a thick cloud.

The two were separated as children due to mysterious circumstances, but they will soon be reunited as adults. Perhaps their misfortune can be changed? Maybe the seeds of calamity will result in the bloom of love?

Anything is possible. No really, *anything*.

Coming June 2021 from Karla Nikole Publishing

# ACKNOWLEDGMENTS

To the wonderful people who helped shape The Vanishing:

Madeline, thank you for being both an incredible cheerleader and my most valued critic. I couldn't have done any of this without you.

Alex, thank you for being my very first fan.

Maia, thank you for being so invested in Cellina and Giovanni's story.

Julianne, thank you for being fixated on "the underneath."

Megan, thank you for our morning pandemic walks that kept me sane.

Jericho, thank you for your kind support in guiding me to develop a better story, and for taking a chance on a stranger.

Lindsay, thank you for being honest, hilarious and not shy about sex commentary.

Toby, thank you for cleaning up my stories to help make them presentable to the world.

Lorenzo, Elaine and Junko, thank you for lending your beautiful language fluency to help bring my characters to life.

# ABOUT THE AUTHOR

Karla Nikole has a long-standing love affair with Japan. They have always been very good to each other. Having lived in the country for two years and taken several extended vacations there, she is deeply inspired by the culture, language, landscape, food and people. A trip to Italy in 2018 for a wedding breathed new fire into her writing, eventually leading to the birth of Nino Bianchi and Haruka Hirano—two love letters to these beautiful countries. She has also lived in South Korea and Prague, and currently resides in the USA (although Milan is adamantly calling out to her).

 facebook.com/LoreAndLust

 instagram.com/karlanikolepublishing

Made in United States
North Haven, CT
13 February 2022

15867614R00202